my lies,
your lies

Also by Susan Lewis

SUSAN LEWIS

my lies, your lies

wm

WILLIAM MORROW

An Imprint of HarperCollins*Publishers*

P.S.™ is a trademark of HarperCollins Publishers.

MY LIES, YOUR LIES. Copyright © 2020 by Susan Lewis. Excerpt from FORGIVE ME © 2021 by Susan Lewis. All rights reserved. Printed in the United States of America. No part of this book may be used or reproduced in any manner whatsoever without written permission except in the case of brief quotations embodied in critical articles and reviews. For information, address HarperCollins Publishers, 195 Broadway, New York, NY 10007.

HarperCollins books may be purchased for educational, business, or sales promotional use. For information, please email the Special Markets Department at SPsales@harpercollins.com.

Originally published in the United Kingdom in 2020 by HarperCollins UK.

FIRST U.S. EDITION

Library of Congress Cataloging-in-Publication Data has been applied for.

ISBN 978-0-06-290661-8

20 21 22 23 24 LSC 10 9 8 7 6 5 4 3 2 1

"I'm leaving," he said.

She kept her head down as though working on the pages in front of her. She'd heard the "you" even though he hadn't said it. *I'm leaving you.*

He continued to stand in the doorway, making her wonder if he really meant what he'd said, but she knew that he did.

He'd told her about the affair two weeks ago. She hadn't suspected it, although she probably should have. She'd lost her temper, had even hit him, had told him she didn't care if he was sorry, and that he had to get out.

He hadn't gone then, but he was going now.

She didn't want to look at him; it would hurt too much. She didn't know what to do to repair this.

"Do you have nothing to say?" he asked.

"Is there anything that would make a difference?" she countered, her head still down.

He sighed and she pictured his expression, exasperation, worry, guilt. It was the guilt she couldn't stand to see, because it would confirm that he cared. If he didn't care his eyes would be cold, and she'd never seen his

1

eyes cold. She knew he didn't want to hurt her, had never set out to, but with the way things were between them . . .

The affair had been going on for five weeks.

That was all the time it had taken for him to decide he wanted out of their marriage so he could go to live with her best friend.

No longer a best friend.

"Holly wants to come with me," he said quietly.

A brutal knife in the back, this one almost worse than the other. He was going to take their teenage daughter with him.

Could she allow that? Did she have a choice?

Holly made her own decisions these days and some were to spite her mother, or challenge her, or simply to annoy her.

Did either of them know that her heart had already been broken before they'd taken the pieces and broken them all over again?

Holly would pretend not to care, but she wasn't as unfeeling toward her mother as she tried to make out.

He would care, but she'd never told him how it was with her, what she'd done to blot out the pain, so that was that.

"Please say something," he urged, "even if it's only goodbye." He apparently thought about that because then he added, "You probably don't want to be that polite about it."

Even now, in the midst of this nightmare, he could make her smile. She didn't let him see, but he'd know it anyway. That was how well they knew each other, they could sense things, know things without having to see or hear them.

Finally she turned around and because she loved him so much the hurt cleaved through her. He was tall and rugged with a slow, winning smile and sleepy dark eyes that were as kind as his soul. When they were younger she used to call him Harry because he reminded her of Harry Connick Jr. "Just a shame I can't sing like him," he'd say. She couldn't remember a time when she hadn't loved him, when she hadn't felt complete because of him, when most of her thoughts hadn't found their way back to him. They'd been young when they'd met, but they'd considered themselves mature, as all teenagers did and do, especially those at university. They'd become parents in their twenties and it had brought them closer together. They'd supported each other's careers, understanding one's ambitions were no more important than the other's; they'd hit more highs and lows than she could recall and had always been there for one another.

Now it was all going to change.

"Have you packed?" she asked, and immediately regretted it when she saw him flinch. She didn't want to hurt him really. Why would you want to hurt someone you loved?

"Everything's in the car," he replied.

"Holly too?" *Why would he take her daughter? Why did Holly want to go? What did it say about her? As a mother, as a person?*

"She's almost ready," he said.

She had to swallow a choking buildup of emotion

before she could say, "It's hard for me to imagine being happy without you, but obviously it's not hard for you."

His eyes darkened and they entered a rare moment when she didn't know what he was thinking, although those moments were becoming more frequent now.

He was leaving her today and she wasn't trying to stop him. She could sense his confusion over that, along with the guilt—of course guilt, he'd been sleeping with another woman. And yes, he was hurting, because all their years together had meant something to him too and he'd probably expected her to fight harder to keep him.

He could have accused her of driving him to this, but he never had because that wasn't his style. He didn't blame others for his actions, whatever the provocation. He was a decent man, not a coward who hid behind excuses. In some ways that was a failing, for often he claimed responsibility when there was no need to.

Superhero dad, protective husband, respected boss.

"You're not angry anymore," he stated, and she heard his surprise and pique.

She was angry all right, so angry she could turn violent simply to think of him with another woman—especially that one—like she had when she'd first found out. A lot had been smashed that day and she didn't doubt that more would go the same way during the darkest moments ahead.

She was going to hate sleeping in their bed alone, not hearing his key in the door at the end of the day, pouring only one glass of wine, not having him to talk to or watch TV with. For as long as she could remember they'd been the closest couple among their friends, no one had expected this to happen, theirs was the marriage that would go on to the end.

It would have if it weren't for the affair . . .

It would have if he'd been there for her when her world had spun out of control, when she'd lost the sense of who she was, and asked herself what point there was to anything anymore.

Maybe he would have been if she'd told him, but she hadn't, because she couldn't, and wouldn't.

Some things were just too hard.

And so he was leaving.

CHAPTER ONE

1968

The really cool thing about teasing Sir (Mr. Michaels the music teacher) is the way it makes him blush. It starts under his collar and creeps out like mischief, slowly, cautiously, as though checking to see who's looking before suddenly revealing itself with rosy abandon over his neck and cheeks. It makes him seem younger, closer to our age in a way, but not so close to give him the air of a teenager, or someone lacking in worldly sophistication. He definitely isn't, for he seems to know everything and isn't easily shocked, only easily thrown or discomfited by a roomful of fifteen-year-old girls intent on claiming his attention.

He's not tall exactly, but few of us girls can look him directly in the eye—I don't think he'd allow it even if we could. We're too challenging, too full of ourselves and determined to score points over one another at his expense. I can tell he understands that and he never assists. I'm not one of the girls who dares to throw myself at him—no one does really, at least not in an actual physical sense. However, some are brazen enough to try and treat him to glimpses of their stocking tops or to ask if he thinks they should wear lipstick when kissing a boy.

"Sir, do you believe in free love?"

There's a big, exciting world out there, beyond the walls of our boarding school, where people are drawing power from flowers and "finding themselves' as though they've been lost, and we just know that in his free time Sir is one of them. There's more to him than his beige corduroy suit and deep brown eyes that try not to twinkle (and rarely succeed)—and his love of music.

"Sir, did anyone ever tell you that you look like Andy Fairweather Low?"

"Who?" he asks and we almost riot, before realizing he's teasing us back.

We're all mad about Amen Corner's lead singer, so for most of the girls this is the biggest compliment we can give Sir, but in my opinion he looks more like George Harrison. Or he did before George let his hair and beard grow long. Sir's face is always shaved, but it has a similar sculpted look to George's and in my opinion he has the same air of secrecy about him.

What are his secrets?

How we all want to know.

Actually, Sir is much more thrilling than a pop star, mostly because he's *here* and so accessible, possible even, and because he's willing to treat pop music as if it's as important as any other kind. Our lessons are called music appreciation, so I guess that makes sense, although I can't imagine our previous teacher, Mr. Maugham, even considering the hit parade to be part of his lessons. Much less can I imagine him picking up a guitar, or any other instrument, to play "Hey Jude" while we writhe around in time to the slow-motion beat and shake our hair loose as if we're at a wild party, or even a ritual coming-of-age.

With Sir we get into deep discussions about the lyrics of pop songs and why we think one instrument has been used over another. Sometimes he breaks it all down on the piano and gets us to sing phrases that sound silly out of context and we end up laughing so hard that someone knocks on the next-door wall to tell us to pipe down.

Sir's classes are the last period on Wednesdays for our year, and no one ever misses them, not even on the weeks it's all about classical pieces by long-dead composers. Sir has a way of talking about music that holds us all rapt, as if we're small children caught in the melodies of a lullaby. He even manages to bring obscure, centuries-old symphonies to life by playing snatches on the piano while telling stories about how, where, and why the score was composed. He tells us about first performances in exotic-sounding places, conjuring images of the crowds and the acclaim, or sometimes the horror and the shame. He delights us with the tale of Mozart composing the overture for *Don Giovanni* on the morning of the opera's premiere while he had a terrible hangover.

"Have you ever had a hangover, Sir?" Mandy Gibbons asks him cheekily.

Sir gives her a look that's both playful and mock scary and everyone laughs.

I remember us being electrified by the tale of John Rutter fancying John Tavener's girlfriend when they were at school together, and we wanted to know how things had worked out.

"Did they fight?" someone asks.

"Which one did she prefer?"

"What was her name?"

"I've never even heard of them."

"Have you ever fancied someone's girlfriend, Sir?"

He never answers those sorts of questions; he just carries on as if they haven't been asked. I guess he thinks we're all pretty childish and stupid, and of course we are, but we're old enough to have sexually charged crushes, that's for sure. I wonder if they're even more intense at fifteen, given their newness and ripe hormonal *appassionatos* and *attaccas*. They could easily run out of control with lots of girls and considering the times we're living in—I've already mentioned free love and most of us are dying to be a part of it. I'm sure we would be if we weren't locked up in this school during the week. We are on the periphery of an explosion of newness—a revolution some are calling it, an emancipation say others—and though we don't really understand it we still vibrate with the excitement of it.

I will readily confess to the frissons of lust I feel going into Sir's class minus my bra sometimes. He doesn't know, obviously, no one does, but later, as everyone around me in the dorm is falling asleep I imagine how it might have been if he had known. It makes me breathless and hot and excited to go even further the next time, although I never do.

I'm still a virgin. I haven't even kissed a boy properly, much less let one put his hand up my skirt or inside my bra. Tricia Hill, whose bed is next to mine, claims she did things with her cousin's friend during a weekend home visit, and Mandy Gibbons, who's the most rebellious of our group, came back after one weekend swearing she'd gone all the way with her new boyfriend. Her eyes were glittering so brightly and her cheeks were so flushed that it was easy to believe she really had allowed that first barrier of resistance to be breached. And by someone who was virtually a stranger! How courageous and erotic that made it seem.

"Did it hurt?" we all want to know.

She shrugs as if she's a grown-up now, and we are mere tadpoles in the pond of life. "Only a bit," she admits, "and not for long."

"Did you like it?"

With a dreamy sort of smile she says, "It was wonderful." (Personally, I reckoned it had hurt, but she didn't want to tell us. She might even have been lying, and I think she was because we'd all read parts of *Lady Chatterley's Lover* by then, and I'm sure it inspired her fantasy.)

"Did you take all your clothes off, or just some of them?" Tricia asks.

"Did you feel embarrassed?"

"What happened after?"

"What if you get pregnant?"

"Are you going to do it again?"

We have so many questions, and we're so stimulated by the things she tells us that it isn't long before Sir's name is mentioned. It always is at some point, whatever the conversation, because it's as though everything we discuss is a prelude to get to him.

We'd all long since agreed that he'd probably had sex hundreds of times so he would be an expert at it. When we talk about this we pause, eyes closed, to imagine ourselves with him, and then we dissolve into riotous giggles when someone makes noises as though it's really happening.

11

We aren't the only ones who fancy him. Some of our younger female teachers do too, you can see it in the way they break into smiles when they spot him coming their way, or are always willing to join in any project suggested by him. Some even openly flirt with him, like Mrs. Blake, the PE teacher, who sometimes joins our special Wednesday classes to show us how to dance like the Go-Jos or Pan's People. She's really good with the moves, whether she's dancing to something slow like "Honey" or wild like "Jumpin' Jack Flash." No one can take their eyes off her, except me, because I'm watching Sir and the way he looks at her makes me certain he's had sex with her. I'm furious about it. She's married and has no right to him. I will her to fall over or break wind or do something to make herself ridiculous or disgusting in his eyes. The only thing that allows me to forgive her is her praise of my dancing. She says I'm one of the best in the class, a natural, and if I carry on this way I'll end up on *Top of the Pops*.

"Don't you agree, Mr. Michaels?" she asks him, and without quite looking at me he smiles and says something like, "absolutely," or "she certainly has talent." Of course I love it when he agrees, but it upsets me that he doesn't really seem to be paying attention.

"It's because he's not seriously into the same sort of pop music as us and Mrs. Blake," my friend Joy says when I complain to her, and I think she's right.

As far as pop goes, Sir is mainly into Jimi Hendrix and Pink Floyd, the headbanging stuff that makes a lot of the girls shudder and groan. I don't mind it, but I especially enjoy it when he puts it on the turntable and laughs when everyone boos and cries "Off, off, off." We all love it when he laughs. It's as infectious as measles, and no one wants a cure.

One day he plays us "The Gaelic Blessing' and asks us to write down the images it evokes for us. I think it's a strange choice, but he's like that, always throwing something different at us, and collecting up our reactions as if they're musical notes he's going to use for a symphony he's composing.

When the piece has finished he asks Prunella Jones to read out what she's written, but every time she tries she bursts out laughing.

"It'll be something rude," someone calls out.

He moves on to Tricia Hill, who gets booed when she says it made her see churches and choirs and hymn-books.

"Stating the obvious," Mandy Gibbons informs her loftily, and rolls her eyes as if Trish is an idiot.

Trish throws her exercise book and pen up in the air. "So let's hear yours, if you're so brilliant," she challenges.

Mandy's eyes sparkle and we all know something outrageous is coming, but before she can read out a single word, Sir says,

"What about you? What did you see?"

Startled and thrilled that he's asked me, and embarrassed and desperate to impress even though I know what kind of reaction I'll get from the others, I tuck my long blond hair behind my ears (I always wear it down for Sir's class) and begin. "I saw myself floating over a meadow like a bird," I read out loud. "I was a weightless ballerina looking down at the flowers in the grass and up to the sun and out across the sea to where angels were beckoning to me to join them."

A couple of girls actually clapped, but more gagged and Sir says, "Very good."

He's not looking at me and I wonder if he means it.

I feel upset, rejected even, but then I comfort myself by thinking of a time when he was looking at me. It was when I was playing hockey in the top field and during a pause in the game I happened to glance back across the pitch toward the main school building. I'm not sure if I actually *felt* him watching me, and that was what made me turn around, you know how that happens sometimes, or if it was just coincidence that he was standing at the music room window and caught my eye as I glanced his way. He didn't look away and as I stared back at him I stopped feeling the chill air on my bare thighs and panting breath in my lungs.

I think that was when his lessons first became the true light at the center of my week and I, like a moth, circled it constantly, so drawn to him that each Wednesday afternoon was like being burned with the intensity of my own feelings.

Today, as we file into his class, there is a buzzing anticipation infecting us all, for it's one of our pop days, as we call them, and several of us have brought in the new records we bought while at home over the weekend.

The night before, in the dorm, we'd taken bets on what he would or wouldn't like.

"A shilling says he'll love 'People Got to Be Free' by the Rascals, or 'Stoned Soul Picnic' by the 5th Dimension."

"Sixpence says he'll hate 'Mony Mony' *or* 'Sunshine of Your Love' by Cream."

They're all wrong about "Sunshine of Your Love," apart

from me, because I knew from the minute I first heard it on my parents' record player that he'd love it. My parents are groovy people. At weekends when their friends come over wearing bright-colored caftans and fake roses in their hair they drape themselves around the place like exotic furniture to chill out, smoke weed, and drink gimlets or whisky sours. They talk about Vietnam or cricket or how to change the world. During the week, my mother is a senior civil servant writing speeches for ministers and my father is a lawyer specializing in tax and finance. They morph into hippies on the weekends and immerse themselves in the same sort of bands that Sir likes, which is how I knew he'd dig "Sunshine of Your Love."

There really is no other teacher in the school like him. He feels more like a friend than someone who's supposed to instruct and discipline us. I've never heard him tell anyone off, not even when some of the cheekier girls ask him for a kiss as a reward for saying something to impress him. He just arches an eyebrow in a comical way, almost as though he hasn't heard, but the color that rises over his neck gives him away. It's why we do it, to see the little telltale spread of embarrassment that, according to most, proves that he really does want to kiss them.

I have no idea when class starts that day that I will remember it forever. It's not my choice of record that changes the background music of schoolgirl crushes and improbable dreams, it's Mandy Gibbons's. She's brought "Young Girl" by Gary Puckett and the Union Gap. It was released a couple of weeks ago, but this is the first chance we've had to play it with Sir, and every one of us secretly thinks the song is about her and him.

We can hardly wait for Mandy to slide it from its paper cover and put it on the turntable. She's allowed to do the honors while Sir peels off his corduroy jacket and drapes it over the back of his chair.

Mandy sets the needle carefully on the revolving disk, stands back with taut anticipation and as those two magical words—young girl—fly into the room with all their tragedy and passion Sir lowers his head. We're all watching him, waiting for the blush, certain it will come and it does. What I don't expect is the way his eyes find their way to mine. I can feel my heart pounding as the song tells me to get out of his mind, that his love for me is out of line, I'm too young and he needs to run. I feel the heat of the moment, intense and fateful, while in possession of all the charms of a woman.

Did the others notice? They're dancing, eyes fixed on him, but not on me. I don't dance, I just watch him turning away, his movements seeming to happen in a strange slow motion.

When the song finishes everyone's waiting to hear what he has to say about a man trying to resist his love for a much younger girl.

He doesn't say anything. He simply applauds, and his eyes are laughing as if admitting that he's got the joke, but he's not going to be baited, and now it's time for someone else to share a record choice.

Tricia Hill steps forward with a Turtles EP she's borrowed from her older sister. I don't take much notice of it, I'm too distracted by the way Sir looked at me, during "Young Girl." I can't seem to shake myself free of it. He's moved on, he's talking about the Turtles, and making everyone laugh when he tries to play one of the tracks on the piano and gets it wrong. He does that sometimes, and we know the mistakes are on purpose. It's his way of trying to change the mood if things have become too chaotic or flirtatious or intense.

It usually works and it does today. He can play us as smoothly as he strums his guitar or as skillfully as he masters the flute. We are innocent, uncomplicated notes on an elementary score; his humor and charm provide the sophistication we believe to be ours. We think ourselves clever and irresistible, but I sense that for him we're merely girls with crazy hormones and dangerous dreams. He talks and sings and laughs, holding us all in his thrall. He doesn't look at me again, not even when I ask if he can talk to us some more about the Moody Blues album *Days of Future Passed*. I know he's fascinated by some of Justin Hayward's work, the bringing together of orchestral compositions and modern rock, and I can sound reasonably intelligent about it, because my parents are big fans too. They discuss it a lot and I take it all in.

Sir is happy to change the subject, but he still doesn't look my way so I sit feeling crushed and confused and even slightly angry. I'd felt us connect over Gary Puckett's song, and I know he felt it too, but now he's pretending it didn't happen.

I was too young then to realize what his studied lack of attention meant, but I did find out. I can feel myself smiling now as I recall those times. The early memories are the most beautiful, the most thrilling; the sweet percussive notes of a love song before the rest of the orchestra is brought in to provide the darkness and tumult of the drama to come.

CHAPTER TWO

Joely was on a train heading away from London still not sure what to expect when she arrived at her final destination. She was trying not to think about it too much, although creating scenarios for what lay in store was infinitely better—and probably healthier—than tormenting herself with what she'd left behind. Better still, at least for the moment, might be to create a little fantasy around the attractive bloke sitting opposite her.

It was a good try, but it took next to no time for her mind to circle back to Callum, her husband, who'd left her two weeks ago.

He'd actually left her.

She'd never imagined he would, had always believed in their marriage so completely that she still couldn't make herself accept it had happened.

She wasn't sure he'd accepted it either.

"So what's this assignment you won't tell anyone about?" he'd asked when he'd called by the house only yesterday, using his key to come in as if he still lived there. His deep brown eyes had shown only amusement, a gentle tease; an invitation to trust him to keep the secret if she was willing to share. If he'd felt anything deeper she hadn't been able to detect it, but in spite of everything she was sure that he did. Why else was he finding it so hard to stay away?

She knew he was put out that she'd declined to share the details of her new assignment. Nowhere near as put out as she was that he was now living with another woman. It was all wrong, and she couldn't believe that he didn't think so too. Even if he did, it remained a reality. He'd actually given up the beloved home they'd created in the Artesian Village of Notting Hill to go and live in Hammersmith with Martha. Clearly this meant that he now preferred Martha's company, Martha's body, Martha's love, Martha's everything in fact. She'd become so important, so *vital* to him that he'd put aside twenty years of marriage as though for him it had amounted to little more than a book that had been enjoyable but had come to an early and unsatisfactory conclusion.

Was that really how he saw it?

Needless to say, Martha was no longer a friend. Callum, however, remained the big love of her life and she had absolutely no idea how to remove him from that space. She was crushed by the weight of pain and grief that had accompanied her every move and thought since he'd told her he was leaving. It even hurt to breathe. He wouldn't know that, because she had no intention of letting him see how afraid she was of trying to move forward without him. She had her pride and a few shreds of dignity left—and now she had a new assignment.

"I don't understand," he'd said, "why it has to be so hush-hush. Is it dangerous?"

Joely had walked to the table—the one they'd had specially made to fit their kitchen, had sat around with their families at Christmas and for birthdays; it was

their daughter's homework desk and often where
Callum had spread out his own work if Joely was using
their shared study. She picked up the mug he'd filled
with coffee when he'd come in and rinsed it.

She turned to face him. He was still sitting at the
table looking faintly baffled and far too *present*, too in
charge, too much as if he'd never gone away. His hands
were bunched loosely in front of him, large, masculine,
not beautiful or straight, just *his* hands—the ones she'd
gripped during Holly's birth, that had folded her to him
on their wedding day, that had aroused her in so many
different ways, had stroked and comforted her through
the wrenching grief of her father's death. There they
were now looking as though they had nothing to do,
that they might even be contemplating a way back to
her, but really they were momentarily resting or waiting
before returning to Martha.

She could see them on Martha's skin, brushing lightly
over her hair, touching her face . . .

How could imagining something hurt so much? It
was like taking a flame to her insides and holding it
there. Wasn't reality painful enough without using her
own mind to make it worse?

"What are you doing here?" she asked. She hoped
her moss green eyes showed only impatience and
perhaps a hint of distraction. *I'm busy, I really don't
have time for this.* Her shoulder-length sandy hair was
a mess, twisted awkwardly into a knot at the back of
her head, and she knew her face was strained because
she could feel it. He wasn't seeing her at her best, but
it hardly mattered anymore.

"Holly mentioned your assignment," he explained,

"and I thought . . . Well, I wondered why you're not telling her what it's about."

She said, "The client has requested confidentiality, which I'm respecting. As the producer of highly sensitive documentaries, I'm sure you understand that. Now, can I remind you that you have a new life? You left this one, remember? So please see yourself out and the next time you come you'll find I've changed the locks."

He looked startled, and hurt. "It doesn't have to be like that," he protested. "I thought we could be friends."

Were all men so naïve, delusional, stupid?

She turned abruptly away and switched off the coffee machine.

"Are you going back to reporting?" he asked. "Is that what this new assignment is about? Are you going undercover or something?"

She almost wanted to laugh. He knew very well that her reporting days were over, that she was well established in her new career as a ghostwriter so this was a transparent attempt to provoke an answer.

More minutes ticked by until, with her back still turned, she said, "I'm leaving tomorrow and as yet I'm not entirely sure how long I'll be gone. I'll be on my mobile in case of emergencies, but I know Holly will be fine with you." She didn't add, and Martha—that would have been too hard. And if Holly wasn't fine with them, she'd go to her grandma, Joely's mother, where she had her own room, an intergenerational best friend, and even easier access to school.

As Callum got to his feet she could see his reflection in the window and knew he was casting around for a way to make this right. He'd never liked loose ends, he was used to being able to fix things, including those he'd broken himself. People found it easy to forgive him: colleagues, family, friends, no one ever had a problem believing that he hadn't meant to hurt them, because he wasn't someone who deliberately hurt anyone. Even when he'd set out on an affair with his wife's best friend he wouldn't have been doing it to cause pain to Joely. That wouldn't have been his intention at all. In fact he probably hadn't as much as thought about her until after the crime had been committed. That was the way those things usually went, wasn't it? Satisfy the insatiable urge now, deal with the consequences later.

Yes, that was definitely the way it went.

"Joely," he said softly.

"For God's sake, Callum," she cried angrily, and grabbing her phone she answered an incoming call when she probably shouldn't have.

"Yes, this is Joely. I'm fine. How are you?" It was the publisher who'd given her the new assignment. As he spoke she was so aware of Callum watching her and listening that she missed most of what was being said.

When she was finally able to ring off, she put the phone down and turned around. Callum was holding his coat but making no move to put it on.

"Was that about your new project?" he asked.

"Yes, if you must know."

He nodded, waited, and finally accepting she was going to say no more, he attempted a smile. "I hope it goes well," he said, and after more moments of awkwardness he left.

Now here she was on a train staring out of the

window watching fields and hedgerows passing by in a frantic blur, and feeling thankful that it wasn't possible to read someone's thoughts, or see inside their hearts. She wouldn't want anyone around her to know why she was so glad to be escaping London, while feeling utterly desperate to return.

The train plunged into a tunnel, turning the windows into mirrors and she gazed at her ghostly reflection seeing some of what others saw, she supposed. A normal, nonthreatening woman the wrong side of forty with soft honeyed curls and a smattering of freckles over a delicate nose.

Callum used to say she was beautiful. "When I put my arms around you," he'd say, "I feel as though I'm capturing the impossible, because no one can capture the ethereal or the magical, and yet here you are."

He could be very romantic, if a little corny, could Callum.

She wondered how he described her now, apart from as his ex. He might say he'd opened his arms and she'd simply flown away, the way ethereal things do. No, he wouldn't be so whimsical or poetical about her these days. In fact, he probably didn't talk about her at all if he could help it; it wasn't a subject he and Martha would be comfortable with.

What did it feel like when he put his arms around Martha? Could he actually get them all the way around? *You're being a bitch, Joely.* Martha wasn't fat, exactly, she was strong-boned with masterful shoulders and sturdy legs. Her attraction would be of a more earthy nature, so did he feel as though he was embracing a tree, perhaps? Or a small truck?

23

Slagging her off isn't going to change anything. He chose her; you didn't try to stop him, so now you have to live with it. Just like you have to live with everything else.

They emerged from the tunnel and she watched the world outside rushing by, rushing, rushing into the past. There it went, like her life, her marriage, her dreams. There one minute, gone the next.

"Excuse me, can I get you something from the buffet?"

Joely started. The handsome man opposite was looking at her, clearly expecting an answer.

"Uh, um, no, I'm fine, thanks," she stammered.

He smiled and wound his way through to the next car, tall, athletic in black jeans and matching T-shirt that looked as though it had swirled out of a glossy magazine with him in it. She wondered why she hadn't asked for a coffee when she was dying for one. Now she wouldn't be able to have one at all.

What she could have though was a few minutes imagining her return to London with the handsome stranger as her main squeeze (she could hear Holly cringing, *"no one says that anymore, you* muppet!") glowing with happiness, as radiant as a new bride fresh from an exotic and erotic honeymoon, and totally over all the shabby misery the ex-husband and ex–best friend had inflicted, because she had a much better life now.

Yes, that was a fantasy she could happily run with to distract herself from her own guilt, the part she'd played in the breakdown of her marriage because it had never been put into words.

Or she could try to use up the time testing out various

scenarios that might crop up over the next few weeks in order to prepare herself for all eventualities. She wasn't nervous about her new assignment exactly; in fact she was quite excited by it, and grateful that it had come her way at this time when she'd so badly needed the distraction. Regrettably, her heartache was coming too, there was no leaving it in a cupboard at home, or burying it in a time capsule to be dug up by strangers a century after her death.

Before leaving this morning, in a fit of despair and utter stupidity, she'd composed a text to Callum: *I've told Holly she can get me on my mobile if she needs to. If you happen to come to your senses while I'm gone please know it's already too late. You're stuck with Martha and her moustache.*

She hadn't actually sent the last two sentences, but it had given her a momentary satisfaction to see them there until she'd realized how pathetic they made her look. Although Martha really would have a moustache if she hadn't shelled out for several sessions of electrolysis some years ago.

And she was definitely fat.

What are you talking about, Martha, you're absolutely not fat. You're curvaceous and sexy and totally scrumptious, which is what all men love—and honestly they don't look at ankles.

What a wonderful best friend she'd been, always ready to stretch the truth to make Martha feel good about herself.

Callum had texted back: *Are you going to tell me where you're going? Are you all right?*

She hadn't replied to that, mainly because she wanted

him to feel intrigued and worried and guilty and altogether sick of himself for breaking up their home and their family and taking their daughter with him.

"I think it's best if I go," Holly had sighed when Joely had gone into her room the day they'd left to ask her to stay. She'd seemed unfocused, earbuds in, suitcase half full, decisions in progress.

"But why? This is your home. I'm your mother."

Holly turned to regard her own lovely face in the mirror, innocent, almond-shaped eyes, exquisitely wide sculpted mouth, silky blond hair drawn over one shoulder. So much beauty and sophistication in one so young, except Joely wasn't fooled. No matter how grown-up and worldly she looked, or liked to believe herself to be, at heart Holly was still a child.

"Is that who you are?" Holly asked, still gazing at her own reflection, not at her mother's.

"Holly, please . . ."

"It's best I'm with Dad."

Joely wondered what she'd done to alienate her daughter, what had happened to the closeness they used to take for granted, the easy laughter, shared clothes, and long-into-the-night confidences. These days she was almost impossible to get close to.

"What can I do to make things right between us?" Joely asked, unable to let her go like this.

"You're asking me? Why don't you ask yourself?" She could be so sharp at times. An overprivileged, over-beautiful teen who hadn't yet learned how easy it was to hurt people. Maybe because she was hurting too.

"Holly, that's enough with the attitude," Callum inter-rupted, appearing in the doorway.

Throwing out her hands, Holly cried, "You're treating me like I'm the one to blame around here, but it's *her*. It's like we've all stopped existing, we don't matter anymore!"

"I said enough. Your mother loves you and she's going to miss you, so try to be nice before we leave."

Holly's frown darkened as she muttered, "From you, that's great, but *whatever*."

Later, when Holly was outside in the car waiting to go, Joely used pride to suppress her tears as she looked at Callum, still not quite believing he would go through with this. They belonged together; surely he felt that as deeply as she did. They'd shared so much, had digital albums full of it, and what about all the dreams they had yet to see through? He was going to find out pretty soon that he was making a mistake. Martha wouldn't rub his back when it ached the way Joely did. She'd balk at cutting his toenails, and hate the way he hawked and coughed like a stuck volcano in the mornings. She already didn't share his love of France and fine wines— Martha liked Spain and beer. What sort of woman preferred beer? Not Callum's sort, that was for sure.

Maybe she'd never known him.

"Come on, Dad," Holly shouted from the car.

Finding his brown eyes waiting for hers to reach them Joely turned away. Too many rows had already bounced around the walls of their beautiful home, she didn't want to be left with the echoes of yet another as he walked away.

He was now living at Martha's Edwardian end-of-terrace in Ravenscourt Park, Hammersmith, where, over the years, Joely and Martha had spent hours, days, weeks, trying to work out why Martha had so much bad luck with men. Joely had always been there for her, turning up at a time of crisis with boxes of Kleenex, an overnight bag, and a loyal friend's shoulder. She brought wine and beer and vodka and all the support and advice she could muster.

She'd always known that Martha would die for someone like Callum. That was how Martha used to put it, that she'd die to have a man as successful and sensitive, as sensual and masculine as her best friend's husband.

Now she'd taken not only him but Joely's daughter as well. She'd given Holly the entire loft conversion as her own private space where Holly could hold sleepovers and take drugs. (To be fair, she hadn't actually offered the option of drugs, nor had Holly ever shown any interest, but it could come and how was Martha going to cope with that?)

More to the point, how was she going to cope without a best friend to pour her heart out to, to bring booze and love and even laughter to a nightmare that couldn't be borne alone?

The first call she'd received after the car had pulled away had been from Callum to check she was all right. He couldn't have gotten much farther than the end of the road. Then Holly had rung to say sorry for being so mean, probably because Callum had told her to, but at least she'd sounded as though she meant it. Minutes later Martha had rung, but Joely hadn't picked up.

She'd stopped taking calls until the next morning when her mother had finally gotten hold of her.

She'd been standing in the kitchen staring at empty porridge bowls like a tragic, dumbstruck Goldilocks.

"I had a text from Holly," her mother said gently, "so I know it's happened. Are you OK? No, obviously you're not. What did he have to say before he left?"

"Nothing really."

"Do you want me to come over? I can stay for a few days, longer if you like."

Tears had stung Joely's eyes. Her mother was her real best friend and always had been, so why had she wasted her time with Martha? "It's OK," she said. "We'll only end up going round and round in circles and we've already done enough of that . . ."

"But I don't like to think of you on your own."

"I'll be fine, honestly." She probably wouldn't, since right at that moment she felt like killing herself, but her mother was a busy woman. Marianne Jenson might have retired from her job as the most glamorous and popular head teacher the local primary had known, but she was now a top part-time sales exec for an upmarket estate agent specializing in high-end properties, and with the way things were going in that world she was having to work extra hard.

Sighing, her mother had said, "I know it feels awful right now, but to be honest I really don't think it's over. He'll come to his senses, I'm sure of it."

How loyal and lovely of her to say that. It was the kind of thing you said as a parent who was also hurting, because how could you not hurt when your child was suffering?

"And if he doesn't?" Joely asked crisply, unable to be kind. Was everyone destined to hurt their mothers? First Holly had hurt her and now here she was doing the same . . .

29

"It'll take time, but you'll get over it," her mother said.

Such a platitude. It was outrageously insensitive and not what she'd have expected from her mother. "You mean the way you got over Dad?" she shot back, and instantly regretted it, because her mother really hadn't deserved that. "Sorry," she said, before her mother could respond.

"Your father died; that was quite different."

Yes, it had been different. No rejection there, just an awful, wrenching grief that he'd been taken from them too soon, and an emptiness where he'd been that never went away, sometimes seemed even bigger, and then so big . . . No one had told her that losing her father would be so destabilizing that it would change her in ways she didn't even begin to understand, make her do things she could never excuse.

What she wouldn't give now, sitting here on this train, to be on her way to her father, to know that he was probably already waiting at the station, an hour in advance, not wanting to miss her. He'd cry, "Ha! Ha!" when he saw her and envelop her in an embrace that would shut out all the bad things and make her feel loved and safe and able to cope with anything as long as he was there.

Feeling the burn of self-pity in her eyes she blinked quickly to check her mobile as it rang. Seeing who it was, she felt the tug of a smile pulling her out of the gloom and clicked to answer right away.

"Hey you. Mum tells me you've already set off for your secret assignation."

Joely had to laugh. Her brother Jamie was as special

to her as their father had been to them all. "You're making it sound romantic," she chided.

"You mean it isn't?"

"Nothing like. How are you?"

Affecting a southern Irish accent, he said, "We're all great over here. Clare and kids send their love and we all want to know when you're coming to see us."

She'd always loved going to visit her brother in Dublin, Callum had too. "I'll be there as soon as this job is over," she promised. "I feel in need of a you-fix."

"Same here. How are things with Callum, as of today?"

Steeling herself, she said, "We're kind of speaking, but he's definitely with her."

Jamie sighed. "I can't help thinking there's something I'm missing in all this, because it's not making any sense to me. Are you sure you wouldn't like me to have a chat with him?"

Joely's eyes closed. He'd made the same offer several times now, and while in some ways she'd love her brother to be able to fix things, she knew it wasn't fair to drag him into it. "You're just like Dad," she told him, aware of the catch in her heart, "which is probably why we're all so mad about you."

"Well, you know I'm always here for you, and don't forget to stay in touch while you're on this clandestine mission. Clare and I are dying to find out who you're going to be working for. Mum says you haven't even told her."

That wasn't strictly true, for she'd realized it would worry her mother terribly if she had no idea at all of where her daughter would be for the next few weeks so she'd divulged as much as she could. Clearly her mother was keeping her confidence, unless Jamie was trying a double bluff. It didn't matter, she was more than happy for him to know what she'd told her mother.

After ending the call with more promises that they'd see each other soon she checked the text that had arrived while they were speaking. Though she wasn't expecting it to be Callum or Holly, she couldn't help the disappointment when she saw it was neither. However, it did manage to lift her spirits a little.

Hi, just checking your train's on time and you're still able to stay over tonight. Happy to take you wherever you need to go in the morning. Excited to see you and dying to hear more about the new job. Who's the client? Axx

CHAPTER THREE

Now here was someone Joely would never have any trouble calling a friend. Standing at the station entrance searching the crowd as travelers streamed by, and looking every bit as gorgeous as Joely remembered her, was Andee Lawrence. Never mind that they hadn't clapped eyes on each other for the best part of ten years, or that being at opposite ends of the country meant they hadn't been there for each other during many of the most critical times in their lives, the point was they'd never lost touch and Joely couldn't imagine they ever would.

Smiling as though there wasn't even the trace of an ache in her heart, she dropped her bags and walked straight into Andee's embrace. God, it was good to see her, better even than she'd expected.

"You look amazing," they said in unison, and laughed and tried again. "It's so good to see you."

Reminded of how they'd often said the same things at the same time, they hugged again, delighting in the enjoyment of years melting away to free up the many memories along with the easy rapport that had brought them together in the first place.

"I can't tell you how happy I was when you said you were coming," Andee told her, grabbing the larger of Joely's two bags. She was taller than Joely by a good two inches and everything about her was as effortless and captivating as it was calming. "You should be bottled and sold," Joely used to tell her back in the day when Andee had been a detective constable with the Met and Joely was making a name for herself as a crime reporter on a respectable paper. Police and print media didn't usually work well together, and nor had Joely and Andee at the beginning, but it was during a harrowing search for a missing toddler that they'd found their instincts chiming in a way that not only led them into confiding in each other, but had resulted in the arrest of the abductor. Afterward, they'd become friends, often meeting for drinks at the end of hard days, and frequently passing each other information to help solve a case for Andee and provide an exclusive for Joely.

"The car's out the back," Andee told her, pointing the way, "so not far. Are you OK? Did the journey seem endless?"

With an arched eyebrow, Joely said, "I managed to entertain myself and luckily they have lock-down on trains now, so no chance of hurling myself out of the window."

Andee slanted her a look.

Joely slanted one back. "Joking," she assured her, and was abruptly almost blown off her feet by a savage gust as she stepped out of the station.

"So do I get to meet Graeme while I'm here?" she shouted through the hair plastered to her mouth, referring to Andee's live-in partner.

"Later," Andee shouted back, catching her scarf as it tried transforming itself into a noose. "He's looking forward to meeting you, having heard so much about you."

Grimacing, Joely decided not to ask for any detail on that in case it covered her personal chaos, and after hefting her small bag into the boot of Andee's car she practically hurled herself into the safety and calm of the passenger seat. "Nice weather you're having," she commented as Andee got in next to her.

Andee laughed and started the engine. "We ordered it in specially," she replied. "It was either that or a marching band."

Loving how similar their humor was, Joely fastened her seat belt and settled into the luxurious leather surroundings as Andee drove them out of the car park.

"I can't believe this is your first time in Kesterly," Andee declared. "I know I've invited you . . ."

"And I've always intended to come," Joely broke in hastily, "but you know what life's like, it gets in the way and before you know it we're in our forties, our marriages have broken up, and our children have left home. Or have yours done the boomerang thing?"

Andee slowed to a stop at a traffic light and waved to someone she knew. "Luke's in Africa saving endangered species," she answered, referring to her son, "and Alayna's landed a job with the Royal Court in London, although it's getting off to a tricky start. Can you believe they're twenty-four and twenty-two already?"

Marveling at how fast time had flown them through the years, Joely said, "That's what you get for having them so young." She recalled the teenagers she used to know, great kids, easygoing, uncomplicated, loving toward their mother—or certainly they had been then.

"It's good to hear they're doing so well," she said, meaning it. She hadn't forgotten how hard it had been for them, Andee too, when their father had taken off to go and pursue the call of a midlife crisis. It was the abandonment that had persuaded Andee to leave London and join Kesterly CID so her parents, and Martin's, who all lived locally, could help out with the children.

"So no longer a detective?" she commented, turning to watch a homeless woman trying to keep hold of her junk-filled pram.

Andee inched the car forward and let out a groan as the lights returned to red before they could get through. "I'm not sure I was ever really cut out for it," she admitted, frankly, "and then one day I ran into a child murder too many. It affected me badly, they always did, but it got worse with each one, so in the end I decided for the sake of my sanity, and my family, I needed to change my life."

Having no trouble understanding that, Joely regarded her fondly as she said, "So do you miss it?"

"Not as much as I expected to, although in some ways you might think I'd never given it up, because I keep getting involved in cases, locally, that the police don't have the resources for." She smiled and grimaced. "My children think I should set up as a private investigator, but I don't see myself doing that. I'm quite happy working as an interior designer, which is mostly what I do now, and using my contacts to help those who can't help themselves when they need it."

Joely smiled. "You always were a thoroughly good person," she told her.

Andee laughed. "Glad to know the illusion is working. Now tell me about you and—"

"Hang on, I haven't finished. I want to know what happened when Martin got over himself and came back. You told me in an email a while ago that you'd married him, but you're not with him now so I guess he flunked his second chance?"

Andee's smile was wry. "I'm not sure I'd put it like that. He really wanted to make it work, and I guess I did too, but I'm afraid marrying him turned out to be a mistake. I'd already met Graeme by then and although I ended it between us when Martin asked me to give things another go for the children's sake, the feelings for Graeme didn't go away. So we came to a point when I had to tell Martin I was sorry, that I'd always love him just not in the way he wanted me to."

Flinching, Joely imagined Callum saying the same to her. He hadn't in so many words, but from the way he was behaving he might as well have. "So how did he take it?" she asked. "I can't help remembering how gorgeous he was . . . A shit, obviously, for doing what he did, but I'm guessing he wasn't used to being dumped. I bet it hit him hard."

Andee didn't deny it.

Unable to resist feeling sorry for him, Joely said, "It sounds like you're still in touch."

"We are. In fact, we're quite good friends, and he and Graeme often work together. You know Graeme's into property development, and Martin's taken over his father's construction business. Actually," she said brightening as they finally cleared the lights to head out onto the Promenade, "he met someone lovely about six months ago and I think it could be serious."

Joely gave a groan. "Why doesn't that cheer me up?" she grumbled. "I should be happy for him, for everyone who's happy, but I find it only gets on my nerves."

Andee cast her a glance and they both laughed.

Sighing, Joely gazed out at the bare trees lining the boulevard and the dismal spread of the sea beyond. "God, it's horrible, isn't it?" she murmured, quickly adding, "I mean being dumped, not this lovely seaside town that clearly has so much going for it."

Andee's eyes shone with humor. "You're not seeing it at its best," she responded, "but I doubt it would ever be top of anyone's list for a romantic getaway or dream vacation."

"But you like it here?"

Andee nodded. "I'm used to it; Graeme's here, so's my mother—my father died, did I tell you that?"

"You did and I sent a card, but I don't expect you to remember. It was a difficult time for you all."

"Actually, I do remember, and you're right about how hard it was. And now you're going through it. How are you coping?"

Joely swallowed. "I could lie and say fine, but I still miss him all the time. It's hard to believe more than a year has gone by since Dad went; sometimes it only feels like days. I kind of lost the plot for a while, I got angry and confused and frightened . . . I did things . . ." She stopped, took a breath, and pressed on. "It was like I was back to being a child. I even seemed to forget how hard it was for Mum and Jamie."

"I think we all become a bit insular when we lose

someone we love. How are your mum and Jamie now?"

"They don't seem too bad, considering how devastated they were at the time. I know Mum hides it a lot, but it hasn't stopped her from getting back out there. She plays tennis three times a week, runs most mornings, regularly comes to the gym and yoga with me. She also has a job selling houses and a social life that puts mine to shame. No men. She says she's not interested in meeting anyone else, but I guess we'll see."

"If she's still as gorgeous as I remember, I can't imagine she'll be on her own for long."

Joely smiled. "She takes good care of herself, it's true, and she still looks at least fifteen years younger than she is. How about your mum? How's she these days?"

Andee sighed. "Not too bad. She's had a few health issues lately, but she's in Majorca with Martin's mother at the moment, otherwise I know she'd love to see you."

Joely looked around at the wider and clearly wealthier streets they were passing through. "I'm guessing this is Kesterly's answer to Holland Park or Knightsbridge," she commented drily.

Andee laughed. "It has a long way to go before it can boast that sort of status," she replied. "It's called the Garden District, and along here," she added taking another left turn, "is where you're going to be staying."

Joely gazed admiringly—and sadly—at the elegant Regency houses they were passing, tall and white with smartly painted front doors and grandiose eaves. They weren't so dissimilar to her own house, the one she and Callum had bought and renovated during the years before Holly was born—and ever since. They were always doing something to it. She wondered about the people living here, behind those benign and beautiful facades, and hoped that none of them was feeling as wretched at the core as she was.

"Here we are," Andee declared, pulling into a resident's parking spot outside the final house. It was double-fronted, with a black front door between tall sash windows and a private garage to the left that separated it from the elaborate entrance to the Botanical Gardens.

Inside, the house turned out to be every bit as welcoming and tastefully decorated as Joely had expected, given Andee's new career, and she couldn't help but feel a little prideful when she discovered that she'd chosen the same wallpaper for her kitchen in Notting Hill as Andee had for hers here in Kesterly. The only difference was the color—hers being teal green, Andee's a silvery blue.

"This is a beautiful room," she declared, looking across the large center island to three sets of double doors in the back wall that opened out to a small courtyard garden. "Did you knock it through like this to include a sitting room, or was it already done when you moved in?"

"We did it last year," Andee replied, signaling for Joely to take off her coat. "We spend so much time in the kitchen that we decided to make it more comfortable. Now, if you go and sit by the fire—it looks like it's still going—I'll make some tea, or would you rather see your room first and freshen up a bit?"

"What I'd really love," Joely confessed, sinking into a sumptuous raw silk sofa beside the hearth, "is a great big glass of wine." She pulled a face. "Is it too early?"

Andee's eyes sparkled. "Red or white?"

"Whatever's open."

After hanging the coats in a hall cupboard, Andee took a bottle of French Merlot from a well-stocked rack, uncorked it, and filled two glasses.

"Heaven," Joely declared, taking a first sip and feeling the wine's warmth and flavors running through her like liquid comfort. She looked up and upon finding Andee watching her a surge of emotion threatened to overwhelm her. "God, it's good to see you," she said, "I think I feel better already."

Andee smiled. "It's good to see you too." Putting her glass on the coffee table, she threw more logs onto the fire and folded her long legs under her as she settled into the opposite sofa. "So where do you want to start?" she asked gently.

Joely's eyes widened, feigning surprise, but then they wandered to the flames as she shook her head. "Not with them," she replied, trying not to see Callum and Martha in her mind's eye. "I told you the worst of it on the phone, and going over it won't change anything. I'm so glad to be away for a while. Except it travels with you, that sort of thing, doesn't it? I guess it's just good to know that he won't be dropping in whenever he feels like it."

"Does he do that a lot?"

"Less now—and goddamn him, I'm starting to miss it." She sighed and took another sip of wine. "He came yesterday, actually. I told him I'm going to change the locks and I think I should."

Andee sat quietly watching her, and Joely felt her cheeks start to glow in the warmth of the fire. She couldn't

41

put into words how much she missed Callum, how wrong this breakup felt, but she was sure being left never felt right for the person it had happened to. And it would serve no purpose to talk about it, other than to keep him there in her mind, and what was the good of that?

In the end, clearly picking up on Joely's thoughts, Andee steered them away from the subject, and said, "You asked if I miss being a detective. Now it's my turn to ask if you miss being a journalist?"

Joely's eyebrows arched as she looked down at her wine. Everything always came back to Callum, for he'd been a journalist too. Still was, in fact, although he was the co-owner these days of a highly regarded independent production company. However, he'd been a reporter once, on a paper, like her. "Not really," she replied, mentally shaking herself. "The job changed and not in good ways. Everything happens online now, almost no human interaction, and the paper's new owner is much more interested in snappy celebrity chit-chat or scandal than in-depth investigative reports." She smiled wryly. "I'm not into soaps, I'm afraid, and as for delving about in social media looking for stories . . . It wasn't what I wanted to do."

"So you became a ghostwriter and you already have quite a few successes under your belt. Sportsmen, a celebrity cook, a national treasure, and now this intriguing new project."

Enjoying the prompt, Joely stretched out her legs and let her head sink against the side wing of the sofa. It was so cozy here, felt so like home that she already wished she was staying longer. "And now you're going to ask me who it is." She smiled.

Andee waited, her eyes filled with teasing expectation.

Joely said, "Please tell me you've heard of F.M. Donahoe."

Andee looked impressed. "The writer? I have to admit I haven't read much of his work, but there was a TV adaptation of one, wasn't there? I remember finding that, dare I say, easier than the book?"

Joely had to laugh. "I agree, the books are definitely cultist—and actually he's a she, but don't worry I wasn't sure myself until her publisher called to sound me out about the job." She took another sip of wine. "Turns out her name is Freda, she's a very private person and she lives just outside of Lynton and Lynmouth, so not a million miles from here. It's actually one of the reasons I took the job, knowing it would give me the chance to see you, but I have to confess I'm curious to find out why Ms. Donahoe wants a ghostwriter, given that she's never used one before. It could be what she's really after is some help with research. We'll see."

"So is it another novel? A biography, maybe?"

"Her publisher, Sully—Sullivan Thorpe—says she wants to write a memoir focusing on a certain period of her life. I don't know any more than that at the moment, although it seems her aim is to right a wrong, set the record straight, reveal the truth about something that happened when she was younger. She's invited me to stay at the house, which, to quote Sully, is amazing— better not give him a job as an estate agent—and I'll have the use of a car, which is why I came by train."

"So how long will you be there?"

"About a month, Sully thinks, maybe longer depending on how many hours my client wants to work in a day.

I'm not sure how old she is, Sully isn't certain either, but somewhere in her sixties, possibly seventy. There's surprisingly little about her personal life online. I had to dig pretty deep for an entry that gives her full name and confirms she's female."

"Any idea why she's so reclusive?"

"Sully thinks it's probably all tied up in the tragedies she's experienced in her life—nothing about that online either, or not that I've found so far. However, he says I'm not to worry about her being morbid or frail or deaf or bitter or any kind of weird. He says she's very sociable when she wants to be, quite eccentric, and she always gives the impression of enjoying having company when he goes there, so he sees no reason why it would be any different for me."

"Does she live alone?"

"Yes, but she has a housekeeper who goes in most days and a handyman who keeps an eye on things and drives her if she wants to go anywhere. She offered to send him to the station to pick me up, but I said I'd find my own way there."

Andee sat forward to top up their glasses.

"Do you know Lynton and Lynmouth?" Joely asked, swallowing a yawn. "Aren't they twinned in some way?"

"They're on the coastal edge of the moor," Andee replied. "Lynton, which is more of a town, is at the top of the cliff, and Lynmouth, which has the harbor and beach, is at the bottom. There's a funicular—a kind of Victorian railway carriage—that runs up and down the rock face to connect them. My kids used to think it was better than a fairground ride when they were small."

Joely smiled. "Sounds quaint. Actually, from what

I've read about it, the whole place sounds lovely, although I wish I was going at a different time of year. I imagine deep winter can get quite savage thrashing itself out between the sea and the moor."

"I won't deny it," Andee replied. "But don't worry, if there's a storm, or the funicular isn't running for some reason, there's a road that connects the two. It's steep and winding, and you can even walk it, but personally I'd only do it going down."

"And if it snows I guess the whole place gets cut off?"

"Almost certainly, but they're used to it and they keep up with the forecasts to make sure they have what they need."

Joely pulled an awkward face. "Are you sure about driving me over? I think it's quite a bit farther than I realized, I mean across the whole of Exmoor—which is pretty wild from all I've read."

Amused, Andee said, "There are roads these days with white lines down the middle and helpful signposts to tell you where you're going. And truly, I don't mind. It'll give us more time to chat. Now, unless I'm mistaken, that sounds like Graeme coming in."

As they got to their feet the hall door opened and a tall, distinguished-looking man with silvery, dark hair and a close-shaved beard broke into a welcoming smile as he came through. "You must be Joely," he declared, coming to take Joely's hands in his. "I've been hearing so much about you I feel I already know you."

Not a bit surprised that Andee's partner was so attractive and charming, Joely treated him to a playful scowl. "Whatever my friend here has told you," she said, "it's probably all true, so if you'd like me to leave now . . ."

Laughing, he pressed a kiss to Andee's forehead and pointing to the wine said, "Is there enough for me, or shall I open another?"

Going to fetch a glass while he took off his coat, Andee passed it to Joely to fill and reached for a second bottle. "I thought I'd cook dinner," she told him as she picked up the corkscrew. "It'll save us going out in this weather."

"Great idea," he agreed, circling around her to go and wash his hands at the sink. "Are we still vegetarian, or have we gone vegan now?"

Andee said to Joely, "We're cutting back on meat, so I hope you're OK with aubergine and sweet potato curry."

"Sounds scrummy," Joely responded, meaning it. She and Callum had given up meat altogether last spring, but she expected he was back on it now, with Martha being a carnivore.

She wondered if Holly had taken it up again too, and felt suddenly so sad that it was a moment before she realized Graeme was toasting her. She smiled and tapped her glass to his. "Thanks for letting me stay," she said. "You have a lovely home."

"Mostly thanks to Andee," he assured her, and gestured for her to sit down again as he took Andee's spot opposite. "So the mystery assignment . . ."

"It's F. M. Donahoe," Andee told him, filling small plates with quail eggs and stuffed cherry tomatoes for them to snack on. "And in case you didn't already know, she's a woman."

Graeme looked surprised. "I'd always assumed it was a man," he admitted. "Have you read the books?"

"I've been working through the 'Moths' as they're known, these past few weeks," Joely replied.

Graeme frowned. "Moths?"

"It's what the literary world calls her best-known novels, because they focus on nonentities who lived, loved, worked, schemed around the great luminaries of history. Moths to candles. They're pretty heavy going, but once you're into them the drama and unusual slants on well-known stories can be quite gripping."

Graeme nodded thoughtfully. "Have you met her yet?"

Joely shook her head. "To be honest, I'm slightly nervous about it, though don't ask me why. Maybe it's because I've never met a recluse before."

Irony shone in his eyes and she laughed.

"OK, I get that's the point with recluses."

"She wants Joely's help to pull together a memoir," Andee said, carrying a loaded tray to the table, "and we're guessing that it might throw light on the *tragedies* plural"—she glanced to Joely for confirmation and, receiving it, continued—"she's experienced in her life. Whatever, she's planning to right some sort of wrong, presumably by telling the real story of something that happened?" Again Joely nodded, enjoying having her task outlined with more clarity than she'd managed herself so far. "And maybe," Andee said, "we can assume it'll be sensational in some way, or what would be the point of it?"

As intrigued by that as if she'd not already thought of it herself, Joely said, "So will it involve someone famous? Or retell an event that everyone believes happened one way, but in fact there was some awful government cover-up to make it look like something else?"

Graeme said, "There was a disastrous flood in 1952 that devastated Lynmouth and killed over thirty people."

Andee regarded him curiously.

He shrugged. "I'm only saying, if there's going to be a retelling of a big event, could that be it?" Realizing he was losing his audience he said, "OK, maybe there was a major extraterrestrial incident that's been passed off as some kind of special forces activity?"

Andee said, "And F.M. Donahoe knows about it because . . . ?"

"Well, how do I know? I've never met the woman and I know absolutely nothing about her life or her tragedies. I thought we were searching for ideas."

Laughing, Joely said, "I think it's safe to assume that her own experiences and what she knows, or at least believes, to be true will be paramount to the memoir. And as we know, tragedies have a way of reshaping our lives, so writing a memoir can often be about revisiting past traumas to try and exorcise them."

Andee looked faintly alarmed.

"Bad choice of word." Joely smiled. "But you know what I mean. Although I have to say, Graeme, I like your theory of UFOs if only because it's not something I'd thought of myself. Is there a lot of that sort of activity around the moor?"

"Depends who you talk to," he replied drolly.

Joely's smile faded as her phone buzzed with a text. She knew it wouldn't be from Callum—and if it was she needed to tell him to stop contacting her.

It turned out to be . . . she froze in furious astonishment. It was Martha the meat eater wanting to

48

know if she could share any details of her mystery assignment yet.

As if she'd share them with bloody Martha.

"Is everything all right?" Andee asked curiously.

Joely put away her phone. "The minor-role actress, aka my ex–best friend, seems to think she still has the part," she replied smoothly. "Sorry," she said to Graeme, "nothing worse than a bitter female. Now, enough about me and my next job, let's talk about you."

CHAPTER FOUR

Have I already told you that I call my parents the weekend hippies? It always makes them laugh; I think it's a label they're quite proud of. They're very easygoing and probably overindulgent where I'm concerned, but they work hard during the week at jobs that call for a lot of discipline, so they make it a rule for us all to let our hair down at weekends. I'm not allowed to be at most of their parties, it's all too grown-up for me, they say, but I'm usually in the house so I know what's going on. They smoke a lot of weed and trip out on acid, and everyone seems happy and in love so they take off their clothes and have orgies.

They are surprised and thrilled when I tell them I want to learn the piano. I haven't shown any interest in it before, but that doesn't matter; all that does is the satisfaction of knowing I'm happy at school and focused on doing well even in subjects I've shown little aptitude for in the past. They are keen for me to explore every avenue that's open to me, and aren't at all judgmental or disappointed when things don't turn out so well. We know already that I'm never going to be an athlete, or a scientist; I probably won't make much of a pianist either, but they consider it a wonderful skill to have even if I'm not going to be the next Clara Schumann. Everyone agrees with that—it was discussed among their guests during the weekend I broached the subject—and before I returned to school on the Sunday evening many piano recitals were played on the new stereo-master that Daddy bought for Mummy's birthday. It looks like a small sideboard and has taken the place of Grandma's old writing desk in the niche to one side of the marble fireplace.

The question of who is to teach me was never in doubt. My parents have met Sir on visits to the school and were as charmed by him as they are by anyone who has kind things to say about their daughter. (I don't think Sir ever utters a bad word about anyone, it's not in his nature, but his praise for me is fulsome enough for my parents to feel certain he'll do a magnificent job of bringing out any hidden talent I might have.)

"Have you got a crush on him?" Mummy asked when she came into my room to help me pack for the return to school. She's lovely and willowy, eyes deep, dark pools of dreaminess, wide lips always slanting toward a smile. "I know I would have if I were you," she confides with a laugh that seems to float on her perfumed breath.

I tell her I might have if he weren't so old and she laughs again. "He can't even be thirty yet," she gently scolds. I don't tell her he's twenty-five because I see no reason to. She comes to clasp my face between her delicate hands and gazes into my eyes. Her own aren't fully focused, which tells me she's stoned, but I'm used to her being that way and usually love her even more when she is. "Do you think we should invite him to one of our weekend parties?" she whispers mischievously. "Would you like that?"

Knowing I'd rather keep him to myself than share

51

him with my parents' promiscuous friends, I say, "The taxi should be here any minute."

She laughs and hugs me close. "You're a beautiful girl, my darling, probably more beautiful than you know, but you will soon and when you do you'll begin to understand how powerful you are. Don't squander that power; use it wisely and you'll make all your dreams come true."

During the journey back to school I sit staring at the passing countryside, thinking over her words, and trying to understand what they really mean. Was there something tucked away in between them that I'm not clever enough to catch? We've had plenty of chats about intimate things; in fact, thanks to their parties, I know quite a lot about sex without ever having experienced it. I've even been invited to join in on occasion, but Daddy is having none of that.

"This is for the grown-ups," he tells me, sending me back to bed, "and you're not there yet, my angel."

"Your first time," Mummy sometimes says when we're lying together on her bed chilling out to Cream or Hendrix or the Doors, "has to be special and with someone who matters to you and cares about the way he takes your most precious gift."

"Did Daddy take yours?" I ask.

She smiles and stretches like a cat. "Yes, my darling, he did and we both treasure that truth, that memory almost as much as we treasure you."

There's so much to think about on my return journey, much of which I don't really understand even though I think I do.

Now here I am in the music room with Sir having my

first private lesson. School has finished for the day so everyone else is either in the dorms or at their own after-hours activity leaving this wing of the main block quite quiet. Sir is sitting beside me at the piano showing me how to find middle C and explaining its importance. His voice is soft and low, and I wonder if he knows the real reason I've asked for these lessons.

I listen closely to what he's telling me, catching the words in a web of understanding that is uncomplicated and complex at the same time. I ask questions such as "Is middle C always played with the right thumb," and "Why does the scale begin with C and not A?"

He smiles at that and says, "I've never tried to find out the reasoning behind the keyboard being set up the way it is, but I can tell you it was invented by an Italian, Bartolomeo Cristofori in the sixteen hundreds."

"Bartolomeo Cristofori," I echo in a whispery attempt at an accent, and as my eyes go to his a smile remains on his lips even though he blushes and looks away.

I'm not sure why he blushes, but I think I do too.

He puts a sheet of music on the stand in front of me and points out middle C so that I can see how it appears between the five lines. I look at his hand, his long fingers and short, clean nails. I follow it as he reaches across me to begin playing a scale, his hand cupping as though, he explains, he is holding a ball. I can feel his chest close to my arm, his breath on my hair. My heart is beating hard, and I wonder if he can hear it over the notes he's playing. On E he tucks his thumb under his fingers to reach F, and on the way he back he crosses his middle finger over his thumb at the same place to end smoothly back on C. It's simple and almost tuneless, and yet this is the foundation, the start of everything he is going to teach me.

He encourages me to play the scale myself, and a hint of humor comes into his voice as he tells me to relax my thumb. I press the keys awkwardly at first, but then experience a childlike pleasure as I travel steadily through the eight notes and back again.

I hope he's pleased by my dexterity. As I look at him to check the door opens and Mrs. Green, the new English teacher, comes in. She asks if she can have a word with him out in the corridor, so he tells me to practice the scale again until he comes back.

I'm not worried that there might be something going on between them because Mrs. Green is at least as old as my grandma and has a hairy wart on her chin. And she's married, although that probably wouldn't count for anything if she were young and attractive.

I think about asking Sir if he's married, but I know I won't. Mandy Gibbons is sure he has a girlfriend, but I think she's making it up, because how would she know?

I play the C major scale again, slowly at first, bringing flexibility into my fingers and thumb, then I go faster and faster making my fingers fly over the keys like a practiced musician. When I stop abruptly the notes take a moment to fade into silence, which isn't silence at all, because many sounds are drifting in through the open windows. A netball game in the distance, a car driving away, girls laughing, footsteps, a radio playing "Hurdy Gurdy Man." I can smell the grass, fresh and sweet, and feel the penetrating gaze of classical composers watching me from the walls of the room. Mozart appearing pleased with himself; Beethoven looking slightly mad; Vivaldi a bit female; Debussy handsome and not unlike Sir.

I wonder what's taking so long, but then the door opens and he comes back apologizing and making a joke that I don't really understand, but I laugh because he does.

He returns to the chair that's next to my stool and I play the scale again, quickly and fluidly as though I've known it all along.

"You're a natural," he tells me and we laugh again.

I want to touch him, and at the same time I'm terrified that he might touch me. If he does I shall start to shake and the sensations throbbing like bass notes at the join of my thighs will explode.

"Will you play?" I ask him.

He looks surprised.

"I don't mean scales, I mean something by one of them." I wave toward the long-dead men in the posters.

"But how are you going to learn if I do the playing?" he asks lightly.

I can't tell him that I want to watch his hands moving over the keys, his body swaying and his eyes closing as the music transports him to a place of pleasure. I don't even know how to put it into words, but it's what I want.

When I look at him he seems confused, but there's more. I catch the slight tremble of his lower lip as he traps it between his teeth. A kind of energy flows between us like music, gentle chords and scales that only we can feel or hear. I think he's reading my mind, I can sense the thoughts going to him, reaching him like a song.

He knows why I've asked for this private tuition. We both do.

His eyes drop to my mouth and I think he's going to kiss me.

"Are you sure you want to do this?" he asks quietly.

I know he could mean the lessons, but he doesn't.

My voice catches like a quaver on a whisper as I say, "Yes."

CHAPTER FIVE

Exmoor was proving every bit as bleak and dramatic as Joely had expected, flowing and stretching its uncompromising landscape to each horizon with the sea crashing onto the cliffs to one side and stark acres of bracken and gorse giving way to cultivated fields and feeding livestock on the other. The road they were traveling was a long, winding ribbon of gray threading through mile after mile of steep inclines, twisting bends, dense forests and seeming for a while to have no end.

Andee slowed as they passed a handful of red deer grazing a nearby bank, every one of them appearing oblivious to the moving vehicle only feet away. Joely relished being this close to wildlife, taking in the stags' antlers curling imperiously from slender handsome heads, and the females' sleek bodies, smooth and lush and lithe.

Minutes later they stopped for an Exmoor pony to amble across the road to join the rest of the herd, and around the next bend there were sheep with horns coiling out of their heads like fancy hairdos.

They passed signs to places with quaintly intriguing names such as Dunkery Beacon, and Lorna Doone Farm Shop. They glimpsed old villages, drove through fast-gushing fords and all the time Joely drank in the austerity of the wintry landscape as chill as the empty sky, as forlorn as the abandoned picnic tables and lookout spots.

"It's eerie," she decided, "but beautiful and compelling and kind of otherworldly." She considered this a moment and added, "I don't have to ask if it's haunted, I can already feel it."

Andee smiled.

Joely turned to her. "What am I going to do if Freda Donahoe's place is full of friends from the other side? Who might not actually be friends?"

Andee had to laugh.

"You might think it's funny," Joely retorted, "but me and ghosts, we're in the same place as me and Martha the man stealer. I don't want them anywhere near me, and any attempt to speak to me . . . Well, it won't end well, I can tell you that."

Andee laughed again. "Given your occupation, I'd have thought you'd have an affinity with them."

Joely threw her a look. "Ha, ha," she responded, smiling in spite of herself.

"Well, if Dimmett House does turn out to be haunted," Andee said, steering around a sweeping bend that ended with a breathtaking view of the Bristol channel, "and I'm sure it won't, you can always say you want to stay in a hotel. There are several places in both Lynton and Lynmouth."

"Which might be haunted too," Joely mumbled, absorbing the magnificent vista ahead where bold cascades of sunlight were streaming through dark, dense cloud into the sea. "It must be wonderful here in summer," she stated, although this was pretty spectacular too.

"It is," Andee assured her, "and if you're still around

by then, who knows, it might be because you've met your very own John Ridd."

Joely wrinkled her nose. "Who? Oh, you mean from *Lorna Doone*. I'm not sure I can remember the story, and I missed the TV series. Does it have a happy end?"

"Eventually."

Joely's heart tightened as the flippant talk of romance pulled her back to the very place she was trying to escape. Cal had texted this morning to have another go at being friendly in much the way Martha had last night: *Don't forget to let us know about your assignment, and wherever you are, take care of yourself.* She had no idea whether the "us" referred to him and Martha, or him and Holly, perhaps it was all three. What she did know was that it had cut deeply into the sadness she was feeling, and ludicrously, she'd felt she really didn't want to take care of herself at all.

Childish and attention-seeking, she'd scolded herself, and knowing she could do better she'd composed a message back to them both saying, *Leave Me Alone.*

And she'd sent it!

It had felt good at the time, but it didn't feel all that great now.

What felt better was the message she'd received from Holly shortly after midnight saying, *Good luck tomorrow.*

She'd stared at the words for a long time, pretending to herself that Callum hadn't talked their daughter into sending them.

She wondered if it might be easier if he was being mean to her, or carrying on as if she'd stopped existing.

"Distraction," she announced, as they began the

descent from the moor. "That's another very good reason for taking this job. I can throw myself into work for the next few weeks and by the time I look up again who knows where we might be?"

A few minutes later as both Lynton and Lynmouth came into view, seeming almost too much too soon, Joely said, "OK, you need to slow down, because this is seriously lovely."

With a smile Andee did as she was told, giving them as long as she could for their northerly approach from the moor to take in the small sprawl of a town at the top of the cliff, and the seaside village at the bottom. For the moment Joely was fixed on Lynmouth where the tide was lapping over two rocky beaches that fanned out like skate wings from the river at their center making its way through to the sea. There was a small scoop of a harbor, with gray stone sea walls surrounding it, a Rhenish tower, and a handful of single-mast boats moored in the mud. A long, thatched terrace of white cottages, a pub, a café, and shops slanted up an incline alongside the harbor, and the rest of the shore village curved around the seafront like a protective arm.

After crossing the West Lyn river, Andee steered the car to the left to begin a steep and winding drive up over the cliff, home to hotels, B&Bs, and guest houses, to the high-perched town of Lynton. Joely felt herself smiling as they meandered along the main street taking in the olde worlde charm and narrow streets that tumbled away to one side as if pulled in by the moor, while on the other more hotels and guest houses towered over the village and sea below.

"We're going to need further directions soon," Andee said as they drove out the other side of town where green fields jostled for space in the rough and undulating moorland.

Calling up Sully's email on her phone, Joely looked around again as the GPS instructed them to keep going straight and her eyes grew round as they entered what could only be the Valley of Rocks. "Wow," she murmured as they moved slowly through a lunar-like landscape where vast tors of jagged stone patched with grass and lichen soared skyward on one side, and dry, bristled slopes of flinty terrain rose majestically on the other.

"The largest rock there," Andee said, pointing to the right, "is known as Castle Rock, and the one over there, to the left, is Devil's Cheese Rock. Legend has it, if you walk around it a certain number of times, probably under a full moon, Satan will appear."

Deciding she probably wouldn't be giving that a whirl anytime soon, Joely returned to Sully's directions. "OK, we need to follow the road all the way through the Valley of Rocks to . . . Oh my God, are they goats? Yes, they're goats. They're so sweet."

"They live here," Andee told her, steering around a handful of the small, feral beasts that had broken off from the main gang.

After taking in more of the scenery, Joely continued with the directions. "OK, there's a small track at the end of the valley that eventually leads to a spiritual retreat. We're to take that, but about twenty meters in we'll see another track to the left that we should follow all the way along the ridge to the next vale."

Soon after passing the spiritual retreat in its haven of natural beauty they began a gentle descent from the next hilltop into an enclave of clifftop moor where black-faced sheep were grazing the sloping fields on one side and immense tors clustered like giants to block the sea on the other. Between the opposing swells of nature was a sprawling green meadow rich with tall grass that appeared at the farthest point to dip down to a cove.

As they drove slowly on they finally realized that down to their right, tucked securely against the protective wall of rocks was a house where it seemed no house should be.

"Wow," Joely murmured again, taking in the pale-colored limestone exterior with three stories of tall shuttered windows facing out over the meadow, and a bold, square tower at the far end with a gray slate conical roof. In spring the entire facade would be covered in wisteria; now there was only the climbing ramble of naked branches not at all ready to flower. On the ground level of the tower was a patio with large stone pillars holding up another gray slate roof, and all along the front of the property were clusters of rich green foliage belonging to rhododendrons and camellias.

"OK, this is awesome," Joely stated as the road curved around allowing them a fuller front view of the house.

"It certainly is," Andee responded, and pressing gently on the accelerator she made a 180-degree turn into the drive that ran parallel to the meadow's edge. They came to a stop in a large space next to the house where an old red Jeep was parked in front of a row of garages.

As Joely looked at the black front door at the side

of the house she felt a flutter of nervous anticipation come to life inside her. "How far are we from town?" she asked, as Andee began turning the car around to face back down the drive.

"Not much more than a mile," Andee replied, stopping when they, like all the windows at the front of the house, were gazing out toward the dramatic rise and fall of the cliffs that stretched along the coast beyond the meadow. The sea was enchantingly visible thanks to a large V in the rugged landscape, while the tors protecting the house from fierce southwesterly winds hugged up closely behind it and into the far side of the tower.

"So it's walkable," Joely stated. "That's good." She was looking now at the random arrangement of garden beds framed by small rocks and filled with succulents, heather, faded hydrangeas, daffs, snowdrops, hellebores, and even palm trees.

"You have to wonder what it's like inside," Andee commented. "If it's as well tended as the exterior."

Joely turned to her. "I wish I could invite you in . . ."

"It's OK, I understand that she doesn't want visitors."

Joely glanced over to the front door again surprised that no one had come out to meet them. Or maybe her host was waiting for the uninvited guest to leave before welcoming the one she was expecting. "I'll take photos if I can," she said, "and maybe when I've gotten to know her I'll be able to invite you for tea."

Andee smiled. "Do you want me to help you carry your things to the door?"

"It's OK, I can manage," Joely assured her, mindful of a meeting Andee had to get back for.

After taking her bags from the trunk she hugged Andee warmly and walked back to the driver's side with her. "Thanks for bringing me." She smiled. "And for all the moral support."

"It's always yours," Andee assured her. "Stay in touch, won't you?"

"Are you kidding? Of course. If you're free, let's make a tentative arrangement to have lunch next Saturday. We can call or email to confirm when I've got a clearer picture of what my schedule's going to be."

"It's a deal!" Hugging her again, Andee slid into the car and started back down the drive.

As Joely watched her turn at the end to start along the track toward the Valley of Rocks she gave her a wave and only then realized it might have been a good idea to establish that someone was actually at home before she'd let Andee go.

To her astonishment there wasn't.

She could hardly believe it, but the white envelope in plastic wrapping that she found attached to the panel of the doorbell with her name handwritten on the front, told her it was true.

My dear Joely,

Please forgive me for not being here to greet you, but I've been called away unexpectedly and I was unable to get hold of you on the phone. I expect you were crossing the moor where there's little if any mobile reception.

Don't worry, I shall be back tomorrow—

Tomorrow!

—and I've left a key under the pot to your right so you can let yourself in. Please make yourself at home. You'll find more helpful instructions in the kitchen, which is at the far end of the house on the ground floor of the tower. You simply follow the corridor from the entrance hall all the way through to the last door which is facing you. There is plenty to eat courtesy of my housekeeper Brenda Bambridge, who you'll meet in due course.

I am very much looking forward to working with you.

Freda M. Donahoe

Not at all sure how she felt about this, apart from distinctly weird, Joely glanced at her mobile, saw *no service* in the top corner, and having to fight down a surge of annoyance at being cut off in a strange place she accepted there was little else she could do right now but retrieve the key.

It was the smell of the place that greeted her first, kind of musty with drifts of wax and wood smoke and something sweet and flowery. She looked around the spacious entry hall with its wide ornate wooden staircase rising from the center up to a half landing where it divided and disappeared from view. The floor was laid with an intricate mosaic of earth-colored tiles, and the cream-colored paint on the walls was flaking in places and darker in others where smaller paintings had taken the place of larger ones. The magnificent windows that occupied the front wall were like masterpieces in their own right with such stunning views in their frames.

She glanced at the double doors in front of her, wondering what might be on the other side, but felt uncomfortable about snooping (in case she ran into someone or was even being watched). So she followed instructions and walked the long corridor at the back of the house through to the kitchen. It was high-ceilinged and bright thanks to a set of large French doors that led out to the vine-covered patio. The floor was laid with pale flagstones, the many cupboards and units were in honey-colored oak, and there was a long refectory table at the center of the room, and an enormous inglenook fireplace built into the far wall with an armchair on either side of it. There were other doors, presumably leading into a pantry, a utility room, and maybe one of them led to the base of the tor outside. Above the one she'd entered through was a quaint row of four brass servants' bells and since they were labeled *den, front door, music room, library,* and *bed,* she suspected they might work, and was already praying hard that none of them rang while she was here alone.

Maybe she'd go to a hotel and come back in the morning?

Easier said than done with no reception on her phone.

It's not that the place is spooky, she told her mother in her head, *because it isn't, but like any empty house it has the potential to be and given how remote it is I'd really rather not be here alone.*

Silencing her misgivings—or at least storing them until she got to speak to her mother—she picked up a neatly written page from the table containing further instructions.

Dear Joely,

If you're reading this then you're in, so please let me welcome you to Dimmett House and I apologize again for not being here to greet you in person. Brenda has prepared the blue bedroom for you, which you'll find at the top of the main staircase, first door you come to. There is a bathroom en suite and the French windows open onto a balcony that's over the front porch (probably for warmer days).

The library and my writing room are in the tower, I will introduce you to them on my return.

For many years I have been vegetarian so Brenda has prepared a jackfruit, mushroom, and cheese bake which we hope you will enjoy. There is enough for six, so we'll probably be eating it until Friday. Ha ha! You will find plenty of fresh veg to accompany it and Brenda has whisked up a delicious tiramisu for dessert, one of her specialties.

I hope you'll be warm enough, but do light the fire if you'd like to. You'll see a generous supply of logs beside the hearth, with lots of kindling and old newspapers in the cupboard to the right. On the chair closest to the logs I have left a large envelope containing a couple of chapters that I have compiled in readiness for your arrival. I thought it might help to start our discussions. I will explain more about my plans for the memoir when I get back.

Lastly, and I know this will be important, I have put the WiFi code at the bottom of this sheet. Unfortunately, it's more miss than hit out here, but if you don't get a connection right away please be patient because one will come along.

I hope to be back before eleven tomorrow.
Yours truly,
Freda M. Donahoe

Joely looked up from the note and took in her surroundings again. Through the French windows she spotted a rabbit bounding through the long grass and a wooden bench turned toward the sea. It looked bitterly cold out there and dismal in the sleeting rain that had begun to fall. Any thoughts of trudging back to town for the night were fading fast, for if the wind picked up, and she could see from the slant of the trees that it was already starting to, it would slice the skin off her bones before she got to the Valley of Rocks, and no way did she want to walk through there in the dark.

Spotting an electric kettle beside the Aga with an array of brightly colored mugs hanging from the base of the cabinet above, she decided to make herself a cup of tea.

While she waited for the water to boil she entered the WiFi code into her phone and within seconds she was receiving texts. Five came through straightaway: the first two from Sully explaining that Mrs. Donahoe wasn't going to be at home to meet her. The third was from her mother wishing her luck and telling her to call as soon as she could. The fourth was from Callum claiming to understand how badly he was handling things, but could she please be in touch. The fifth warmed her. It was from Holly, saying, *I know you think Dad told me to send the text last night and you're right, he did. Joke! I did it myself because I feel bad about leaving you, but I had my reasons. If you think that's a bit cryptic you should try living with you. Oh you do, I forgot ☺ Anyway if you think I'm missing you you're wrong but I reckon I will if you stay away long enough. H xxx*

The clumsy attempt to ease the tension between them, while warning her not to make too much of it, caused Joely to feel a deep longing for her daughter and the closeness they used to share. It was without doubt the nicest message she'd received from her since Callum had gone, and while she wondered what had really prompted it she knew better than to ask. The wiser course would be to wait a few hours before texting back to say something like *Have I been away long enough yet?* It would make Holly smile in spite of herself, and if Joely could achieve that then there was a good chance they'd start to find their way out of this thorny patch they were trying to get through.

After making some tea she sat down at the table to call her mother.

"Hi, darling, how are you? Where are you?"

"I'm at the house," Joely replied. "Mrs. Donahoe has been called away and won't be back until tomorrow."

"Really? So who was there to let you in?"

"She left a key. I'm here alone."

The connection failed so Joely moved about the kitchen and eventually her mother was back again. "Sorry, I lost you," she said. "Did you get that I'm here alone?"

"Yes, and I said I'm not sure what to make of it. It seems an odd way to greet someone. Are you all right?"

"I think so. There are lots of instructions on how to make myself at home, food in the fridge, a log fire to light. It's a fabulous place, actually, or what I've seen of it is."

When her mother didn't respond she realized she'd been talking to herself for a while.

"Are there neighbors?" her mother suddenly asked.

"Not unless you count the wildlife. Actually, there's a deer in the meadow outside even as we speak, but the town, which is very small, is about a mile away."

"Has she kept her promise about a car?"

"There's a Jeep outside, but she hasn't mentioned it in her note so I wouldn't want to use it, even if I knew where the keys were, which I don't. Anyway, tell me, how things are with you?"

Sighing, her mother said, "Busy, but not in a good way." She disappeared again and came back saying, " . . . so there's no way I'll meet my target this month."

Joely said, "I don't know why you put yourself through the stress of it when you don't actually need to work. Dad left you pretty well off . . ."

"I'd drive myself crazy if I didn't have something to do and you know it. Did you remember to send my love to Andee, by the way?"

"Of course, and she sends hers. Have you been in touch with Holly?"

"Yes, she texted me this morning to ask if she could come and stay for a while."

Joely's heart missed a beat. "So things aren't going so well in her loft?" she said hopefully.

"I don't know if it's that. Apparently Callum and

Martha are going away for a couple of days and she doesn't want to be there alone."

Joely had to swallow as she struggled with the concept of her husband and ex–best friend on a romantic break together. For a moment she felt oddly panicked by it, as though she had to stop them, but how on earth she was supposed to do that she had no idea.

"I shouldn't have told you," her mother said ruefully.

Though Joely wished she hadn't, she said, "It's OK, I'd probably have found out anyway." She wouldn't ask where they were going, there was no point doing that to herself, because if it turned out to be somewhere she and Callum had been together, or had always wanted to go, she didn't think she could bear it.

" . . . are you going to do until your client gets back?"

Joely started to answer but a strange sound suddenly clanged out of nowhere and she froze in shock.

"Joely? What is it?"

Joely turned to the servants' bells. There was a light above one and as it rang again she stepped back as though it might spring from its base to attack her.

Realizing it was the front door, she said, "Someone's here. Stay on the line while I go to find out who it is?"

"It's probably the postman," her mother assured her.

Spurred by the likelihood, Joely went back along the corridor to the front door where her bags were still parked where she'd left them. "Who's there?" she called out, putting an ear to one of the panels.

"Florist," came the reply. "I have a delivery for Mrs. J. Foster."

Blinking in astonishment, Joely whispered to her mother, "Did you hear that?"

"I did. You'll have to open the door."

Joely did as she was told and found herself confronted by a spotty youth brandishing a fulsome bunch of bright yellow daffodils.

"No signature," he told her, and thrusting them into her hand he sprinted back to where he'd left his van.

"Who on earth is sending me flowers?" she said, unable to stop herself thinking of Callum. Obviously they wouldn't be from him, he didn't even know where she was, and anyway, why would he?

"Is there a card?" her mother asked.

Finding one, Joely tugged it free, opened it, and read aloud, "'Daffodils symbolize new beginnings, creativity, and inspiration. Freda Donahoe.'"

"Gosh, how thoughtful," her mother commented.

"Mm," Joely responded, thinking the same, along with something else she couldn't quite define. "I should go and put them in water. I'll call again later if you're not going out."

"I should be home by six. Speak to you then."

An hour later Joely was curled up in one of the armchairs, snug and warm in front of a real fire and pleasantly full after a helping of Brenda's delicious jackfruit bake. She'd have followed it with a spoonful of tiramisu if a rogue memory of sharing the dessert with Callum on holiday in Sicily hadn't shunted her appetite into the deadening plains of her heartbreak.

She understood, she really did, why some people were driven to drink when trapped in all this pain, how the hurt and anguish of it all could send them out of their minds, because sometimes she could feel it happening to her. It had happened when her father died, although that had probably been worse, for she really had lost her mind for a while.

She closed her eyes, knowing that the best way through it was to try not to think about it, consuming though it was, and since one of the main reasons for taking this job was to refocus her mind, she turned to the pages Freda Donahoe had left for her.

By the look of them, they'd been composed on an old-fashioned typewriter that possibly wasn't even electric. Joely found this quaint and even admirable, though she was relieved she'd brought her laptop for she couldn't imagine trying to create a single sentence of her own without the luxury of delete, cut, and paste.

If Callum and Martha were words just think what she could do to them; certainly she wouldn't pair them with "and" in the middle. More likely she'd put them on separate pages, probably even in separate books, or she could simply dump Martha in the trash.

Sighing, she turned to the first page of Freda Donahoe's memoir and started to read.

Half an hour later she went back to the beginning and read through both chapters again, this time asking herself what kind of input Mrs. Donahoe might be hoping for from her.

"There's not much of it yet," she told Andee when she called to find out how Joely was settling in, "but what there is paints a pretty clear picture of a teenage girl on a mission to seduce her music teacher."

"And the girl is her?"

"I think we can take that as read."

"Is the teacher male or female?"

"Very definitely male. It's possible he's encouraging her to come on to him, that actually he's the real manipulator of the piece, but at fifteen she's not mature enough to understand that. It'll be interesting to see where it goes."

"Or ends? I'm thinking of the tragedies you mentioned."

Joely nodded thoughtfully. "An affair with an underage pupil would be a crime, consensual or not, and might indeed impact the rest of the girl's life. Anyway, I don't actually know yet if it does develop into an affair. It's left with some pretty powerful chemistry doing its best, or worst, during a private piano lesson, but so far no physical contact."

There was a smile in Andee's voice as she said, "Have you googled the music teacher yet?"

"No, but I will when I get a decent connection— although it's possible she's using a pseudonym." She started as a gust of wind suddenly rattled the French doors and howled eerily around the tower. "Are you having a storm over your side of the moor?" she asked, staring out at the turbulent shadows of twilight and hoping she didn't spot anything she'd rather not.

"We are," Andee confirmed, "but it's forecast to blow itself through by morning. Have you explored much of the house yet?"

"Actually, no. It's so cozy in this kitchen that I haven't wanted to move, but I suppose I ought to go and check out the blue bedroom where she's put me before it gets dark. I hope she doesn't get power cuts here, that would freak me right out."

"Maybe you should try to find some candles or a torch in case you need them," Andee advised.

"Good idea. I'll do it now, but I swear, if she keeps them in the basement they'll be staying there."

Still smiling at Andee's laugh as she rang off, Joely unraveled herself from the chair and keeping the warm fleece around her shoulders she began rummaging about for a form of emergency light in case she needed it. Fortunately she came across a torch that worked in a table drawer, and spotting an old photograph beside it she took it out and held it up to the light. It was of a small girl, probably no more than three or four, sandwiched between two boys, one not much older than her, perhaps six or seven, the other closer to eleven or twelve. She guessed from their similar shocks of blonde hair and round faces that they were related, probably brothers and sister, though there was nothing written on the back to identify them or the date of when it was taken.

Freda's children when they were young? They might even be grandchildren.

Reflecting on how sorry she was that she and Callum hadn't been able to have more children she put the photograph back in its place and closed the drawer. Time, she decided, to make her first foray up the stairs before it was completely dark outside.

CHAPTER SIX

When Joely woke in the morning it took her a while to remember where she was. She peered around the shadowy room taking in elegant antique furniture, a washstand in one corner with polished brass taps and a flowered porcelain bowl, a wooden armchair, her bags on the carpeted floor half unpacked and partly strewn over an indigo rug. All the time her mind was reconnecting with the blue bedroom, Freda Donahoe, a memoir, here alone . . .

Pushing back the sumptuous duvet with its royal blue cover and hand-crocheted throw, she swung her legs over the side of the bed, and since they didn't quite reach the floor she stumbled as she reached for her phone on the nightstand.

No service.

Sighing, she glanced at the heavy azure curtains where chinks of daylight were brightening the edges. She listened for the sounds of a storm but heard only gulls and a distant sibilance that could be the wash of the waves.

Padding over to the window she pulled one of the curtains aside and because it had been too dark when she'd drawn them last night to get a real sense of the view, she blinked in surprise. It was truly enthralling, all the way down over the grassy meadow to the glimmer of a small sandy beach tucked into the heart of a cove. From there the cliffs, shadowed and brooding, undulated along the coast like fortified barriers to the vast expanse of sea, swelling with life and glistening benignly in the soft morning sunlight.

How could she not think of Callum when confronted with such a romantic view? She wanted him to be here with her, to drink it in, to wrap up warm and walk the coast path with her, climb the rocks and try to remember poems they knew about the sea. Callum, bizarrely, could recite whole verses of the *Ancient Mariner* and she just knew he'd make her listen to them all until he'd finished, all the time hotly denying it when she accused him of going wrong.

"Tell me your favorite love poem," he'd challenged her once, a long time ago, while they were traveling back from a concert in Oxford.

She'd said, "*When I'm sad and lonely, and I feel all hope is gone, I walk along our street and think of you with nothing on.*"

How he'd laughed, and she wasn't sure he'd ever believed that she hadn't made it up. But it was a real rhyme, slightly doctored, that she'd once found in a velvet-covered volume of little-known verse.

Stepping back from the window she let the curtain fall closed and returned to the bed to check her phone again.

Still no signal, so no messages of any kind from anyone; but it was already nine thirty and Freda Donahoe was due back by eleven. She needed to be showered, dressed, and ready to meet her with something intelligent to say about the chapters she'd read.

How weird it was going to seem, welcoming her host back to her own home.

When she'd finished in the blue-and-white-tiled en suite bathroom and had pulled on some jeans and a sweatshirt she ran swiftly down the stairs and straight to the corridor. Halfway along she registered the sound of voices coming from the kitchen and felt momentarily unsure of herself not wanting to barge in on anyone. However, it was probably the housekeeper and her husband, and they must surely know she was here, so they were hardly going to be surprised to see her.

As she pushed open the kitchen door with a gentle half knock she was immediately assailed by the mouth-watering smell of hot toast and fresh coffee.

"Ah, Joely, here you are. Good morning, good morning. Come along in."

The woman who'd spoken so welcomingly was tall and willowy with mannishly cut silver hair and exquisite feminine features. It was hard to tell her age when the years had clearly been kind, but she was certainly over sixty. Her eyes were almond-shaped and blue, surrounded by small webs of faint lines that deepened when she smiled. Her mouth was large and shapely, also troubled by lines but it retained some of the sensuousness it must have exuded when she was young. "I hope we didn't wake you," she said, coming to usher Joely further into the kitchen. "I'm Freda, as you've probably already guessed, and this is Brenda."

"It's lovely to meet you," Joely responded to them both, her eyes widening slightly as the very large Brenda gave her a bawdy sort of wink. She was almost as broad as she was tall, with plump, veiny cheeks and curly gray hair that looked as lively as her chocolate brown eyes.

"It's lovely to meet you too," Brenda declared, as though this very moment had long been on her bucket list. "We're ever so happy to have you here at Dimmett House. I hope you slept well and I see you had some of my jackfruit bake last night. Not a veggie myself, but Mrs. D tells me it's scrumptious."

Enjoying the cozy-looking woman's West Country burr, Joely said, "You're lucky there's any left it's so good, but I thought I ought to share."

Clearly appreciating her sense of humor, Brenda chuckled her way back to the Aga where she appeared to be concocting another culinary delight.

"Do sit down," Freda urged, waving Joely to a place opposite her own at the table. "Would you like toast or crumpets? There's plenty of both, or I'm sure Brenda can rustle up . . ."

"Toast will be fine," Joely assured her, not wanting to put anyone to any trouble.

"There's wholemeal or white," Brenda piped up, passing over a small breadbasket full to the brim and covered by a checked napkin. "The jam's homemade by yours truly—strawberry or crab apple jelly—and the butter's fresh from Pete Miller's farm. There's not a lot of fruit in season, but help yourself to what's there in the bowl. It's all from round here, apples, pears, and some lovely juicy oranges grown in Ann Granger's magic greenhouse. That's what we call it, because that woman can grow anything in there, probably even drugs. Coffee or tea?"

Laughing, Joely said, "Coffee, thank you," and feeling

Freda Donahoe watching her as though curious to see how she was responding to Brenda's touch of local color, she smiled at the woman and helped herself to a half slice of wholemeal followed by a knob of butter and spoonful of crab apple jelly.

Freda said, "As you can see I'm back earlier than expected, and I'm sorry again that I wasn't here to greet you. I'm glad the flowers arrived as ordered. Well done for finding a vase, and you managed to choose exactly the right one."

Joely glanced at the daffs she'd more or less plonked in a white pitcher that she'd found in one of the cupboards. They were now on a low windowsill, beside the French doors, moved from the table where she'd left them, presumably to clear a space for breakfast.

"Did you remember to trim the stems?" Freda asked, eyes lowered as she spread butter over a crumpet.

Thankful that she had, Joely smiled. "My mother is always very strict about that. And I popped some sugar and cider vinegar into the water to make them last longer."

Freda was clearly impressed. "Another little trick of your mother's?" she asked with a crispness that was somewhere between interest and irritation.

"Well, I . . . Not hers, exactly. I—"

"Oh, everyone knows about that," Brenda chirruped as she plonked a large jug of orange juice on the table. "Have you taken your pills yet this morning, Mrs. D? Shall I fetch them for you?"

"Thank you," Freda replied gratefully. To Joely she said, "Hypertension, I'm afraid. It runs in the family, although my husband suffered from it too, and from quite a young age. Do try the orange juice and tell me if it isn't the best you've ever had."

Obediently Joely filled a glass and after taking a generous sip she was more than ready to agree. It wasn't only sweet and cool; there was a hint of tartness to it that whipped up her taste buds with a longing for more. "The very best," she confirmed, after draining the glass.

Freda gestured for her to take a refill and said, "Now will you have some more toast? Half a slice doesn't seem very much."

"Thank you," Joely replied, and helping herself to another half from the basket she set it down on her plate and bit into the first one to experience yet another heavenly assault on her taste buds. "This jelly is delicious," she told Brenda, dabbing crumbs from the corner of her mouth. "Is it your own recipe?"

Brenda beamed as she passed Freda a large pill organizer with a different color for each day of the week. "My grandmother's," she confided. "We've got a secret ingredient that stays in the family, but it makes all the difference."

"We're very lucky to have some," Freda declared. "Brenda's jelly sells out before she's even made it, so I feel very fortunate that she keeps a jar or two back for me."

"Course I do," Brenda smiled fondly. "Can't have you going without, can we? Now make sure you get it right, taking these pills can be a complicated business."

Freda's expression was droll as she obediently popped the medication and washed it all down with a mouthful of juice. "Do either of your parents suffer with the same affliction?" she asked Joely. "It's very common amongst us older people."

Surprised by the question, Joely said, "I'm pretty sure my mother's blood pressure is OK, and my father's no longer with us."

Freda immediately looked sad. "I'm so sorry to hear that," she said. "Was it recent?"

"About eighteen months ago, but we still miss him."

"Yes, I'm sure you do. It's never easy when a loved one passes. Do you have brothers or sisters?"

"A brother, Jamie. He lives in Dublin with his wife and two children, so we don't get to see him as often as we'd like."

"Dublin?" She sat with the word or notion of it for some time, before suddenly continuing. "That's a shame, although I'm sure it's a perfectly nice place. Is he older or younger than you?"

"Older."

Freda nodded and fell silent again as though this was information that needed deeper consideration, or perhaps her mind had moved to other things. Whatever, she seemed not to hear when Brenda said, "Mrs. D is always interested in people's families, aren't you, dear?"

When Freda didn't respond Brenda put a finger to her lips as if to say they wouldn't go any further with the subject for now. "All right, so I've got a lovely leek and potato soup going here for your lunch," she announced, turning back to the bubbling pot on the Aga. "There's plenty of crusty bread in the box and a nice chunk of local cheddar if you want it. Mrs. D isn't vegan, but she's very strict about where the dairy products come from. We don't look much farther than

North Devon for supplies and always from farms we know treat their livestock well."

"You haven't asked Joely if she'd prefer to have meat," Freda pointed out. "If you do," she said to Joely, "I have no objection, but . . ."

"No, really, I'm vegetarian," Joely assured her. "I care about animals too, and the planet."

Freda smiled. "Of course, the planet," she echoed and seemed to sink into the timeliness of the reminder. Then suddenly banging her hands on the table, she said, "I think we're going to get along well. I told Brenda we would. Didn't I say that, Brenda?"

"It's exactly what you said," Brenda confirmed. "Mrs. D and Edward carried out a careful search before settling on you," she informed Joely. "They had to be sure it was the right person or it wasn't going to work."

Joely said, "Edward?"

"My nephew," Freda explained. "He did most of the liaising with my publisher, and when they presented me with a shortlist I had a feeling right away about you. Naturally, I had to read some of your work first, and I'm delighted to say I was most impressed, particularly by the fiction you've helped to produce. It wasn't possible to tell how much of the books was ghosted— my guess is quite a lot—and if I'm right about that it means your talent for capturing your client's style is exceptional. Not once did I feel a stranger's presence creeping into the prose, something that always makes me shudder, nor were there excessive amounts of sentiment in the autobiographies. In fact, in my opinion, they were far better served by the kind of subtlety and restraint that I'm certain was your careful hand, because the official authors I'm thinking of are not known for those qualities." Her smile was roguish and infectious. "So, my dear," she continued, "I say that you have precisely the right sort of skill to undertake a memoir such as mine."

Pleased by the praise, and even faintly embarrassed, Joely said, "I'm glad you think so, and I'm looking forward to starting—"

"But you've already started," Freda interrupted in confusion. "I take it you read what I left for you yesterday?"

"Yes, of course," Joely assured her, not wanting to think of how this might now go if she hadn't, "and I was left wondering why you need me when you're writing it so well . . ."

"It's only the beginning. There's a long way to go, and beginnings are always easy. You are to be my objectivity. I want you to tell me what you thought of those first pages, but not in the way you've just tried, using flattery and self-modesty, and not now. I'm tired after my early start this morning so I'm going to lie down for a while."

Joely watched her get up from the table and hold her coffee mug out for Brenda to refill. In a softer tone she said, "I have some documents I'd like you to look through and sign if you're willing. You're probably familiar with NDAs—nondisclosure agreements?"

Though Joely certainly knew what they were this was the first time she'd been asked to sign one. "I'll be happy to," she replied, thinking of what she'd already discussed with Andee and though it wasn't much, at least Andee was someone she could trust to keep things to herself.

"The forms are there," Freda said, nodding toward a buff file at the end of the table. "When you're done, give them to Brenda and she'll send them off to the lawyer." She checked the time. "Let's say we meet back here at one thirty for some soup before we get started. Now, if you'll excuse me . . ."

After she'd disappeared through a door in the corner Joely looked over at Brenda, who was once again busying herself at the Aga as if nothing unusual had happened—and in truth Joely couldn't say that it had. What was more unusual, now she came to think of it, was the fact that she hadn't been asked to sign an NDA before. It would make sense if the client was anxious to stop her going to the press before he or she was ready to reveal all they had to tell.

Maybe they'd instinctively trusted her, and with good reason, for it had never occurred to her to try to make money out of selling someone's secrets.

"Can I get you more coffee?" Brenda asked, coming to clear Freda's side of the table. "It's still hot."

"Thanks." Joely smiled and held out her mug.

Taking it, Brenda clutched it in both hands and stood gazing at Joely as if she were some sort of prodigal returned. Then she said, "Mrs. D can be a bit different sometimes, changeable like, and she gets lost somewhere inside her own head, you know, the way writers do, but take it from me she's a wonderful woman. I've worked for her over twenty years and I wouldn't ever want to work for anyone else. My Bill feels the same. That's my other half. He takes care of the maintenance and garden around here and drives her if she wants to go anywhere."

Mindful that Freda hadn't mentioned where she'd been until this morning, Joely said, "Did he drive her yesterday?"

"Oh yes, and waited overnight to bring her back."

"So where did they go?"

Brenda tapped the side of her nose. "Oh now, that's not for me to say. Anything she wants you to know she'll tell you herself. That's the way it is, and I respect that." She raised the mug. "I'll get that coffee."

Not sure whether she'd been scolded or warned or simply brought up to speed, Joely reached for the file, but before starting to read she said, "Can I ask one thing? Mrs. D mentioned her husband—"

"Oh, he's gone." Brenda sighed sadly. "We lost him about three years back. Terrible it was, and him still so young, relatively speaking. It's when she stopped going out, not that she was a gadabout before that . . . Well, like I said, whatever she wants you to know she'll tell you herself, and," she added with a twinkle, "I daresay you'll end up knowing a lot more than me once this memoir's done. That's provided she tells you everything— and how would we know if she doesn't?"

"I guess," Andee said, when Joely called her from the thatch-roofed pub on the harbor front to tell her about the NDA, "the question is, do we want to know?"

Puzzled, Joely said, "Don't we?"

"Only teasing." Andee laughed. "Of course we do, and I'm more intrigued than ever now you can't talk about it. I take it you signed."

"I didn't see any harm in it, so yes." Thanking the barman as he put a small glass of local ale in front of her, she said, "I can't help wondering where she went yesterday."

"Does it matter?"

"No, but why not just say?"

"I'm afraid I can't answer that, apart from to remind you that you're dealing with an obsessively private person. Can you hang on a moment?"

As she waited Joely sipped the ale and smiled her appreciation at the barman who'd offered her a glass on the house as a welcome to Lynmouth. Whether he did this for every newcomer she had no idea, although she doubted it, considering what a popular tourist destination this was. So it probably meant that word had got out, presumably through Brenda, that Mrs. Donahoe had a rare guest who should be treated well.

She'd walked into town, wrapped up in a padded coat, scarf, and hat, enjoying the brittle, bright winter sunshine and how much less eerie the Valley of Rocks felt when under a blue sky. Still otherworldly, that was for sure, the kind of place where cults would come for midnight rituals and poets for divine inspiration. The towering rocks were like monarchs gazing Canute-like out to sea, and the valley itself, sheltered from the elements, was a dry, stony bowl in the landscape that had the feel of an amphitheater, or, as she'd thought yesterday, a place on the moon. The only sounds came from the low burble of hikers as they passed through, the cry of cormorants, and clatter of goats' hooves as they scrambled over scree and slate and dilapidated walls.

Going through the clifftop town she'd passed the new and old cemeteries, a school, and the Convent of Poor Clares that appeared deserted, so where were they now?

There was an abundance of teashops and coffee bars, Victorian town houses doubling as hotels and B & Bs, a candlemaker, an art gallery, a beautiful old church, and a filigree archway leading to the famous funicular. Riding down over the cliff face in the quaint green carriage had been utterly joyful, not unnerving at all in spite of the twenty-nine-degree angle and a teenage wit telling his friends they were going to crash.

"Hi, sorry about that," Andee said, coming back on the line. "So where are you now?"

"At the Rising Sun, next to the harbor," Joely replied, drinking more of the Exmoor ale and thinking she could get to like it as much as the pub with its low white ceilings, crisscrossed with black beams, undulating stone walls, and notice for ferret racing at Brendon Town Hall. "Did you know you can see Wales from here? Well, yes, of course you did, and the Rhenish tower on the harbor wall used to be where they stored water for indoor baths. That was before it got itself a lightbulb and became a beacon."

"Are you reading from a guidebook?" Andee asked drily.

"How did you guess, but it's fascinating stuff, or I think so anyway."

"Great, now tell me more about Freda Donahoe. Are you going to get along with her?"

Pulling a face, Joely said, "I hope so, but I don't think she's going to be easy. Still, show me a client who is, and I'll show you someone who doesn't care about the end result. She was married, by the way. Her husband died about three years ago, I think unexpectedly, but the housekeeper was sparing with details."

"So one of the tragedies?"

"Quite possibly, because apparently that was when she became a recluse, but the parts of the memoir I've read date back to the late sixties. Still, it's only the beginning so the end could have happened three years ago."

"A long way to go. Listen, I'm afraid I'll need to ring off in a minute, but are we still on for meeting up at the weekend? I don't mind driving over there again, but I'll wait to hear from you about your schedule."

Talk of the weekend inevitably turned Joely's thoughts to Callum and the couple of days away he was planning with Martha. It made her feel so lonely all of a sudden, so cut off from their life together, from the joy they used to gain from shared experiences, and now here she was, all on her own in a new place she knew he'd love.

Andee said gently, "Are you still there?"

"Yes, I'm here," Joely replied brightly.

"Any news from London?"

Joely's heart twisted and sank. "None so far today. I'll text Holly and my mother before I go back to the house; the others will just have to find a way to live without me."

Sounding sympathetic, Andee said, "I know this isn't much comfort, but they seem to be having a hard time living with themselves after what they've done."

"And I'm supposed to feel sorry for them?" Joely countered.

"Not at all, but try not to make things worse for yourself by creating scenarios in your head that are probably a long way from the truth."

Knowing how caught up she was in that very form of self-torment Joely felt her tension begin to unravel. "Thanks for that," she said, "and now I should probably let you go."

After ringing off she sat quietly finishing up her ale, enjoying the peace and quiet of a near-empty bar, the only sounds coming from the clank and rattle of a delivery going on somewhere outside and the noisy birds around the shore. Then she picked up the sough of the waves and hum of voices outside; the salty scent in the air wafted in as someone opened the door and mingled with the yeasty smell of beer. Although she couldn't seem to stop fixating on Callum and how sad she felt that he wasn't here, she was also aware of how relieved she was to be so far away from him and Martha-the-manta-ray with lovely horn-shaped fins and twenty-foot width.

Stop being childish, Joely. Focus on this assignment instead, because after this morning's brief meeting it's clearly going to be far from dull.

She looked down as her phone buzzed with a text.

I know you're not going to answer this, but I wanted to let you know that Holly's gone to stay with your mother. I think she misses you, as do I.

The last three words hit Joely hard. Why had he added them? What was the point when he didn't mean them, probably hadn't even thought about them, merely done what he always did as though nothing between them had changed? *Damn you, Callum,* she seethed inwardly. *Damn you for making me think there might still be hope when you're about to go away with Martha. What the hell is wrong with you?*

She tensed as another text arrived. If it was from him, she was going to ring and tell him to stop messaging, that she didn't want to hear from him and anything important about Holly she could hear from Holly herself or her mother.

Are you somewhere in the house, or have you popped out? FMD

Not sure whether she was relieved or angry that it wasn't him, she checked the time and noting that it was still more than an hour before she and Freda had agreed to meet in the kitchen, she sent a reply. *On my way back. Walking, so should be there by one thirty.*

She wasn't expecting a response to that so was surprised when one came saying, *You should have taken the car.*

Since it wasn't possible to tell whether this was a rebuke or simply a kindly reminder that it was at her disposal, Joely swallowed the rest of her drink, zipped up her coat, and after thanking the bartender she started back to Dimmett House.

CHAPTER SEVEN

"Hey Jude" was playing in the kitchen when Joely returned, the slow, mournful chords coming, she realized, from an iPad propped up on the dresser. She hadn't imagined Freda being into gadgets, much less knowing how to download music onto a tablet.

It just went to show how mistaken first impressions could be.

Freda was at the Aga stirring the soup and humming along, glancing up only once to let Joely know she'd heard her come in.

Remembering that the song was mentioned in the memoir's first chapter, Joely wondered if this was her host's way of reminding her they had work to do. Well, Joely was here now, and she wasn't late, so she didn't need to apologize for keeping her client waiting. She simply removed her coat and scarf and hung them on the back of the door.

"Is there anything I can do?" she offered, going to the Aga.

Freda seemed on the point of replying when she lifted her head and sniffed the air. She turned to Joely curiously. "Have you been drinking?" she asked, still holding the stirring spoon.

Flushing, Joely said, "I was invited to try a local ale at the Rising Sun."

Freda nodded thoughtfully, and instructed Joely to sit down as she picked up a ladle to fill a bowl from the pot.

Doing as she was told, Joely said, "I'm sorry. I don't want you to think that drinking at lunchtime . . ."

"Were you offered one of Auntie Marian's hot pickled onions?" Freda interrupted, setting a serving of soup in front of Joely.

Startled, Joely said, "No."

"Mm, shame. They're very good." She went to fetch some soup for herself and settled down at her usual place. "The next time you're at the pub," she said, picking up a napkin, "perhaps you'd be kind enough to bring back a bottle of Exmoor Gold for me."

Thrown, not only because she was sure she'd earned her first black mark but apparently hadn't, but also because it sounded as though Freda actually went to the pub herself on occasion. Joely asked if it were true.

"Rarely," Freda replied, unrolling her napkin. Then changing the subject, "I don't have a computer, but I do have this iPad. Edward talked me into it and I must say I find it a very useful research tool." She took a mouthful of soup and continued. "I've compiled the music mentioned in the first two chapters of the memoir. I thought it would provide a good backing track to our discussions. Get us in the mood, so to speak, maybe even transport us back to that time." She laughed, and corrected herself, "Well, me anyway. You're far too young, obviously. Bread?"

She drew a large wooden board containing several crusty slices toward them as "Hey Jude" faded to a merciful end and what Joely guessed to be "The Gaelic

Blessing" began—a sweet and melancholic melody that was quite hypnotic, she found.

To Joely's surprise Freda began singing softly with the choir while looking across the table, almost as if serenading her.

"'Deep peace of the running wave to you,'" she sang. Unsure where to look or what to do Joely was relieved when it finished and Freda started her soup.

"Rather fitting for where we are in our acquaintance, don't you think?" Freda asked. "And for where we are on this beautiful planet we're so keen to save."

Though it was an unusual next step in their acquaintance Joely had to agree that actually it did seem quite fitting on both counts, and feeling safe now to pop a spoonful of soup into her mouth she did so, not having wanted to during Freda's performance.

"Sunshine of Your Love" was next, and Freda's shoulders moved with the beat as she ate her meal and broke apart a chunk of bread.

"He loved this," she said, casually.

Joely swallowed a mouthful of soup, realizing that they must be talking about Sir. She placed her spoon gently back on the table, eager to hear more. But Freda just continued to boogie and eat, clearly enjoying herself immensely. At least until, to quote from her memoir, the first two magical words of "Young Girl" flew into the room and a change came over her that Joely found quite strange—as if the whole thing wasn't strange enough. Freda became very still as though trapped in the words and their resonance, carried away into memories they seemed to stir . . . Was it pleasure or pain?

She put down her spoon and ran her knotty fingers

through her hair. She seemed to be shaking as she sat quietly throughout the song, and when at last it played out she sat still for a while, staring at her bowl, until finally she looked at Joely with an expression that somehow managed to be both sad and faintly self-mocking. "If ever there was a theme tune," she murmured.

She was right, it could have been written especially for young Freda and her music teacher, and how power-fully it must have captured them when it was released at the very start of their . . . affair? It must have been that, surely, it had to be where the story was going, but perhaps more than an affair considering the need to write about it all these years later.

After a while Joely ventured, softly, "Do you know where he is now?"

Freda frowned, not in confusion but in something more like disapproval. "We'll get there," she replied, "and please don't ask me questions like that again."

Stung, Joely continued her soup and quietly listened to the piano recital now playing—Debussy's "Clair de lune," Freda informed her.

Halfway through, Freda said, "Tell me what you think of the writing style I've adopted. Do you find the first person, present tense an approach that works, or would you advise something different?"

Thinking fast, Joely lowered her spoon and said, "The way it is brings the reader right into the moment, so I wouldn't change it."

Freda considered this, tilting her head to one side as she smiled in apparent satisfaction.

Another piano recital began. "Chopin Nocturne Number Two in E-flat Major," she said. "I've selected these pieces at random because they're well known. I don't actually remember what was played at the parents' house the weekend private piano lessons were discussed. Do you think that matters? The fact that I've . . . improvised?"

"Not at all," Joely replied, unable to understand why it would.

"I deliberately didn't say fictionalized, but would you agree that sometimes, in a memoir, it's necessary to help the facts a little, either to make them more interesting, or to bring clarity to a complex situation? Or simply to move things along."

"Ye-es," Joely replied, drawing out the word and hoping it was the answer her client was looking for.

Freda nodded and nodded again. "What do you think of my parents and their friends?" she asked bluntly. "Do you find them appallingly debauched and irresponsible?"

Mindful that it was never a good idea to be critical of someone's relatives, Joely said, "I think they were people of their time and probably very interesting parents to have."

Freda chomped on a mouthful of bread as she absorbed this, then asked, "Would you say that Mother was in favor of an affair with Sir? That she tried to nudge me into it even?"

Judging it wise to counter this with a question of her own, Joely said, "Why would you think that?"

"Well, she knew I wanted private lessons and asked me if I had a crush on him. If she thought that, wouldn't finding another teacher have been the right thing to do?"

Thinking she had a point, Joely said, "Do you blame your mother for . . . what happened?"

Freda eyed her beadily. "You don't know what happened," she reminded her.

"No, but I'm presuming there was a relationship that . . . didn't end well?"

Freda didn't deny it, she simply got up from the table and carried her bowl to the sink. The music changed to a ponderous recital—Erik Satie's Gymnopedie No. 1, Freda told her, and added, "He could play everything you've heard. He was very talented."

Was she using the past tense because he was no longer alive, or because it had happened a long time ago? She ought to be able to ask, but her client had already made it clear that she was not receptive to questions that would reveal any detail of where her story was going.

She watched as Freda stood listening to the melancholic melody and wondered what she was seeing and thinking as she gazed down across the meadow toward the cove.

After a while Freda checked the time on her watch, then put her hands in her pockets as she continued to stare at the outside world. It was as though she was expecting someone to arrive—or the tide to come in? Suddenly she turned around.

"Tell me what you were like when you were fifteen," she said as though it were a perfectly natural question to ask—and maybe it was.

Joely began struggling for an answer, wanting to make herself sound interesting, or at least a little more colorful than the predictable, studious, hardly rebellious spirit she'd been.

Freda said, "Were you promiscuous? Maybe you had a crush on a teacher."

"No and yes," Joely replied. "I was quite shy, actually, but I remember having some pretty lurid fantasies about the PE coach."

She couldn't tell whether Freda was still listening; her back was turned again and it was a while before she said, "We're none of us really as fascinating as we like to think we are. Would you agree with that?"

Doing her best to keep up, Joely said, "Probably."

Freda picked up a bowl of apples and brought it to the table. "Did you visit my library yesterday?" She plonked the fruit down, her eyes were burning with interest.

Joely said, "In your note you mentioned you'd intro-duce—"

"Then let's go," Freda interrupted. "I want you to see where I write, and if it appeals to you I shall invite you to work there while you ghost."

After disposing of her own soup bowl in the sink, Joely followed Freda through the door Freda had disap-peared through earlier this morning and up a narrow staircase to another door with the same cast-iron handle and thumb latch as many others around the house.

Clicking it open, Freda stepped into a large square room and threw out her arms. "Here we are," she declared, spinning around as she indicated the book-shelves so crammed and weighted by publications of every shape, size, and color that there was no room left for anything else but two tall arched windows over-looking the meadow and cliffs beyond, and another door.

Joely took it all in, mesmerized by the collection of so many novels and biographies, reference works, volumes of poetry, plays, bound manuscripts, foreign-language editions of Freda's own literary creations. There was so much, and as far as she could tell everything was categorized and alphabetized, there was even a rolling librarian's ladder parked in one corner and an exquisite though worn leather reading chair complete with lamp and footrest.

"My husband had this part of the house added on for me," Freda told her. "He designed it himself. He found it amusing to gift me an ivory tower and I admit I found it amusing too—until I saw it and then, of course I fell in love with it. How could I not? It provides me with all the privacy and quiet I need to work, or to relax, and naturally one never tires of the view. It changes every day, and it nourishes me in ways nothing else can. It's my great love now, this library, and my writing room." She moved to the opposite door, but before thumbing down the latch, she pointed to a sign and read out the words, "*Schauen Sie tief in die Natur, und Sie werden alles besser verstehen.* Do you know what that means?"

Joely shook her head. "Is it German?" she ventured.

Freda gave a laugh of approval. "It's a quote from Einstein," she replied. "*Look deep into nature, and then you will understand everything better.*" Another gift from my husband, and when you go up to the writing room you'll understand why he considered it to be appropriate."

At the top of the next staircase, the upper level of the square tower, there was another door, this one already half open and as Joely followed Freda through she saw right away why Mr. Donahoe's wife loved it so much. It was surely every writer's dream to have a place like this. Though it was smaller than the library, and with only a few select books on the shelves, the sense of calm, the light, the sheer essence of the room must surely be as invigorating and inspirational as any writer could ever wish for.

"Special, isn't it?" Freda commented.

Joely nodded, still taking it in. There was a day bed draped in white muslin against one wall, an armchair that matched the one downstairs, a marquetry cabinet, and an Edwardian leather-topped writing desk with bow legs, five drawers, and small brass ring handles. On top of the desk was an old-fashioned Remington typewriter with a blank sheet wound into the roller and a box full of black spooled ribbons beside it.

"I order them from America," Freda replied to Joely's unasked question. "The machine itself was my father's. I know there are easier ways to work these days, but I'm attached to it."

Tearing herself from the fascination of a bygone era Joely crossed to one of the windows, wanting to get a closer look at the balcony that hugged it. It was large enough to stand on, she discovered, though perhaps not when it was so cold outside, and even then she felt sure that being out there would give her vertigo considering how high they were. She looked ahead at a whirling formation of seabirds and on to the restless waves glittering in a sudden burst of sunlight. *Look deep into nature, and then you will understand everything better.* From here there was only a look into nature.

She turned to find Freda watching her.

100

"Is this somewhere you'd like to work?" Freda asked hopefully, generously. "You can bring your laptop, but I shall ask you to use a font that is similar to my Remington's. After all these years I find it easier to read—and I'd like you to print out the pages when you've finished so I don't have to critique on a screen. Is that acceptable to you?"

"Of course," Joely replied, "but do you have a printer?"

"I don't, but Edward has organized for one to be delivered sometime today." Her eyes performed a slow progress into twinkle. "And once you're underway in here I shall wait with bated breath elsewhere in the house for you to bring me your literary interpretations of our discussions. Is that acceptable to you? Will you take notes, or did you bring a voice recorder?"

Not a little daunted by this on several levels, Joely tackled the unstated one first. "Are you meaning that you want me to continue the first draft?" she asked.

No hesitation. "Correct. With the first two chapters I've established a style for you to emulate, and I have every confidence that you'll do so with great skill and sensitivity. Taking a step back like this will allow me to call upon a more objective viewpoint, and at the same time it'll give me an idea of how you see my life." She gave a sudden laugh that softened her features and seemed to dispel the strange air of intensity. "Don't look so worried," she chided. "Before you write anything we'll talk, at length. I'll tell you everything that happened and you'll transform it into words that everyone will believe I've written myself."

It wasn't as though Joely hadn't worked this way before, often because the client was either too busy or too lazy to do it themselves—and just as often because they had no writing skills. None of these applied to Freda M. Donahoe, who was an established author of a literary standard that Joely wasn't at all sure she could emulate, much less meet.

"It'll simply be a first draft," Freda reminded her, picking up on Joely's misgivings. "When it's done we'll review and edit it together and if need be I'll take over from there. Would that suit you?"

Joely said, "Yes, I'm sure it will. I just . . . Well . . ."

"Don't be intimidated," Freda instructed. "I have no doubt that we'll soon fall into a pattern that will work extremely well for us both. I don't want you to be shy about making suggestions, and you must feel free to give me your opinions on certain behaviors. I asked you about my parents earlier, and what sort of people you considered them to be. It's going to be helpful to me to see them—and myself—through your eyes. Did you warm to young Freda?"

Wishing she felt better prepared for this, while realizing she had to get herself off the spot before she came out with the wrong thing, Joely said, "I'd like to have some time to think about that," and before Freda could respond she pointed to a door beside the day bed. "What's through there?" she asked.

Unruffled by this small distraction, Freda raised her eyebrows humorously. "A WC," she replied, and glanced over her shoulder as a voice carried up from downstairs.

"Yoohoo, I'm back."

To Joely's relief it was Brenda, who'd returned to clear up after lunch and to take away any laundry that needed doing. At least while Freda was busy with her, Joely would have a little time to collect her thoughts and maybe even read through those first two chapters again. She'd had no idea she was going to be questioned about them in quite such a personal way, and nor had she expected to be writing the rest of the first draft herself. If anything, after reading the first chapters, she'd imagined her role was going to be more of a sounding board, a researcher, perhaps even a line editor, with some occasional ghostwriting. However, if she'd learned anything from this past half an hour with Freda Donahoe it was that if she, Joely Foster, wanted to make an impression on her unusual and clearly unpredictable client she was going to need all her wits about her.

"So," Freda said with a smile as they settled down at either side of the kitchen fireplace after Brenda had gone, "have you decided yet whether you're warming to the young Freda?"

Used to clients referring to themselves in the third person, especially when discussing behavior or events they might not be proud of, Joely said, "I'm still forming an opinion, but she certainly intrigues me." And before Freda could take the ball back to her court she said, "What do *you* think of her?"

Appearing surprised by the question, but ready to take the challenge, Freda said, "I think she's vain, ignorant, and arrogant."

Joely hadn't expected that. "Harsh words to speak about yourself, especially when you were at such a tender age."

"Do you think I have to like who I was back then?"

"No, but if you're still angry with your fifteen-year-old self it'll come through and—" She broke off as Freda waved a dismissive hand.

"I was naïve," she declared, "vulnerable and hormonal. I thought I knew more than I possibly could at fifteen, and my parents encouraged me to believe it."

"So you're still angry with them?"

Freda's eyes shifted to the flames as she considered this. It seemed to take a long time for her to formulate an answer, until in the end she folded her hands almost prayer-like and began to shake her head. "I loved my parents," she said softly. "I loved them very much and they suffered in ways no parent should ever have to."

Joely held her silence, and even her breath. She pictured the raucous weekend parties and motherly chats that had influenced and confused a young girl; the respectable tax lawyer and his wife the civil servant who wrote speeches for ministers. Could they still be alive? They'd be very old if they were. What had happened to them? What had happened to the husband, and was there any other family today besides the nephew?

Freda spoke again, this time in a tone that was light, even bordering on playful as she said, "How do you feel about explicit sex?"

Joely stared at her.

"Writing it, I mean."

Joely swallowed, and tried to work out what the right response should be.

"Do you think sex should be portrayed in graphic detail?" Freda inquired. "Or should it be approached with the use of subtle innuendo and metaphor?"

Still not certain of herself, Joely said, "Probably the latter?"

"Mm," Freda murmured. "I suppose it's not really possible for you to give an intelligent answer, is it, until you know what happened after the piano lesson."

Smarting at the *intelligent answer*, Joely reached for her notebook and recorder as any good ghostwriter should.

CHAPTER EIGHT

I shall not be the first girl in our year to lose my virginity, but I shall be the first—and only one—to lose it to Sir. No one knows that. I'm not stupid, I realize he could get into a lot of trouble if anyone found out and I'd hate for him to be sent away. I wouldn't want to go on living if that happened. I'd be like Cathy in *Wuthering Heights* after Heathcliff left, it would make me very ill and when I die Sir will have visions of me until he dies.

A savage book.

I don't believe they were vampires.

I wonder if Sir thinks they were. I shall ask him when we have our next private piano lesson.

I haven't been able to stop thinking about him since the first one. I'm so full up with thoughts of him that I can't listen in my other classes and I'm not interested in my friends. They don't understand what it's like to be in love, I mean *really* in love. They're too immature. The boys they like are unformed men whose voices are squawks and who have no idea how to behave with a girl.

Sir didn't kiss me at the end of our last lesson but I *know* he wanted to, and he would have if we hadn't heard Mandy Gibbons and Tricia Hill giggling outside the window.

How childish they are.

After that Sir said, "I'm sorry," but I'm not sure what

he was sorry for. His cheeks were red and as he turned away from me I saw his hands clench tightly closed. I think it's because they wanted to touch me, but he had to make them stop.

I want him to touch me more than anything. I lie on my bed imagining it; I go through lessons almost feeling the brush of his fingers on my skin and his mouth on mine. While I was at home for the weekend I wrote him letters to tell him how much I was missing him. There were lots of other things I wanted to write, but I didn't quite have the nerve.

My parents went out to an exhibition of photographs taken by the friend of a friend who knows the Beatles. Left alone in the house I took off all my clothes and walked around talking to Sir in my mind and imagining him watching me. I saw myself as Juliette in my parents' favorite old film, *And God Created Woman*. My hair is blond like hers, and my legs are long. My nipples stand out large from my breasts and when I touch them I pretend my fingers are Sir's.

I enjoy being naked almost as much as I enjoy thinking about him.

I play a game writing both our names on a sheet of paper and striking out all the letters we share. I go through those that are left, *he loves me, he loves me not*, and it ends with *he loves me*.

I'm going to keep that piece of paper forever.

I've decided that when I go for my next piano lesson I will keep my hockey kit on after the practice game that comes before. The pleated skirt is very short and I can open my shirt buttons so he can see my bra. I won't wear the boots. I'll change back into my plimsolls and short socks and I'll pretend I didn't have time to go back to the dorm to put on my uniform.

It's the night before my private lesson and Sir has come into the boarders' recreation hall where most of us fifth formers, after finishing an hour of prep, are playing our records and dancing. (First- to fourth-year girls have already gone to bed and the sixth formers are either in their cubicles or their common room.)

"Bend Me, Shape Me" is on the turntable and I'm not sure whether I'm relieved or sorry that he didn't come in before while we were playing "Let's Spend the Night Together." We'd all be put in detention if anyone heard us playing this record so it's quite scratched because of how often we have to whisk it off and turn it over to "Ruby Tuesday."

I think Sir would have been embarrassed if he'd walked in on us dancing to that, but I don't think he'd have given us detentions.

He's blushing now because a couple of the girls are gyrating up to him and trying to get him to join in to "Bend Me, Shape Me." I can tell he thinks they're juvenile and wishes they'd leave him alone.

"Come on, Sir, we know you can dance, Sir."

I carry on as if I don't know he's there, jerking my arms and legs to the beat, writhing my hips and throwing out my hair. I think of him bending and shaping me however he wants me, and me telling him that as long as he loves me . . . A hand touches my shoulder. As I turn around I'm singing " . . . it's all right." And then I can't find my words because I hadn't realized it was him.

"Sorry to interrupt," he says in my ear. The music is loud and some girls are singing along at the tops of their voices. That could be one reason he's so close to me . . .

My heart is pounding like the drum in the song and I can feel certain eyes on us. Eyes that belong to jealous and gossipy girls who'd kill to have Sir talk to them.

His hand is still on my shoulder and he's leaning in to me again. He says, "I'm afraid I have to cancel our lesson tomorrow," and when I realize what he's said I want to shout, *No! You can't. I won't let you.* I see myself in my hockey skirt, my shirt open, his eyes on my skin, his hand moving on my thigh . . . It all flashes in front of me and I realize everyone's looking at us. There's fire in my cheeks, and shaking in my hands.

He says something else. I don't catch it so he says it again, softly and very close to my ear. "Better run, girl," and only as he walks away do I realize it's a line from the song "Young Girl."

CHAPTER NINE

Joely had finished ghosting her first pages for Freda's memoir, pages that had contained no sex, explicit or otherwise. In fact, to Joely's mind, they didn't contain very much at all. Apart, she supposed, from a further glimpse into young Freda's character, and the blurring of lines around who was the real seducer.

Perhaps there was more there than she was allowing for, something more subtle that would gain its proper significance the further into the memoir they went. As it was, having been given so little information during their discussion it hadn't taken Joely more than a day to produce the few paragraphs she'd felt it warranted. After, she'd gone back over them several times, comparing them with Freda's opening chapters to check that the style was similar enough for Freda to deem them worthy of use as a first draft. (It was Joely's secret hope that Freda would find them so convincing that she'd feel confident enough to let them pass as her own work.)

In the end, having decided that her efforts portrayed young Freda in the light her older counterpart had intended—vain and arrogant, certainly naïve but perhaps now there was the suggestion of her being as much a victim as a predator—she'd handed over the pages for inspection (feeling a little apprehensive, she had to admit, given how keen she was to impress).

Freda had thanked her politely, said she would read with interest and had promptly taken herself off to her room.

Twenty-four hours later she was still there.

They couldn't be that bad, surely.

"Mrs. D won't be joining you today," Brenda had informed her again this morning. No explanation, or indication of when she might expect to see her host, simply, "More porridge? Did I tell you the honey's from Bob Allsop's hives and a sweeter concoction you won't find anywhere."

After breakfast Brenda said, "How about a little tour? Of the house."

Whether this was at Freda's prompting, or it was Brenda simply wanting to show the place off, Joely had no idea. It hardly mattered, since she was keen to find out what lay behind at least some of the closed doors she kept passing on the way to and from her bedroom.

And of course there was the mysterious third floor where no one ever seemed to go.

They began in the long corridor, where Brenda opened up the room next to the kitchen first, turning on the overhead lights as they stepped inside so they could see where they were going.

"I won't bother opening up the shutters in here," Brenda said, "they're a bit stiff and I can't always get them closed again. Anyway, this is the 'den' where Mrs. D watches TV when she's in the mood for it."

It was an old-fashioned room with fading wallpaper and an eclectic mix of furniture including a large Oriental-style cabinet beside the empty marble fireplace that presumably contained the TV.

"She's got a *big* collection of DVDs," Brenda boasted,

111

pointing Joely to the built-in shelves on either side of the hearth that were packed with movie choices. "She's keen on old films and documentaries, but there's a good selection of all sorts, some belonged to her husband, and some are her nephew's."

"Does he visit often?" Joely asked, skimming over titles: *Doctor Zhivago, Out of Africa, Hangover III, Bridesmaids, King Lear, North by Northwest*. All randomly placed, and giving no clear indication of ownership or character insight.

Brenda said fondly. "Not as often as he'd like, he always says, but he's a busy man, being a lawyer, in London."

"What sort of lawyer?" Joely inquired. *Brief Encounter, The Ides of March, I, Claudius, Mrs. Miniver. The Killing* box set.

"I think he deals mostly in brands and intellectual something or other," Brenda replied, dusting off a stray DVD with her apron and slotting it back onto a shelf. "That's him over there," she said, pointing to a row of photographs on the mantelpiece. "Looks a lot like a young Cary Grant, I reckon, or that's what I tell him and he says I shouldn't flatter him or it'll go to his head."

Picking up one of the photos, Joely studied it for a likeness to the movie star, and while she couldn't really find one, she had to admit that the dark hair and strong jawline were impressive, and there was a certain ease about his smile that made him look friendly and fun. In fact he reminded her of someone, perhaps not as old as Cary Grant, someone more contemporary but for the moment she couldn't think who it was. In the next shot she picked up he was younger and glowering at the photographer in a way that reminded her of a schoolboy being forced to do as he was told. The man with him had a hand on his shoulder, and was laughing as though he was sharing a joke with the photographer, one that a bad-tempered Edward might be the butt of.

"Is this his father?" she asked Brenda, holding up the photograph.

Looking at it Brenda said, "Yes, that's the two of them together, bless their hearts. They look alike, don't they, and you can see the family resemblance to Mrs. D. Edward's father was her brother."

Joely placed the photo back on the shelf, and said, "Are there any of Mr. D?"

"Not in here," Brenda replied, straightening up the frame. She walked back to the door and lifted a hand to the light switch. "There's this room done," she declared. "Let's move on to the next, shall we?"

Keen to learn more about the family, especially Mr. D, Joely followed Brenda along the corridor to the entrance hall, where the housekeeper pushed open the set of double doors that had caught Joely's interest the night she'd arrived.

Like the den it was in darkness, but in here Brenda unbolted and unfolded the tall wooden shutters allowing sunlight to flood into the room and Joely saw right away that it was all about music. She gazed around at the many instruments, an electric keyboard on cross-hatch legs, a collection of violins in cases, a cello, guitars, an African drum, a saxophone in a display case, and at the center of it all a magnificent grand piano.

"No one ever comes in here now except me to clean," Brenda told her sadly. "It was Mr. D's special place where he'd play and listen and compose, and the music would roll out over the meadow down to the sea when the windows was open . . . Magical it was, absolutely magical."

Finding that easy to believe, Joely said, "Was he a professional musician?"

Brenda chuckled. "You could be forgiven for thinking so with all this, but no, he wasn't. It was his hobby, well, I suppose you'd call it his passion. Yes, it was definitely a passion." She walked across the room and slid open the doors of a cupboard that took up most of the back wall. "Have you ever seen a collection of vinyl like this outside a shop?" she asked, seeming almost as proud of it as its owner had surely been.

"They're in alphabetical order," Brenda informed her, "and there's everything from classical to pop to jazz and country and western. He loved all sorts he did. He'd shut himself away in here for hours and hours losing all track of time. Sometimes Mrs. D would come in and they'd sing together or dance, and you never saw anything so romantic the way they moved together." She smiled fondly. "They was always ravenous when they came out from one of their listening sessions so I'd make sure to have something ready to go on the table. They used to eat meat back then and he was very partial to game pie or a goulash."

Joely wandered over to the piano so polished it shone like a mirror. There was a music sheet on the brass stand—"While My Lady Sleeps" (Phineas Newborn Jr.)—and the stool was slightly askew as though someone had just popped out for a moment. She wished she could read music, or better still listen to someone playing this seemingly abandoned piece. "So what was his profession?" she asked, feeling an urge to press the keys but not daring to.

Brenda nodded meaningfully toward the paintings that were hanging over the fireplace and around the walls. Having been so entranced by all the musical instruments Joely hadn't noticed them until now, and as she gave them more attention, she began to frown in confusion.

"Recognize them, don't you?" Brenda stated with satisfaction. "Monet, Bonnard, Cézanne, Matisse."

Joely continued to study them, going closer to one that depicted a naked woman standing beside a chaise longue and half turned toward a French window. Surely all the great Impressionist works were in galleries and museums. Certainly the ones she was seeing here were.

"He was a copyist," Brenda explained, "and a very talented one as you can see. If you look more closely at that one you'll spot that the woman is a young Mrs. D. He used to do that, just for them—paint her into famous pictures. The ones he sold were proper copies of the impresarios and people were willing to pay a lot for them."

Not correcting the mistake, Joely roamed the display taking in more of the familiar works and seeing that many of them did indeed feature a much younger Freda. Not as a girl, but as a twenty- or thirty-year-old woman with an exquisite body and such luxurious long blond hair it seemed almost to have a life of its own.

"Is this him?" she asked stopping at a smaller portrait of a strikingly handsome man with penetrating eyes and a roguish sort of smile.

Brenda came to stand beside her. "Yes, that's him," she said affectionately. "A real looker, isn't he? And charm like it was spring flowers in bloom. He had a temper on him though, not that he ever turned it on any of us, it was always when he was trying to write some music or paint a picture and it wasn't properly working out that he went off on one. We called it his artist's temperament."

"Didn't they have any children?" Joely asked, still intrigued by the man captured in oils who seemed so alive, so ready to walk into the room and play one of the many instruments.

"No, it never happened for them," Brenda replied, "and it's a shame because I think they'd have made good parents, the two of them."

Joely turned around to see if there was any more she'd missed in the room.

"His painting studio is upstairs next to the tower," Brenda informed her. "We keep it the way he liked it; only me and Mrs. D ever go in there, me to clean, obviously, and she says it makes her remember him better when she's where she used to pose for him."

Apparently deciding they'd had enough of the music room, Brenda closed and locked the shutters and led the way back into the hall where she pulled the double doors gently together again.

"What's on the top floor?" Joely asked as Brenda used her apron to wipe a smear from one of the windows.

"Oh, there's only more bedrooms up there," the housekeeper replied. "None of them get used now, so we've got them all shut up."

Joely paused as she caught the sound of someone singing at a distance and looked up the stairs as she realized it was coming from somewhere much deeper in the house. She listened harder and felt an odd chill go through her as she recognized "The Gaelic Blessing." Why was Freda singing it now, and why was she, Joely, feeling spooked by it?

She turned to Brenda, but the housekeeper was already on her way back to the kitchen, saying it was time for her to get on.

Not knowing what else to do, Joely followed and after Brenda had left she tried to get better reception on her mobile. It was no good, no matter where she went in the house the signal simply wasn't strong enough to make calls or receive emails, she couldn't even send a text. So apart from being unable to contact her mother or Holly, she could also forget about googling Mr. D, or his wife's nephew, Edward.

How frustrating and even disorienting it was to be without the Internet and phone, especially in a house that was positioned with its back to the nearest town and seemed so packed full of secrets. She really wasn't enjoying feeling this cut off; it was bizarrely like being in a different time zone, another dimension even, and she wasn't quite sure what to do to make herself feel more grounded. Or less unsettled by her peculiar client.

In the end she drove into town and downloaded her messages in a bustling café over a coffee and muffin. There were plenty, mostly work-related (though no actual offers at this time) and a couple from friends wondering when to expect her back. There was nothing from Callum to say he was still missing her—*as do I*—or from Holly on whether she'd moved to her grandmother's yet.

From her mother there was a brief text saying *Hope it's going well. Call when you can.*

She tried her mother's number but went straight to voicemail. "Hi, no news," she said, "just getting in touch while I can because the signal where I'm staying is next to useless. Is Holly with you now? Hope she's OK. Love you both. Speak soon."

On returning to Dimmett House she went straight through to the kitchen hoping to find Freda ready to give some feedback on the latest paragraphs, or perhaps to reveal more for the memoir, but there was no sign of her. She toyed with the idea of going into the den to watch a movie or boxed set, but as she hadn't actually been invited to make use of that room she decided to curl up in front of the fire with one of Freda's books instead. It turned out to be a gothic tale of necromancy, illicit pleasure, and treason, and like most of Freda's works was hard going and unsettling, although Joely's concentration was poor. Her mind was flitting between the music room and its paintings, and her host somewhere upstairs silent and uncommunicative, apart from when she was singing.

Joely had been around publishing—newspapers and books—for long enough to know that some editors kept writers waiting simply because they hadn't had time to read anything yet; or because they were so baffled or appalled by what they'd read that they didn't know what to say. Some did it because they were sadists. But Freda wasn't an editor, she was an author, she'd had plenty of time to read, and what Joely had put on the page was neither baffling nor appalling.

So did that make Freda a sadist?

A bit of an extreme conclusion, however she'd certainly know how stressful it could be waiting for a response.

I'm making this too much about myself.

This was possible, but Freda was definitely a strange woman, unpredictable and eccentric—and fixated. For instance, why did she keep her husband's things exactly as they'd been at the time he'd died? Did she have a purpose for that? Was this her way of freezing time? What had happened to him? And was the nephew Edward likely to turn up while she, Joely, was here?

Where were Callum and Martha going for the weekend?

"Grandma, are you OK?" Holly asked, glancing up from her mobile as she wandered into the kitchen. "Why are you staring at your phone like that?"

Marianne Jenson sighed and put down her mobile to pull her granddaughter into a hug. "I didn't hear you come in," she said. "Is Dad with you?"

"No, he dropped me off and ran. He said to tell you he'll see you later when he brings my stuff. Can I get something to eat?"

"Help yourself. So are you here just for the weekend, or to stay? You know you're welcome. Your room's always ready for you."

"Cool, thanks. I think I might stay. It's kind of weird being at Martha's, and I definitely don't want to be there on my own while they're away."

Understanding that, Marianne said, "Have you heard from Mum recently?"

Holly slotted two slices of bread into the toaster as she shrugged. "Kind of. Why? She's OK, is she?"

"I'm sure she is, it's just that she's not easy to get hold of at the moment and I'm used to speaking to her every day." She left it there, not wanting to confide any deeper concerns in her granddaughter for fear of making her worry too. Not that Holly was worry-free where her mother was concerned, far from it given the breakup of her parents' marriage. However Holly was currently handling it in her own way, which didn't include discussing it with anyone until she was ready. "My reactions, my trauma, my timetable," was how she put it, and they all knew better than to try arguing with her.

"Are you doing anything this evening?" Marianne asked, tugging a band from her hair to let it tumble around her shoulders.

"Yeah, I'm meeting up with some friends," Holly replied. "How about you?"

Marianne checked the time. "I need to leave in half an hour to make a viewing in Knightsbridge. After that I've got a session with Ryan Philips, so I won't be back until around eight."

"Ryan Philips being one of your private students?"

"I'm helping him with expository writing."

Holly pulled a face. "What's that?" she demanded, fetching a jar of peanut butter from the fridge.

"It's what they call factual compositions at the school he's going to be attending when his family move to the States," Marianne explained. "Did Dad say what time he was coming back with your things?"

Holly shook her head and checked her phone as a text arrived.

"Doesn't sound as though I'll see him," Marianne commented, and hoisting a basket of fresh towels onto her hip she took it upstairs with her, needing to shower after her run.

Ten minutes later, dressed in slim-leg navy pants and cream cashmere sweater, she returned to the kitchen to find Holly already on her way out. "Back by nine," she said, as Holly planted a kiss on her cheek, "and please wear a coat."

With a roll of her eyes Holly grabbed the black pea coat she'd draped over a chair and with a winning smile she blew another kiss her grandmother's way before heading out of the door.

As soon as she was alone, Marianne picked up her mobile to call Jamie.

"Hey, Mum," he said cheerfully. "What's up? I'm about to go into a PTA meeting, but if it's urgent . . ."

"It's not," Marianne confessed, "I only wanted to know when you last spoke to Joely."

"Uh, let me see, it was when she left to go on her new assignment. I rang to wish her luck. Why? Has something happened?"

"Not that I'm aware of. But I can't help worrying about her. I'm even starting to wonder if the assignment is really a cover for her needing to get away for a while. You know how she's been lately . . ."

"Sure I do, but she's had a lot to deal with, and she told you who she's working with so I don't get why you think the job isn't real."

Marianne sighed. "I guess it is, but she took off so

soon after Callum moved out that I still haven't been able to talk to her about it. She doesn't usually keep things back from me, but I'm certain she is now, and we've agreed many times that she's been different since Dad died."

"It's true, she has, but not in a way that I think you need to go worrying yourself about. We all took it hard, and we've all got our own ways of dealing with it. Joely's has been to shut down for a while."

"I know, but I'm afraid it's the reason behind Callum leaving. Or at least part of the reason."

"Have you asked him about it?"

"No, but I intend to as soon as I can. Holly's staying with me now, by the way, I guess until Joely comes back."

"Which will be when?"

"I don't know. She hasn't been very specific." She paused, not sure whether to ask the next question, but in the end decided to. "Jamie, do you think she might have found something out about Dad after he died?"

"Like what? There's nothing *to* find out, is there?"

"Not that I know of, but the way she's been . . . Have you ever told her about the talk you and I had with Dad?"

"No, you thought she didn't need to know so I've never mentioned it."

Marianne nodded. "OK, so it won't be that and anyway I can't think why it would make her pull away from us, and especially not from Callum. Even Holly's felt it . . ." She stopped, not entirely sure what else she wanted to say, how to put into words her mother's instinct that she was missing something that she needed to get hold of.

"Mum, I have to go, but I'll be home in an hour if you want to call back."

"Thanks, but you've got enough going on and I don't want to bother you again."

"It's not a bother. You're my mother, she's my sister. I'm here for you, OK?"

With a smile Marianne said, "Love you, Jamie Jenson," and after ending the call she grabbed her keys and coat, deciding to try Joely again as soon as she returned home.

"Mrs. D sends her apologies," Brenda said as Joely entered the kitchen, "but she won't be joining you for breakfast and she doesn't want to work today."

"Is she unwell?" Joely asked, as concerned as she was baffled by this prolonged absence.

Brenda simply shrugged and carried on stirring milk into the porridge she had simmering on the Aga.

Joely wasn't sure what to say. Something was odd about this, something she couldn't fathom, unless her client was ill. Even if she wasn't, if she didn't want to work, she, Joely, was hardly in a position to insist. Sitting down at the table, she said, "Please tell Mrs. D that if she doesn't like the pages I wrote then I'm happy to discuss them and try again." She was irked by her admission of insecurity, and it wasn't helped by the time it took for Brenda to dry her hands on a tea towel before answering.

"Bill's taken the Jeep for an inspection today," she said, "so if you'd like a lift into town I'll be leaving shortly."

Joely drank her coffee, puzzled by Brenda's failure to acknowledge her message to Freda, and wondering

123

if she'd just been told in an oblique way that Freda wanted her out of the house.

In the end, deciding it would serve no purpose to hang around here with nothing to do but get spooked by random singing and her own imagination she accepted the offer of a lift into Lynton. Once there she rode the funicular down to Lynmouth and the National Park Centre to use up some time learning more about the area.

It turned into a fascinating few hours that took her mind off Freda, and even off Callum, who still hadn't texted since his claim that he was missing her. It wasn't that she wanted to hear from him—she did, but only if he was going to say something she wanted to hear. Such as, *I've made a terrible mistake*; or, *How can we work things out?* Or, *I realize now I can't be without you.*

By the time she left the Centre she'd heard all about the great flood of 1952 when a terrible storm had brought trees and boulders crashing downriver from the moor, devastating Lynmouth and killing thirty-four people while making hundreds homeless. She could, she hoped, now identify many of the birds she'd watched flying about the cliffs, and name the wild flowers she'd spotted tilting their colorful faces to the winter sun. She knew that two rivers became one before they reached the shore; that there was a photography competition in need of more entries if she was interested; that someone had sighted the beast of Exmoor only last week (but she was to take no notice of that because this particular naturalist had clocked a couple of mermaids the week before). She also knew where to go for the best cheeses, wines, smoked hams, laver (whatever that was), and cider. It hadn't come as a surprise to learn that the cliffs along this wild and rugged coast were the highest in England. However, later, as she struggled through the wind back to Dimmett House (having taken the picturesque but precipitous coast path as a shortcut instead of going through the Valley of Rocks) she'd have preferred not to know about the woman in a white dress who sometimes appeared out of the mist to tempt passersby off the path to their doom in the icy waters below. (It wasn't until a fourth chilling ghost story had caused the hairs to rise on the back of her neck that she'd realized someone had misunderstood her job title so thought they were being helpful in her search for the supernatural.)

It was now six thirty in the evening and Brenda was putting the finishing touches to a "tasty Stilton and potato pie" while Joely cleaned the greens to go with it.

"Right you are," Brenda declared, popping her artful creation in the oven, "it should come out at quarter past seven. I won't bother hanging around to take Mrs. D's up to her because she's going to come down and join you."

Joely's heart jumped, almost as if she'd been told she was going on a date, or to get some exam results.

After checking Joely had made a good job of chopping the veg, Brenda untied her apron and hooked it inside the pantry door. "Mrs. D prefers the sprouts to be steamed, so you should put the water on to boil about seven," she instructed, zipping up her padded parka. "Oh, and she said to tell you that if you want

125

some wine she'll take a glass herself so best to put a bottle of Clearview red by the fire to warm. You'll find one in the rack over there next to the dresser."

"Don't tell me." Joely smiled. "It's from a local vineyard?"

Brenda's eyes sparkled. "As near as it gets," she confirmed. "The other side of Barnstaple, and I expect Sissy Flood'll be interested to know what you think of it. She's got quite a following around here with her whites, but Mrs. D prefers red."

Once left alone Joely found the wine, uncorked it, and placed it on the hearth as instructed. She stood for a moment gazing at the windows at the end of the kitchen, blackened by night, and showing a ghostly reflection of a fair-haired woman looking lost and indecisive. Picking up her phone she sighed to see that once again she had no service. Still at least she'd chatted with Andee and her mother while she was in the Centre's coffee shop treating herself to cake. She was still feeling disappointed that Andee had had to postpone the lunch they'd penciled in for tomorrow, not until then had she realized how much she'd been looking forward to seeing a familiar face.

Her mother had sounded relieved to hear from her. "It's odd not being able to get hold of you whenever I like," she'd commented. "It makes me worry when I probably don't have to. Are you all right?"

"Yes, I'm fine, but the work's getting off to a slower start than I expected. Is Holly with you yet?"

"Callum brought her last night, but I didn't get to see him unfortunately. Have you heard from him?"

"Only to say that he's missing me as much as Holly

is, and you can read into that as much as you like, except I can tell you he didn't mean to say it."

The signal had failed soon after that, but at least she knew her mother and Holly weren't in any kind of crisis and she still had no idea where Callum and Martha were heading off to for the weekend. Best not to know.

Deciding not to wait to pour herself some wine she went to fetch a glass and was pouring the bottle when Freda appeared through the door from the tower.

"Ah, yes, I think I'll have one of those," she declared, rubbing her hands together. She looked no different from the way she always did, so not ill, Joely concluded, and she didn't seem downcast or disappointed, or querulous, or anything else Joely might need to feel worried about. "Mm, something smells good," she commented, sniffing the air. "One of Brenda's pies, no doubt. Has she gone?"

"She left about five minutes ago," Joely told her, passing over a glass of wine. "Supper is cheese and potato pie and will be ready at seven fifteen. There are sprouts and leeks to go with it—all we have to do is put them on to steam—and an upside-down pudding for afters."

Nodding approval, Freda sipped her wine and strode over to her favorite armchair beside the fire, where she made herself comfortable with one leg crossed over the other. "Are you ready to begin?" she asked as Joely took a wineglass for herself from a cupboard.

Realizing Freda meant to work—*now*—Joely staged a quick gathering of her wits and went to settle into the other armchair.

"Pour, pour," Freda insisted, waving a hand at Joely's empty glass.

Half filling it, Joely was about to attempt a toast when Freda said, "'Better run, girl.'"

Coming with no preamble of any sort it almost sounded like an instruction, until Joely realized what it was.

"You've written," Freda stated, "that he whispered those words in my ear, but that's not what I told you. What I said was I *knew* it was what he said—as in a love-struck girl hearing what she wants to hear." Affecting a high, breathy voice, she said, "I just *knew* it was what he'd said." Back to her own voice, "I understand it's an easy mistake to make, the nuance is a little opaque, but it must be corrected."

Joely didn't protest, in spite of being certain there had been no nuance or lack of clarity when they'd talked; Freda had been quite definite that he'd said, "Better run, girl." However, she was happy to make the alteration if it was what Freda wanted. She said, "If there's ambiguity around the line then I'm presuming you want to keep her in the role of Eve." How much easier it was to use the third person, and an abstract one at that, when making these sorts of comments.

Freda frowned. "You mean Evil Eve. Well, yes, it's what she deserves, to stay in that role. That child—the one I used to be—knew what she wanted, or she thought she did, and I was prepared to believe . . . actually, at that stage, I was fully convinced that he wanted it too." She let go of her frown and took a sip of wine. "Otherwise you've done a good job. I'm sure only experts on my work would know that I didn't write it, or they might think that I did, but perhaps I'd been having an off day."

Smarting at that, Joely stared at her, not sure how to voice any of the tart retorts crowding her head.

"It's thinner than I would have made it," Freda continued, "less texture and depth, a certain amount of rhythm is lacking, but to be honest, I don't think it matters. We've taken the next step in building the picture of a fifteen-year-old girl and her adolescent self-obsession, which is good. What do you think of her now? Do you see her as delusional, perhaps? As a manipulator? How conscious do you think she is of the consequences she and her teacher could face if she gets her way?"

Still not quite over the criticism of her efforts, Joely took a moment to summon an answer that wouldn't sound peevish or defensive. She needed to move on. "Probably not very conscious," she quickly decided. "She casts herself in the roles of two very different fictional heroines, which suggests she's not as connected with reality as she might like to think." When Freda didn't interrupt she continued, "Can you remember how you felt back then? *Were* you aware of the consequences you could face?"

Freda's eyes narrowed as she thought and for a while there was only the hiss and crackle of the fire and haunting whine of the wind as it wrapped around the tower to disturb the silence. In the end she said, "I didn't give them a thought and even if I had I don't think I'd have cared what they might be. Certainly I wouldn't have imagined my obsession—yes, I believe it was an obsession—ending us up where it did." She drank more wine, and Joely could see that she was going to say more. "I was an exhibitionist," she confessed in the same tone she might have used to declare herself a philatelist.

Joely thought of the paintings she'd seen earlier, and since most were nudes it was clear that stripping off wasn't a hobby the young Freda had grown out of.

"That girl," Freda continued, "and I call her that girl because she feels like a stranger after all these years, someone who had nothing to do with me . . . That girl was in love with herself and her body and most definitely with all the new things that were happening to it. When sexual desire first comes alive it has a kind of rawness to it, don't you think, a hunger, a greed that has no recognition of its power, or direction to proper satisfaction. It takes over, consuming the mind and the body—and we have to remember that I came from a home where carnal pleasure wasn't only permissible, it was virtually obligatory." Her eyes sparked as she said, "Put more simply, I was determined to get the man everyone else wanted. I had to have him; it meant everything to me. Not that I could have articulated that to myself at the time. What girl of that age could?"

Not many, Joely thought, remembering how she too had gone through a phase around that age of believing herself to be all powerful where boys (not men) were concerned, and Holly was definitely feeling it. *Please, God, don't let her be trying to seduce one of the schoolmasters.* She said, "I'm still getting the sense that you're angry with yourself, that you detest what you did, whatever it was—so is this memoir about punishing yourself?"

Displeasure flashed sharp in Freda's eyes but was

quickly gone. "Yes, I suppose it is about punishment," she conceded, "but it's also about understanding and truth." She raised a hand as Joely started to speak. "A lot of lies were told back then. Lies that hurt people, *destroyed* people, and they have to be exposed, that's why I say it's about truth. Now, do you think it's time to put the veg on?"

As they worked together around the Aga and set the table Joely found herself wondering if she liked the older Freda any more than the younger one. Actually, she decided she had some sympathy with the fifteen-year-old narcissist for she at least had naïvety on her side. The older Freda had nothing like it, so it was understandably hard to warm to her, and yet Joely couldn't deny that the reason she felt hostile toward her was because of the way she'd so curtly and condescendingly criticized her literary effort.

You need to get over yourself, Joely. This isn't about you, it's about her and whatever it is she needs to get off her chest. It's the only reason you're here, not to like her, or make her your best pal, or be her therapist, it's to play midwife to this burden of hers that she's apparently determined to bring into the world.

"The song, 'Young Girl,'" Freda said as they ate. "Did you know it before you took this assignment?"

"Vaguely," Joely replied. "I had to find it on YouTube while I was in town, to be sure I was thinking of the right one."

"That doesn't surprise me. As far as I'm aware there haven't been any covers and I don't suppose there will be. In this day and age it could be seen as promoting pedophilia, but for us girls, back then . . ." Her eyes drifted as she presumably returned to the past. "We all believed it was about us and not one of us gave a moment's thought to the wrongness of it, I suppose because falling for older men is what girls do, isn't it? And we all know how irresistible most men find young girls."

Thinking that was truer than most would want it to be, Joely said, "I have to ask if Sir found his piano student irresistible, or was it all one-sided?"

Freda regarded her archly, her eyes taking on an intensity that made Joely uncomfortable. "Do you *think* it was all one-sided?" Freda countered. "That only she had the crush?"

"Actually, no, but I'm getting the impression you want her to take the blame."

Freda put down her fork and reached for her wine as she dabbed her mouth with a napkin. "You're running ahead with all sorts of assumptions," she accused. "I don't blame you, it's human nature to try to work out where a story is going, what the outcome will be. We do it all the time when we read books or watch films, we're always trying to second-guess the writer as though we have to prove that we're cleverer than him or her. I wonder why we feel compelled to do that? Is there something wrong with just waiting for the narrative to unfold?"

Taking it as the criticism she knew it to be, Joely said, "OK, I won't ask again what comes next. I'll wait until you're ready to tell me."

Freda continued to eat. "Would I be right in saying that so far you're considering *Sir* to be a victim?"

Joely said, "I don't think he can be that, given his age and position, but he could be considered prey."

132

Freda broke into a smile at that. "Yes, prey," she agreed. "He was her prey—until he wasn't anymore."

Joely continued to eat, presuming Freda was going to expound on the verbal trickery.

"Nabokovian games," Freda stated.

Having no idea what that meant, Joely helped herself to more pie.

"You know who Nabokov is?" Freda asked.

"Didn't he write *Lolita*?"

"Yes, he did. Have you read it?"

Joely shook her head.

"Humbert—you know Humbert is the main protagonist—he claims to be a hebephiliac. This is someone who has a sexual preference for children in early adolescence, usually up to fourteen, but I think we can stretch it to fifteen. A pedophile is generally recognized to be a person whose attraction is for prepubescents. Eleven and under."

Wanting to be sure she was following this, or maybe she didn't want to follow it at all, Joely said, "So are you suggesting that a hebephiliac is more acceptable than a pedophile?"

"Don't you think so?"

All Joely could really think was that she'd rather not be having this conversation, but she said, "I guess I'd prefer it if neither of them existed."

Freda didn't appear to disagree. "The problem is we don't choose our sexual proclivities, we're born with them—or are we conditioned into them?" She puzzled that for a moment. "I'd say both are possible, but for the purposes of this discussion let's just deal with those whose chemical makeup comes into the world with

133

them. They don't at any point in their lives make a conscious decision to become a monster, if that's how you're going to view men whose predilections are for children. Do you have any, by the way?"

Startled by the question, Joely said, "Presuming you mean children, I have a fifteen-year-old daughter."

Freda's eyes widened with interest. "Is she healthy? Normal? A pretty girl?"

"I'd say all of the above."

"So if an older man found himself attracted to her, would you consider him a monster?"

"I'm sure I would if he did something about it."

"But what if you found out she'd instigated it? Do you think it would be fair for him to be labeled a pedophile for the rest of his life when her sixteenth birthday might be just around the corner and she made all the running? She's not under eleven, she's practically old enough to get married."

Becoming increasingly uncomfortable with this, Joely said, "I'd rather we didn't bring my daughter into it, if you don't mind."

Freda's expression darkened, although her words were mild as she said, "It's a difficult subject. We naturally feel very protective of our children, but we have to accept that very few, probably none of them, are angels. What they do when their parents aren't looking is very often something the parent would rather not see, that way they can perpetuate the myth of their offspring's innocence and believe them blameless if something happens to them that shouldn't have."

Since there was no arguing with that, Joely didn't try. She was intrigued though to realize that Freda was putting up a bizarre sort of defense for Sir, which at least provided some indication of where the story was going.

"Young Freda's parents—my parents—were hedonists, dedicated to the experiments of free love. They set no rules or none that were clear enough to help keep a fifteen-year-old out of trouble. They accepted, *encouraged*, nudity and much more at their weekend parties, and seeing all this with impressionable eyes we have to ask ourselves, was it any surprise I went on to behave the way I did?"

Joely said, "So you're not only blaming yourself for whatever it was you went on to do, you're blaming your parents?"

"Precisely."

"And you're not holding him, the hebephile, responsible at all?"

"Oh yes, he has to be responsible, after all no one forced him. He didn't have to get involved."

"But he did."

"I could say as a hebephile he couldn't help himself, but let me tell you what happened after he canceled the piano lesson, then you can take your time while writing it up to decide what you think of him."

CHAPTER TEN

Today I'm having my second private piano lesson and Sir says he's really impressed by all the practice I've put in; he's proud of me and sorry he had to cancel last week.

"It was a family matter," he explains, "but everything's fine now."

I want to look at him just to see his eyes but I carry on staring past my hands on the piano keys down to my bare legs. I'm wearing my hockey kit and my skirt has wriggled all the way up. I imagine him putting a hand on my thigh, running it under my hem and over my knickers, and I feel a quickening like electricity flicker through me.

He says softly, "Why don't you show me more of what you've been practicing?"

I play "Twinkle, Twinkle, Little Star" with both hands and it makes us both laugh.

I love it when he laughs. It changes his face in a way that lights him up from the inside and makes me feel as though I know him even better than I know me. His eyes crinkle up at the corners and his white teeth that are slightly crooked are beautiful. The sound of his laugh is deep and quiet and I want to tell him that it's like a different, but better kind of music.

I carry on looking at him, but his laughter dies and he turns away.

I think to myself, *Better run, girl.*

I'm completely sure now that's what he said when he came into the rec room to tell me he couldn't make our lesson. He's scared of his feelings for me, and I understand that, I'm scared of mine too, but I don't think that's any reason for us to hide from them when we're alone together. In another few months I'll be sixteen, old enough to get married, and he's definitely who I want to marry.

Mummy says I shouldn't be thinking about going down the aisle until I'm at least twenty-five, even thirty, and it makes me want to cry when she says things like that. It's as though she doesn't understand how I feel about Sir, but I know she does.

Last weekend, after he'd canceled our lesson, she said, "It's only this once, sweetheart, and I'm sure he canceled for a good reason. You'll have plenty more opportunities to swoon away to your heart's content; you can even flirt with him, you little minx, but if you do you mustn't be too hard on him."

"You said once we could invite him here to one of your parties. Can we do it?" I asked.

She laughed at that and said, "We'd have to be on our best behavior if we did, and I'm not sure we're capable of that when it's the only time we get to relax."

"He wouldn't mind about the pot. He's really hip and I expect he smokes it anyway."

"The answer is still no, my angel . . . No, no, please don't pull that face. Daddy would never allow it even if I would, so we must stop talking about it."

I cried so much that weekend, and I didn't really stop until yesterday, the day before my next private lesson.

Everyone thought I was having my period so I let them; I wasn't going to admit how terrified I was that he'd cancel again. Just in case he wanted to I avoided any places I might run into him. I even said I was sick to skip his music appreciation class but then I wished I hadn't because all I did instead was lie on my bed wondering if he was falling for someone else because I wasn't there. It drove me crazy, I wanted to scream and kick my feet, and I knew I'd kill whoever it was if she even mentioned his name.

Now I'm here and although I'm listening to everything he's telling me I'm not taking much of it in. I can feel him next to me, his breath on my cheek, his fingers so close and even sometimes touching mine. I hear him when he says that it's a pleasure teaching someone so dexterous and who has a good ear, and it makes me glad that I've practiced so much in my spare time in order to show him how important it is to me. I want him to know that it's only because of him that I'm doing so well.

After an hour of being close to him, of listening to his voice, of breathing in the scent of him, and learning about flats and sharps he looks at his watch and says, "It's time for the lesson to end now."

I don't want to go. I can hardly make myself move, but I have to. I say, "Do you promise not to cancel next week?"

He doesn't answer straightaway, he stares at nothing, it seems, but then he's staring at me. "Next week when you come," he says softly, "you mustn't wear your hockey kit."

I leave in a hurry so upset and angry that I think he

should be punished for being mean to me, something to make him sorry so he'll never make me feel stupid again. I go up to my dorm thinking up ways to hurt him as much as he's hurt me, and I decide that one of them could be to report him for putting a hand on my leg while I was practicing my scales. Or I could say that he tried to kiss me when he leaned forward to point out the bass clef symbol on the sheet music. That would definitely get him into trouble, a lot of trouble, but then our private lessons would be stopped and I couldn't stand for that to happen. I know I've only had two so far but already I live for those lessons. Nothing else matters.

It's lesson three and I'm wearing my usual school uniform of navy kilt and pale blue blouse. I've rolled my waistband over a few times so my hem is above my knees and when I sit down I toss back my hair and say to him, "Is this better?"

He looks puzzled.

"You told me not to wear my hockey kit," I remind him.

"Ah, yes."

"Would you prefer it if I didn't wear anything at all?" I say and I can hardly believe the words have come out. My nerves are suddenly jumping around inside me, and I can tell by the way he's looking at me that I really did speak out loud, and I don't know what he's thinking.

In the end he leans forward and opens the piano lid. He speaks so quietly that I can hardly hear him. "That's a very beautiful image you've created for me. Thank you."

I swallow, shocked and disbelieving—and elated that he thinks the image is beautiful. I want to say it again and again, but my heart is beating too fast, everything is jumbling up in my head. I want to show him the real thing. Should I offer to? I could go to the store cupboard at the back of the room and take off my clothes.

Would he like that?

Would I have the courage?

"Shall we begin?" he asks.

We start the lesson as if no wonderful things have been said or even thought about, but my hands are clumsy and when he puts his over them, like bigger shells protecting small ones, I stop and wait for him to tell me what to do.

He doesn't say anything and nor do I as we sit there next to each other staring at our hands and the piano keys as if they might play themselves.

I can feel my chest going up and down as I breathe and I think I might be shaking.

He says, "Perhaps we should end the lesson now."

"No," I cry. In a panic I turn my hands in his and hold onto them.

He doesn't pull away, he lets me hold on to him until finally I let him go. I lower my head so that my hair is falling around my face. He pulls it back and when I look at him he says in an odd sort of voice, "Can something be impossible if it's already happened?"

I don't know what he means so I don't try to answer, I just carry on looking at him.

"I understand what you want," he says softly, "but you know it can't be."

"Why?" I ask in a croak.

His smile makes my head spin and as he watches his hand touch my hair I feel sure he wants to kiss me. If he does I know my heart will explode.

He says, "You have no idea what simply looking at you does to me. It's why we shouldn't continue this."

Terrified he's going to cancel our lessons, I say, "Please don't send me away. I won't be able to stand it. I'll kill myself."

His eyes roam my face as if he's imprinting every part of it on his memory. "I'm trying to be strong, but you're making me weak," he tells me.

Encouraged, emboldened by this, I say, "I want to learn everything you can teach me. Please teach me."

He doesn't speak and I think he's going to tell me to go now, or pretend he doesn't understand, but then he says, "I'm going to teach you the piano."

The lesson continues, but again I find it hard to concentrate and I think he's finding it hard too. He repeats a number of things he's already said, and sometimes his voice seems to catch in his throat.

At the end of the hour I say, "I wish I didn't have to wait a whole week to see you again."

He smiles and I'm not sure if he understands how I feel.

My next words flutter out of me like small butterflies searching for nectar. I can't stop them, they have their own life. "Please will you kiss me?"

I hear him swallow. I think he wants to move away, but he doesn't. He says, "Not here."

Shocked that he wants to and desperate for it to be now, I cry, "Then where?"

He tells me where and I say,

"Do you promise you'll be there?"

"I promise."

I stand up to go and he takes my hand. "Come with me," he says, and he leads me to the store cupboard, where he stands aside to let me go in first. He doesn't close the door, he doesn't even speak as he reaches under my skirt and pulls my knickers down. They fall to the floor and he holds my hands as I step out of them.

He stoops to pick them up and says, "I'll return them the next time we meet."

The incident in the storeroom didn't happen, but it's what I've been imagining every minute of every day since he promised to meet me.

Shall I tell you what I do as I wait for the day to come around, the lessons I don't listen to, the games I can't play, the girl chats that are all nonsense to me? Shall I describe my school, my friends, my daily routine? Would you like to hear more about the music I listen to that makes me think of him, because everything does?

No, I won't tell you about any of that because it's not what you're interested in, is it? All you want to know is where we are going to meet and if he keeps his promise.

It's the weekend now and I'm on the train to London, as I always am on Saturday mornings. Other girls are with me, we travel together, but their stops are before mine, so I am the only one who goes to the end of the line. My parents aren't expecting me; I told them I'll be spending the weekend with Mandy Gibbons. They won't check, because I've stayed at Mandy's before and they think I have a crush on her brother.

I walk out of the train station taking the exit he told me to and as I round the corner I see him waiting beside his car and I am so relieved and afraid and happy that I stop walking. I can't move because I'm suddenly trapped between wanting to run to him, and away from him, and at the same time I want to laugh. He's different; his clothes are modern and stylish, a patterned waistcoat over his open-necked shirt, a large belt buckle at his hips, his trousers are white and tapered to his legs. This isn't Sir, this is a real man away from the school and I feel so nervous I am finding it hard to breathe.

He comes to take my hand and as he looks at me I want to put my arms around him: I want everyone to look at us, to see that we are together and we don't have to worry about hiding anything, because I look much older than my age.

"Are you sure?" he asks.

I nod and, still dazed that he's actually here I say, "I was afraid you wouldn't come."

He puts his fingers under my chin and tilts up my face. His eyes seem to sink into mine as though he can see right into me. He murmurs something that I don't quite hear, but I think it's "How could I not?"

He drops my bag into the back of the car and I slide into the passenger seat. When he gets in beside me he doesn't start the engine, he just sits quietly for a while, staring straight ahead until he says, "I need to be certain that you're sure."

I turn to look at him and when I say yes, I'm sure,

he puts a hand on my face. His eyes stay on mine and it's like I can feel them. He leans forward to kiss me. It's not the first time I've been kissed, but it is the first time I've felt the onrush of so much emotion. It's flooding through me so fast and powerfully it's making me dizzy. His aftershave is spicy and leathery and I feel it swirling around my senses making me intoxicated by it and by him.

"I've wanted to do that since the first time I saw you," he says in a whisper.

I remember that day in his music room at the start of the school year when he introduced himself to us and asked us to do the same. It seems incredible that when I'd told him my name he'd been thinking about kissing me because that was what I'd been thinking about him.

He looks down at my psychedelic mini dress and white knee-high boots. I felt like a model when I put them on, one that dances the twist and who knows how to have fun, but now, because of the way he's looking at me I feel self-conscious and worried that I might have chosen the wrong thing.

He starts the car and turns on the radio. It's crackly and loses the station now and again, but we can tell that the record playing is "Something Stupid"—and because it's about saying "I love you' we both blush as we smile.

He blushes so easily.

"Where are we going?" I ask as he drives away.

"To a place where no one knows us," he tells me.

Quite soon the record changes to Percy Sledge singing "Dock of the Bay" and because we've sung it in his appreciation class we sing along now, knowing all the words, and we continue singing when the Beach Boys come on with "Good Vibrations." I get quite excited when the Doors' new one plays, "Hello, I Love You," and he drums his hands on the steering wheel while I dance in my seat. I don't feel worried or shy or afraid anymore, I only feel so happy I could fly.

We drive for a long time, much longer than I expected to, sometimes singing, other times just listening. I know we're heading south because I recognize some of the signposts, but then I stop recognizing them until we pass one for Brighton. We don't follow that turnoff, but soon after we take another and wind through country lanes, so narrow that we have to pull over sometimes or reverse to make way for cars and tractors coming in the opposite direction.

We stop in front of some tall wooden gates and he gets out to open them. At the same time he pulls letters from a mailbox. Once we're through the gates he stops the car again to go and close them and then he drives us along a narrow lane lined with trees and wild flowers. At the end, in a small clearing is a house that's more of a cottage with a thatched roof and ivy-covered walls.

"Is this where you live?" I ask, starting to feel nervous again. I know he has a flat in the town near school, but so do lots of teachers who have other places they go to at weekends.

"It's my uncle's," he tells me. "He's in Asia on tour and while he's away he lets the rest of the family use it."

He tells me later that his uncle is a famous conductor and that he travels all over the world. His mother is an opera singer and his father a concert violinist. He has a brother who's in America learning about jazz from

145

black people in the south, and a sister who's traveling around India with some friends.

I must admit I'm finding it hard to take everything in. I'm thrilled and daunted and bemused and excited. I miss my parents, but obviously I don't want them to be here. I feel I've entered another world as I follow him inside the house and help to open the curtains and windows. It smells of dust and lavender-scented polish. The ceilings are high and crisscrossed with dark oak beams; the walls are crammed with shelves of books and long-playing records and piles of glossy brochures. These turn out to be the concerts his uncle has directed from Berlin, to Hong Kong, to London, New York, Buenos Aires, and Cape Town. There is a wooden bar to separate the kitchen from the sitting room, and in front of some French windows there is a beautiful grand piano.

He's brought a picnic basket in from the car and we take it into the back garden, where magnolia trees are coming into flower and the lawn needs mowing. He points out a gazebo that he and his brother used to defend from dragons and monsters when they were small.

We spread a tartan blanket under the trees among daisies and dandelions, and after we sit down he pours us some cider and lemonade to drink. I tell him I've had cider before, so he lets me have some of his. He's brought pork pies and cheese sandwiches, bags of ready salted crisps, apples, grapes, and chocolates. The May sunshine is too warm for me to keep my boots on so he tells me to take them off and lay them down next to his shoes. He goes back inside and a few minutes later the sound of some classical music (Mozart's Piano Concerto No. 19

in F Major, he tells me when he comes out) drifts down over the lawn as lazily as the breeze that's tilting the grass and cooling my legs.

We eat and drink, look at each other, blush, and laugh. He tells me that the music we're listening to now is Mendelssohn's Violin Concerto in E Minor conducted by his uncle, with his father playing lead violin. I can tell how proud he is of them, and I feel proud that he wants me to hear it. I ask about his mother, the opera singer, and he laughs as he says she'd be very cross if she knew he'd told me about her brother and husband before telling me about her.

His family sound exciting, clever and different. I imagine them meeting my parents and I know they'd all get along because my parents love music of all sorts even though they don't play any instruments them- selves.

He lights a cigarette and when I see it's a joint I ask if I can have some too. I know how it's done, I've seen it often enough at home, but this is the first time I've tried it. Though I choke on my first inhale, the second and third are fine and as my head starts to swim with words and joy I can feel myself drifting and flying like a jubilant bird in currents of music and air. I wonder what I'm doing here in this strange and beautiful garden, but there is nowhere else I want to be.

I look at him and we laugh and laugh rolling around the blanket, convulsed in our merriment until the music stops and the cigarette runs out—and the bird is finally caught in his gentle hands.

CHAPTER ELEVEN

Joely looked up from her laptop, blinking to draw focus on the real world that surrounded her, consisting of winter-torn sea, cliffs, and tors, not a sunny back garden with magnolia trees and picnic rugs. She'd been so engrossed in the latest part of Freda's story that she hardly knew how long she'd been here in the writing room, perched like a ghost in a lonely observatory. Long enough for her limbs to feel stiff and her stomach to cramp with hunger.

Sitting back in the chair she stretched her arms overhead and noticed there was rain on the windows and a small flock of cormorants was gliding on invisible thermals over the cove. Although in many ways this was a perfect place to write, isolated, calming, and nourishing, she'd become so captivated by the story and how best to tell it that she'd actually lost the sense of where she was some time ago. Even now, in her mind, she still couldn't quite shake free of the teacher and student who were sparing no thought for the future, or for anything beyond the new intimacy of that early summer day.

Even before starting to write she'd known she would find it hard to get beyond this point. The notes were there in front of her, Freda had told her everything, how Sir had unzipped the psychedelic dress and helped to remove it; how he'd undone her lacy bra and slipped off her panties and while she'd lain naked on the grass his eyes had drunk her in as he'd removed his own clothes, but Joely couldn't find the right words to tell the story as Freda wanted it told.

Freda had gone into some detail about the tender exploration of unfamiliar bodies, hot, breathy kisses and the breaking of the final barrier that had allowed him to take her completely. She'd even talked about the tears of happiness and the music he'd chosen to celebrate the momentous event. Nothing triumphant or rousing, as Joely might have expected, but the *Allegretto scherzando* from Saint-Saëns Piano Concerto No. 2 in G Minor—a gentle, playful piece, Freda had told her, that he'd performed himself, seated, still naked, at his uncle's piano. At the same time his young student, also still naked, had stood behind him with her hands on his shoulders as she swayed and listened and adored him.

Joely didn't normally consider herself a prude, but she simply didn't want to write sex that left nothing to the imagination, which was what Freda had requested. All she felt comfortable with was capturing the essence of it, laying down the structure, and if graphic was what Freda wanted she must fill in the bold detail herself, or the innuendo, or the artful metaphors. It would be her choice.

Sighing, Joely pressed the heels of her hands into her eyes as though to push out the tiredness. It was the weekend and she needed a break, although she had no idea what she was going to do, given that Andee wasn't free and Freda hadn't shown any signs of wanting to be social.

She glanced at her phone in the vain hope it might have a suggestion, but as usual there was no signal.

So, Callum and Martha had no doubt already taken off for their romantic break while she was here in this ivory tower feeling unsettled by the shenanigans of a precocious fifteen-year-old girl and the older man who'd submitted himself to her so readily.

"Submitted" wasn't the right word, she knew that as surely as she knew that he'd orchestrated the entire seduction. And yet it wasn't him she was feeling so bothered by, she realized, it was the older Freda who seemed to want her to feel more tenderness and under-standing for Sir than he surely deserved. Her client's manipulation hadn't succeeded, exactly, but there was no doubt that Freda's dislike of her younger self struck an odd contrast to the affection, even love that she still seemed to feel for her old music teacher. And wasn't it interesting that she'd gone on to marry someone who shared Sir's passion for music—unless, of course, Sir and Mr. D were one and the same person.

Now that was a twist to the tale she wouldn't have predicted, nor would she dare to suggest it, given her client's aversion to second-guessing.

"I'd rather not talk this evening," Freda announced as Joely emerged from the tower staircase into the kitchen. "You probably consider that rude, but there it is. If you wish to go out to find more entertaining company, be assured I shall not feel offended."

Since Joely had no one to go out with, and certainly didn't want to sit in a bar or restaurant alone thinking of Callum and Martha somewhere together, she accepted the silent rule as they ate the spicy pasta dish prepared by Brenda and cooked by Freda.

"Why don't you join me in the den to watch a film?" Freda offered when it came time to clear away their plates.

So Joely did, and was neither surprised nor put out to discover that Freda had already decided on their viewing. It was only when she realized what the film was that she wished she'd said she'd go to her room and read.

And God Created Woman, the erotic story of a young girl with abundant sexual energy who causes havoc in three men's lives. An old favorite of the parents' if Joely remembered correctly.

So were there more men to come after Sir? Or was this Freda's attempt to get her ghostwriter to visualize her young self as a nymphet not unlike Brigitte Bardot?

Who knew what went on in that woman's head?

The film wasn't particularly engaging; really nothing more than a vehicle for Vadim to show off his sex-kitten wife, Joely thought, and by the end, though she'd enjoyed the cinematography, she was struggling to stay awake.

Clicking off the TV, Freda got up to pour herself a whisky from the decanters arranged in front of the shuttered windows.

"Would you like one?" she offered.

Stifling a yawn Joely shook her head. She'd never liked whisky and besides she really wasn't up for some sort of head-spinning discussion about the film's morals and purpose, which was what she feared Freda might be about to embark on.

"Good night then," Freda said abruptly, and turning her back she downed the single measure in one and poured another.

Almost laughing at the summary dismissal, Joely picked up her phone and shoes and started for the door.

"How far have you got with it?" Freda suddenly asked.

Knowing she meant the memoir, Joely tensed slightly as she said, "To the picnic in his uncle's garden." *She's now going to ask how much detail I've gone into and I will have to tell her that I'm finding it difficult to write about the private parts and orgasmic achievements of my employer even if it did happen over fifty years ago. They're still her private parts and her molto orgasmic stringendos.*

Freda's pale eyes drifted to the dying fire as she presumably recalled, maybe even relived the occasion that she'd described so vividly during their talk. In the end she said, "You're going to think this slightly mad, but while you've been writing about him I've been feeling jealous that you're in his company."

She was right, Joely did think that was mad, but also sad that Freda was so deeply affected by revisiting her past. She apparently did still love him, and missed him, or that was Joely's reading of it so far, but she wasn't going to ask who he really was.

"Do you like him?" Freda asked.

Joely admitted that she did, "But I think," she continued, "it's what you want, and I can't help wondering if you're setting me—or the reader—up for a twist in the tale that might change . . ."

Freda's smile was thin. "This isn't a novel," she interrupted sharply, "and you're aware of how I feel about jumping to conclusions," and with a dismissive wave of her hand she helped herself to a third small measure of Scotch.

"God, you don't know how glad I am to see you."

It was the following day and Joely was at the Rising Sun greeting Andee after receiving a text during a short burst of connection first thing to let her know that her old friend was free today if that was of any interest. "I feel I'm going off my head for so many reasons that I don't even know where to start."

Laughing, Andee asked the waiter for a glass of whatever Joely already had—a chilled Chenin Blanc—and shrugging off her coat she sat down at the window table. "If I'd known you were so desperate to see someone," she remarked drolly, "I'd have made sure to come sooner. So what's been happening?"

"No, no, tell me about you first . . ."

"Really not interesting, so?"

Joely threw out her hands. "I've signed an NDA so I can't tell you anything, but I swear it's not that big a deal. So many years later? I mean, really? Unless 'Sir' turns out to be someone famous."

"The music teacher? You don't know his name yet?"

"David Michaels, but she doesn't use it much and I'm pretty sure it's made up anyway, which could support the possibility of him being recognizable." She twinkled mischievously and drew in a little closer. "So, here I go breaking my agreement," she whispered, "but I know I can trust you."

Andee glanced up as her wine arrived, thanked the waiter, and turned back to hear more.

153

"Last night," Joely continued, "she got me to sit through the movie *And God Created Woman*. Have you seen it?"

"With Brigitte Bardot? No. Is it any good?"

"Not unless you're a Bardot fan, or into gorgeous shots of the French Riviera. The point is, I think she wants me to portray the young her in the same way as Vadim portrayed Juliette, the film's main character. High-octane sex appeal, no inhibitions, too beautiful for her own good, basically someone who doesn't have much of a relationship with everyday morals."

Andee looked impressed and intrigued. "Is that how she talks about herself during your discussions?" she asked.

"Kind of, but not always. To be honest, I never really know what she's thinking, apart from the fact that these many years on she's pretty disdainful of herself. Anyway, from the way she tells it she was definitely in love with him, insofar as any girl that age can be in love, but here's the thing: I reckon she still is. In fact, I think it's very possible she married him."

Andee blinked in surprise.

Joely threw out her hands, indicating her own surprise. "I know it might sound crazy, but her husband had a serious passion for music; there's a room in the house where his piano and other instruments are still in the positions they were in the day he died, three years ago. It's like a shrine, I suppose. I don't know how often she goes in there, the housekeeper does to clean, but the shutters are always closed and I think the doors are kept locked."

"But if she married him, where's the scandal, or drama—or tragedy? Aren't we looking for a tragedy?"

"Listen, I've no idea if I'm right. It's just a guess. I mean, I get that her first love and her husband both having an affinity for music doesn't make them one and the same person, I'm only saying that they could be."

"So you've got no idea yet what happens next?"

"I dare not ask. She's made it abundantly clear that she detests second-guessing in readers—in ghostwriters it could be a capital offense. Now here's the other thing, this story is starting to get to me in a way it probably shouldn't, and I think that's for two reasons: one is being shut up in that house, gorgeous as it is, with no one to talk to apart from the chess master of mind games, namely my host. The other is, she has a way of telling her story, when we're talking, that makes me feel as though I'm involved, it could even be me she's talking about."

Andee pulled a face. "You really are starting to sound crazy now," she commented drily.

Joely laughed. "OK, we know the power good story-tellers can exert over readers, they toss us around, get us onside only to throw us onto the horns of dilemmas before snatching us back because they've introduced someone or something new. They can totally wring us out. Of course, generally we're reading a book that we can put aside and forget about for a few hours while we think about something else. That's what I keep trying to do with this, but the problem is, my something else is always Callum and Martha, who I'm also starting to see in scenes she's described—which is really horrible, let me tell you. And now let me show you this. It's a text that managed to get through to me last night from Holly."

As she passed over her phone she took a large sip of wine and felt grateful all over again that Andee had been able to make it today.

Andee read aloud, "*Turns out they haven't gone away for weekend. Went to pick up some stuff and they were there, so obvs trying to get rid of me.*" Andee's eyes showed both confusion and concern as she looked up.

"I tried calling her," Joely said, "but the signal wasn't good enough, so I ended up speaking to Mum from the Valley of Rocks."

"Are you serious?"

"That's how far I had to go before I could make a decent connection. OK, the very last place you'd expect to get one, but it happened, and take it from me, that geological wonder is not a soothing place to be after dark. However, after receiving that text I needed to talk to someone; Holly was unavailable by the time I got a signal, probably because she's tripping out on acid somewhere—that's Freda's influence, so forget that." She clasped her hands to her head. "See, I'm starting to think my own daughter is taking drugs and probably getting off with her piano teacher, that's how much this story is getting to me—and she's not even learning piano. Anyway, Holly wasn't answering her phone, but Mum did. Apparently Holly went to Martha's row house . . ."

"Row house?"

"It's a derogatory term for terraced house. When she got there, she saw straightaway that both Callum's and Martha's cars were outside and the lights were on downstairs. So she peeked through the window and saw them sitting on the sofa sharing a bottle of wine—

and we can only feel thankful that's all they were doing, given his daughter was the peeping Tom."

Andee pulled an expression of wry distaste.

"Precisely," Joely responded, hurting far more deeply than she was showing. "So they lied to get rid of her; she knows it; she's furious, devastated, Mum says, and swearing she'll never go back there again in her life. My dilemma now is should I go home to sort her out or let Callum deal with it?"

Andee took the menu a waiter was passing her. "I'm guessing," she said, "that you already have an answer."

Joely had to smile. "Not me, my amazing mum. She says she can deal with Holly even though she knows there's probably a scene brewing between her and Callum. She thinks I should let him make a mess of it, because we're sure he will, and when the time is right I can sweep in to sort it all out."

"And take Holly home with you?"

"That's my second-best outcome. My best is that he comes too and we go back to being a family."

Clearly hearing the catch in her voice, Andee reached out to squeeze her hand.

Joely put on a laugh, and knowing she ought to get off the subject now, she said, "Have you tried the mussels in this place? They're the best I've ever had."

Andee studied the menu and after deciding to have the same as Joely she said, "I get the feeling there's something you're not telling me."

Joely feigned confusion. "You mean about Freda?"

"No, about you. I'm not sure . . ."

"Honestly, there's nothing." Joely insisted. "Stop looking so worried, everything's fine with me, apart from my marriage breaking up, obviously, and this bonkers assignment I'm trying to work my way through."

Though appearing reluctant to let it go, Andee finally said, "OK, going back to the husband and whether or not it's Sir. Have you googled him? Do you even know his name?"

"I didn't, but I tried a different search this time, remember I've already googled her a few times, and before the connection dropped on me I discovered he is called David—not Michaels, but Donahoe—and he was a renowned copyist, particularly of the Impressionists. That chimes with what I already know about Mr. D. She hasn't mentioned anything yet about Sir being into art, but it might come."

"So if Michaels is a pseudonym, perhaps she did marry him. That's definitely not where I was expecting the story to go."

"Me neither."

"Did it say how David Donahoe died?"

"It seems there was an accident at sea in which another man also died. Nothing suspicious that I could find, just an accident in which two old friends out for a sail ran into trouble."

Andee was looking pensive.

"Are you putting your detective hat on?" Joely asked hopefully.

Andee smiled. "Go on," she prompted. "Who else have you googled?"

"No one, because the WiFi is rubbish, but on my list are Sir's parents and uncle. The trouble is, if she's using a pseudonym I don't have anywhere to start."

"Is his family relevant?"

"I don't know yet, but the fact that she's talked about them . . . The uncle was/is a conductor, the father a concert violinist, and the mother an opera singer. There's also a brother who was in the American deep south during the late sixties, and a sister traveling the world."

Andee said, "Would you like me to see what I can find out?"

Joely was about to leap at the offer, but then wasn't sure. "She's presumably going to tell me everything sooner or later," she said, "and if we dig around too much now it'll be like turning to the back of the book when we've only just gotten started. God, I'm beginning to sound like her now, and I can only imagine what she'd think if she knew I was conducting an electronic delve into her past. Actually, I'd rather not imagine it."

Andee smiled. "Well, if there is anything you want me to find out, let me know. If nothing else I have a way better Internet connection."

Joely laughed and checked the text that had arrived as they were speaking.

Dad's acting really strange. Hx

Nothing like a bump back to reality—and worry. After showing it to Andee, Joely messaged back saying, *In what way?*

He keeps on about wanting to know where you are.

That shouldn't be strange; nevertheless Joely's heart skipped a beat simply to know that he was asking. *What did you tell him?*

That I don't know, because I DON'T. So that's both of you acting weird. Def staying with Grandma forever.

Have you seen Dad this weekend?

You mean apart from through the window drinking wine with Martha when he was supposed to have gone away for the weekend? No. He texted me just now to ask about you AGAIN. I've told him that he needs to contact you himself because I'm too busy for all this crap.

"She has attitude," Joely murmured as Andee read the last text.

"So why is Callum so interested to know where you are?" Andee wondered. "And why is he dragging Holly into it?"

Joely's heart twisted as she guessed at least part of the answer. "He's probably checking the coast is clear to go and pick up some more stuff," she said, not even wanting to imagine it. "It makes me doubly glad I'm not there." She looked at her phone again, expecting the latest text to be yet another from Holly, but it turned out to be from Freda.

When he was asked about it later he said we experienced a coup de foudre. *Did I tell you that? FMD*

Joely showed the message to Andee and said, "A *coup de foudre.* Love at first sight."

"Or literally translated, a lightning strike."

Joely sat staring at the message thinking how odd it was that Freda should fire off a text as though they were in the middle of a chat. "She's at home thinking about him, reliving it all . . ." She lifted her gaze to Andee's. "Did I tell you what she said last night? She said she feels jealous of the time I'm spending with him, just by writing about him."

Andee frowned.

"I know, weird to say the least." Joely checked her phone again as another text came through,

I believe you're having lunch with a friend. I hope you're not discussing the memoir. If you are you'll be in breach of our contract. FMD

CHAPTER TWELVE

I learned so much from Sir that first weekend we were together—not in the way you're probably thinking, but yes that too. Definitely that. I didn't realize until after he'd made me his—that was the phrase he used—that I could love him even more than I already did. Each time I looked at him I felt as though I was breathing him in, that every part of him was reaching every part of me. He was in my eyes, my mouth, my heart, all over me. He was tender and rough, playful, happy and curious to know what pleased me. He showed me pleasure to degrees that made me cry out for him to stop even as I wanted more. He was like a painter taking a brush to canvas, bringing it to life with expert strokes, teasing touches, and bold, purposeful embraces. He wanted me to be naked the whole time so I was, thrilling at the sensation of cool air on my skin when we were outside, and the caress of his eyes as he watched me. I've always loved to be naked, to be admired, and it seemed he loved it too.

He played the piano—Elvis, Johnny Cash, the Everly Brothers, the Beatles—we sang and I danced. He changed to classical—*La Campanella* by Liszt; Beethoven's *Moonlight Sonata*; Tchaikovsky's Concerto No. 1—and I twirled, stretched, pirouetted, pointed my toes, and swept my arms in circles like a ballerina. His passion for playing was as consuming as his passion for me; when he pulled me to him, hungry and masterful, we made sweet, thunderous music of our own.

He taught me about jazz and the differing stories of its origins; he told me about his plans to join his brother in America to support the fight for civil rights. (I will go with him, naturally, because now I know more about it I also care very much about black people and the oppression they are suffering.) He talked about his parents and what it was like growing up in a household where music mattered more than food. We played symphonies conducted by his uncle, a recording of his mother in the role of Tosca: and of course violin concertos performed by his father.

The weekend was ours alone, perfect and full and over so soon that the end still felt like the beginning. On Sunday evening he drove me to London to get the train back to school, stopping on the way to kiss me and remind me of the promises we'd made to each other. We knew how to behave during the coming days, and we knew that next weekend couldn't come soon enough.

All that week I felt as though I was floating on air, somewhere distant from my friends though I could see and hear them and even respond to what they said. My thoughts were solely for him, each one made lustrous and sensual by the memories of all we'd shared, and would share again soon. The days passed in an agony of slowness only made bearable by the excruciating thrill of anticipation and longing. If we saw each other at a distance we looked the other way; if we were close we smiled as we had before our worlds had combined, and passed on by.

In his class I watched my friends flirt with him in their usual way, and when they danced to "Do Wah Diddy Diddy" and "These Boots Are Made for Walking," I did too, joining in the laughter as we'd decided I should, and hardly looking his way. It wasn't until we were alone together for our private lesson and he taught me to play Mozart's *Night Music* with my right hand that he was able to tell me how he couldn't stop thinking about me. As he spoke and I played his hand moved around my waist causing me to make mistakes and he corrected me as he might any other student. We changed the exercise to my left hand and I was able to touch him discreetly in a way I knew he liked. Before the lesson was over we went to the store cupboard and though it was over quickly it was beautiful and necessary for we were unable to wait any longer.

The next weekend, just like the last, I told my parents I was going to Mandy's and Sir met me at Waterloo. The drive was too long, but eventually, when we walked into his uncle's house I made him wait while I put on the record I'd brought with me. Tricia Hill had played it during his appreciation class, now I was playing it for him, and as he realized what it was his eyes lit up with laughter.

"Then He Kissed Me."

It rained that weekend, but it didn't matter. It wasn't cold and we enjoyed being naked in the downpours as much as we did in the sun. He'd brought food and wine and cigarettes, most of them hand-rolled with pot as the main ingredient. When we weren't making love, sleeping, or eating we listened to his uncle's jazz records and talked about so many things, music of course—he even taught me how to play "She Loves Me" that weekend—about our favorite books (his was *The Martian Chronicles* by Ray Bradbury, mine was *Dr. Zhivago* by Boris Pasternak). His favorite film used to be the 1955 version of *Bel Ami* but now it was *And God Created Woman*, he said, because I remind him of Brigitte Bardot. I tell him my favorite is the same as his and because we haven't made love for a while we stop talking and do so.

After, over cheese on toast and red wine, we smoke more pot and discuss the incredible plans for a moon landing. This moves on to the places we long to visit, together—his first choice is New Orleans and mine is Paris. He says he'll take me after school has broken up for the summer—and I can tell he means it.

Keeping our secret was easier than you might think; either we were good at hiding our feelings while others were around, or everyone was too wrapped up in their own lives to worry much about ours. My parents were sad that I wasn't going home as often—of course I went sometimes, I had to—but they were busy and liberal-minded and most of all trusting. My mother guessed I'd fallen for someone, she could see it in my eyes, she said, and in the way my skin glowed. When she asked if I was being careful I said I was, and it was true, we were. She didn't insist on meeting him, or on hearing anything about him until I was ready to tell. That would have to wait until I was sixteen, naturally, but the weeks and months were passing and though sometimes it felt as though October would never come, like Sir I treasured the private time we had at his uncle's place when it felt as though we were the only people in the world.

We didn't always go to the cottage. One weekend there was a hotel in Brighton where we booked in as brother and sister with adjoining rooms and he spent the night on my side of the connecting door. There were trips to the cinema, walks on beaches, out-of-the-way music recitals or concerts where I watched him become so enthralled by the performance he almost forgot I was there. Once we even went to the Albert Hall where his uncle was conducting Handel's *Messiah* and his mother was singing soprano. They didn't know we were right up in the gods and I could hardly see them, but knowing they were his family and that he wanted me to be with him while he watched them perform, told me again how much he loved me.

I was never in any doubt of that.

He didn't allow me to be.

Do you know what he said, later, I mean much later? He said, "She was very young, and yet not young at all—and I was so captivated by her that I could think of nothing else but making her mine."

That was what he said.

He never denied he loved me.

He would never have done that.

Joely stopped typing and stared down at her now silent recorder. There was no more, only the echo of Freda's voice as she'd ended their last discussion with the words *He would never have done that.* Her tone had been low and reflective, even faintly incredulous, as if she still couldn't quite believe it. Joely remembered feeling moved at the time, and she did again now. Wherever this was going she was in no doubt that they'd loved each other then.

Looking up from her laptop she gazed at the bleak

landscape stretched out before her, swathed in turbulent shadow, impervious to the gusts that were howling and sighing all around it. She watched the sea swallowing up white horses and pushing out more, and after a while she became aware of music playing somewhere in the distance.

Realizing it must be coming from inside the house, she made her way down to the library and listened. It had stopped, and as seconds ticked by she wondered if she'd imagined it. She turned back to the stairs to return for her phone and laptop, then she heard it again, low and melodic, a single hand playing Mozart's *A Little Night Music*.

The hand of young Freda in her private piano lesson all those years ago.

Joely stared at the book-filled wall that separated this room from the studio where David Donahoe had produced his copies of the great Impressionists. Was there a piano in there? There must be, because someone was playing it. The notes were being picked out carefully, sometimes incorrectly, and the longer she listened the more she realized how easy it would be to believe that it was the ghost of a young girl bringing those long-ago moments to life.

The playing stopped and silence followed.

Joely remained where she was, sensing someone was still in the studio. She wondered about calling out, but as she took a breath she noticed that the books on the wall in front of her were moving toward her.

Shocked, she stepped back, not sure if she was imagining it, until realization dawned. It was a hidden door and someone was coming through.

"I—I'm sorry." Joely tried to laugh, as Freda came through and regarded her with wintry eyes.

"What for?" Freda demanded.

Joely had no idea. "I didn't—I didn't know there was a door. You startled me."

"Then I'm the one who should apologize. Are you all right? You've gone quite pale."

Joely might have asked her host the same question, for she was as white and oddly opaque as a sea mist. "I'm fine." She smiled. "I've just finished for the day. I haven't printed anything out yet, but I can do it now."

"I won't read it tonight so there's no rush."

Joely watched as Freda walked to the door that led down to the kitchen, but when she tried to open it she couldn't.

"Blasted latch has jammed again," Freda snapped irritably. "You must pay attention to that. Make sure the door isn't fully closed or, like once happened to me, you'll end up locked in here until someone comes and lets you out. Wait there, I'll go down to the kitchen and come up the stairs to sort it out."

She disappeared back through the bookcase door so swiftly that it was already shut before Joely realized that she was now trapped in the tower with access only to the writing room above.

A wave of unease swept over her.

She took a breath, and another.

It was crazy to think that Freda had just imprisoned her. Why on earth would she do that? She wouldn't, of course. Nevertheless Joely wasn't responding well to being shut in here with no way of contacting someone on the outside apart from during the random moments her phone connected to the WiFi. She ran up to the writing room to get it, not because she needed to call or text anyone now, Freda was on her way to open the door, it simply made her feel better to have it with her.

Long minutes ticked by—many more than it would take for Freda to descend the front stairs and walk along the corridor into the kitchen. Joely tried the door; the latch wouldn't budge. She listened hard, expecting to hear footsteps on the stairs, but the only sound that reached her was the wind whistling in from the sea, up over the cliffs, and around the tower.

This was crazy. She wasn't locked in here.

She rattled the latch, and was about to shout out for Freda when the door suddenly opened and Freda was there.

Feeling foolish as her panic subsided, Joely quipped, "I thought you'd forgotten me."

Ignoring the comment, Freda said, "I won't be joining you for dinner tonight, but Brenda has something prepared. Please bring your printed pages to breakfast tomorrow." And with a strange little gesture that might have been a wave, she returned to the stairs and disappeared down them.

Still shaken, Joely took a Larousse encyclopedia from a bookshelf and propped the door open while she returned to the writing room to send her day's work to the printer. She had no idea what the last few minutes had been about, the music, the opening of a hidden door, keeping her waiting so long in a locked room. Perhaps they were about nothing at all and she was spooking herself into creating discomfiting scenarios where they had no place to be.

CHAPTER THIRTEEN

Joely, can we talk. Please call me. Cx

Joely looked away from the text she'd received while in town earlier and stared at the flames in the kitchen hearth. She hadn't replied yet, and had decided she wouldn't until she was sure of what *she* wanted to say. There was so much going around in her head, words inflamed with anger, softened by sadness, riven with guilt even, and she didn't think any of them belonged in a text. Or in a phone call. They needed to see each other face-to-face for what she had to say, and whatever he had to say would have to wait until she was ready.

Freda was sitting in her usual chair, apparently lost in her own thoughts as she too watched the fire. It was listless, yellow flickers rising from a glowing pile of hot, scorched logs. There was a mouthwatering aroma emanating from the Aga, one of Brenda's flavorful veggie concoctions, and Joely found herself remembering what her father used to say to her mother when something smelled delicious.

"It makes you want to take a bite out of the air."

She missed him so much; the grief was as tenacious as the bond they'd shared, as consuming at times as the need to hold on to him, but he'd gone and she felt as though she was clutching at air.

She shifted slightly in her chair and glanced at the time. Brenda had left several minutes ago and neither Joely nor Freda had spoken since assuring her they understood what time the pudding was to come out of the oven, and yes, they'd be sure to have a lovely evening, thank you.

Freda's legs were stretched out toward the fender, the latest pages in her lap, but Joely had no idea yet if she'd read them for she'd done another of her disappearing acts for the day. However, Joely had spotted her standing at the end of the meadow earlier, staring out to sea. She hadn't moved, had seemed oblivious to the wind that was buffeting her short hair and padded coat as she fixed her gaze on whatever she was seeing in the waves.

The next time Joely had looked out of the window Freda had no longer been there.

She'd turned up here, in the kitchen, about ten minutes ago, bringing only her iPad, which she'd put on the table before coming to sit down. It was very possible, Joely realized, already bracing herself, that at some point, probably while she was being subjected to more of Freda's stinging criticisms, they were going to listen to the music that had accompanied the start of Sir and young Freda's intimate affair.

More minutes ticked quietly by and Joely's thoughts wandered to her mother, who hadn't sounded her usual self when they'd spoken last night. (Not from the Valley of Rocks this time, but from the small, square balcony over the front porch, which Joely had accessed through the window of her blue bedroom. She'd managed to get two bars of reception and had frozen half to death during their short conversation. It hadn't been easy to hear either, thanks to the combined roar of wind and waves.)

"A bit of a cold, that's all," her mother had insisted when Joely had asked if something was wrong. "Nothing to worry about. How are you?"

"I'm fine," Joely replied, glad her mother couldn't see how the bellicose weather was tossing her about like a piñata. "Still not sure how much longer I'll be here," she shouted.

"Is she treating you well?" her mother shouted back.

"I guess so. She makes sure I'm fed and lets me use her writing room, which is pretty amazing."

Though her mother responded, Joely didn't catch the words and when she asked her to repeat them her mother simply said, "It was nothing. I just wish . . ." Whatever the wish was Joely still didn't know because they'd lost the connection then and she'd been unable to get hold of her when she'd driven into town earlier.

Certain now that her mother was wishing she'd come home because Holly was being difficult, Joely decided she needed to try and call again later to find out what was really going on. It might be true that Holly was usually an angel where her beloved Grandma was concerned, but considering how unsettled she was by her parents' breakup she couldn't be relied upon to be at her best. And who could blame her for that?

"Is something wrong?" Freda asked, gaze still fixed on the flames. "You seem . . . agitated."

Wondering if Freda had superpowers, Joely tried to think how to answer, but before she could, Freda said, "Is my memoir bothering you? I think you might disapprove of young Freda. You're right to. Or perhaps you're afraid of what's coming next."

Irked by the assumption that everything was about her, Joely bit back a tart response—after all, everything was supposed to be about Freda. However, it would do the woman no harm to realize that her ghostwriter had a life beyond that of some fancy form of messenger. "Actually I have a few issues going on at home," she confessed.

Freda didn't break her gaze as she gave a brief grunt. *Definitely everything has to be about Freda.*

More emptiness passed with a backing percussion of heavy rain and a howling wind until Freda finally said, "I thought as much. Now that you've brought it up, would you like to talk about it? I can be a good listener." She paused as though considering the truth of this, and apparently coming to a positive conclusion she added, "It can help to confide in someone who has no agenda."

Joely couldn't help it; she said, a touch wryly, "You mean you can be objective, the way you're hoping I can be for you?"

Freda's eyebrows arched, and only then did Joely notice how pale and tired she seemed, and as she wondered if reading the latest pages had been a strain for her she wondered too what had been on Freda's mind when she'd stood in the meadow staring out to sea.

"Tell me why you're upset," Freda prompted. A smile hovered close to her lips. "Age and experience might count for something, so perhaps I can give some useful advice."

Joely found herself considering the offer and what

detail she might go into, and since there was no one else to talk to right now, and because she needed to hear herself voice her concerns, she said, "My husband's left me for my best friend; my daughter's obviously having difficulties with it; I think my mother's stressing about my daughter; and my husband wants to talk to me—I don't know what about, but it could be divorce."

Freda withdrew her hands from her pockets and rested her elbows on the chair arms, linking her long fingers together. She allowed several moments to pass as she considered what Joely had told her and finally said, "The heart of the matter is your husband's betrayal."

Although Joely hadn't expected that, it about summed it up.

"Or is it the loss of your best friend that's causing you the greater sadness?"

Joely thought of Martha, detested her, and was about to speak when Freda said, "She'll never be your best friend again so you might as well forget about her."

Well, that was Martha dealt with, and fleetingly sorry that Andee wasn't around to be amused by Freda's directness, Joely said, "She'll have to be in my life going forward because my daughter's father is with her . . ."

Freda's hand went up. "Let's talk about him and you, not her. We need to sort out the betrayal, and being someone who has known it, *suffered* it, many times in her life, my first piece of advice to you is to stop jumping to conclusions you have no evidence for, especially if they cause you pain."

Joely frowned. "It happened," she said. "I'm not imagining it."

"Has he mentioned divorce before?"

Realizing her mistake, Joely shook her head. "But it has to come up at some point."

"Why does it have to? And why put yourself through the torment of imagining it when there are other things that should concern you more, such as who else is suffering because of this betrayal?"

Not having expected that Joely sat quietly thinking of Holly and her mother. Jamie too, because they always worried about each other.

"You believe that you and your husband are the main players in this—though you acknowledge that your daughter and ex–best friend are also involved—but in your mind it's really about you and . . . What's his name?"

"Callum."

"Callum. Of course it is about you two, because if you can resolve your issues the hurt will go away for those around you—apart from the best friend, but I don't think we're very concerned about her. She's no more than a moth."

Joely blinked before remembering that this was a reference to Freda's literary works. "When you write," she said, "you usually turn moths into the main players."

"But they're still moths, and if you're familiar with my books you'll know that they're drawn to the luminous aura of success, love, power—you and your husband would have represented at least two out of the three for your friend—but moths are always burned when they go too close to the source of their fascination. They don't survive."

Finding this thought quite pleasurable, if a little extreme, Joely said, "In this case the moth has put the light out and is creating a new light of her own, so maybe I'm now the moth."

Clearly unimpressed by that, Freda said, "Only if you choose to be. The question is, do you want to resolve your issues with Callum?"

Liking that she might have the option, Joely said, "As far as I was concerned, we didn't have any, but obviously he wouldn't agree with that or he wouldn't have gone." She didn't have to go into the entire truth of it all and the part she'd played herself, this was deep enough.

Freda gave a small sigh and checking the time on her watch she got up to go and take the pudding from the oven. After placing it to cool, she returned to her chair, dropping another log onto the fire before sitting down. "My husband and I didn't have any 'issues' as you put it," she said, "our marriage was sound, our understanding of each other had few flaws—I say few because I never did understand why he was unfaithful to me. Do you understand why yours was unfaithful to you?"

Joely shifted uncomfortably, not willing to take any blame in spite of knowing she should.

As though reading her mind, Freda said, "I'm not going to tell you what to do, I'm going to tell you what I did with my husband and you must decide for yourself if it was the right thing."

Still suspecting that Sir and Mr. Donahoe were one and the same, meaning Freda was about to jump forward many years in the story, Joely was eager to listen.

"I knew before we were married," Freda began, her

eyes starting to lose focus as her lips trembled slightly
and her fingers tightened their hold on each other, "that
he had a roving eye. I don't think he actually misbehaved
during our courting years, at least not in the biblical
sense, but he was always very comfortable in female
company. He adored women, revered them, and I know
he adored me. That never changed. We always loved
each other from the time we first met right up until the
time he died. I still love him, of course, feelings that
deep don't disappear because someone has stopped
living, we all know that. What I hadn't realized until I
lost David was that in some ways they seem to get
stronger, which makes them even harder to let go of."

David. So it was Sir.

And he'd turned into a serial adulterer.

"Certainly I've never been able to let go of mine, but
I confess I don't want to. They're what hold me together.
He was everything to me, and he always will be. Of
course I've loved others, my family naturally—my
nephews are the only ones still alive and I care for the
youngest as much as if he were my own son." She broke
off for a moment, pressed a hand to her brow as though
smoothing out the frown and continued. "Each one of
my husband's affairs broke my heart and he knew it.
He hated himself for hurting me, swore it would never
happen again, but it did. Sometimes he'd leave me for
a few weeks, even a few months, and my despair was
so great that my family would fear for what I might
do if he didn't come back. He always did and I always
opened my arms to him, because I knew he'd realized,
yet again, that nothing would ever mean as much to
him as the love we shared. Other women were like a

drug, you see. It was the forbidden fruit, the risk, the danger even, and there was plenty of that. He craved it as profoundly as the music he loved. He tried hard to control the urges, he really did, and I did everything I could to help him, but he was a handsome and fascinating man with the kind of magnetism that made him irresistible to everyone who knew him, not just women. You could say that he was the candle burning bright, and we were his moths—and no amount of pain could force us to protect ourselves from him."

She paused, touched a hand to her mouth and continued. "Unlike other addicts he didn't have to go out looking for his drug of choice, because it—they—came to him." She gave a small, humorless laugh. "The women, tall, thin, short, blond, English, foreign . . . Each of them with their obsessions, beliefs, delusions, and most of all their temptations . . . In trying to help him I agreed to go through a period of isolation with him. We stopped our friends coming to the house and we didn't go out unless it was locally and together. It didn't last; he simply wasn't cut out to be reclusive. He loved to socialize and entertain, and so did I. At weekends our home was always full of guests. We'd throw parties in the meadow, or on the beach, grand dinners in the dining room that's now the den, or intimate soirées in the music room. He loved to play for our friends, and there were many who could take up instruments too and the rest of us would dance and sing and drink cocktails into the small hours."

She raised a hand to her face again and Joely saw how shaky it had become. She even wondered if there were tears in Freda's eyes, but there was no sign of any when she looked up, only of a small, knowing sort of smile.

"Aren't you going to ask about my pride?" she challenged. "How I was able to bear my own weakness, and let him trample all over me like that?"

Though Joely had wondered about it, she simply shook her head. It hadn't felt like the right thing to ask before the story was finished.

"He never cheated on me here, in this house," Freda went on as if she hadn't interrupted herself. "He always went away somewhere, I rarely knew where, but it hardly mattered. He was gone, I tried to believe he'd be back, and while I waited I wrote my books to distract myself, but the fear was always there, eating me up in a terrible, soul-destroying way. That this time I might be wrong. This might be the woman he finally leaves me for."

She seemed to hold her breath as she turned her hands over, looking at them as though they'd been holding something precious that had somehow vanished. "That woman did come," she said quietly. "It was inevitable, I suppose I always knew that and he did too, but what he hadn't expected was that she wouldn't want him. He would have left me if she had. He wasn't only infatuated with her, he was obsessed with her, I think he even stalked her until her husband threatened to report him to the police. Even that didn't stop him wanting her, if anything it made him more determined to win her. He was, quite literally, crazy about her and when I found out who she was . . ." She broke off and her quiet laugh was drowning in sadness.

"I advised you a moment ago," she said, "to think

179

about the others who are being hurt by the betrayal. Your family will always feel your pain, even after it's over for you. For them the trust will never come back, and even if you can forgive your husband don't expect them to do the same. In my case, it was my brother who couldn't go on watching me suffer each time David went away. They used to be good friends, but he couldn't stand what this new obsession was doing to me. He wanted to confront him, to tell him that it had to stop, and though I didn't think it would do any good I agreed to let him try."

Freda paused for a beat before continuing, her hands shaking slightly.

"He and David were both keen sailors," she continued, speaking faster now, "so it wasn't unusual for them to take a boat out together. On this particular day, less than a week after David had been threatened with the police, the conditions were perfect for a bracing sail out into the channel. David had no idea that my brother had other things on his mind, and I don't know if he ever got to find out what they were . . . but I suspect he did." She swallowed and took a shallow breath. "We'll never know for sure what happened—a fight must have broken out, and one of them went overboard. And then when the other tried to rescue him . . . I'm sure there would have been a rescue attempt, no matter who went in." She said this more to herself than Joely. "The police and coast guard were alerted. Their bodies were found not far from each other, about a mile along the coast from here. The search took hours."

Joely sat watching her, sensing the ache in her heart, the terrible fear she'd have known during the wait for them to come back. It seemed to be with her now, the pain of losing two people she loved so deeply that it had obviously changed her life, turned her into a hermit to live with a grief that she hadn't even tried to escape.

Joely understood now why she'd advised her to look at who else the betrayal was hurting. "Your brother," she said softly. "You haven't mentioned him in the memoir."

Freda shook her head for some time and when she finally looked up there were shadows in her eyes that Joely didn't understand. "Christopher wasn't a part of that story," she said, "and I realize you think David is Sir, but you're wrong. They shared many of the same qualities, for sure, their passion for music, their gentleness of character, and the same name, but they are not the same person."

For some reason the admission caused Joely's heart to twist. "So is any of it true?" she asked, suspecting she'd been deliberately misled to this point and knowing she'd be angry if she had.

"About my husband and brother? Every word of it."

"And was your husband's name really David?"

"Yes, but we called him Doddoe. David Oswald Douglas Donahoe. It was a name he got at school and it stuck."

Yet throughout the story she'd just told, she'd referred to him as David, so she had been deliberately misleading.

"Are you disappointed?" Freda asked. "I think you are, but this is what happens when you make assumptions, you get it wrong. Or you could say I set a trap for you and you walked into it."

Joely couldn't deny it.

"I've told you about my husband now," Freda continued, "to make you forget your belief, or suspicion, that he and Sir are one and the same. Sir was somebody else entirely . . . Somebody who made the world a beautiful place to be, as long as he was close. He didn't have to try to do that, it just happened. He shaped my young life . . ." Her breath caught in her throat. "Sometimes I wonder if I loved him even more than I loved my husband, if perhaps it was because of him and what happened to him that I'm who I am now." She seemed to consider this for a moment, though Joely suspected it was a question she'd asked herself many times before. "Losing Sir, and in the way I lost him . . ." Her words were swallowed by a swell of emotion. "He didn't deserve what happened to him," she said softly, "and nor did I."

Joely was in her room sitting cross-legged on the bed as she thought back over what Freda had told her, still unsure of what she was supposed to have taken away from it all other than the warning about the damage betrayal could do to the rest of the family. And the disclosure that Sir, David Michaels, was not David Donahoe.

After, when they'd settled down to dinner Freda hadn't wanted to talk any more about her own family, or Joely's, instead she'd wanted to listen to the music Joely had written into the memoir's most recent pages. *Moonlight Sonata,* "She Loves You," a selection of American jazz, an aria from Handel's *Messiah,* "Then He Kissed Me" by the Crystals.

Before they'd gone their separate ways to bed Freda had said, "You're doing a reasonable job with the story so far, but your coyness isn't serving reality. If we were writing about a young nymphomaniac I'd understand your reticence, since it's an illness that requires sensitive treatment, not salacious exploitation. The child we're writing about"—she put a hand to her chest—"the one who acquired more decorum and morals later in life, was little more than a very beautiful, self-absorbed slut at fifteen."

Startled by the harshness, Joely countered, "But one who was capable of love. You said yourself that you loved him."

"Yes, yes, I did, but I believe at this point in the relationship the physicality of it was the most important part of it, so I think it should be written that way. Use words that shock you, disgust you even, they will bring you closer to the truth."

"The truth," Joely murmured to herself as she slid under the duvet, abandoning all plans to chance calling her mother from the balcony tonight when the rain was coming down in torrents. What was the truth? She guessed she'd find out when Freda was ready to tell it, however, she was still determined that Freda herself would have to provide the more sensational aspects of the memoir. She, Joely, was a ghostwriter, not a purveyor of porn, even if that was how young Freda and Sir had conducted themselves. Who didn't in the privacy of the bedroom? (She hoped not Callum and Martha, though knowing some of his more exotic tastes . . . No, she couldn't go there.)

Anyway, she could tell that on some level—perhaps many levels—she was being manipulated by Freda and not always in a way to serve the memoir. It seemed more to serve Freda's own sense of . . . what? Power? Control? Perhaps they were one and the same thing. She was such a peculiar woman it was hard to work out what was really going on, and right now Joely was too tired to try. She was simply going to close her eyes and fall asleep doing exactly what Freda had warned her against, trying to guess what had happened to Sir and young Freda that they hadn't deserved.

CHAPTER FOURTEEN

"My nephew is coming today," Freda announced as Joely joined her for breakfast the following morning. The kitchen was bright with sunlight, the meadow outside a carpet of wildly glittering frost.

Immediately interested, Joely said, "Is that a surprise, or were you expecting him?"

"Here we are," Brenda announced, passing Freda a plate of scrambled eggs sprinkled with freshly cut chives and grilled tomatoes.

Thanking her, Freda reached for the salt and pepper mills and said, "He rang last night." Her voice took on a droll lilt as she said, "He didn't say as much, but he's coming to find out how we're getting along with the memoir."

He rang last night. Joely hadn't got past that yet. "Does your mobile work in the house?" she asked. "I can't ever get reception . . ."

"He called on the landline," Freda informed her. "There's a telephone there," she pointed to an antiquated piece that Joely had assumed was a nostalgic ornament, not something that actually worked. "The other is next to my bed," Freda added.

So there was contact with the outside world, although she'd never heard a phone ring.

"Are you going to have some eggs, dear?" Brenda

offered, holding up the pan ready to load more onto an empty plate.

"Lovely, thank you," Joely replied. "Your apple and caramel pudding last night was delicious by the way."

"She had a second helping," Freda informed the housekeeper.

Joely's eyes rounded, since it was Freda who'd gone back for more.

Freda gave her a wink, startling her even more with this rare display of playfulness—apparently the prospect of her nephew's visit was lifting her spirits. "When was the last time you saw him?" she asked.

Freda helped herself to a mouthful of eggs as she thought.

"It was the week before Joely arrived," Brenda reminded her. "He came and stayed the night to make sure you were serious about going through with the memoir."

Intrigued by that, Joely regarded Freda as she said, "Of course. And we went to Bistro 7 in Lynmouth for dinner so you could have a night off."

"Or you could have a night out," Brenda countered. "You'll like Edward," she informed Joely, "he's one of those easygoing types who never seem to be in a rush even when they are."

"What a curious observation," Freda commented, although she didn't correct it. "He's Christopher's son," she told Joely, and a shadow passed briefly over her eyes. "Losing his father was a terrible blow for him. They were very close. As a family we always have been. Would you say your family are close?"

Joely took her plate from Brenda as she said, "Yes,

I would, and I can sympathize with your nephew's loss. It hit us very hard when my father died unexpectedly."

"Mm, yes, I think you've already mentioned that. Was he a good man?"

Wondering what on earth she expected to hear, Joely said, "Yes, he was. Everyone who knew him had a lot of affection for him."

Freda continued to eat. "What did he do?" she asked after a while.

"He was a doctor. A surgeon."

Freda picked up her coffee, drank, and turned to Brenda. "Is there a room made up for Edward? With Joely in the blue room we'll have to put him somewhere else if he decides to stay."

Brenda said, "I've already taken fresh laundry to the bedroom next door ready to make up the bed. I'll do it before I leave. What time are you expecting him?"

"Not until sometime this afternoon."

"And is he coming alone?"

"I imagine so. He didn't mention bringing anyone with him. Oh, and don't go to the trouble of cooking something especially for him, if he stays he knows he'll have to do without meat for tonight. Or perhaps he can take you to the Bistro?" she said to Joely.

Joely started to protest, certain he wouldn't want a stranger foisted on him any more than she wanted to be foisted.

"He'll probably have to rush back to London," Freda went on, "so you don't have to make a decision now."

"Wouldn't you like to come with us, if we do go?" Joely asked.

Freda sighed. "All this talk of the past is wearying

me more than I'd expected it to, but yes, I probably should. It'll stop you trying to wheedle information out of each other."

Finding that interesting, Joely said, "So Edward doesn't know what the memoir is about?"

"He probably thinks he does, but he's wrong. No one knows, apart from you, and obviously you're only aware of a part of it so far."

Joely was still searching for an appropriate response when Freda suddenly said, "He's not married, and he's not gay."

Feeling as though she'd hit turbulence, Joely said, "Well, that was subtle."

Freda's laugh was girlish and lit up her features in a way that let the young beauty she'd once been shine through.

"OK, ladies, I'm off upstairs to sort out that bedroom. If you want anything else you know where to find it, or me. Oh, and my Bill's down at the beach collecting up laver so we'll be able to have some with our dinners once I get round to cooking it."

"Laver?" Joely asked after Brenda had gone.

"Seaweed," Freda explained. "It's delicious the way Brenda prepares it. Now, I saw that you were a little surprised to discover that Edward doesn't know what we're writing about."

"Yes, I was. Didn't he help Sully, your publisher, to find you a ghostwriter?"

Instead of answering right away Freda tilted her head back as though studying the ceiling, or considering the question, or perhaps she was trying to recall exactly what she'd told her agent and nephew. Finally, she said, "I believe both men have assumed I'm writing about the boating accident that robbed us of Christopher and Doddoe." She stopped as though shocked at having said it so matter-of-factly. "Sir is my secret," she continued in a softer tone, "but now I'm starting to share. Does your family have secrets?"

Startled by yet another unexpected question, Joely was immediately consumed by her own secret, buried deep, needing to stay there . . .

"Every family has them," Freda informed her.

Joely supposed that was probably true, but some were a lot worse than others.

"Would you agree with me," Freda continued, "if I said it's not always good to know the truth?"

Joely put down her fork and reached for her coffee. She wasn't entirely sure what she was going to say, if indeed she was going to say anything at all until the words started to come of their own accord. "For most of my childhood," she said, "I knew that there was a rift in my grandmother's family, between her and her brother. I had no idea what it was about and I kept pestering my mother to tell me. Her answer was always the same: your grandmother says that if we knew what was behind it we'd wish we didn't. Of course it made me more curious than ever. I knew instinctively that asking my grandmother was out of the question, and in the end it went to the grave with her. I've come to realize since that sometimes that's the best place for secrets."

With arched eyebrows Freda said, "So you don't feel inclined to go looking for them anymore?"

Joely shook her head.

"Hah," Freda laughed. "A very good ruse of your mother's to stop you asking her what she might be hiding. Do you think she's got something squirrelled away in the past too?"

Though Joely doubted it, she said, "If she does and she wants to keep it there, then I'm OK with that."

"Do you think your father was always faithful to her?"

Bristling, Joely wanted to say, *Not every husband was like yours*. Instead she said, "I'm sure he was, but we both know that marriages can go through difficult times. If either of them was ever unfaithful they obviously made it up, but frankly I don't think they were."

Freda nodded, as though having no dispute with this possibility. "Were you never tempted to ask your grandmother's brother, your great-uncle, what the rift was about?"

"We didn't see him and he died not long after Granny did."

Joely could see how intrigued Freda was by this, mulling it over, trying out various scenarios that might cause such a rift until she said, "Your grandparents must have been about the same age as my parents. Were they hippies, do you know?"

Wondering if there was some bizarre kind of one-upmanship going on here, Joely said, "If they were, she never said, but I believe they were people of their time, smoking dope and going to concerts . . ."

"You're making them sound rather dull. A secret has the potential to make them much more interesting. A secret that has gone to the grave makes them fascinating. Surely you agree?"

"Clearly you think so."

"And you don't?"

"I've let it go, because I understand that not everything needs to be revealed."

"So you think I'm wasting my time with this memoir?"

"Not at all. If you want to tell a story, it's your prerogative, and I'm sure no one would argue with that."

Freda nodded, seeming pleased with this approval. "Some awful things happened back in the sixties," she declared suddenly, seeming to have several incidents in mind. "People suffered a lot for the mistakes that were made."

Joely didn't comment because she was sure it was true. After a while she said, "Is your memoir going to cause anyone in your family to suffer?"

Freda's smile became thin and sad as she said, "Those who might have suffered, who did suffer, are no longer with us."

"What about Edward and your other nephew?"

"Yes, they're still here, and yes, perhaps it will . . . What will it do to them?" She didn't answer her own question, merely sat contemplating it as though it might not have occurred to her before.

"What about Sir—David Michaels," Joely prompted, "and his family? Will they survive it?"

Freda's eyes flashed with a sudden sharpness, but then it was gone and her voice was even, almost toneless as she said, "They were completely crushed by it."

Joely's heart gave an unsteady beat of pity for people she didn't know, but who she couldn't help but feel for.

"And now we will end this discussion," Freda stated,

pushing away her plate. "Paris is next on our agenda for the memoir. Perhaps we can do that this morning, in the den. We should be finished before Edward arrives."

"Of course," Joely agreed, "but now I know there's a phone here, I'd like to make a quick call to my mother to make sure everything's all right at home."

Freda stared at her hard, and for one strange moment Joely thought she was going to refuse. "Your mother," she repeated, as if taking the time to recall that Joely actually had a family. "Yes, certainly, but wasn't it your husband who asked you to call?"

"He did, but I don't want to speak to him yet."

Freda grunted and got to her feet. "Help yourself," she said, waving a hand toward the vintage contraption with rotary dial.

After she'd gone Joely spent a ludicrous few minutes trying to master the old-fashioned technique of dialing a number on a circular pad, until eventually she connected with her mother's mobile.

"Hello, darling," came the sotto voce reply. "I'm in a meeting. Is everything OK?"

"Yes, fine. I was a bit worried about you, that's all."

"No need to be. Do you know when you're coming back yet?"

Joely was about to respond when she felt sure someone had picked up an extension.

"Are you still there?" her mother asked.

"Yes, yes, I am. Is Holly all right?"

"She is, but have you spoken to her, or Callum?"

Joely was immediately anxious. "Why?"

"Callum is putting pressure on us to find out where you are. I wish you'd tell him, or at least call him.

Listen, I'm sorry, I have to go now. Call later if you can. Or call him."

Ringing off, Joely waited a moment to see if the phone in front of her pinged with the sound of an extension going down. It didn't, but she remained convinced that someone had listened in to her call. And who else was there but Freda?

Deciding she probably ought to give Callum a try regardless of eavesdroppers, she had better luck with the rotary dial this time, but ended up going straight to his voicemail. As she waited for his short greeting to play out she became certain someone was listening again. "I don't know why you're so keen to speak to me," she told him, "but please stop pressuring Mum and Holly. Neither of them knows where I am, and I really don't see that it has anything to do with you." There was more she wanted to say, a whole lot more, but she'd already decided it wouldn't be on the phone, and certainly not while Freda Donahoe was listening.

"I'm not sure," Freda stated, cranking open the shutters in the den as Joely settled onto a sofa with her notebook and recorder, "how necessary the trip to Paris is to the overall story. I've been going through it in my mind and I wonder, were I an editor, if I'd be saying 'Where is this actually taking us?' 'What more are we learning about the relationship that's serving the memoir?' But Paris is Paris, would probably be my reply. Everyone wants to read about Paris."

She stood staring out of the window taking in the day as she quietly assembled her thoughts. "Memories," she said softly, "are like this meadow, don't you think, filled with as many nettles and stones as precious flowers and sweet-smelling grass. It's all there but we prefer only to look at what pleases us." Going to the mantelpiece she picked up the photograph of her nephew and regarded it pensively before holding it out for Joely to see. "He's a good-looking man," she said. "Would you agree?"

"I would," Joely confirmed.

"He's the image of his father, Christopher. I sometimes find it hard to look at him without seeing my brother at that age and remembering . . ." She broke off and went to replace the photograph on the mantelpiece. "We won't talk about him today," she said, "there's no reason to," and going to an upright armchair she pulled a blanket over her knees and folded her hands in her lap.

"We drove to Paris," she said launching straight into her story. "We put the car on a ferry, and when we got there . . ." A hint of irony twitched at her smile. "The riots were more or less over, which he was very disappointed about. He'd wanted to take part, to show solidarity with the students, because he was like that, young and revolutionary, or antiestablishment in spite of his family . . . Anyway, it didn't stop us from having a good time. He never let anything get in the way of that. He'd rung ahead to book us into a small *pensione* on the Left Bank . . . It was on quite a famous street called Rue Mouffetard. Do you know it?"

Joely shook her head.

"I believe that even now it's still full of cafés, food shops, bistros . . . Typical bustling Parisian life. There was a wonderful market, I recall, with every type of

194

fruit and vegetable you can imagine, and the colors . . . They were so bright they hardly seemed real, and the smells coming from the many food stalls made you permanently hungry. Naturally there was the obligatory Frenchman in striped shirt and beret playing the accordion on the street corner, and onion sellers. They seem like clichés now, but back then they were everywhere. We looked down on it all from our *pensione* window, waving out to people if they glanced up, while doing things to each other out of sight below the sill that excited us tremendously. I expect you can imagine the kind of things and if we do decide to keep this in I hope you'll leave the reader in no doubt as to what they were."

Certain she'd be leaving that task for the second draft, Joely simply pretended to note it.

"We were Monsieur et Madame Bardot," Freda continued joyfully. "We were there for the weekend before traveling south to continue our honeymoon on the Riviera. I don't recall anyone regarding us suspiciously, I was mature for my age and we were in Paris, the city of love. We were welcomed by all and treated to copious amounts of cheap red wine in smoke-filled cafés where old men played *bezique* or dominoes, and *l'Anglais*, as they called him, struck up tunes on dusty pianos. He sang in French, all the classics by Edith Piaf of course and everyone joined in. 'La vie en rose.' 'Je ne regrette rien.' 'La Foule.' One night in our room he taught me the words to 'I Love Paris in the Springtime' and the next day we went back to our favorite café and sang it together. In English, obviously—the French would have been too difficult for me—but everyone seemed to know it anyway, and even if they didn't they hummed and swayed and asked us for encore after encore.

"We saw the sights, lay on the grass in the Jardin du Luxembourg, and ate oysters at Le Train Bleu. Once we had sex in an alley close to Montmartre. I made it happen. I loved to take those risks, to feel the warm night air on my skin and know that I was driving him so wild with desire that he'd do anything to please me." She tilted her head as though considering that for a moment, and added, "Yes, he really was willing to do anything, and of course it was the same for me. Our love was becoming deeper and bigger and more consuming by the day. As Madame Bardot I was his wife and I knew that as soon as we could make it a reality we would, except I would be Mrs. Michaels." She smiled. "It doesn't have quite the same ring, does it, but it meant everything to me. It was all I wanted, all I ever thought about.

"One morning he took me to an antique market. I forget where it was exactly, it could have been Les Puces de Saint-Ouen, but I can't be sure. He bought me a small, art deco–style moonstone ring and said that every time we looked at it we'd remember our wonderful first trip to Paris."

Realizing she was more inside the memory than the present, Joely let several minutes pass before she said softly, "Do you still have it?"

Coming out of her reverie, Freda took a breath and shook her head. "I'm afraid not. It . . . I can't remember what happened to it." She got up and paced over to the window, where she stood staring out at the chill sunny day. Her arms were folded in front of her, and her shoulders seemed stiff with tiredness.

"So what do you think?" she asked without turning around. "Should Paris make the final cut, or do we drop it?"

Although virtually nothing had happened to make it worthy of inclusion Joely could sense how precious those days were to her client, so she said, "It's a very romantic interlude, and everyone loves romance, especially one set in Paris."

Freda nodded and when she turned around she was smiling. "I've probably made it sound as much of a cliché as the accordion players and onion sellers," she said, "but that's what we do with memories that hold a special place in our hearts, isn't it? We want to present them in a way that will make everyone love them as much as we do, or envy them, perhaps, or even doubt them for their perfection. It doesn't matter. There was a trip to Paris, a lot of wine was drunk, many songs were sung in cafés, and dances danced on the banks of the Seine—and our love-struck fifteen-year-old who'd drawn everything into her passionate embrace with all the naïvety of her age never spared a single thought for what could go wrong."

"But it did go wrong?"

"Not there, in Paris. Paris *was* perfection, provided we discount the petty jealousy that made me try to stop him from phoning his mother to wish her a happy birthday. He made it, of course—he had no time for jealousy—and the abominable child sulked until he persuaded her to make up the way they always did."

Joely said, "Had you felt jealous of his family, or anyone else before that?"

Freda shook her head. "Oh, the girls at school," she admitted dismissively, "all that ridiculous flirting . . . I don't think they realized how foolish they made themselves, but they're not important. We've moved on to the summer and Paris—and all that followed . . ." She stopped, as if unsure how to continue. Her memories were obviously going to a darker place for the frown between her eyes deepened even as they filled with tears. "When we got back," she said softly, "it was two weeks later, he . . . he told me something . . . I didn't want to believe him, but I could see it was true, and so I . . ." she swallowed hard, "I did something so terrible . . ."

Joely waited, knowing better than to interrupt now.

Freda shook her head. "When you think back to yourself at the age of fifteen," she said, "does that girl feel like someone you know? Or does she feel like a stranger?"

Joely gave it some thought and realized that perhaps she didn't identify with her younger self quite as closely as she might have expected. She'd grown, changed, her ideas and ambitions were different, she was less opinionated, she hoped, and less naïve. She simply wasn't that person anymore.

"When I think of what happened," Freda said quietly, "when I view it from a distance of these many years it almost feels like a fictional story, that she is a character I've made up . . . I don't want her to be me; it's easier to imagine her as someone separate, to talk about her that way . . ." She continued to gaze out of the window, not moving, not even raising a hand to wipe away a tear that fell onto her cheek. In the end she said, "When I tell you what she did you will judge her, you will judge him too because what he did was also terrible. You will listen and then you will understand why I can never forgive her for what happened, why all these years later I still hate her and I will never stop."

She turned around and Joely was unsettled by the disturbing mix of bitterness and sadness in her eyes. "I want you to hate her too," she said, making it an instruction. "As my ghostwriter I will rely on you to make sure it's the same for every reader. We will publish the truth and the real punishment for the terrible crime committed against an innocent person will begin.

"Now Edward is here, so I must go to greet him."

CHAPTER FIFTEEN

Joely had been in the writing room for almost three hours by now committing the trip to Paris to her laptop, doing her best to conjure both the heady romance Sir and young Freda had enjoyed, and the sublime location. The task might have been easier if she didn't already know that something awful was to follow, if she could actually stop herself creating scenarios in her head for what it could be. Actually, just as much of a challenge, if the truth were told, was containing her irritation at being sent off to do this now. It was like being ordered to bed so the grown-ups could talk in peace.

"We have a lot of things to discuss," Freda had announced as her nephew's car had pulled up outside the front door, "so it would be a good time for you to go and transcribe our little chat this morning."

And so, without even being introduced, Joely had climbed the tower staircase, propped open the library door with a well-thumbed Gibbon's *The Decline and Fall of the Roman Empire*, and settled herself down to the task at hand.

Now it was more or less finished, and she was feeling absurdly reluctant to go downstairs in case showing up unannounced angered Freda. If there were another way out of the tower she'd happily take it, for it was a beautiful day, almost spring-like, and she hadn't yet taken a walk down to the beach. Or she could take the section of coast path that fronted the Valley of Rocks. From there she could make her way into town for a cup of tea in the inviting-looking tea shop at the top of the funicular ride and have a private chat with her mother or Andee on the phone.

Had Freda really been listening in to her call earlier? If so, what on earth had she hoped to hear?

Anyway, her host's peculiarities aside, good manners— or something like that—had her trapped up here like she was some embarrassing guest who had to be kept out of the way in case she disgraced herself.

Well, the heck with that.

Sending her afternoon's work to the printer, she picked up her phone and bag and descended as far as the library before coming to a cautious stop at the sound of raised voices down in the kitchen. Certainly one of them belonged to a man, and the other, though quieter was unquestionably Freda's.

Reminding herself that it was outrageous to eavesdrop, she tiptoed to the top of the next staircase where she could hear much better.

" . . . tell me the truth, Freda. I'll find out anyway, you know that so . . ."

"Edward, please stop bullying me . . ."

" . . . let's be sensible about this. I care about you, for heaven's sake, you're the only family I have now that . . ."

"You have a mother," Freda cut in sharply.

" . . . who we haven't seen in decades. Freda, if you're as . . ."

"Stop, I know what you're going to say, you think I'm about to die and that's why I'm trying to finish this memoir. Well, I'm not that sick, Edward, and I'll thank you for not calling my doctor again to find out when I last saw him."

"If I hadn't I wouldn't know that you'd been, and you never go unless it's serious."

"Well, it turned out not to be. I'm fine, or better than you seem to think, and this memoir is something I've been planning for a very long time, so you could say I've been working on it for years. So there's no urgency about it, it's just . . . time to get it out of my head and onto the page."

"OK, then explain to me why you won't tell me anything about it. Why do I have to wait until it's published to find out whatever the big secret is? If it concerns Dad, surely I have a right to know."

"It doesn't concern him, or Doddoe. It's something that happened a long time ago and it's time I set the record straight."

"About what?"

"We're going round in circles. Let's stop and have some tea."

Joely stayed where she was, listening to the sound of the kettle filling with water and a chair being dragged from the table.

"So how's the ghostwriter working out?" Edward asked, his tone less stringent now, more conciliatory.

"She's good," Freda replied. "Better even than I expected, but we still have a way to go."

"Where is she?"

"In the writing room. I know you want to meet her,

and I'm sure she wants to meet you too, but if I allow it you are not to bully her for information. She's signed an NDA and I'm sure you don't want her to be in breach of her contract."

With a laugh, Edward said, "Who did you get to draw that up for you? I know it wasn't anyone in my office or they'd have told me."

"Precisely, which is why I went to a firm in Taunton."

"Did she mind signing it?"

"I don't think so."

His voice lowered in a teasing, conspiratorial way, "Were you a spy, back in the day? Are you revealing some sort of government secrets in this tell-all of yours?"

"That's it," she gasped in mock horror. "You've guessed. Now let's talk about you. Are you planning to stay tonight?"

"If I'm allowed to."

"Good, a room's been made up for you, but you'll have to eat in town. I was planning to come with you, but I have a few things to do here so perhaps you'll be kind enough to take the ghostwriter with you. Before you answer, I want your word that you won't fall for her, or try to make her fall for you."

Sounding amused, Edward said, "Do you always call her the ghostwriter? Isn't her name Jodie Something-or-Other?"

"Joely Foster. She's very attractive, smart, and she's on the rebound, so she really doesn't need to be discombobulated by a playboy like you."

As he gave a shout of laughter Joely's eyebrows arched. This was a different tune to the one Freda had played earlier when she'd announced that her nephew was single and not gay. She'd sounded then as if she wanted to push them together, but apparently not.

And *playboy*?

Deciding she ought to go down before the mood changed against her, she resisted the urge to check herself in a mirror—easy since she didn't have one—and then promptly made an idiot of herself as she slipped three steps from the bottom and thumped into the kitchen door.

Luckily there wasn't enough room for her to go all the way down to her knees, and by the time Freda came to investigate the thump she was fully upright and ready to say, "Sorry, just a little advance warning of my arrival."

Freda regarded her curiously and stood aside for her to enter. "Joely, my nephew, Edward," she said, smoothly. "Edward, this is Joely."

Since she'd already seen a photograph of him Joely wasn't as affected by his good looks as she might have been, although she did find herself warming to the easy charm he seemed to emanate as he rose to greet her. *Definitely not my type,* she was thinking as she said, "It's lovely to meet you."

"And to meet you," he responded, closing his long fingers around hers in a grip that wasn't exactly too tight, but very definitely firm. "I've been told that you're doing great work with the memoir."

"I'm simply typing it up," Joely assured him, glad to have her hand back, for he seemed to have held it slightly too long.

"I've warned him not to quiz you about it," Freda

informed her, going to take the kettle from the heat. "He knows about the NDA. Would you like some tea?"

"Actually," Joely said, "I was thinking about walking into town so I can make some calls."

"But there's the phone," Freda objected, pointing her to the museum piece with working extension.

"I could do with the exercise." Joely smiled. "And it's such a lovely day."

"Maybe I could walk with you," Edward suggested. "It's been a while since—"

"We have a lot of paperwork to get through," Freda reminded him. To Joely she said, "Do you have anything for me to read?"

"It's on the printer," Joely replied. "I'll go and get it—"

"No need, I can pick it up myself. If you're walking into town now, perhaps you can meet Edward there later, for dinner. I recommend the Bistro as a change from the Rising Sun. Edward, you can drive over so you'll have the car to come back in."

Clearly amused by being bossed around, Edward said, "I wonder how I manage without you when I'm in London."

"Mm, yes, I wonder that too," Freda muttered. "Why don't you meet at seven? Edward, you should ring up to reserve a table."

Laughing at his ironic smile Joely started for the door, and as she closed it behind her she heard Freda say, "I told you she was attractive."

"But that's not why you chose her."

"No, you're right, that's not why I chose her."

*

205

In spite of the brilliant sunshine the air was bitingly cold as Joely climbed out of the Valley of Rocks to start along the coast path toward Lynton. As far as she was concerned it wasn't much more than a ledge in the cliff face with mighty tors rising up on one side and a slope so steep and unnervingly mesmerizing on the other that she couldn't allow herself to look down. One slip, or one ferocious gust of wind, and there was very little or nothing at all on that barren hillside, to break a fall into the foaming waves below. And how far away was the coast guard? With so many cuts there might not be one at all.

Every so often she met some hikers loaded down with backpacks and wasn't especially impressed by the way every one of them stepped over to the tor side as they passed, an invitation for her to take the killer drop side.

Fortunately the path soon became wider, or maybe she got used to it, and as her tension eased she allowed herself to think beyond the instinct to keep herself alive. Although the sheer beauty of nature's showy mid-winter display with so many wild flowers springing into bloom and the coconut scent of gorse in the air was still distracting.

So too was the text that had pinged into her phone from Holly.

Deciding that no matter what the path was doing now it was still too risky to attempt walking and reading at the same time, she hurried to the next memorial bench and sat down to look at the message again.

Dad has moved back into the house, and so have I. Hx

Joely's gaze drifted from the words to the glittering stretch of channel in front of her where huge swathes of indigo formed island patches in the aqueous blue. Overhead a rowdy flock of seagulls dived and soared around the cliffs and in her head, like the lapping tide below, questions formed and dissolved and formed again.

In the end she half-walked, half-ran to the sea view hotels on the edge of town, and as soon as there were enough bars on her phone she connected to Callum's number.

As she waited for him to answer she began priming herself to leave a message on his voicemail, but then he was there.

"At last," he said, sounding both relieved and irritated. "You are impossible to get hold of . . ."

"Is it true you've moved back into the house?" she demanded, turning her back on a couple who threw her a curious glance.

"Yes, I have, but only . . ."

"Then you can leave. I don't care what's going on with Martha, or anyone else, you are not . . ."

"Joely, it's my house too, and you aren't using it at the moment. For God's sake, I've been trying to get hold of you to ask . . ."

"And the answer's no. You made a decision to leave . . ."

"Joely, please. I understand you're angry, you have every right to be, but can't we at least discuss this? I'm prepared to come to wherever you are . . ."

"I don't want to see you, and I don't want you in the house . . . Please tell me Martha's not there too. If she is . . ."

207

"She isn't, but Holly is. I can't just leave her . . ."

"She can go to my mother."

"It's her home. She wants to be there, and you can't keep relying on your mother."

"Don't tell me what I can and can't do with my mother."

"She's not well, Joely. It might only be a cold, but it's a pretty bad one, and she doesn't need to be coming home from work to cook and God-knows-what-else for Holly. So I've moved back in to take the load off her . . ."

"So you haven't actually left Martha?"

"Yes, I have. I realize—"

"And you think that gives you the right to carry on as if nothing happened? Well, it doesn't, so please don't be there when I get home."

After ringing off she strode on along the path in front of the hotels and up the steep incline to the town. When she reached the café next to the funicular station, she ordered herself a cup of tea and glass of wine and sat down at a table outside. The view was spectacular, and the sun was much warmer here, but she was hardly noticing either as she connected to her mother.

"If you're not well you shouldn't be at work," she barked as soon as she received an answer.

"I'm not that bad," came the reply. "I'm guessing you've spoken to Callum."

"I have and—"

"Joely you're sounding angry so please calm down—"

"Wouldn't you be angry in my shoes?"

"Maybe. I—"

"If Dad had ever cheated on you, you'd know how

I feel." *Where had that come from? She'd never said anything like that to her mother before.*

"Well, he didn't, but that doesn't mean I don't understand. Callum's hurt you very badly, and I honestly don't know—"

"Our marriage is over." Her head spun at the sound of the words, and she immediately wanted to take them back.

"I don't think you believe that," her mother responded, "but even if you do I don't see anything wrong with him being at the house while you're not there. If you want to give us some idea of when you'll be back I'm sure he'll be able to make some alternative arrangements . . . No, don't interrupt," she scolded as Joely drew breath to protest. "You know it makes sense this way and if you don't want to be under the same roof as him when you come home you can always come and stay with me."

"Oh great, so now I'm the one who's moving out." Her mother sighed.

Realizing that venting at her mother this way was doing neither of them any good, Joely took a calming sip of wine, and attempted to start again. "So what happened with Martha? Do you know?"

"All I can tell you is what Holly told me, that he's an effing idiot who was led by his . . . Actually, her language is too colorful for me to repeat. However, she did say that her father told her to ask *you* why things went wrong."

Joely's mouth fell open as an uncomfortable heat spread through her. But Callum didn't know what she was hiding, he couldn't, and besides *he* was the one at fault here. "So he's blaming me for him going off with my best friend?"

"I don't know what he's doing, but you have to admit, Joely, that there are always two sides to a story and now we know that Callum has his."

Later, sitting opposite Edward Martin in the Bistro—a quaint little place set back from the harbor with shiny brass rails and cozy booths—Joely was doing her best to put the conversation with her mother out of her mind. In fact, rather than deal with it, she'd spent the time waiting for Edward wondering about the other story occupying her world right now and how Sir might tell his side of it if he had the chance.

She wondered if he was still alive, and if so, where he might be. And did he have any idea he was being written about? What would it do to him and his family once the memoir was published? Was Freda protecting them with pseudonyms, or was Michaels their actual name?

"I'm ready to accept," Edward said, after ordering the wine, "that I might not be the most fascinating company, but in my defense you haven't given me much of a chance yet."

Joely had to smile. "Sorry, just a few things going round in my head, nothing to do with you. In fact, I've been looking forward to meeting you."

His eyes lit up in a way that made her laugh. "Freda's always so secretive," he said, "that I'm amazed you even knew I existed. Or maybe you didn't until you heard I was coming."

"I knew," she assured him. "Not that she told me

anything about you. Brenda was more forthcoming, she says you're very easygoing and you remind her of Cary Grant."

His laugh was one of true amusement. "Tell any of my children that and they'll say Cary who? and probably think it's a girl." He leaned in conspiratorially, "I think everyone under forty reminds Brenda of Cary Grant and I don't have the heart to tell her I'm past it."

Chuckling, Joely said, "How many children do you have?"

"Three. Two sons with my first wife, aged seventeen and fourteen, and a little cracker of a nine-year-old daughter with my second wife. None with my third wife, but as we've recently embarked on an amicable split I'm not expecting any from that quarter to add to the number."

Joely's eyes were wide. "You've had *three* wives," she cried in amazement. *Definitely a playboy and quite possibly a serial adulterer.*

Appearing perplexed, he said, "Do you think I might not be cut out for marriage? That's what each of them has told me and I'm beginning to think they could be right."

"I think there's a very good chance of it," Joely informed him drolly, and felt more than a little relieved that he definitely wasn't her type. The last thing she needed right now was to be struggling with an attachment to a very handsome, but clearly totally untrustworthy womanizer.

On the other hand, introducing him to Callum could be fun.

Immediately as the thought occurred to her she felt

her smile fade—did she really think she'd get some pleasure out of hurting him?

After sampling the wine and approving it, Edward waited for their glasses to be filled and proposed a toast. "To you," he declared, "and I hope whatever's bothering you can be quickly resolved."

Surprised, she said, "What makes you say that?"

"It's in your eyes. They're very expressive, and perhaps because my aunt happened to mention that you're on the rebound. I'm sorry about that."

Joely had to smile. "It's hardly your fault, and I'm not sure I'd call it the rebound, although I've no idea what else to call it. It's complicated and I'd rather not talk about it if you don't mind."

"Not a bit. Why don't we choose what we're going to eat and then you can tell me all about this memoir."

Realizing he was baiting her, Joely shot him a look and turned to the menu.

After they'd ordered—pork medallions for him while Joely went for the mushroom stroganoff—he sat back in his chair and regarded her with frank interest. Before he could speak she said,

"It's no good, I'm not going to betray her confidence . . ."

"I don't expect you to. I'd simply like to be assured that she's not writing herself into some kind of trouble."

Joely screwed up her nose. "It's hard to give you that assurance when I've no idea if the names she's using are real—apart from her own—and I've yet to find out why she feels the need to do this."

"Have you asked her?"

"She says she wants to put the record straight—and even if I knew what about I wouldn't tell you because I've signed an agreement."

He weighed the answer, and said, "So is it about Doddoe? Her husband. He was a terrible philanderer, you know. That's an old-fashioned word, isn't it, but it certainly suits him."

"No, it's not about him. It's something that happened when she was much younger . . . Now, that's all I'm saying. Let's talk some more about you and all your marriages . . ."

"I'm sure you're much more interesting."

"Not true. I've only tied the knot once, and actually I'm still married, I just don't know for how much longer."

"Do you have children?"

"A daughter who'll be sixteen in a couple of months. I found out shortly before coming here this evening that she and her father have moved back into the family home."

"Which means they must have moved out at some point. Will they be staying once you return?"

"Holly will, I'm sure, but as for Callum . . ." She sighed and took another sip of wine. "He left me not long before Christmas to be with my best friend."

"Ouch."

She nodded. "Apparently it hasn't worked out for them so . . ." She threw out a hand. "I've no idea where we're supposed to go from here, but he's somehow made my mother believe that our breakup is partly my fault."

He frowned. "Mm, not very chivalrous, considering what he did."

She didn't meet his eyes as she said, "No, it isn't."

His scrutiny was making her uncomfortable now, although he'd have no way of knowing what she was hiding, what she couldn't even bring herself to put into thoughts, never mind words.

"I have an aunt who's very big on protecting secrets," he reminded her, "and I have no problem with it. I get that some are better left untold, while others can do a whole lot of good if they come out. I guess you know which category yours falls into."

"The former," she assured him, and keen to change the subject she said, "we seem to be having a very personal conversation for two people who've only just met. So, how about we get onto slightly less delicate ground and talk about hobbies, likes and dislikes, where we go for holidays, that sort of thing?"

With a laugh he raised his glass and said, "Skiing, sailing, music, loud people, usually Italy, but sometimes further afield. How about you?"

Enjoying the throwback, she said, "Skiing, horseback riding, cinema, cheats, usually France, sometimes Spain."

He nodded, clearly satisfied. "So now we have that out of the way, what shall we talk about next?"

"Stop being difficult," she chided. "Since we both enjoy skiing why don't you tell me where you go, or let me guess, Aspen, Verbier, Whistler?"

He looked amazed, although she could tell it was mock, but actually it turned out that he did frequent some of the world's most luxurious resorts. She, for her part, had never been to any of them, since she and Callum usually went somewhere way less pricey either in Austria or Eastern Europe, or France if they could get a good deal.

She couldn't imagine they'd be going this winter, at least not together. Maybe one of them would take Holly if she was up for it.

The food arrived and they continued to chat easily and humorously and in a way that made her realize that she hadn't felt this relaxed in a very long time.

"You just smiled," he told her as their coffees arrived. "Did I say something funny?"

"No, it was something that occurred to me." She narrowed her eyes as though warning him not to ask. "I've really enjoyed this evening, thank you," she said. "No offense to your aunt, but it's good to get out of the house now and again—and to have someone to talk to."

His dark eyes twinkled. "So she's not proving a great conversationalist? It doesn't surprise me. She never had much time for chitchat even when my father and her husband were alive. Since we lost them she's all but shut up shop in a social sense, as you know. She had a breakdown right after it happened, she couldn't handle it at all. We had to check her into a clinic for a while. Personally, I think she's still finding it hard to accept that Doddoe might actually have left her if the accident hadn't happened. It would have broken her, that's for sure, she was completely devoted to him. Now she just writes, listens to music, and writes some more. It's actually quite good to know that she's finally allowed someone over the threshold, never mind into her precious inner world. I think having you there could be doing her a lot of good."

Recalling what she'd overheard earlier, Joely said, "Is

215

she all right? I'm sorry, but I can't help wondering if she's doing this memoir because time isn't on her side."

"She had a bleed to the brain several weeks ago," he told her. "It gave us a bit of a scare, but fortunately, she came through without too many complications. She has to keep a close eye on her blood pressure now, and luckily Brenda's very good at making sure she takes her medication. I expect you can guess that it's the main reason for bringing you in to help with the memoir. Frankly, I never imagined she'd go for it, but actually it was her idea, so at least we know she's taking her condition seriously. Now, I think we should be heading back to Dimmett House, unless you have some calls to make first. I'm happy to wait if you do."

Deciding that actually she didn't feel like talking to Callum again tonight, or anyone else come to that, she thanked him and got out her purse to pay her share.

He was having none of it, but only got his way when he said, "How about we make it your treat the next time I come?"

Finding herself hoping that might be soon, Joely put away her card and followed him out into the wintry night, where his car—she'd had no idea until today that Porsche even made SUVs—was parked nose on to the river.

The journey back to the house took no more than ten minutes and as they pulled up at the end of the drive Edward said, "I'll be taking off early in the morning, so I probably won't see you. But here's my card." He handed one over. "Give me a call when you're back in London, or before if you're concerned about Freda."

Joely thanked him and as she got out she glanced up

at the tower. Though it wasn't late, just after nine, she was surprised to see lights on in the writing room. Then she spotted Freda sitting at her desk, a small figure darkened by the brilliance around her like a moth trapped in the heart of a flame. A second later the light went out, making it seem eerily as though Freda herself had been extinguished.

CHAPTER SIXTEEN

It's almost the end of summer and I can hardly wait to go back to school.

I'll see much more of Sir then, even though I won't be able to speak to him privately very often, or touch him whenever I want to, unless we can snatch some secret moments together. (We've talked about that and I've come up with some good ways that we'll find exciting and daring and necessary because it's hard for us to keep our hands off each other.)

Paris was wonderful, fab, everything I ever dreamed of and more, but it seems such a long time ago now. I've seen him since, of course, I've gone to him every time I could, even while I was on holiday with my parents in Wales. They were staying at a big house near the west coast, and Sir drove all the way over just to see me. I escaped without anyone even asking where I was going; they were too chilled out on pot, loud music, and hot sun even to notice I'd gone.

I met him in a layby about a mile away from the holiday house and we drove to a deserted beach I'd spent days finding for us. He'd brought a picnic, the way he always does at his uncle's cottage, but we didn't eat straightaway. Instead we stripped off our clothes and ran into the surf, splashing and leaping about in the waves, laughing and screaming over the roar until he carried me onto the sand and lay me down. Beaches are not good places to make love, we soon discovered, but he'd brought a blanket and towels and soon we were as together as it is possible to be.

He misses me every bit as much as I miss him when we're apart; he says he thinks about me all the time and I know I can never think about anything else. He's written poems for me to read when I go to bed and they're so beautiful that sometimes they make me want to cry. I picture him in my mind, seeing him as he is when we make love; it's like he's lost in his favorite music. As it grows louder and more forceful his eyes close and all the muscles in his face tighten until he's carried into the very heart of the symphony.

Today we're going to the cottage for the first time in several weeks. His uncle's been using it over the summer, but he's gone away again now, to Argentina, I think, or Buenos Aires, which actually might be the same place. My parents are back in London after our holiday and they think I've gone to stay with Mandy to plan which clubs and teams we want to belong to during the coming school year. First day of term is less than a week away, but Sir wants me all to himself one last time before the summer is over. He also wants to talk to me, because he has something important to say. At first I think it's going to be one of his little pep talks about taking extra care when we're at school.

"It's more than that," he says when I tease him that I already know what it is.

I think about it for a while and find myself starting to smile as I work out what it's most likely to be.

In a little over a month it'll be my birthday and he's said so many times that he wishes I was sixteen.

We'll be able to get married then, or live together—some people are doing that now without trying to hide it—but I'd rather be his wife and have him as my husband so the whole world will know that we belong to each other. It won't happen straightaway though, because I know my parents will be upset if I don't complete this last school year to make sure I'll at least have some O levels to my name. So do you know what I think he's going to do today, I think, I'm *certain* he's going to propose to me so that when we go back for the new term we'll have our secret as well as our love to keep us together.

When we get to his uncle's the first thing we do is make love, as we always do, and after, because he loves it so much, I put on a long white dress he bought me in Paris that's as soft and transparent, he says, as a butterfly wing. He loves to watch me dance when I wear it, writhing and pirouetting, stretching tall and curling to the floor in a ball. Or he sits me in front of a mirror and brushes my hair like it's the most precious part of me, down over my shoulders until it and his hands are covering my breasts.

"Sometimes," he says, "I feel as though you might float away, disappear into nothingness like notes already played, and I couldn't bear that."

I couldn't bear that either, but he doesn't seem as melancholy today as he was when he said that, so I unpack our picnic and he puts on a record. I recognize it right away as one of his favorites: "Blowin' in the Wind" by Bob Dylan. I love the song most when Sir plays it himself on the guitar, but today he stands quietly listening to it as though it's making him think about it in a way he hasn't before. Perhaps he is a little bit melancholy after all.

When it finishes he puts on Mozart's *Night Music* and it makes me smile because I can play it much better now, and with both hands. Of course this is the orchestral version, nothing like my amateur flailing around the basic keys, nevertheless whenever I hear it, it reminds me of the first time he put his hands on mine to teach me.

We eat and listen to more music and I notice after a while that he isn't saying very much. He definitely seems sad about something but when I ask what it is he just shakes his head. I think he's worried about us going back to school and how difficult it's going to be pretending we don't mean anything to each other, so I go to sit on his lap and put my arms around him.

He catches my wrists in his hands and holds them between us as he looks into my eyes; it's for such a long time that I start to feel nervous. It's like he's seeing me for the first time, or that he doesn't really know me . . . I don't know what he's thinking.

He says, softly, "I'm not going back for the new term."

I hardly have time to take this in when he says, "I'm going to America to join my brother."

I feel confused, frightened even, but then I realize what he's waiting for me to say so I say it quickly. "I'll come too. I don't care about school . . ."

"No, listen," he interrupts. "Your schooling is important . . ."

"No. I'll come . . ."

221

"*Cherie,* you can't. You must try to understand that there cannot be a future for us."

I shoot up from his lap, crying, "No! You don't mean that. You want us to be together. You're always saying it . . ."

"In a different world, at a different time . . ."

"Stop!" I cry, covering my ears with my hands. "You can't go to America and leave me here, I won't let you. I'll come too. I want to come . . ."

"Sssh, I know you do, but it isn't possible. You're too young, and this, what's happened between us, it's more beautiful than I can ever put into words, but it should never . . . It wouldn't have . . ." He pushes a hand through his hair, and I grab it harshly.

"Please let me come," I implore him. "It's what you promised, that we would go to America together . . ."

"No, I didn't say that. I know it's what you've told yourself, but . . ." He grips my shoulders as I start to sob hysterically. He shakes me and holds me tight until I quiet down and when I look at him I can see how hard he's struggling, how much he hates himself for doing this—but not as much as I'm starting to hate him.

I want to lash out at him, to smash all the records and pummel my fists into his face and into my own. I can't bear it. I have to make him understand that I can't stay here without him, I have to go too. "Please," I beg, choking the words into his chest. "Please take me. I'll do anything."

"I can't," he says and it sounds so final.

"Why? I don't understand . . ."

He takes hold of me again and says, "You know how hard it can be to tell the truth sometimes?"

I want to say that I don't, that I just want him to stop.

"Well, this is one of those times." He drops his head but I know there are tears in his eyes and it's making me panic.

"There's someone I've never told you about," he says. "I know I should have, but . . . I . . ." He can't get any more words out and I'm trapped in the silence like a terrified mouse before the spring comes down. "I have a girlfriend," he whispers, "and she's coming with me."

Shock pushes the blood from my veins. I stare at him, unable to believe what he said because it doesn't make any sense. He's lying, because how can he have a girlfriend when he's been seeing me during almost all of his free time? He took me to concerts, to Paris; he came to Wales . . .

"Her name's Linda," he says. "She's been traveling around India for the past three months with my sister. They're coming back next week and in September we're joining my brother in Georgia."

Joely stopped typing. Young Freda's devastation was flooding through her. The lies, the false promises, and brutal crushing of her dreams were too much for anyone, never mind someone so young. It might be true that she'd talked herself into believing in a future he'd never actually promised, but he'd never, until now, said it was impossible either. Nor had he ever mentioned a girlfriend.

He was weak, a coward, and worst of all he was cruel.

In her mind's eye she saw the older Freda's face as

she'd recounted the scene all these years later, her eyes moist, her mouth twisting with remembered pain. She'd said only a few more words beyond those that Joely had already transcribed, but they were perhaps the most devastating of all.

I hate him, I *hate him*. I want him to die and I want to die too, because I can't live without him. I need to find out who Linda is so I can kill her. They won't be able to go anywhere then. He'll have to take me. I know he wants to really, but he can't now, because I've already told Mummy and Daddy what he did to me. I was crying so hard when I got home that I had to tell them. I've never seen Daddy so angry. He sent me to my room and now he's saying that he's going to destroy "that pervert." That's what he called Sir. A pervert. Good, because after the way he's treated me he deserves to be called vile names. He's going to find out that he can't just throw me away like a used-up toy.

Mummy's been in touch with the school to tell them I won't be coming back for the new term and why. She insisted they sack their music teacher before he corrupts any more young girls.

Daddy called the police just now. I heard him on the phone and I'm so scared . . . I suddenly want to see Sir, but then I remember he's got Linda and I'm so full of hurt and pain and fear that I don't know what to do with myself.

"They're sending some officers to talk to you," Daddy tells me, not even knocking before he comes into my room. "You understand that what he's done is rape, don't you?"

Joely paused again, and instead of typing Freda's account of what came next she decided to listen to it first, needing to be sure she'd heard it correctly, although she knew she had.

"I accused him of raping me," Freda had said hoarsely. "Of course it went without saying he was guilty of that in a statutory sense, but I told them, my father and the police, that he'd forced me . . . I lied to make sure that when he went to prison he would go as a rapist in the truest sense of the word. I knew, you see, that it would destroy him, and that was what I wanted." A long pause followed and Joely recalled the odd way Freda's hand had fluttered through the air as she'd said, "Except it wasn't really me who lied, it was the moth," and with a small puff of breath she snapped her fingers together as though extinguishing the illusion.

CHAPTER SEVENTEEN

Joely was sitting on the harbor wall huddled into her padded coat, hair fluttering about in a sprightly breeze. The Rising Sun was behind her and in front a handful of small boats was anchored in the mud waiting for a tide and better days. As she gazed out at a bruised and belligerent sky, her eyes half-followed the gulls and cloud shadows as they passed over the rocky headland of Foreland Point. She was thinking about Holly and occasionally confusing her with young Freda; then of Callum, which caused the ache in her heart to deepen and swell with the pain and knowledge of how even the deepest love could go wrong.

Martha had messaged to say she understood they couldn't be friends again, but if Joely ever changed her mind . . .

Joely was sure she wouldn't, so she hadn't messaged back.

She still had no idea what had actually gone on there, but for the moment she wasn't particularly keen to find out.

She sighed, and like leaves resettling after a gentle gust her thoughts returned to the memoir. She still hadn't transcribed all that Freda had told her, but since Freda seemed in no hurry for it, and had so far shown

no inclination to explain her bizarre excuse for the monstrous lie, it could wait.

I didn't do it, it was the moth.

What the heck had she meant by that?

Was she losing her mind? Had she somehow got her own life confused with the characters she'd created? Joely had even begun to wonder if the memoir was actually another work of fiction dressed up as fact, but that didn't seem to make much sense. Freda was using her own name and she must surely be aware of how hard it would be for anyone to admire her once they knew what she'd done. She'd even admitted it was a form of punishment, so she seemed to want to be despised and scorned in the worst and most humiliating way.

" . . . I lied to make sure that when he went to prison he would go as a rapist in the truest sense of the word. I knew, you see, that it would destroy him and that was what I wanted."

The most devastating revenge, and yet she'd said, *I didn't do it, it was the moth.*

So did she have some sort of alter-ego she was trying to blame? An invisible friend who urged her to do things that her real self knew to be wrong? Clearly time had done nothing to ease her normal conscience, if anything this project proved that she was deeply troubled by what she'd done.

So many questions in need of answers, but one thing appeared certain, Freda's aim with this memoir was to try to clear the name of the man she'd set out to ruin.

Taking out her phone she looked down at the screen and wondered if she should ask Sully to find out who David Michaels really was. If she was helping to create

an unexploded bomb for some unsuspecting politician, movie star, business leader, or leading churchman, didn't he at least deserve to be warned that his past was going to be brought back into the public eye? He very likely had a family now who might know nothing about his affair with a fifteen-year-old girl, or of his time in prison.

However, if Freda had used a different name where would Sully start? In fact, was it even necessary to find the man if Freda was protecting him with a pseudonym?

Realizing there was probably only one person who could help her with this, even though it would mean breaking her NDA, she connected to Andee's number.

"Hi, it's me," she said to the voicemail. "I'm in need of a detective, or at least some friendly advice on how to go about finding someone. No rush, whenever you can get back to me. Or given my circumstances, I'll try you again later."

Later in the day Joely was sitting with Freda in the kitchen not entirely sure how much more she wanted to hear, or even how willing she was to stay on and complete the assignment. She only knew that the disturbingly darker turn things had taken was making her uneasy.

Speaking into the silence, her voice dry and distant, Freda said, "What he did, the way he led on a silly, naïve young girl, was unforgivable, of course it was. There's no excuse for a grown man to behave in such a manner, or to expect any sort of forgiveness . . ." She took a breath and another before forcing herself to go on. "He didn't receive any, from anyone . . ."

Joely watched her swallow and press her fingers to

her mouth as though not wanting any more words to come.

But they did.

"I don't suppose I expected it to go so far, but once the police became involved . . ." Her voice broke and as tears welled in her eyes she began to shake her head.

Joely fetched her some water, and set it on the kitchen table in front of her. "Maybe we should take a break for a while," she suggested.

Freda stared at the glass and many minutes passed before she spoke again. "He said later, 'I was besotted with her. I just couldn't resist her even though I knew it was wrong.' He never tried to deny that the affair had happened, or that he'd broken all his promises along with every possible rule. The law too, of course. He behaved as honorably as he could in the circumstances. He accepted that he'd never be able to teach again, that he'd have to suffer unimaginable public disgrace . . . He even wrote to me to say sorry."

"Do you still have the letter?" Joely asked.

Freda didn't answer, her eyes were glazed, her thoughts clearly elsewhere. "He was a good man," she said quietly, "and his life was ruined by a lie. Nothing can change that, we can't turn back the clock to correct mistakes or untell lies, but we can punish the person who committed the crime."

After Freda had disappeared to her room Joely stayed where she was in the kitchen, concerned by Freda's state of mind, and even afraid of how far she intended to go to punish herself. She wondered if she ought to alert someone to how worried she was? It seemed a good idea to call Edward and ask for his advice, so she decided that as soon as she'd transcribed the last few minutes with Freda she would drive into town and do that. She didn't want Freda listening in to a call she made from the house.

As she passed through the library on her way to the writing room, she paused to prop open the door and thought she heard someone moving about in the studio on the other side of the connecting wall. She listened, trying to catch the noise again, but there was nothing so she continued up the stairs.

It didn't take long to draft the lines containing young Freda's remorse. Joely even added a few to make it seem more heartfelt and genuine. She had no details yet of the arrest, or the police interviews, nevertheless, simply to think of how shocked and afraid that young man must have felt when the police had come for him caused Joely's heart to twist with the angst of it. On the other hand, in today's world he'd be considered a predator, even a pervert, someone who deserved everything that came to him, and Joely couldn't bring herself to argue with that. She wondered if Freda would want to fictionalize the detention part of the story—she wouldn't have been there, so she couldn't know for sure what had happened.

Now that all her notes were on the screen she glanced up to clear her mind of the words and her heart practically leapt from her body as she caught sight of Freda's ghostly reflection in the window.

"I'm sorry," Freda said from the doorway, "I thought you must have heard me come up."

Still recovering, Joely attempted a smile as she turned around. "Is everything all right?" she asked, aware that this was the first time Freda had joined her in the writing room while she was working.

"Yes, everything's fine," Freda assured her. "I wanted to let you know that Bill is driving me into town so if there's anything you need . . ."

"Uh, I don't think so, thank you. I might go myself when I've finished here."

Freda nodded and came forward to peer at the computer screen.

Resisting the urge to cover up what she'd done so far, since she hadn't read it back yet, Joely waited tense and curious. There had to be another reason for Freda coming up here when she could easily have left a note in the kitchen to say she was making a rare excursion into town. So what was this really about?

"Please print out what you've done so far," Freda said. "I'd like to read it through properly."

Reluctantly, Joely did as she was asked and handed the pages over.

Without any thanks, Freda returned to the door. "You really haven't worked out who the moth is yet, have you?" she asked, seeming almost irritated by this.

Joely frowned and felt unease coming over her again.

"You surprise me," Freda stated. "With your compulsion to try to work everything out before you're told I thought you would have by now."

Joely's tension was building. There was something different about Freda now, something that she couldn't fathom but knew she didn't like.

"The moth," Freda said bitingly, "or young Freda as we've called her in the story, is your mother, Joely," and turning around she started quietly down the stairs.

CHAPTER EIGHTEEN

Joely stared at the empty doorway, immobilized by the shock of Freda's revelation. Common sense was telling her that it couldn't be true, it was crazy even to think it, Freda didn't even know her mother.

Maybe she, Joely, was being gaslighted as a character study for a new novel? Maybe Freda had turned herself into some sort of literary Frankenstein to find out how a subject would react to extreme and untenable suggestions.

Joely took a breath and pressed her hands to her cheeks.

There was no way her mother could be young Freda. It made no sense at all. And as for doing such a despicable thing to a man . . . No, it simply hadn't happened. Her mother was *not that person.*

So what the hell was Freda's game?

What was she expecting her ghostwriter to do now?

Where had she gone?

What was taking her into town?

Joely tried clearing her head to make herself think more rationally. The accusation about her mother was nonsense, she was in no doubt of that, but there had to be a purpose behind it. Freda clearly had something in mind, so now it was Joely's job to figure out what it was . . .

No, actually, all she had to do was get the heck out

of here. This project, this game or whatever it was had gone too far and she really didn't want to be a part of it anymore.

Closing down her laptop, she picked up her notebook and recorder and made her way down to the library. She saw right away that the door to the kitchen staircase was closed, and her heart gave an uneasy twist, for she remembered propping it open with *English Medieval Literature*—which was now cast aside farther along the floor.

She tried the door and felt another stab of fear when it wouldn't open. This surely had to be a mistake. Freda wouldn't have shut her in here on purpose, it would be an insane thing to do, and yet there was no getting away from the fact that the makeshift doorstop wasn't where she'd left it and the latch on the stairway door was firmly shut.

"Freda!" she shouted, directing her voice down to the kitchen. "Freda! Let me out of here."

There was no sound from anywhere else in the house.

She pummeled the door's solid wood panels, battered the latch with a heavy book, but it wouldn't budge.

She looked at her phone, but it was useless.

Her mind spun with disbelief and horror as she tried to think what to do.

Suddenly remembering the hidden door in the bookcase she began pressing random volumes and panels to activate the mechanism, but nothing happened. She tore books from shelves searching for hinges, a concealed handle, some sort of button, but she could find none.

"Freda!" she yelled, banging a fist on the wall. "Let me out of here! This is crazy."

She waited for an answer but beyond her own breath everything remained silent. She stared at the door to the kitchen again, still hardly able to accept that it wouldn't open, then a sound reached her from the next room and she spun around.

"Freda," she called out. "Are you in there? Please let me out. Whatever you . . ."

Suddenly music began to play, an orchestra swelling out of the silence so loudly that it drowned her cries. She couldn't even hear her hands thumping the wall.

"Freda! Stop this, please! I'm begging you."

Realizing from the volume that there must be hidden speakers in this room she ran up to the writing room and closed the door.

She was breathing hard, too hard. She was also shaking as much in fear as in shock. The music was just as loud in here, but she couldn't see any speakers.

She needed to stay calm.

This was obviously some sort of temporary madness on Freda's part. It would be over soon, all she had to do was block her ears, hold on to her sanity, and wait it out.

"Thank you, Bill," Freda said as her gardener-cum-chauffeur opened the car door for her to get out. "I'll only be a moment."

Leaving him waiting at the curb she went into the post office and handed over a small parcel for special delivery, paid what was required and returned to the car.

"Everything all right?" Bill asked as she got into the front passenger seat.

"Indeed it is," she confirmed.

He drove away and five minutes later they came to a stop outside the railway station.

"You don't need to help me any further," she told him, as he came to open the door. "I can manage."

Lifting her small suitcase from the boot he said, "It's platform two that you want. The train's due in about ten minutes, so enough time to get your ticket."

She smiled gratefully, and took her suitcase. "Enjoy your holiday in Spain." She smiled. "Brenda will enjoy the break, I'm sure."

"It's very generous of you . . ."

"Think nothing of it," and patting his arm she started into the station.

Joely kept checking her phone, but as yet she'd been unable to achieve even a single bar of connection in spite of standing on chairs, leaning out of the window, even climbing out onto the balcony.

The music had stopped for a while, long enough for her to shout herself hoarse, but the only response had been the hurling sough of the wind outside and the cries of impervious birds. She'd searched the desk for something to help force the latch on the library door but had found no scissors, no paperknife, not even a ruler. She'd used the books again, banging them into the stubborn metal, but not even the bigger volumes had made a difference and nor had trying to ram the door with a chair.

When the music had suddenly started up again it had seemed louder, more oppressive than ever.

Offenbach, "Hey Jude," "Jumpin' Jack Flash," "The

Gaelic Blessing," Mozart's *Night Music*, "Je ne regrette rien," Chopin, Schubert, "Then He Kissed Me," "Young Girl," Puccini, and the same Puccini again. She'd never considered any of it menacing before, and realized that it was the volume making it so now, but worse than that, far worse, was the fact that Freda was doing this. What did it mean? What was she hoping to gain?

After the fourth time of playing she realized it was on a loop so it was going to play, over and over, until someone turned it off—or until she hurled herself out of the window to escape it. She wouldn't do that, obviously, the only place to land was the rocks at the base of the tower and she'd never survive that kind of fall. If the wisteria was strong enough she might be able to climb down, but she wasn't going to try it now. It was already getting dark, and the wind was so strong it would tear her from the creeper and make her fall as disastrous as if she'd jumped.

Where was Brenda? Why hadn't she come?

Joely had barely taken her eyes off the drive these past few hours desperate to see someone, anyone, but no one had come, or gone, although she was convinced by now that Freda was no longer in the house.

So what the heck was she going to do?

She looked at her computer, thought of her mother and Freda's crazy accusation, but before she could try to attach any sense to it the music suddenly started up again.

She couldn't stand any more of it. She needed to think, to work out if Freda knew where her mother lived, if she could be going there to try and settle some imagined vendetta. What the heck was in Freda's mind?

Without her phone she couldn't warn her mother, but she needed to do something, contact someone, Callum, Edward, Andee . . . There just wasn't a way . . .

Andee looked up as Graeme came into the bedroom and sat down on his side of the bed.

"Who are you calling?" he asked, kicking off his shoes and loosening his watch.

"I'm trying Joely on the off chance I might get her," she replied, mobile pressed to one ear, iPad open in front of her. "Hi," she said to the voicemail, "sorry it's taken me a while to get back to you, we've got a few issues going on here, I'll tell you when I see you. I'm around all day tomorrow so try me when you can."

As she rang off Graeme came to take both phone and iPad from her hands and set them on the nightstand. "I know how worried you are about your mother," he said.

"Alayna too," she reminded him, referring to her daughter.

"Alayna too, but you'll be able to help them all much better, Joely too, if you get some sleep."

Andee smiled as she picked up on the tone of his voice. "And you have just the way to make that happen?" she asked, knowing that he did.

"I do," he confirmed, and turning her over he placed his soothing hands on her back to start the process with a massage.

It was morning.

Joely could hear the birds singing and the distant sibilance of waves. There was nothing else, no music, no voices, only the sound of her breathing and the silence.

She opened her eyes, carefully, nervously.

It was barely light, but she wanted to weep with dismay when she realized she was still in the writing room, curled up on the daybed. It hadn't been a nightmare, it was actually happening.

She picked up her phone, and saw straightaway that the battery was dead.

Doing her best not to panic, she swung her feet to the floor and went to open her laptop. It was six-forty-five, so yes, she'd been here all night. Funny how her brain was finding it so hard to accept it. She was wearing the same clothes she'd had on the day before, her mouth was stale, and her hair was tangled around her face.

She pushed it back, rubbed her eyes, and made her way to the WC, not only to satisfy the need to pee, but to put her mouth under the tap for some water.

She was hungry, so hungry that she had to force her mind away from food at least until Brenda arrived. That should be in about an hour.

Everything would be fine once Brenda got here.

After refreshing herself the best she could she ran down to the library to check the door again. It still wouldn't open and as her frustration threatened to boil over into angry shouts and hot, bitter tears she looked around at the mess she'd created the night before, books all over the place, scattered and damaged like innocent victims of a storm.

What if Brenda didn't come?

There was no obvious way out, she knew that, unless

she wanted to risk her life on the wisteria, and right now she really didn't.

The moth, or young Freda as we called her in the story, is your mother.

The words had gone around and around in her head through the night as the music had repeated over and over, making it almost impossible to think straight.

Right now it was quiet, though probably not for much longer, so running back to the writing room she took a sheet of paper from the printer and wrote *Freda* in the top left corner. In the opposite corner she wrote *David Michaels.*

She tried to remember what other names Freda had mentioned, but could think of none. It was always "my parents," "my father," "his uncle," "his mother." Were there more twists and lies that Freda hadn't yet revealed? She flipped open her laptop to check and as she went through the memoir she discovered that apart from random school friends or teachers, she was right, there were no other names.

Just the girlfriend that hadn't been mentioned until the end.

Linda.

Joely turned cold to her core.

Linda was her mother's name. Linda Marianne.

In one enormous leap her mind reached a conclusion that sent her reeling. Was Sir her father?

She pushed herself away from the desk, needing to escape this insane scenario. Sir couldn't be her father, any more than her mother could be young Freda, or Linda the girlfriend . . . Her parents had nothing to do with this . . .

Oh God, no! No! No! The music was starting up again pummeling the tower, crashing through the silence and tossing her thoughts into chaos.

"Sir can't be my father," she cried into the clamor, "he can't," but with the violins shrieking like demons and heavy drums thundering through her ears she was unable to seize on why it couldn't be true.

CHAPTER NINETEEN

Marianne had just called the office to let them know she wouldn't be in today. She wasn't unwell, nor was she someone who normally shirked work. If anything she embraced it, but not today.

The shock of what was happening, of what had been handed to her by the postman first thing this morning, caused her heart to twist with another sickening wrench of fear.

Going through to the kitchen of her Kensington town house, she picked up the phone to try calling Joely again.

Still no answer.

Ludicrously she made another attempt from her mobile, as if it might have a better chance of connecting than a landline.

Still no answer.

She was becoming more concerned and agitated by the hour. She hated not being able to get hold of her daughter at the best of times, at a time like this . . .

Maybe she should call Callum. She knew he'd come if she asked him to, but he was at work, possibly in a meeting, or even in the studio recording a program. It wouldn't be fair to disturb him when she wasn't entirely sure what she'd say to him. "I can't get hold of Joely" would hardly seem like an emergency when they'd both had such trouble these past two weeks.

She couldn't say any more than that, at least not until she'd spoken to her daughter to get a clearer idea of what was going on.

Her confused blue eyes returned to the screensaver on her mobile—Joely, Callum, and Holly in happier times. Now, Joely had run away to carry out an assignment heaven only knew where and for an author who was as well known for being a recluse as she was for her peculiar books. Marianne hadn't even known F.M. Donahoe was a woman until Joely had told her, and she might not have been particularly interested then had the postman not turned up this morning with a special delivery from F.M. Donahoe.

It was right there on the kitchen table, a large, neat brown envelope with her name and address handwritten on the front, seal broken, closely typed pages tucked back inside, out of sight.

Her mouth was dry as she looked at it. It had come out of the past like a karmic punch to the heart and all these hours later she still wasn't breathing steadily.

She guessed Donahoe was Freda's married name, unless it was a pen name—that was also possible.

Marianne had no idea what to do. There had been no note in the envelope, nothing to tell her what Freda wanted, or what she intended to do with these pages. And where was Joely?

Hearing the doorbell chime down the hall she pressed a hand to her heart to steady it. She wasn't expecting anyone, but it could be Holly having lost her key *again*. Or the postman—please, God, not with another special delivery.

She walked along the hall aware of how dread was

242

slowing her pace; the sudden and brutal thrust into the past was affecting her badly. For whole moments at a time it seemed to distort reality and make her uncertain of herself in a way she hadn't felt in so long.

It had taken years to get over what had happened, and now it was as though she was being sucked back into the very worst of it.

Though she checked the spyhole the person on the porch had stepped aside so all she could see was the shoulder of someone wearing a gray coat. She knew she ought to call out to ask who it was, but she didn't want to appear timid or pathetic. So she opened the door wide and stood tall, almost confrontational before the woman whose back was to her.

"Can I help you?" she asked tonelessly.

The woman turned around and as fear bloomed in Marianne's heart she felt her senses swim.

"Hello," Freda said smoothly. "We've never met, but I think you know who I am."

"What do you want?" Marianne's voice was clipped, too defensive, she needed to calm herself, handle this in a way that wouldn't antagonize the woman, that made it clear she wasn't afraid of her.

"Aren't you going to invite me in?" Freda responded.

Battling with her conflicting instincts, Marianne stood aside and gestured for her to go into the sitting room. There was no point trying to avoid this, not while she couldn't get hold of Joely.

The sitting room was large with a high corniced ceiling, two tall sash windows at the front, a white marble fireplace over the hearth displaying an assortment of family photos, and three neatly arranged lemon-striped sofas around a glass coffee table.

"Is this where your children grew up?" Freda asked, taking it all in and pulling a face that showed as much disdain as interest.

"Where's Joely?" Marianne asked.

Freda sat down on one of the sofas and crossed her legs. "You'll have read the memoir she's been working on by now," she said, folding her hands in her lap. "I think . . ."

"Where is she?" Marianne repeated.

With a small sigh, Freda said, "We have some things to discuss, you and I . . ."

"I am discussing nothing until you tell me where my daughter is."

Freda waved a hand as though batting the words away. "She's perfectly all right, and you'll get her back as soon as you've done as I ask."

Get her back? Marianne's heart began to thud. Freda was holding Joely hostage? "Tell me where Joely is," she growled, "or I'm calling the police."

Freda laughed. "To tell them what, exactly?"

Marianne opened her mouth, but no words came out.

Freda's eyes became opaque, glassy, unreadable, as she said, "You must have known the day of reckoning would come, Linda."

Marianne still couldn't speak. Inside she was shaking, as much in anger as in fear. What did this woman want? Why couldn't she have left the past where it was? What did she hope to gain from raking it all up again?

"Yes, tea would be very nice, thank you." Freda

smiled. "Milk, no sugar," and, as if Marianne really had made the offer, she settled back more comfortably in her seat, waiting to be served.

The music had stopped.

Joely's eyes opened slowly. The powerful voice of a gifted soprano who she suspected might be Sir's mother was still echoing in her ears. It was fading now, the applause of an ecstatic audience drifting like mist into nothingness and leaving her to confront the awful suspicion of why Freda had ended her torturous loop with this particular aria. Joely was familiar enough with Puccini's works to recognize "Vissi d'arte" and to know that at the climax of the opera Floria Tosca threw herself from a tower to her death.

Wishing that thought had never occurred to her she picked herself up from the daybed and made her way to the desk. Outside storm clouds were gathering like ghouls over the channel, blackening the sky and casting the cliffs in oppressive shadow.

She was so hungry that the pangs were making it almost as difficult to focus as the music when it was blaring, but she forced herself past it and opened up her laptop.

After taking a few more moments to collect herself she began again.

According to the memoir, Sir was twenty-five in 1968, which meant he'd been born in . . . 1943. If he was still alive today he'd be . . . seventy-seven.

Her father had been born in 1947 in Australia, and had lived there until 1967 when he'd come to England to attend medical school. His family had immigrated in the mid-1970s, which was when he'd met his future wife, Marianne. In 1968 he would have been . . . twenty-one. He'd died three years ago at age sixty-nine.

He had never been a music fanatic, or even much of a concertgoer.

The dates and ages were all wrong, plus he'd never worked as a teacher, much less in a girls' school, or made a habit of telling lies—as far as she knew.

She took a breath, let her head fall back to clear it of rogue doubts, and started again.

Sir was definitely not her father.

Her father was not Sir.

Her mother, on the other hand, had been fifteen in 1968. Her name wasn't Freda, but obviously Freda had used her own name to make the story seem like a personal memoir until she'd decided to reveal the fact that it wasn't.

So what was it, exactly?

Putting a label on it hardly mattered; what did was the reason for doing it at all, and what she was planning to do now—apart from imprison her ghostwriter in a tower, play music to her at full volume as if to blast out her brains, presuming she didn't starve to death first, or do a Tosca out of the window . . .

Realizing hunger, fear, stress were combining to make her delirious, she took some more deep breaths, and went to drink from the tap before returning to the desk.

How long was Freda planning to keep her here?

Where was she? What was this really all about?

Rain and fierce gusts of wind were battering the windows now and the temperature in the room had noticeably dropped.

Joely returned to her computer and began working on the theory that her mother was "young Freda" to see if it flew.

Her mother, aged fifteen . . . From the photos Joely had seen of Marianne in her teenage years she'd certainly been beautiful, she still turned heads now, but a young Bardot?

Had she gone to boarding school?

Yes, she had, and it had been a weekly one as far as Joely could recall, but the way her parents, Joely's grandparents, had been portrayed . . . The self-centered, hedonistic, neglectful, narcissists . . . That certainly didn't chime with the people Joely had known, but they'd been so much older by the time Joely had come along . . .

How had Freda known them?

There wouldn't have been a trial if Sir had pleaded guilty, so nothing could have come out about them then . . .

She'd have to come back to that; she was trying to deal with her mother for now, the statuesque, elegant sixty-six-year-old transformed into an immature, over-confident, and self-absorbed teenager who'd fallen victim to her fixation on a handsome young teacher. It happened, back then and now, but even if she'd been some sort of Lolita once, it still didn't explain why Freda was writing about her now.

Nor did it provide an identity for Sir.

What was she missing?

It had to be there, she was sure of it.

Scrolling back to the start of the memoir she began reading it again, making sure she was taking in every

247

last detail, checking her notes, analyzing Freda's tone and nuances in the recordings, but she got no further than the first few pages before the music started up again, snatching at her thoughts, and making concentration impossible.

Tears filled her eyes and her heart almost burst with frustration as she returned to the daybed and put a pillow over her head to help block out the deafening concert.

"Did you read to the end of what I sent you?" Freda asked, sounding only mildly curious as she replaced her teacup on its saucer and put both on the coffee table.

Marianne simply stared at her. She had no intention of answering anything until she knew what this woman was up to with Joely.

"I'm sure you did," Freda continued, "but even if you didn't you already know everything that happened, what you said and did, the lives you destroyed . . ."

Biting out the words, Marianne said, "What you've written . . ."

"What your daughter wrote," Freda interjected. "They're her words, not mine, at least most of them. Obviously, I gave her some guidance. I can't help wondering how she feels now she knows that she's the author of her own mother's sexual exploits with a much older man."

Hating the very idea of Joely even knowing about it, never mind being tricked into writing about what had happened back then, Marianne rose to her feet. "It's time you left," she said with so much steel in her voice it caused Freda's eyebrows to arch.

"It's uncomfortable, isn't it," Freda said, "thinking

of your own flesh and blood engaging in a sexual act with you, even if only in a literary sense. However, I believe incest isn't a stranger to your family. Didn't your mother mistakenly sleep with her own brother at one of the famous orgies?"

Marianne's eyes flashed with rage. "That was an ugly, vindictive lie spread by a girl who was jealous of my mother," she cried furiously. "It wasn't true, but it was vile enough to make it impossible for my mother and her brother to see each other again."

"Really?" Freda said disbelievingly.

"I don't care what you think," Marianne spat dismissively. "I don't even care how you know . . ."

"Sit down," Freda told her. "What your mother did or didn't do with her brother is of no interest to me. I'm only interested in what *you* did to mine."

Marianne glared at her as the past crackled like sparks in the air between them. David Martin—or Michaels as he was called in the pages she'd read—the man who still haunted her dreams to this day, was this woman's brother. Marianne had never imagined that she and Freda would meet, not back then, or now, but here she was sitting on the sofa and clearly proud of the way she'd tricked Joely into telling the terrible story of her mother's teenage mistakes.

"You know what you did to him," Freda said, her tone seeming oddly distant and yet horribly present. "He was a good man, a decent man with his whole life ahead of him."

"He was . . ."

"He wanted to teach. It was his dream and he had so much to offer . . ."

"Why are you doing this, Freda?" Marianne cried. "*Why* are you here?"

Freda regarded her with incredulity and scorn. "You know the answer to that," she retorted. "I want the truth, Linda Barnes—or I believe they call you Marianne now. I want your name in that memoir, not hidden behind a law that protects minors . . . You're going to finish the story with a full and unambiguous admission of who you are and what you did to my brother."

Marianne didn't hesitate. "I'm not doing anything until you tell me where Joely is. I need to know she's . . ."

"I don't care what you need to know . . ."

Marianne turned on her heel, walked to the kitchen, and snatched up her mobile.

Moments later she was upstairs closing the bedroom door behind her, and going swiftly to the bathroom she locked herself in. Her hands were shaking so badly it took longer than it should have to connect to Callum. *You've got to answer; you've just got to.*

"Hey, Marianne," he said cheerily.

"Callum, do you have Andee Lawrence's number?"

"I'm sure I do, but is everything all right? You sound . . ."

"I'll explain later. Text it to me, please. Do it right away."

It came through in seconds and moments later another voice was at the end of the line: "Hi, this is Andee."

"Andee, it's Marianne, Joely's mum. I'm sorry to be abrupt, but do you know where she is?"

"I've been trying to get hold of her, but I'm guessing she's at Dimmett House."

"If you know where that is, please can you go to check if she's all right?"

Immediately concerned, Andee said, "Yes, of course. Why has something . . ."

"I just need to know that she's OK. Call me back when you . . . How long will it take you to get there?"

"About forty-five minutes. I'll leave now if it's urgent."

"Please—I'd be very grateful if you could. Thank you. I'll wait to hear from you."

After ringing off, Marianne tried Joely's number again. Once more she went straight to voicemail. She turned to stare at herself in the mirror. Her face was flushed and stricken, her eyes glittery and wide with fear. *It's all right,* she tried telling herself. *Andee will be sure to find her, then you'll be able to deal with the rest.*

Taking a breath, she unlocked the bathroom door, and pulled it open.

Freda was standing right outside.

CHAPTER TWENTY

As Andee started out to her car she connected to her own mother, Maureen, to let her know that something had come up but she'd be with her as soon as she could. Though Maureen assured her it wasn't a problem, Andee knew how worried she was about the biopsy results she was expecting tomorrow. She ought to be with her, and she would be, provided Joely turned out to be at the house and nothing untoward had happened.

The drive to Lynton took only forty minutes, most of which passed Andee by in a blur as she worried about her mother, and her daughter, who was having a difficult time at work, and her sister, who was always a concern. She tried Joely's mobile several times, but knowing there was little or no reception at Dimmett House she wasn't surprised when she was repeatedly bumped through to voicemail.

When at last she turned into the drive she saw right away that all the shutters were closed, apart from in the tower, and there were no cars to be seen. She pulled up outside the front door and went to press the bell, hearing a distant ring somewhere far deeper inside.

When there was no sound of anything happening, she pressed the bell again and walked along the front of the house, whose windows looked like blind eyes, to a covered patio at the base of the tower. There were no shutters here, but the French doors were firmly shut, and not wanting to set off an alarm by trying to force them, she rapped hard with her knuckles while calling out Joely's name.

"Hello! Is anyone at home?" she shouted, knocking again. Cupping her hands around her eyes she peered through to what was clearly a kitchen. No sign of anyone, so she took a few steps back and assessed the upper levels of the tower.

No sign of anyone there either, and everything was silent.

She looked around at the benign and beautiful surroundings, and spotting a trail running through the long grass of the meadow she decided, in the interests of being thorough, to follow it.

It took only a couple of minutes to reach an incline that sloped in rugged tiers down to a small sandy beach. There were only the tide's latest offerings to see on the sand that nestled between the huge, imposing cliffs rising up on either side of the cove.

Turning back to the house, Andee checked her phone, and seeing she had no signal she decided to cut diagonally across the meadow back to her car.

Before leaving she pressed the doorbell again, several times, but she was clearly wasting her time. There was no one at home.

Joely was coming awake, stiff and cold, head throbbing, threads of music still seeming trapped in her ears. They'd begun to echo on long after the concert had ceased, weaving through her mind and her dreams, as present and persistent as the reality of silence.

She sat up, pressed her hands to her face and tried to make herself think. Before the last musical onslaught she'd remembered the photograph she'd found in the table drawer the day she'd arrived at Dimmett House. A small girl with two boys on either side of her. She'd come to the conclusion that it must be the real young Freda with her brothers. Christopher and David.

Freda was Sir's sister.

The music was playing again, but differently, distantly, like a bell until suddenly realizing what it was she leapt up from the bed and ran to the window.

There was a car on the drive, heading away from the house.

"No," she cried frantically, and heaving up the heavy frame she scrambled out onto the balcony. "Don't go," she screamed into the wind. "I'm up here."

The car was already turning out of the drive onto the road.

Realizing who it was, Joely yelled, "Andee! I'm here. Please don't go."

Moments later there was no car, no one to hear her, or to see her as she stood helplessly and desperately at the top of the tower buffeted by icy squalls of rain and watched by a solitary deer at the heart of the meadow.

"What are you doing?" Marianne cried, experiencing a bolt of terror when she found Freda blocking her way from the bathroom.

"You didn't flush," Freda told her.

Marianne stared at her, hardly knowing what to say. For one wild moment she considered trying to shove her into the bathroom and locking her in, but the bolt was on the other side—and besides it wasn't going to help her find out what was happening to Joely.

Pushing past the woman, she stalked across the room and out along the landing, moving fast so Freda couldn't get too close behind and push her down the stairs.

Why would she do that?

Why would she do anything?

When they got to the sitting room Freda went to stand at the window, gazing out at the street, and Marianne watched her not knowing what the heck to do.

Several minutes ticked by until finally Freda turned around and said, "Do you have a computer?"

Marianne didn't reply.

"I'm sure you do," Freda decided. "If you get it we can continue with the memoir, or maybe we should call it a confession from now on." Seeming to like the idea she said, "You can write down everything that happened to you after my brother's arrest, telling us why you lied, and continued to lie and perhaps we can detail your parents' shameless hypocrisy in the way they condemned your affair with my brother when your mother as good as approved it."

"That's not true," Marianne snapped before she could stop herself. "The way you've portrayed my parents . . . You knew nothing about them. They weren't those people . . ."

Freda waved a hand, cutting her off. "They were well known for their lifestyle, even my parents were invited to some of their parties. They never went. Orgies weren't their scene. But your parents and their low morals aren't really the issue. It's what you did that we need to get straight. Tell me, how much of the affair have I got right?"

Strengthening herself with thoughts of Joely, Marianne said, "Why don't you tell me where my daughter is first, then I'll answer your questions."

Freda shook her head. "I want a full and frank confession out of you before I do that. For now, all you have to do is sit at your computer and—"

"It's not going to happen, Freda. I'm not doing anything until I know Joely is safe."

Freda's eyes flashed. "Then we are at an impasse. I want the truth, you want your daughter, who's going to give in first?"

Realizing she had to play for time at least until Andee rang with some news, Marianne's hand tightened on the phone in her pocket as she said, "The girlfriend who returned from India. Her name was Dinah."

Freda's eyes narrowed with a humor that seemed sly and triumphant. "So it was," she agreed, and Marianne realized she'd always known it. She must have changed it to confuse Joely.

"Dinah," Freda repeated and her expression turned mournful. "Did you ever know, or even care about how your lies affected her? No, I don't suppose you did. I'd be surprised if you spared her as much as a single thought. She wanted to stand by him, you know?"

Marianne swallowed drily. It was true, she'd never thought, or cared, about Dinah.

Freda said, "I've lost touch with her now, but she

came to—" She broke off as Marianne drew her phone from her pocket.

It was a text from Callum. *Did you get hold of Andee?*

Tucking the phone away again, Marianne fixed Freda with a contemptuous stare.

Apparently unfazed, Freda shrugged. "I don't have anything to fear," she said, "so if you're calling for help, or waiting for someone else to arrive, that's fine. I won't be going anywhere until I have what I came for."

Still stalling for time, Marianne said, "Why now? After all these years, why are you doing this now?"

Freda smiled. "There are two answers to that," she replied. "The first is the simplest: I do not intend to die without clearing my brother's name." She glanced down at her fingers as she stretched them out. "I could say," she continued, "that I'm sorry for what it might do to you, being branded a liar and having to face the truth, but I would be lying."

Marianne sat very still, already sensing what was coming next.

"The second answer," Freda said, "is that I think it's time I met my nephew, don't you?"

Joely's head was throbbing, and her heart kept racing as though trying to catch up with itself. The adrenaline rush of seeing Andee had subsided now, leaving her feeling more vulnerable and desperate than ever. Why hadn't the music been blaring while her friend was here? She'd have known right away that something was wrong. But it hadn't and Joely wanted to sob and rage at the sheer bad timing of it.

Aware that her physical strength was starting to wane, she told herself she must begin assessing exactly how she was going to clamber over the balcony and lower herself down onto the winter-bare wisteria. How thick were the branches, and were any of them strong enough to bear her weight? How could she find out without testing them, and when she did would it already be too late?

Staring down at the ground from the balcony, her stomach twisted—with both hunger and dread. She remembered reading once that hunger could change the pathways to the brain, making it hard to reach decisions. Did her fears for her mother even make sense? She was becoming increasingly convinced Freda had gone to see her mother, but what was she hoping to achieve? Was it revenge she was after? What else could it be? What had happened to Sir? Where, who was he now?

Unable to answer these questions, she became sure of one thing—she couldn't bear to stay in this tower much longer. Should she write a letter to Holly, her mother, and Callum, in case the worst happened? The music would start again any minute, and there was a lot she wanted to say to them. She had to make sure they knew how much she loved them. And there was something she'd never told Callum, something that made her feel so sick inside that she wasn't even sure she could tell him now.

Did he need to know?

No, was the answer. She would take it with her if she fell, and if she didn't . . . Maybe she'd tell him herself the next time she saw him.

She'd barely got started on a letter to Holly before the

music boomed back to life. She did her best to keep going through bass beats and unstoppable voices, but it simply wasn't possible, so pushing away from her computer she went into the tiny bathroom and closed the door.

Andee was in the car park just past St. Mary Magdelene Church in Lynton. She'd paused to send a text to Marianne—*She's not at the house. Let me know if any more I can do. Ax*—and after making sure it had gone she put the car into gear to start the drive back across the moor.

Nevertheless, she was aware of something niggling away at the back of her mind about Joely, she just couldn't quite grasp what it was.

As Marianne put her phone away, Freda said, "Does Joely know that she and her brother have different fathers?"

Marianne looked up, her expression revealing nothing of what she was feeling inside, but both the text and the question were upsetting her badly. Even harder to deal with was just how crazy, even dangerous, this woman might be.

"Perhaps what I should be asking," Freda continued, "is what my nephew knows . . ."

Marianne snapped, "Tell me where Joely is."

Freda spread her hands in a helpless sort of way. "Write the truthful version of what happened when my brother ended your affair and you'll have your answer."

Marianne hesitated, but only for a second. "Your brother was a—"

"—rapist, yes in the statutory sense he was, but you

259

didn't let it end there, did you? He'd have gone to prison anyway, but *you* made up a story—"

Marianne shot to her feet.

"Where are you going?" Freda asked as Marianne walked out of the room.

Moments later Marianne was back with her laptop. Opening it, she clicked to a fresh screen and said, "You want the truth, you'll have it."

Joely was staring at her undies drip-drying over a luke-warm radiator. Dealing with the discomfort of being in the same clothes for so long had provided a bizarre distraction from the last assault of music, but at least it had reminded her that the normal, rational part of her mind was still functioning.

She'd washed herself and her underwear while trying to sing along with "Young Girl" and hoping she never heard it again in her life. Worse, always worse, was the passionate, heart-wrenching soprano that had turned to screams in her ears.

Everything about her situation was driving her closer to the brink.

She had decided that the best way down would be to climb the wisteria around the tower until she was over the tiled roof of the kitchen patio. It would still be a long way down, but at least if she fell there it wouldn't be onto rocks.

She'd wait until the next assault of music was over, dress, and pray to God that the wind didn't pick up. And that the wisteria would hold her weight.

*

As Marianne's fingers flew over the computer keyboard she was trying not to engage with the words. She couldn't, wouldn't, think about how deeply the memories were affecting her; the private lessons, the uncle's cottage, and those wonderful, unforgettable days in Paris. She could see his eyes more clearly than the page in front of her. She'd loved him so much . . .

She imagined him telling Freda about their affair—it was the only way she could have known so many details—and was able to hear his voice, soft and melodic, wry and endlessly sad that everything had ended the way it had. Her son reminded her of him in so many ways that at times it had been almost painful to look at him. She'd learned to live with it, and Lionel, her husband, had shown far more patience and understanding than she'd deserved. He'd been such a wonderful father to Jamie, the only one Jamie had known, or wanted to know. As a child he'd never asked about the man who'd come before his daddy, although in later years he'd been interested to know that he was the son of a gifted musician. Jamie loved music too, but he wasn't as passionate about it as David had been.

Joely knew Jamie was a half brother, of course she did, but she'd shown no more interest in it than Jamie had. As far as she was concerned they were a family, and her father was Jamie's every bit as much as he was hers.

Marianne wrote none of this in the "confession' Freda was demanding. She kept her regrets, longings, guilt, and pain closely locked inside, although aware of it tightening and tormenting her heart as each new memory unfolded. He was there at the center of it all and feeling so real that he could almost have been guiding her fingers over the computer keys, as he once had over the piano. She felt fifteen again and wanted to rest her head against him, inhale the familiar scent of him, and feel the warmth of his skin in the places that it touched hers. If only she'd been able to talk to him; if her parents, his family, and the lawyers hadn't kept them apart at the time of his arrest and sentencing . . . She'd had no idea back then that during those terrible months following the breakup, she'd been suffering as much from a form of post-traumatic stress disorder as she had heartbreak. None of them had even heard of PTSD, but the sheer wretchedness she'd felt, the shame and guilt of the affair, the lie she'd told mixed in with all the passion and longing had made her feel at times as though she was dying. As though in some terrible, undefinable way he was killing her.

Eventually her hands left the keyboard. She had no more to say, it was all there for Freda to read, exactly how it had happened, and struggling to hold herself together she passed the laptop over.

CHAPTER TWENTY-ONE

We're at his uncle's house and I want to leave. As soon as he tells me about Dinah I'm desperate to go home to my parents. I feel betrayed and angry and filled with hate toward him and toward her, even though I've never met her. He's lied to me all along, tricked me into believing things that were never going to come true. It was all pretense and now everything's spoiled.

"Don't go like this," he begs me, catching hold of my hand.

I try to break free, but I can't. I'm sobbing so hard I can hardly breathe. He pulls me in even closer, pinning my arms to my sides and me to him. I can smell him and it's the worst and most wonderful smell in the world.

"Let me go," I cry, struggling to break free. "I hate you. Let me go."

"*Cherie*, please calm down," he whispers in my hair. "I'm sorry. I shouldn't have told you like that . . ."

I wrench myself away, but he catches me again.

"If you were older," he says, holding my face in his hands, "it would be different, I swear, but I can't let you leave school . . ."

"I can do what I like," I rage, "and I want to come with you. Please, please say I can."

"It's not possible. I wish it were . . ."

"Why do you have to go with *her*? Why didn't you tell me about her before?"

"She has nothing to do with us. What we have is special, so special I can hardly bear to let you go, but I have to. It's why I can't come back next term. We have to stop seeing . . ."

"No we don't. I'm not going to let you just throw me away. I'll make sure you can't. I'll tell everyone what we've been doing . . ."

"Sssh. You know you don't mean that."

"Yes I do. I'm going to tell . . ."

He presses his mouth to mine so I can't shout anymore, and his hands are so strong on my arms that I can't break free. He pulls me down to the floor and lies on top of me. I'm sobbing and telling him no, but he says he wants to show me one last time how much he loves me. I still say no, but he's not listening. He's kissing me, holding me, telling me he doesn't want to be without me . . .

Then suddenly he stops and as he starts to get up he says he's sorry, he lost his mind. I can see he's distraught, shocked, but so am I. I pull him back. I don't want him to go. I'll do anything to keep him. He's mine, we belong to each other.

When it's over he holds me close and wipes away my tears. "Are you all right?" he asks gently. "Maybe that shouldn't have happened."

"Don't say that," I whisper and he kisses me again. I like being in his arms, but I'm not sure about what just happened. It felt different and I'm afraid it's because it really was the last time.

"I'll drive you home," he says and pulls me to my feet. I want to take a train, but I don't know where the

station is and he's already putting my things in the car.
I can't bear to look at him; it's upsetting me too much.
He's going to take me to my parents and leave me. I'll
never see him again after that and it makes me wish I
was dead.

As he drives us he says, "I'm sorry about just now.
It shouldn't . . . I don't know what to say . . . Please tell
me I didn't hurt you."

"You didn't," I assure him, though he did, but not in
the way he's meaning. I start to ask him, beg him, to
change his mind, to say that he will come back to school,
that his girlfriend means nothing to him, but he only
shakes his head.

"I'm sorry," he says, over and over. "One day you'll
understand. You'll thank me for letting you go."

"I never will," I cry in anger, but he keeps telling me
I will.

When we arrive at the end of my street he stops the
car and takes my hand. "I'll send a postcard from
Georgia," he says. "Would you like that?"

He'll be there with his girlfriend so no, I wouldn't like
it, but I don't say anything.

He turns my face to his and I can see how upset he
is. He says, "You're not going to tell anyone about us,
are you? You know what'll happen to me if you do."

I wonder why I should care what happens to him
when he doesn't care what happens to me.

I get out of the car and take my bag from the boot.
He's still sitting in the driver's seat so I leave him there
and walk around the corner to my home. I hear him
drive away and I want to run after him screaming for
him to come back.

Mummy knows as soon as she sees me that something is wrong. She takes me upstairs to my room and because I'm so unhappy and can't bear to think of returning to school if he's not there I end up telling her everything. She's shocked, but understanding, and she soothes me the best she can.

I don't realize she's angry until later when I hear her talking to Daddy and then Daddy is shouting and the next thing I know there are two policemen in our drawing room.

Mummy holds my hand as she tells them everything I told her. They write it down and look at me from time to time seeming sad but also suspicious. I think they might not believe me, but they don't say that. They ask if he forced me and I answer no.

"You told me he did, sweetheart," Mummy reminds me. "Is that not true?"

I nod, because it is true, at least he started to. I want to explain that he stopped when I told him to, but I can't go into that sort of detail in front of Daddy and the police.

"The point is, Linda," Daddy says sharply, "he took advantage of you in every way, starting with your private lessons, right through to what happened today. He can't be allowed to get away with it. I'll make sure he doesn't."

After the police leave I ask Mummy what will happen next and she says they're going to talk to Mr. Martin—she's still calling him that even though I call him David—and then they'll be in touch with us again.

It's about a week later that Mummy tells me he's been arrested and remanded in custody. Daddy says it's a damned good job he didn't get bail, we don't want him trying to come near me again.

"He's going to prison for a long time," Daddy growls, "a very long time," and he leaves the room.

I don't go back to school at the beginning of the term. I can't face it and Mummy says it doesn't matter because they're making arrangements for me to go somewhere else.

I start receiving letters from girls who used to be my friends, but they hate me now for "telling lies" about Sir. They're glad I'm not going back because they never want to see me again.

I want to see David, but I'm afraid to ask. I know Mummy will say it's a bad idea and Daddy will simply forbid it.

Then we hear that David is going to plead guilty so that I don't have to face the ordeal of going to court.

I cry and cry and cry. I want to tell him I'm sorry, that I wish I could take everything back so he can go to Georgia with Dinah. It would be better than thinking of him locked up in a prison cell for a crime I don't even feel sure he committed.

"You were underage," Mummy reminds me. "That makes it a crime even if he hadn't forced you."

If only I'd never told anyone.

"At least," Mummy adds, "he's done the decent thing by pleading guilty, so it seems there's some honor in him after all."

Daddy says, "He pled guilty to try and get a shorter sentence, nothing to do with honor."

We find out through the lawyer that he receives ten years and will begin to serve the time at Wandsworth

Prison. He might be moved later, but Daddy says we don't need to worry ourselves about that.

I go to my new school—it's close to home so I'm not boarding anymore—and everyone calls me Marianne now. Every afternoon when I come home I write him a letter. I want him to know how sorry I am, how much I still love him, and that no matter what anyone says I am going to wait for him. I send him poems, some that I've written myself, others that I choose specially because I think he'll like them. I copy out the lyrics to some of Bob Dylan's songs and know that reading them will help him to hear the music.

When we find out I'm pregnant I want to write to tell him that too, but Mummy persuades me not to. She says it'll only make things worse for him.

Freda looked up from the laptop her eyes dark with anger. "This isn't what happened," she snarled, her cheeks turning puce. "I came here for the truth, and this is what you give me?"

Marianne simply looked at her.

"You've spun a tale that's as false as your heart."

Knowing Freda would only ever believe what she wanted to, that she'd already set the story in black and white for herself with no shades of gray, Marianne swallowed the tears in her throat and said, "What you have there is exactly what happened. Tell me where Joely is and I'll change it to whatever you want it to be."

CHAPTER TWENTY-TWO

She had to go now.

Waiting for someone to come and let her out could no longer be an option. For all she knew, Freda had no intention of coming back, and it didn't seem as though Brenda and her husband were going to show up either.

One more day of sitting here, worrying about her mother and where Freda might be, or what she could be doing, would drive her mad.

She had no coat, only a thick sweater to protect her from the cold, but at least the wind had dropped and no music was playing. Her core and limbs were strong, thanks to regular yoga classes, and her jeans were two percent elastane, which would help her to move. She'd throw her trainers and socks down first so she'd have something for her feet in the hope she made it in one piece to join them; for the descent she'd decided, based on no knowledge at all, that it would be best to go barefoot. The cold would be horrible, crippling even, and might make her more likely to fall, but she had to risk it.

Her phone was already tucked into a back pocket, but she'd have to leave her laptop behind. Just in case she didn't make it she'd finished the letters to Holly, her mother, and Callum.

Tense with fear, she kicked off her trainers and socks, took several deep breaths, and pulled up the window to climb over the sill onto the balcony. The air was so icy she almost drew straight back inside, but she kept her eyes fixed on the rail, counted to five, and after tossing her trainers and socks she grabbed the rail with both hands and hooked one leg over. She sat astride for a moment, catching her balance and struggling with the wisdom of going on. This was crazy, beyond insane; she was never going to make it.

She didn't dare to look out or down, mustn't allow herself a perspective on how small and vulnerable she was in this wild and wintry landscape, or how exposed and endangered she was going to be clinging to random branches on the outside of the tower.

She must stay focused on what was in front of her, try to remain oblivious to everything else.

Yoga breaths.

Tightening her grip, she swung her other leg over the rail, slotted her heels between the bars, pulled back her shoulders and stood facing the swollen might of the tor. Her hands were clinging so tightly to the bar at her back that she could almost feel the bones cracking. She didn't look down at the boulders below, but was so aware of them that they seemed to generate a magnetic force all of their own.

Slowly, carefully she edged one foot into the next gap in the bars, following it with the other, and kept going until she was at the corner. The cold was so penetrating that already she could barely feel her hands or feet. She couldn't allow them to become numb, but had no way of stopping it.

She needed to move faster, but if she did she'd be sure to make a mistake and any mistake here was going to cost her her life.

Whispering prayers under her breath, she bent her knees slowly and hand over hand lowered her grasp to come level with her eyes. She had no choice but to look down now for she needed to seek out the closest branch that might hold her. To her horror they all looked so flimsy that she knew it would be madness even to test them. But then she spotted one snaking its way around the corner of the tower to disappear beneath the balcony. It was no more than two inches in diameter, but maybe, just maybe, it was tough enough to act as a foothold.

Gingerly she stretched out her right leg, still clinging on for dear life with both hands, until she felt the rough bark beneath the arch of her foot. She pressed down gently. It didn't move so she pressed harder, willing it not to snap or fall away from its mooring. When it held again she allowed more weight to sink into it, careful to keep the bulk of her balance attached to the balcony. Still it didn't give, but how on earth was she going to fit both feet on such a slender stem with no space between it and the concrete wall?

She was doing this all wrong, but had no idea of what was right.

Maybe she should let her hands do the searching instead of her feet?

Or maybe she should try to climb back inside.

Gasping as a gust of wind stole her balance, she half-lunged, half-scrabbled for the nearest vine, grabbed it with both hands and cleaved herself to it as her left foot joined her right on the branch below.

She was now completely free of the balcony and no more than a meter from the corner of the tower. If she could get to it she was sure she'd find many more tentacles, strong and closely entwined on the front side of the building to help her descent.

The wind gusted again, harsh and bitter, either urging her on—or trying to tear her free. She felt sick with fear; hot tears were burning her eyes. She blinked them away, not daring to use a hand. She was crying out silently for Callum. Without meaning to, she glanced down and as she saw the rocks below, lurking like a final resting place, one of the vines snapped.

Freda was pacing, back and forth, back and forth, so agitated that Marianne's own nerves were fraying. An eternity could have passed since she'd added her version of events to the memoir, but it was probably only a few minutes. She had no idea what was going through Freda's mind now, though her anger was plain to see and Marianne could sense it building.

Suddenly Freda's hands flew in the air as though she was trying to shake them from her wrists. "Why won't you admit that you lied?" she cried in despair. "His name, *he,* deserves to be cleared and you know it. So why won't you do it? You're old now. I won't let you die without—"

"I didn't lie," Marianne said quietly, "but if you want me to say I did—"

Freda's head fell back, her eyes closed against a harsh paroxysm of pain.

Marianne said steadily, "You know this has nothing to do with Joely, so why . . ."

Freda spun around. "You destroyed my family," she

cried, "so why would I care about yours?" Her eyes were bright, angry, and tormented. "You are finding out what it's like to feel helpless when someone you love is suffering. It's what you did to us. My parents never performed again, do you know that? You broke them—"

"Where is she?" Marianne interrupted. She couldn't deal with the guilt of what had happened to his parents, not now. "Answer me, Freda, or I'm calling the police."

Freda's face became pinched. "You're already too late," she informed her tartly.

Marianne's heart contracted.

Freda pointed at the laptop. "Do it," she commanded. "Confess to your lies."

Accepting there was no reasoning with her, Marianne reached for the computer ready to do anything she was asked to help Joely, but at the last moment, still clutching her phone, she turned and ran to the door.

She didn't see the laptop flying through the air after her, she only realized what had happened when it hit the wall close to her head and dropped to the floor at her feet.

She stared down at it in shock. If it had hit her . . .

She turned around to find Freda watching her, appearing as stunned by what she'd done as Marianne was. She seemed to twitch and started to speak, but then she stopped. Marianne got the impression she was trying to disconnect herself from the random act of violence, to work out how it had happened even—and yet, when she spoke, what she said confirmed her determination to get what she'd come for.

"Do it," she repeated shakily. "Confess to your lies."

*

Joely was clinging on with one hand, the other was flailing about wildly trying to find something to grab on to. The vines under her feet were starting to bow; they were going to give out at any moment . . .

In one swift, random move she flung out an arm and grabbed hold of a branch. It felt rough and slender in her palm, too slender; she panicked, but it held. She clung to it with all her might, holding her entire weight with her hands as she felt about with her feet for purchase. Her arms and shoulders were on fire, the cold was slicing through her skin; she had so little strength left. The agony and fear were unbearable.

Her right foot, sore and bloodied, found what felt like a sturdy tendril. She pressed down on it and experienced a moment's relief in her arms as her weight was shared. She brought her other foot to the branch and sobbed when it held.

With every fiber of her being she wanted to go back, to end this now, but she'd reached the point where each way was as dangerous as the other.

Inch by inch she got herself to the corner of the tower. She snaked an arm around, scrabbling for another vine, even some wire that guided it, but her hand fell away as her head was slammed into the wall by another blast of wind. She gasped as a dizzying nausea swept through her. Her fingers and feet were so cold now that it wouldn't be possible to hold on for much longer. She had to get herself around the corner and onto the thicker stems where at least if she fell the roof of the kitchen terrace would break the fall.

Blindly reaching out an arm again she fumbled for something that felt solid, closed a fist around it, and carefully moved a foot to follow. She sobbed and choked and whispered brokenly for her father. Was he watching her now? Could he save her? Were his invisible arms waiting to catch her? Her foot wasn't finding any support, it was just moving around the wall brushing over spidery twigs and soggy leaves. She couldn't find anything, so returned her foot to join the other.

She counted again, storing up strength with each beat, and with a quick, awkward twist she somehow hauled the lower half of her body around the corner of the tower and planted her feet on a branch beneath her hands. Her head spun and icy sweat poured from her skin as she tried to catch her breath.

Terrifying seconds passed as she clung on like a petrified animal, shuddering and shaking, crying and praying not to die.

You can do this, she tried telling herself. *You're going to make it down to safety and then you're going to run into the Valley of Rocks to grab a phone from a tourist to call your mother.*

Andee was already turning her car around as she instructed the phone to connect her with Joely again.

Still no reply.

She couldn't believe she'd been so stupid. If she hadn't been so distracted with her own concerns she'd have realized right away what had been bothering her about Joely, and her visit to Dimmett House half an hour ago. As it was she'd got the best part of the way back to Kesterly before it had hit her.

If Joely wasn't inside the house, then the likelihood of her being somewhere else with no signal seemed too implausible. And if she had a signal she'd answer the phone, or make a call.

Andee had no idea why Joely would be shut up in that house, or if she actually was, she only knew that her instincts were telling her to return there and as they'd rarely let her down before, she was on her way.

"You're not writing anything," Freda stated crossly.

Marianne simply stared at the laptop screen.

"Hard to face the truth, isn't it?" Freda snapped scornfully.

"It's much harder to lie," Marianne said quietly.

Freda snorted and Marianne watched her turn away, her demeanor exuding impatience, irritation, and something more that Marianne couldn't quite define. It was as though her taut, willowy frame was about to crack with the frustration she was holding inside.

What was she thinking? What was she really hoping to achieve with this madness?

Marianne's eyes moved to her phone on the floor, and putting aside the laptop she reached for it.

Freda didn't turn around, so Marianne connected to Callum's number and as soon as he answered, she said, "Please come," and then rang off again.

"Who was that?" Freda asked, her eyes still fixed on the window.

Seeing no reason to lie, Marianne said, "My son-in-law."

Freda nodded and inhaled as she looked around the room as if he might already be there, and maybe hiding. "He cheated on your daughter," she stated. "Did you know that?"

Marianne didn't reply.

"Would you like me to dictate the rest of your story?" Freda offered.

Marianne simply stared at her.

Freda's mouth puckered with displeasure. After a moment she said, "My husband used to cheat on me, you know. He's dead now. He was going to leave me, but he died at the same time as my other brother." Her eyes locked onto Marianne's. "Don't you want to know where he is?" she asked brokenly.

Marianne wasn't sure if they were talking about David.

"You haven't asked where he is," Freda cried in frustration. "How can you not care about that?"

"I know where David is," Marianne told her. "I don't need to ask."

As Andee turned into the drive of Dimmett House she searched the front windows for any change in the shutters but found none. Everything seemed exactly as it had before, until her eyes moved upward and she gave a gasp of horror as she saw Joely clinging to the upper storey of the building.

Leaping from the car she almost shouted Joely's name, but realized any distraction could prove fatal.

How the hell was she going to get her down from there?

She needed a ladder, and someone to help. But with everything locked up and no phone signal she had little hope of either.

Moving swiftly across the grass, she assessed the patio roof knowing she'd have to climb up there to try and help her friend down. Whether she'd be able to reach her was debatable, but if Joely could manage to ease herself a little lower . . .

She cried out and broke into a run as Joely's hold on the vine began to fail. Branches were tearing away from the wall, debris was floating, and with a single, helpless cry Joely plunged to the patio roof. She hit it hard, rolled, and as she came off the edge Andee threw herself forward to catch her. They hit the ground together, Andee grunting as the wind was knocked out of her, Joely a dead weight on top of her.

Long empty seconds passed as they lay in a heap on the grass, clouds drifting aimlessly overhead, birds flying past, the sound of waves rushing up from the sea. Eventually Andee took a breath, waited a moment, and when Joely didn't move she said, "Joely, can you hear me?"

For a long moment, there was only silence . . . And then Andee heard a faint groan. Feeling a rush of relief, she carefully eased herself free and rolled Joely onto her back.

Tearing off her coat, she covered Joely with its warmth, saying, "Hold on, OK? You have to hold on while I go to get help."

Joely looked up at her, eyes unfocused. Her face was deathly pale, and the blood running from her temple was filling Andee with fear.

She had no choice. She had to leave her.

Racing back to her car she pressed the SOS button over the mirror and thanked God as it connected to the Mercedes Emergency Response Centre. After giving all necessary details, she ran back to Joely, praying with all her might that it wasn't already too late.

*

"This is Freda," Marianne told Callum as he came into the room looking puzzled and concerned and slightly harried in a way that suggested he'd broken the speed limit to get here.

Marianne was sitting on one of the sofas; Freda was on the opposite one and didn't look up as the introduction was made.

Callum looked from one woman to the other, his frown deepening. "Are you all right?" he asked Marianne, putting his keys on the sideboard. "What's going on?"

"Freda is the author Joely's been working with," Marianne explained. "She's here because she thought I could help with her story."

More confused than ever, Callum said, "And where's Joely?"

Marianne looked at Freda, but Freda seemed not to be listening.

Callum repeated more forcefully, "Where's Joely?"

"She won't tell me," Marianne replied. "Andee's been to the house but she isn't there . . ." She checked her phone as it rang. "It's Andee," she told him and clicked on. As she listened her eyes widened with horror. "Oh God," she murmured, trying to get up. "Where have they taken her?"

Callum caught her as she swayed and took the phone. "Andee, it's Callum. What—"

"She's had a fall," Andee told him. "I'm not sure how serious it is yet, but I'm following the ambulance to Kesterly Infirmary."

Callum's face drained as he said, "What kind of a fall?"

"It was from quite a height. She's conscious, but I can't tell you what her injuries are yet."

"OK. I'll meet you there." Handing the phone back to Marianne, he said, "She's on her way to the hospital. Are you coming with me?"

Marianne looked at Freda and seeing the tears running down the older woman's cheeks she felt her own eyes burn with pity in spite of the anger she felt. Freda was lost, desperate, and seemed to have no idea what her life meant anymore. "I don't know what you did to Joely," she said hoarsely, "but Callum and I are going to her now. You can stay here if you want to, or you can come with us." She didn't add, *The police will want to speak to you,* but it was what she was thinking as she ran to get her coat.

"You still haven't asked where he is," Freda mumbled as the door shut behind them. "Why won't you ask?"

An hour later Freda was still sitting on the sofa, hands clenched in her lap, bloodshot eyes staring at nothing as if a single thought was jammed in her head, or perhaps there were no thoughts at all.

She heard the front door open and close and looked up as a young girl wandered into the room and let her heavy bag drop to the floor. She was strikingly lovely, with long, slender legs, silvery blond hair tumbling in waves to her waist, and features almost too perfectly sculpted.

"Hi," the girl said, seeming unsurprised to see a stranger in the house, "where's Grandma?"

"Who are you?" Freda asked, already certain she knew the answer.

ask at the nurses' station, someone there will tell you where we are."

Joely opened her eyes.

Sorry, Andee mouthed. *Wrong thing to say?*

Not sure of the answer to that, Joely simply shut her eyes again.

After ringing off, Andee said, "They're on their way up."

"My mother and Holly are with him?"

"Your mother certainly."

"So she's all right?"

"I think so."

"Do you know if Freda went there?"

"I've only spoken to Callum, but there doesn't seem to be anything to worry about. Would you like me to leave you alone?"

Joely tried to swallow but her throat was too dry. "No, stay," she said hoarsely. "Unless you want to go. Where's Graeme? Wasn't he here a moment ago?"

"He's gone to see my mother. She's cooking for us tonight and we thought one of us ought to be there."

"Then you must go," Joely insisted. "Please send her my love."

"I will, but I'll hang on to say hi to Callum and Marianne."

Joely frowned as a sharp pain cut between her eyes, but managed a grateful smile as Andee held a glass of water to her lips. "Before they get here," she said, "I need to thank you for saving my life."

Andee laughed. "You're overstating the case," she assured her, "but I will admit that you came down on me like a ton of bricks."

With a smile Joely said, "What I don't understand is how you came to be there. I saw you leave . . ."

"And I came back."

"But why?"

Andee's brows arched wryly. "I guess you could say I followed my instincts—although they were a bit late kicking in."

"But not too late. If you hadn't broken my fall . . ." She stopped as Andee placed a finger gently on her lips.

"I had some help from the patio roof," Andee reminded her, "and now perhaps you'll tell me what the heck you were doing up there."

"She locked me in," Joely replied, "and then she disappeared. I thought she'd gone to see Mum, but you say Mum's here."

At the sound of footsteps hurrying down the corridor outside, Andee got to her feet.

"Joely, thank God you're all right," Marianne cried as she came through the door. "But look at you. Oh, you poor thing. Does it hurt terribly? How can I give you a hug while you're trussed up like that?"

"This hand's not so bad," Joely informed her, holding up the right one covered in bark burns and scratches and smiling at the way her mother embraced it gently, but as if it were long lost and just returned.

She knew Callum was standing at the door looking at her, she could feel his eyes as strongly as she could his presence, but she wasn't able to bring herself to look at him yet. There was too much emotion swelling up inside her, relief that he was here, that she'd survived the fall, that he'd returned to their home, that he was the man she'd married, that she was still married to him . . . She didn't know what to say, or what her heart was really doing, apart from seeming to break all over again. They couldn't pretend the betrayal hadn't happened, *she* couldn't pretend that she hadn't pushed him into it, but even if she had, no one had made him go to live with Martha.

In the end, as Andee said a quiet goodbye, Joely said to her mother, "Where's Holly?"

"We haven't got hold of her yet," Callum replied, "but I've sent a text telling her where we are and that you're going to be all right."

"She'll probably go to Caitlin's or Tasha's for the night," Marianne added.

Joely gave a nod and closed her eyes. "They're keeping me in until the morning," she said.

"We'll stay with you," her mother assured her. She glanced over her shoulder at Callum. "Or I can go to get us some drinks while you two . . ."

"It's OK, I'll go," Callum said, and Joely knew he understood that she didn't want to be left alone with him yet.

"There you are," Holly said, putting a cup of tea and a cheese sandwich in front of Freda. "Are you sure that's enough?"

Freda nodded and smiled in a way that made Holly think she was a bit weird, but hey, she'd already come to that conclusion so no surprises there.

"I don't think Grandma will be back until tomorrow," she said, sinking into the opposite sofa, and tucking her long legs under her as she checked her phone again. "My mum's had some sort of fall so they've gone racing

285

off to the end of the world to make sure she's all right. Apparently she is, according to Dad."

"Aren't you worried?" Freda asked.

Holly shrugged. "Dad said there was no need to be."

Freda leaned forward to pick up her plate. "Thank you for this," she said. "I hadn't realized I was hungry until you asked."

Holly shrugged again. "I expect Grandma would want me to look after you while you wait. Sorry, but who did you say you are again?"

"My name's Freda."

"Cool. So, Freda, will you be staying the night? If you are, I won't have to go and crash with a friend. I could stay here with you as my responsible adult."

Freda bit into her sandwich.

Picking up the peanut butter sandwich she'd made for herself, Holly said, "You don't say much, do you? I thought it was supposed to be teenagers who are monosyllabic, or whatever the word is."

"Monosyllabic is correct. You look like your grandmother when she was your age, although you seem to be missing something, I can't quite work out what it is."

Holly frowned in puzzlement. "Was that like . . . Did you just insult me?" she asked.

Freda drank some tea. "I'm not sure."

Holly took a bite of her sandwich and eyed the woman curiously, but as another text turned up on her phone she tuned out of Freda and into the friend who'd messaged. After a while she was bored with him and seeing Freda had finished her tea she said, "Would you like any more?"

Freda said, "Aren't you going to ring your mother?"

Holly glanced at her phone. "Yeah, I expect so, later."

"You don't sound as though you care for her very much."

Holly's blue eyes darkened as she scowled. "She's my mother, of course I care for her."

Freda said nothing.

"She's just a bit," Holly shrugged, "you know, like a zombie sometimes."

"She didn't seem like a zombie to me," Freda said.

"You mean you know her?"

Freda nodded. "I locked her in a tower so she couldn't get out, but it seems that she did."

Holly balked and blinked. What the heck was this woman on? "You locked her in a tower?" she repeated.

Freda nodded.

She couldn't be serious. "When? Why?"

"It's quite a long story, but I have it here, all written down if you'd like to read it."

Deciding she probably needed to get away from this nutjob, Holly said, "Well, actually, I think I might . . ."

"It's about your grandma when she was your age," Freda interrupted. "Your mother has been helping me to write it. We've made quite a lot of progress, but it isn't finished yet. Please say you'll read it."

"And if I don't you'll lock me up in a tower too? I don't think so."

Freda laughed. "I promise not to."

Holly regarded her carefully, torn between the instinct to get the heck out of here and an odd sort of fascination to find out what other freaky stuff she might say.

And if she had a story about Grandma . . . That could be interesting. "So it's you Mum's been working with on this mystery assignment?" she probed.

Freda nodded. "It had to be secret or we couldn't have surprised your grandmother. She knows about it now, but we haven't got the end quite right yet. We were almost there, but then Marianne had to rush off."

Holly's attention was caught by her mobile phone again, and by the time she'd finished a fast-moving group chat with her closest mates she'd half-forgotten what the old lady had been on about.

"Here it is," Freda said, pushing a large brown envelope toward her. "You sit there and read it while I go into the kitchen and wash up these few dishes."

It was shortly after nine the following morning when Andee turned up at the hospital with a bag full of essentials. "Jeans and sweater from my wardrobe," she announced, dropping the bag onto a chair next to Joely's bed, "plus newly bought undies from M&S. I'm not sure how well any of it's going to fit, but it'll be better than going home in that."

Joely arched a brow as she glanced down at her white paper gown. It was crumpled and spotted with blood from her scratches, and torn under her good arm. It was also very revealing at the back.

"You'll also find an assortment of cleansers, deodorant, moisturizers, that sort of thing in there," Andee added.

Wincing at the pain in her shoulder, Joely said, "I hope Mum or Callum paid for it all. If not . . ."

"They did, apart from the jeans and sweater, but you

can send them back when you have no more need for them. How are you feeling?"

Joely grimaced. "You mean apart from as if I've fallen from a great height, bounced on my shoulder, and landed on my life-saving friend? Not too bad."

With a laugh, Andee said, "You've definitely got more color than when I left you yesterday, most of it black and blue, I admit, but your eyes are brighter."

Joely batted her lids and almost wished she hadn't. Her head was still pounding and moving her limbs wasn't a pleasant experience either. Still, the painkillers should kick in again anytime now, and after she'd managed a shower (with a nurse's help) she should be ready to leave. "Is Mum still at yours?" she asked, maneuvering her legs over the side of the bed and grimacing at all the scrapes and bruises. Marianne had gone to Andee's around three in the morning to get some rest while Callum had stayed to keep an eye on a sleeping Joely. Though he was nowhere to be seen now, having slipped out during the early morning checks, he'd been there when Joely had woken up, fast asleep in the chair.

Everything felt all right with him here, even though it wasn't.

"She's probably on her way here by now," Andee replied. "My mother's bringing her."

"That's kind of her."

"She wanted to say hello to you, but she has an appointment at the renal clinic in about an hour."

Joely frowned. "Is she OK?"

"I'm sure she's fine, but they've run some tests because she's been a bit under the weather lately." She checked her phone as a text arrived. "Callum's gone to fill up the car," she relayed. "Are you sure you're OK to go back to London today? You're very welcome to stay . . ."

"I'll be fine," Joely assured her, "and we've already put you out enough. I don't suppose anyone's heard from Holly this morning?"

"Not that they've mentioned, which reminds me." Reaching into her bag she pulled out Joely's mobile. "The screen's cracked, I'm afraid, but Graeme thinks it'll probably still work once it's charged."

"Thanks." As Joely took it she wondered why it, more than anything else, was transporting her back to those terrifying minutes before the fall. She suddenly felt nauseous and dizzy and put a hand to her head as she tilted forward.

"Take it easy," Andee said, catching her gently. "Maybe you should lie down again for a few minutes?"

"I'm OK," Joely said weakly. "I just . . ." She attempted a smile. "I think I'll be haunted by the great escape for a while to come." After waiting for her senses to settle she said, "I should try to get hold of Edward, her nephew . . . Does anyone know where she is?"

"I haven't heard anything," Andee replied. "You said last night that you thought she'd gone to see your *mother*?"

Joely glanced up as a nurse came to check on her and gratefully accepted more painkillers. Once she and Andee were alone again she explained as quickly as she could about the real purpose of the memoir. By the time she'd finished Andee was frowning worriedly.

"Do you have any idea where the other brother is now?"

Joely shook her head. "I'm pretty sure he went to prison when it all happened, and considering what he went in for there's a good chance he changed his name when he came out to try and start a new life."

"So do you think he might be behind this memoir in some way? I mean, could it be his idea?"

"I guess anything's possible. All I can tell you for certain is that she told me 'the moth' was my mother, and the next thing I knew she'd locked me in the tower and disappeared."

"And you presumed she'd gone to see your mother, but Marianne's here. Have you asked if she's seen her?"

"I haven't really had the chance, but . . ."

"Maybe we should start by getting someone to go and check if Freda's back at the house."

"And at the same time they could pick up my things? I really don't want to go back there myself anytime soon."

Andee turned around as another nurse came into the room ready to take Joely for a shower.

"Are you sure you can manage?" the nurse asked, coming to help Joely up. "We can easily find you a wheelchair."

"Let me try walking," Joely responded and holding her broken arm and shoulder steady she used her good hand to push herself to her feet. A moment later her mother came in bearing coffees and croissants and Joely sat down again. "Please let me eat first," she said to the nurse. "If you had any idea how hungry I am . . ."

The nurse checked her watch, but made no objection as she went off to fulfill other duties.

"Two life-savers in one room." Joely smiled, taking

one of the croissants, and unable to stop herself she devoured half of it in one bite.

Marianne's expression was wry as she glanced at Andee and offered one to her too.

"Thanks, not for me," Andee replied. "I should go to check on Mum."

"She's in Costa, on the ground floor," Marianne told her. "You will let us know how she gets on with her results, won't you?"

"Of course, and I'll make sure someone collects your things," she said to Joely.

Showering her paper gown with crumbs as she replied, Joely said, "The nephew's card is in my handbag. His name's Edward Martin."

Andee gave her a thumbs-up and Joely looked at her mother to see if anything about the name had affected her, and it clearly had. Joely's appetite faded. "Have you seen her?" she asked, her head starting to pound again.

Marianne shuddered slightly as she nodded. "She came to the house. I didn't . . . I hadn't met her before, but I knew who she was. She'd already sent me a copy of the memoir."

"So you *are* the girl she got me to write about?"

Marianne nodded again. "She wants me to admit that I lied . . ." She pressed her fingers to her mouth. "It was so long ago . . . I've told her what happened, but she doesn't want to believe me."

"Did she . . . ? Where is she now?"

"I don't know. I left her at the house when we got the news about you. I expect she left soon after we did."

Joely swallowed drily and looked up as Callum came

in with more coffees and croissants. Her heart hadn't fluttered this way since they'd first met, and seeing his dismay that Marianne had beaten him with breakfast made it fold around all the love she had for him. "Have you spoken to Holly this morning?" she asked, taking one of his croissants so he wouldn't feel left out.

"No," he replied. "She rang last night to ask how you were and she sent her love. She wants you to call as soon as you can."

"I'll do it now," Joely said and held out a hand for someone's phone.

Marianne passed hers over. "She probably won't be awake yet on a Saturday morning, but I'm sure she won't mind if it's you."

"She'll think it's you," Joely reminded her as she scrolled to the number.

The phone rang several times at the other end telling her Holly probably was still asleep, but then it stopped and Joely was about to say, "Hi, it's me," when to her horror Freda's voice said, "Hello, Marianne. How's Joely?"

CHAPTER TWENTY-FOUR

Marianne's face turned white. "What do you mean, Freda answered?" she cried.

"Are you sure it was Holly's number you connected to?" Callum cut in, scrolling to it himself.

"I don't have Freda's," Marianne told him.

Fear and confusion were welling up in Joely. "What is she doing answering Holly's phone? And why the hell did I just ring off? What a fool. Call back . . ."

"Holly? It's Dad, are . . . Christ, it's her voicemail. Holly, ring me as soon as you get this. I need to hear from you." Clicking off, he stared hard at Joely and her mother. "What exactly is going on?" he demanded, his face tight with confusion and concern. "Who is this Freda person, and what is she doing with Holly's phone?"

"She's the woman you saw at the house, before we left," Marianne reminded him, more agitated than ever.

"The one Joely's been working with?"

"She must still be there," Marianne said to Joely. "We were in such a rush to leave . . . Oh God, Holly must have turned up . . ."

"We need to get back to London," Joely said to Callum, and ignoring the pain she struggled to her feet. "Someone help me into those clothes . . ."

"Is Holly in some kind of danger?" Callum insisted, snatching up the carrier bag as Marianne tore off the paper gown. "Is this woman . . . What the hell is she likely to do?"

"I don't know." Joely grabbed his arm as she stepped into the panties her mother was holding out. "Probably nothing, but she's not . . ." She broke off as a nurse came into the room. "Mum, you tell him," she said, gesturing for her mother to hand the clothes to the nurse.

"Do we need to call the police?" Callum persisted. "Christ, Joely, this is our daughter . . ."

"I know who she is," Joely snapped. "And the woman we're talking about is nuts, so yes, we probably should ring the police. Mum will know what to tell them." She yelped as her damaged left side became trapped between her and the nurse.

"It's her!" Callum cried as his phone rang. "Holly? Are you OK?"

Joely's right hand tightened like a vice on the nurse's arm.

"So where are you?" Callum asked, eyes going to Joely. "And who's with you? She's been there all night? And you've been with her? Is she . . . ? Holly, calm down, I'm only asking. Yes, Mum's fine. We're coming . . . We'll be there very soon. Fine. Yes. We love you." As he rang off, Joely said, "You didn't ask why Freda answered her phone?"

Callum held out his mobile. "Call her back. I'm going to get the car."

"Did she sound all right?" Marianne asked, moving swiftly after him. "I don't think Freda will harm her . . . She had nothing to do with what happened."

"Nor did I," Joely called after her, "and look at me."

*

"Freda?" Holly said, sauntering into the kitchen where Freda was making breakfast. "Why did you answer my phone? I know you did, because I can see there was a call from Grandma . . ."

"It was on the sofa, where you left it," Freda informed her, putting a plate of toast on the table, "and when I saw it was Marianne I thought I'd tell her to hold on while I fetched you. Unfortunately we got cut off. Have you spoken to her now?"

"No, but I have to Dad, and seems like they're all in a flap about you still being here."

"Oh dear."

Perching on one of the barstools, Holly helped herself to toast and coated it with butter. "You know, that story about Grandma is totally awesome," she commented, taking a bite.

"Mm," Freda grunted. She brought mugs and coffee to the table and set them down. "So you've said, more than once. Do all teenagers keep repeating themselves?"

Holly shrugged. "I'm still trying to get my head around her sha— getting it on with her music teacher. And he was your brother?"

Before Freda could reply, Holly's mobile jingled the Dad tone and with a sigh she clicked on. "Hey," she said, crunching into more toast.

"It's me," her mother announced. "Is Freda still there?"

"She is."

"What's she doing?"

"Making breakfast."

Silence.

"Totally amazing story about Grandma," Holly

declared. "I haven't read it all yet, but wow, she rocked when she was young."

"Holly, I need you . . ."

"Oh, sorry, Mum, Caitlin's just texted and I need to get back to her. Glad you're OK, see you later," and clicking off she launched into a lengthy exchange of messages with one of her best friends. By the time she looked up again Freda had disappeared.

Returning to her phone, Holly spent the next ten minutes catching up with other friends while finishing her breakfast and drinking more coffee. It wasn't until she got up to take her dishes to the sink that she realized Freda was standing in the doorway behind her, watching her.

"I wish you wouldn't do that," Holly grumbled. "It's dead spooky." This had to be the fourth or fifth time she'd turned around to catch Freda staring at her, and it was starting to freak her out.

"You can read these now," Freda said, bringing a handful of pages to the island. "You'll probably end up seeing your grandmother in a very different light to the romantic hue you've cast her in now."

Holly glanced at the time.

"It won't take long," Freda told her, and going to close the kitchen door she stood against it, blocking the way out.

With a sigh Holly drew the pages toward her and started to read. She got no further than the first couple of lines before her phone buzzed into life again. "A lot to sort out today," she told Freda, not looking up as she went off on another messaging spree.

Freda crossed over to the sink and began loading the dishwasher.

With more arrangements firmed up, Holly dutifully returned to the pages, reaching behind her head to bring her hair over one shoulder.

A few minutes later, as she got to the part where Sir confessed he already had a girlfriend she started to frown. "Bastard," she muttered under her breath. "Sorry, I know he's your brother, but . . ." She looked up and her eyes widened in shock. Freda was standing with her back to the sink and staring at her so hard it was as if she'd forgotten how to blink. Worse though was the bread knife she was holding up in one hand.

Holly's heart turned over in fear. "What are you doing with that?"

Freda looked at the knife.

"You need to put it down," Holly told her, getting up from the stool.

Freda was still looking at it.

Holly took a step back.

Freda said, "You haven't finished. You must read to the part where her lies began. It's the only way we'll end up getting to the truth."

As Callum drove them back to London, breaking speed limits on both motorways, Joely and Marianne explained about Freda, what she wanted from Marianne, and how she'd used Joely to get it. "It was manipulative to the point of crazy," Joely said, letting her head fall back against the seat as everything throbbed. "She's clearly lost all sense of perspective on what happened to her brother . . . And I still don't know what did," she said to her mother. "Did he go to prison?"

"Yes, he did," Marianne answered quietly.

"I don't care about him," Callum said brusquely. "I'm more interested in my daughter being used to get to you, Marianne. Am I right? Is that what's happening here?"

"I don't know," Marianne replied, anxiously, "but it's possible."

"So damned well give the woman what she wants."

"I will. I'll confirm everything she believes . . ."

"So did he, or didn't he rape you?" Joely demanded from the back seat.

Marianne clasped her hands to her face. "There's so much more to it, Joely," she cried wretchedly. "What happened back then . . . I never . . . He . . ."

Realizing how distraught her mother was becoming Joely said, "OK, we need to calm this down. We've called the police, and we'll soon be there ourselves."

Several minutes passed in silence as they left the M4 and sped across the Chiswick flyover into London. They were approaching the outskirts of Kensington when Callum's temper flared again, "I can hardly believe this, Joely. Not once during all the years you were a reporter dealing with some of the worst types of humanity did it ever come home with you. Now you're supposed to be a safe and respectable ghostwriter and we get this . . ." He broke off as his phone rang.

It was the police calling back.

"An officer has been to the house," a female voice informed them, "but there doesn't appear to be anyone at home."

"Did anyone try to get in?" he almost shouted.

"I believe so, but the doors and windows were locked and there was no sign of a disturbance."

"But I told you, we think someone could be . . ." He stopped as Joely pressed his shoulder.

"We're almost there," she reminded him. "They haven't got in, so there's no point arguing."

Minutes after ending the call he pulled up outside Marianne's house and Joely threw open the rear passenger door to climb out.

"For God's sake," he cried, leaping out to help her.

"Let's just get in there," she said, and hardly feeling the pain racking her shoulder she started up the path.

Marianne was right behind them, taking out her keys, but before she could insert them in the door it opened wide.

All three of them froze.

"Where's Holly?" Joely demanded pushing her way past Freda.

Freda didn't answer, simply stood aside for them to enter as if it were her home they were barging their way into.

"Where's Holly?" Joely shouted, from the sitting room.

Marianne went through to the kitchen. "She's not here," she cried shrilly.

Glaring at Freda, Callum growled, "Where is my daughter? What have you done with her?"

"I know who you are," Freda told him, "you're the cheating husband . . ."

"Freda!" Joely shouted. "Where is Holly?"

"She's gone," Freda replied.

"Gone where?"

Freda fluttered her fingers through the air, and with a small puff of air she flicked them out in a fan.

"Oh Christ," Joely cried, recognizing the movement.

"What have you done to her, Freda? She's only a child. This has nothing to do with her."

"I'll check upstairs," Callum said, and taking them two at a time he threw open the door to every room, but the only sign of Holly was her school bag and uniform dumped on the bed, and the usual clutter of shoes, hairdryer, brushes, and cosmetics scattered about the place.

In the hall, Marianne said to Freda, "I understand what you want, and I promise I'll give it to you, but you must tell us where Holly is."

Freda glanced at Joely, who was using Callum's phone to call Holly again.

"No reply," Joely said, as it went to messages.

"Try texting," Callum instructed from the stairs. "She's better at responding to that."

Joely tapped in, *Where are you?* and pressed send.

She turned to Freda again and found her staring at Marianne. It was disturbing to see how superior she appeared to consider herself in someone else's home, how in control she apparently felt—and how ready she was for this confrontation. Joely's eyes moved to her mother. Marianne was holding the stare with a steel and confidence of her own, and yet there was something deep inside her that made Joely almost afraid to know what she was thinking.

"Why don't you ask where he is?" Freda asked.

"Because I *know* where he is," Marianne replied. Her eyes closed. "Stop this, Freda, please. You don't know everything . . . I know you think you do, but I . . ."

Joely looked down as a text arrived. It was from Holly.

"She's with Caitlin," she told Callum half-collapsing with relief, and she handed him the phone so he could respond.

Freda regarded her archly. "Presumptions, Joely," she stated loftily. "What have I told you about them? Once again you've leapt to an incorrect conclusion and what did it achieve apart from unnecessary fear and distress?"

"For God's sake, Freda," Joely snapped, "this isn't a game," but Freda had already turned back to Marianne.

"Shall we?" Freda invited, gesturing toward the sitting room as if she were the host and Marianne the guest.

Marianne signalled for her to go first and followed.

Joely said quietly to Callum, "I'm not sure what's going to happen now, but I think it's best if you wait in the kitchen."

His eyes searched hers worriedly. "You're exhausted," he said. "You shouldn't—"

"I'll be fine," she assured him, and because there was no more she could say for the moment she attempted a smile and went to join her mother and Freda.

CHAPTER TWENTY-FIVE

Marianne and Freda were already seated on opposite sofas by the time Joely entered the room. It didn't appear as if either of them had spoken yet, although the air was already charged with everything to come.

Joely sat down carefully on the third sofa where she could see both of them, feeling faintly nauseous from pain. She wondered if she should try to start the conversation, but then Freda spoke in a tone that was harsh and slightly mocking.

"Holly knows about your lies," she declared. "She thought you were awesome, that you rocked until she found out what you did to him."

Joely's eyes went to her mother as Marianne said, "Did you let her read what I wrote?"

Freda stared at her. "What you wrote isn't the truth."

"It happened the way I described, and I don't believe he told you anything different."

Freda's head seemed to twitch as she said, "I don't care what you believe, what I know to be true is that we would not be sitting here today if you had not . . ."

Speaking over her, Marianne said, "I don't think he should have been charged with rape. I know some people would disagree with me, especially the way things are these days, but . . ." Her voice suddenly rose. "I loved him, Freda, I mean truly loved him."

Freda's lip curled with scorn. "You were fifteen, you didn't know the meaning of . . ."

"Did you come here for the truth," Marianne interrupted angrily, "or to force me into your version of it? If it's the latter, you're wasting your time. I don't owe you anything . . ."

"He was a decent, honorable man," Freda said fiercely, "who saw it as his duty to protect *you*, from the trauma of going to court. He sacrificed himself for you, and you let him."

"Did he ever tell you why he didn't fight it?" Marianne cried. "You obviously talked to him a lot, that much is clear from your memoir—there are things there that even I had forgotten . . ." She took a moment, pressing a shaking hand to her head and Joely could see she was forcing herself to stay calm. "It's true, he was decent and honorable," she said evenly, "and so much more. You have no idea how much I suffered over what happened to him. Not a single day has gone by in all these years when I haven't regretted—"

"I'm not interested in the pathetic whining of your conscience," Freda cut in sharply. "I just want the truth, not only for me, but for his son."

Marianne flinched as if she'd been struck, and Joely felt the blow too. *His son? Was Jamie . . . ? Of course, it had to be.*

"OK, here's a truth for you," Marianne shot back, recovering fast. "My son was conceived in love and no matter how difficult things were, he was always wanted. It was your family who rejected him, who refused even to see him—their own grandson, your nephew. My parents stood by us. They weren't the people you've made them out to be, all those ugly untruths you've concocted about them taking drugs and encouraging me into a love affair that no parent would ever want for their child. You should be ashamed of those lies, Freda . . ."

"They were hedonists, sybarites, everyone knew . . ."

"They were people of their time but not in the way you've portrayed them and if you think you're going to print with the lies you've invented about them you need to think again, because I won't let you."

Freda scoffed a bitter laugh. "'I won't let you,'" she mimicked sneeringly, as if Marianne had no power at all to stop her. "I'm not interested in them," she spat, waving a dismissive hand. "You can describe them however you want to, it's your lies that we're here to expose . . ."

"All that will be exposed here," Marianne cut in angrily, "is the truth of what happened after I found out I was pregnant, and after David went to jail. You've read up to that point, but Joely hasn't—and I want her to know the truth before we go any further. After that, I'll tell you the rest, but if you're going to keep insisting that anything I say is a lie I will not waste my time."

Joely regarded her mother admiringly; no matter how intimidating and forceful Freda was making herself Marianne was clearly having no trouble standing up to her. And her mother had already written down her account of events—Joely was eager to finally get some answers.

Though Freda's nostrils flared in an expression of contempt she gave no comeback to Marianne's warning, simply folded her hands together to show she was waiting.

Marianne turned to Joely and for a moment Joely wanted to tell her to show Freda out, to say she wasn't going to put up with any more of these absurd theatrics, but it wasn't her place to try and put words in her mother's mouth. "This isn't going to be easy," Marianne said, as if Freda was no longer in the room, "and I wouldn't do it if you hadn't already been dragged into this, but you have and so you need to know the truth."

Joely started to answer, but her mother was getting to her feet. "I'm going to fetch my laptop," she said. "I'll print out what I've already written for you to read, but there's more, which I'll also bring with me and while you and Freda go through it I'll write down the rest. I think I'll find it easier to do that than to speak it out loud."

After her mother had gone, Joely looked at Freda sitting straight-backed and regal and putting on a good show of indifference to all that had been said. She didn't seem interested in either her ghostwriter's evident injuries, or the part she'd played in bringing them about. She had to know what had happened, but it was as though Joely, having served her purpose, had become nothing more than a finished chapter that probably wouldn't even make it to the main draft.

Feeling the need to ask, Joely said, "Did you expect me to try and climb out of the tower?"

Freda glanced at her and away again.

Definitely a finished chapter.

"Did it ever occur to you," Joely pressed on, "that if I did try, and fell, you could have been charged with murder?"

Freda's only reply was the flutter of a hand with a small puff of breath to accompany the final flick of release.

When Marianne came back into the room she was carrying her laptop and a small blue box tied with a paler blue satin bow. She set both down on the coffee table and after untying the ribbon around the box she removed the lid. Joely realized straightaway what she was seeing inside, and when she glanced at Freda she could tell that Freda understood too.

"These are the letters David wrote me from prison," Marianne said, lifting out a small, lace-tied bundle. She turned to Freda. "I know you loved your brother, so reading his words is probably going to be difficult for you. Some of the things he says . . ." She took a breath. "It's up to you, Freda, if you'd rather just read what I write . . ."

"I'll read the letters," Freda retorted stiffly.

Joely watched her mother's delicate fingers untying the bundle. She could see that there was more in the box, not letters, at least not in prison-issue envelopes, but she didn't ask what it was. Her eyes were transfixed by a small moonstone ring. It had to be the one Sir had bought in Paris, and seeing this physical evidence of her mother's connection to the memoir she'd assisted in was affecting her more deeply than she could ever have imagined.

"They're in date order," Marianne said, her voice conveying how precious the letters were to her. "If you don't mind, Freda, I'd like Joely to read them first. When you've finished one, darling, you can pass it to Freda." As Freda made to object, Marianne stopped her with a look. They were going to do this *her* way now, not Freda's. She handed the small bundle over to Joely and picked up her laptop along with a number of typed pages. "You can began with these," she said, passing them to Joely too. "I shall work at the dining table," and walking around the sofa she pulled out one of the high-back chairs and sat down.

As Marianne started to type, Joely did as asked and turned to the typed pages first. Her mother was right, they weren't an easy read, the devastation of a young girl's world, the betrayal and cruel rejection she'd suffered at the hands of a man she'd trusted and loved. Her dreams had been completely shattered that day when he'd told her about his girlfriend, and in what seemed a bizarre attempt to comfort her, to say a fond farewell to her, he'd tried to force himself on her. However, he'd stopped when he'd realized what was happening, and had only continued when Marianne had refused to let him go.

The lines were so blurred around whether or not it really was rape that Joely hardly knew what to think. Surely it would depend on whether or not penetration had taken place before he'd stopped.

As she read on she realized it must have, for why else would he have accepted his guilt so readily? It might have hardened her heart against him had she not then learned that in order to spare Marianne the ordeal of a trial he'd gone against all the advice to defend himself and pled guilty. Of course, he'd have gone to prison anyway because of her being underage, but how could she, Joely, not feel moved by his decision to protect the girl some would say he'd corrupted, but who he'd clearly loved? And how could she remain unaffected by her mother's regret for the part she'd played in him being locked up for a crime she didn't even feel sure he'd committed?

As she put the pages aside Joely looked at Freda sitting aloof and distracted, as if her thoughts were no longer in the room but in some place distant, too superior for anyone else to join her. At her home in North Devon? Or somewhere so far in the past that today had ceased to exist. How had she reacted, Joely wondered, to the fact that her brother had not been the victim of a teenage girl's vindictive and mendacious revenge? Had she believed it? It was easy to imagine that she hadn't when her whole reason for the memoir, and for being here, had been to force Marianne to admit that she'd lied.

Joely took the first letter, crumpled and flimsy like old-fashioned airmail paper, and saw a photograph was next on the pile. She picked it up—and her heart gave an unexpected contraction of emotion. There he was, Sir, David, the man who'd only lived in her imagination until now. He was young and fair-haired, handsome for sure, though not remarkably so, but there was something about him that made her want to carry on looking at him. He was laughing and she could see why Freda had said at the beginning of the memoir that when he laughed it made others want to join in. The enjoyment of it was infectious even through a photograph, even after all these years. He seemed so alive, so present that it would have been easy to believe the shot had been taken only yesterday.

Joely stared at it, realizing she was feeling jealous in a way and protective of her father in case it had hurt him to know about this man. She'd loved her father so much that she couldn't bear to think of anything hurting him, especially not her mother whom he'd adored. But this had happened before he'd come into Marianne's life, and her mother had already said that he knew everything about David. He'd even read these letters, and Joely couldn't remember ever detecting insecurity or strain in her parents' relationship. Her father had been a very special man, tolerant, understanding, and never unkindly judgmental. He'd brought Jamie up as his own and Joely knew how deeply attached her brother had always been to him.

She continued to look at David and as the ghost of her father receded she began to feel as though this stranger wanted her to know him, that he was here or close by as she read his letters. She'd never felt such a powerful connection to someone who was dead before, and she presumed he was dead since both Freda and her mother spoke about him in the past tense.

Going back to the letter she unfolded it carefully, awkwardly owing to her injuries, and studied the handwriting first, thin and slanted to the right with oddly blunt notes in among the more artful script. This, she thought to herself, is *his* handwriting, these words were composed by him for her mother, and with the photograph right there in front of her it felt bizarrely as though she was actually meeting him.

March 1969

My dear Marianne,

It seems strange to call you by that name, but it is a beautiful name that suits you well. I have spoken it to myself several times and I hear its music as I picture your face. Marianne, Marianne.

I think this letter will surprise you, for I'm sure you must have given up hope of hearing from me by now. My lawyer assures me that he has passed on my messages asking you to forget me and to stop waiting. My sentence is a long one, cherie, and you are still so young. Yet you continue to write.

You say you regret telling your parents what happened between us the last time we were together, but it is I who must bear the burden of my actions. You should have no regrets, Marianne, for what you did was right. I could say that I don't know what came over me that day, but I have had much time to think about it, and I have come to realize something I wish I'd known at the time.

The simplest way to explain what I did is to say that I couldn't bear to let you go, but that makes it far from simple. I was trying to make myself let you go, for your sake much more than my own—by then Dinah meant nothing to me. I wish I'd never told you about her, it was foolish to think that you would accept her presence in my life as a reason for us to say goodbye. When I saw how hurt and confused you were I wanted to comfort you, to tell you what was in my heart, but I knew if I did that I would be unable to stop myself from making love to you. As we know, I was unable to stop myself anyway but once I'd begun and you struggled I told myself that I must let you go. I tried, but it wasn't what either of us wanted so we continued.

311

However we want to look at it now, whatever we tell ourselves, you were in that position because I'd forced you to be, and if I hadn't it wouldn't have happened.

By the time the police came to arrest me I'd already made up my mind that I must pay for what I'd done to you. I didn't want anyone to doubt your word, not even for a minute. You didn't deserve to have your honesty questioned, or to be put through the shattering experience of a trial. I simply couldn't let it happen. There were those who wanted me to fight, my lawyer, and my family who refused to believe I'd done it even when I told them I had.

You have said in your letters that you are in no way traumatized by what I did to you, only by my failure to write. My fear, Marianne, is that the effects will make themselves known at a later date, perhaps when you meet someone else. Please keep this in mind, and if you do feel at any time that something is wrong, you must seek help.

I want you to stop writing to me now. For both our sakes please move on with your life and try to put what we shared behind you. You have so much to offer this world with your beauty and intellect, your passion and your love. Don't let what happened between us hold you back.

David

As she finished reading Joely could feel at least some of what her mother must have felt when she'd first read this long-awaited letter. Relief that he'd finally written, devastated that he was trying to make her let go. He didn't appear to know anything about the pregnancy and her mother must have been almost full term by then. She wondered if he'd ever known about his son, and knew she'd feel heartsick for Jamie if he hadn't.

What was it going to be like for her brother once he knew the whole story?

Joely looked at her mother sitting in her chair, typing into the computer for short bursts and occasionally stopping. Beyond what she was seeing, at a distance too far to reach, was a beautiful young girl of fifteen, sixteen by the time this letter had arrived, sitting or lying on a bed in her parents' home poring over every word of this letter, a hand on her pregnant belly, an unbreakable connection to the man she loved.

Had Jamie been conceived the last time young Marianne and David had been together?

Did it matter when it was apparent that his parents couldn't have loved one another more?

Joely's eyes moved to Freda, whose attention appeared to be fixed on the coffee table in front of her, her hands opening and closing as though itching to hold on to something, or maybe to let it go. How was she going to react to this letter, for surely once she'd read her brother's words she could be in no further doubt about Marianne's story?

Or could she?

This was the worrying thing about Freda: she was as unknowable, as unpredictable as the future.

CHAPTER TWENTY-SIX

As Joely picked up the next letter, she was aware of the deep pain in her shoulder pounding in time with her heartbeat and spreading its ache into her neck and her head. It was draining her, making her feel nauseous again, but she was determined to go on. However, she didn't start reading straightaway; instead she kept a discreet and cautious eye on Freda as the older woman's eyes moved quickly over the pages she was holding.

Joely saw her flinch, and her jaw tightened for a fraction of a second before she appeared to return to the start of the letter. She read it again, more slowly this time, taking in all it was telling her, absorbing it into what she already knew. Someone else's story was trying to erase her own, and her own brother was providing a stronger and more honest voice to the events Freda had presumed to know so well.

Eventually, Freda put the letter aside as if it had meant nothing, changed nothing—maybe she was telling herself it wasn't real. Whatever was in her mind, her eyes were unreadable as she stared at Marianne, who was so engrossed in her task that she seemed to have forgotten anyone else was in the room.

Joely fumbled with the next letter and closed her eyes for a moment as a spasm of pain flared through the break in her shoulder. When eventually it receded, she felt her mind start to clear and as she breathed more freely she began to read.

Oh, Marianne, Marianne,

Why have you not told me this before? Why has no one allowed me to know that I am to be a father? Are my parents aware of this? Why would they keep it from me?

You and I have created a child. I want to write those words a thousand times and shout them out loud in joy and in fear.

Since receiving your letter I have experienced more heartache and longing than I'd ever imagined possible—and most of the time I've been in here those emotions have been my constant companions. There have been many others but those two, along with a love as deep as oceans, are what connect me to you.

Yes, my angel, my heart is as connected to you as you say yours is to me. I have resisted telling you this because I didn't want to tie you to me, to give you hope for a future that cannot be the way you want it to be. We will discuss that another time, but right now all that matters is the baby and how much his or her arrival will mean to us both.

You say you are due to give birth sometime in the next two weeks and it is half-killing me to know that I can't be with you. I am already picturing myself holding it in my arms while you look on and our love wraps itself around the tiny being we have created.

Marianne, my beautiful, perfect angel; my joy and inspiration. Since being in here I have been unable to listen to music in the way we used to, and I have written nothing, but now I know that I can. I shall try to compose a melody for our son or daughter and I'll send it to you so you can play it for them. Do you have a preference, Marianne? Would you like a boy or a girl? I keep asking myself that question, and I find that I don't mind at all. Although I can't help imagining a little girl who looks exactly like you. Even as I write that I can hear you saying that you would like to have a boy who looks like me. (Poor him if he does—ha ha! This is the first time I have laughed in so long that it has taken me by surprise and now I am laughing again. This is what you do to me, my Marianne, you bring light into the darkness, and warmth into the chill of these miserable walls.)

My conscience tells me that I should still be urging you to forget me, to stop my selfishness and free you to find the happiness you and our child deserve. But I find myself unable to do it. I have so many letters from you now and your love for me pours out of every line as sweet as music, and as sincere as each beat of your heart. I treasure each one of them as deeply as I do the memories we share. I read them over and over, picturing you, as you write them, hearing you, smelling you and always loving you. They are my sustenance and solace, Marianne, my blessed escape from these hellish times. Yes, I have tried to stop you from writing them, but for your sake, never for mine.

No, I will not do as you ask and tell you about my life in here, it would be like sprinkling a foul disease into a pool of purity and innocence. The time I spend writing to you and thinking about you is my haven and I will not allow anything in here to taint it.

I am sure you've already considered what having a child will do to your education, and I confess it concerns me a lot. You say your parents have been supportive from the start, that they have never tried to persuade you to give the baby up either in the early days or after it is born. Have you discussed your education with them? Will they continue to support you if you want to take your O and A levels and perhaps go on to university? I know money isn't a problem for them, but it isn't for my family either, so I shall write to my parents today to ask them to do what they can to support their grandchild.

I'm sorry I must end this now, my darling girl, as I have duties to fulfill, and also I want it to get to you as quickly as possible. I am sure it will be read by somebody else before it leaves here, but I don't see any reason for anything to be crossed out, or for it to be withheld.

I hadn't realized until now how freeing it would feel to write to you; holding myself back from you has put me in a prison of another kind altogether. By the next time I write I shall have composed a melody for our baby so I will be able to send that too. I only hope that the censors can read music and don't think the notes are some kind of code.

Please put your hands over the baby and sing Bob Dylan's "Paths of Victory." Or, if you don't feel like singing perhaps you will play a recording of Brahms Symphony No. 3 in F Major. I play this often in my head and remember you as my private ballerina. If you have a piano you could play "Twinkle, Twinkle, Little Star'" and remember how you made me laugh the day you surprised me with it.

How long ago that seems.

A la prochaine, ma Marianne,

David

Joely put the letter aside and reached for the photograph again. There was so much in her mind and in her heart—questions, feelings, all kinds of imaginings—that it wasn't easy to go to any one of them first. She wished Jamie was here so he could read this letter too, could know how joyful his existence had made his father, how it had released a young man from his prison, but of course he would read it, if he wanted to. She'd like to call him now, and tell him to come, but that must be her mother's decision.

She looked up as the door opened and Callum came in with a tray of tea and biscuits. Her stomach rumbled reminding her that all she'd eaten during the past seventy-two hours was the croissant she'd had this morning and a snack bar when they'd stopped at a motorway services for fuel. How could she have forgotten about food when it was normally such a passion for her?

"I thought you might be needing this," he said, carrying the tray to the coffee table.

"Thanks." Joely was hardly able to wait, but as she tried to sit forward a burst of pain made her gasp.

"You need to lie down," Callum told her quietly. "You're still recovering from the fall and you look exhausted."

"I'll be fine once I've had some tea," she assured him. She glanced at her mother and saw that Marianne hadn't even registered Callum coming into the room. She was staring at the laptop screen either searching for the right words to help her continue her story, or so lost in her memories that her fingers had simply stopped trying to convey them.

Freda was already filling the cups, again as if she was the host, and after passing one to Callum to give to Joely she helped herself to another. The third was left on the tray for Callum to take to Marianne.

"Thanks." Marianne murmured so softly it was as though she was afraid that any spoken word would interrupt the flow of those in her head.

Going back to Joely, Callum said, "Can you take any more painkillers yet?"

She nodded. "I think so. They're in the kitchen."

He came back with them and a glass of water and perched on the edge of the coffee table in front of her. As he fed her the pills he said, "I'm worried about you. What you've been through . . . Don't underestimate it. You need to rest."

"I will, don't worry." She allowed her eyes to meet

his and felt a swell of emotion as he held her gaze in spite of her first thought going to Martha. When had he last been in touch with her? What had made him end the relationship? And why was she so close to tears?

Tiredness, she reminded herself, and perhaps some delayed shock.

Realizing Freda was watching them she picked up the second letter and passed it over. None of this was going Freda's way, but at least she was hearing the truth from her brother so she could hardly refute it.

"Andee rang," Callum said softly. "She's tried contacting Edward, the nephew. It seems he's skiing in Switzerland, but she's left messages for him to call you or me asap."

Joely nodded and drank some tea. "Did she say how her mother is?"

"Apparently nothing to worry about."

Feeling Andee's relief, she said, "That's good." She looked at him again and was almost overwhelmed by a longing to go and lie down with him, to fall sleep in his arms and wake up to discover that all that had gone wrong between them was a dream. "Have you heard any more from Holly?" she asked.

"Only that she lost her bag but now she's found it again."

With a smile, Joely said, "Sounds like her."

"Your phone's fully charged," he told her, "do you want it in here?"

Joely thought about it. "Not really," she replied. "If Edward calls I'd rather you took it to explain what's happened."

"Sure. I'm making great inroads with my emails out there," and touching a finger to her cheek, he left.

After Joely had drunk the rest of her tea she gave herself a moment to feel its warmth combining with the painkillers to begin reviving her.

She looked over and saw that Freda was frowning deeply as she read David's second letter, and her mother had begun to type again. Joely wondered what this was all leading to, if Freda would be able to accept that she'd got it wrong about Marianne, if the false narrative she'd constructed for herself was going to feel as though a main character had turned on her to take over the story and leave her . . . where?

Returning to the bundle she opened the next letter and saw that it was dated a month after the last one, so the baby would have been born by now.

My darling Marianne,

Thank you for bringing our beautiful son to meet me; and thank you for letting me choose his name. Are you sure you like James? Or Jamie if you prefer. As I said while you were here I didn't want to name him after a relative or a favorite musician, I want his name to be completely his. I'm sorry I forgot to laugh when you suggested we call him Wolfgang in honor of Mozart, I was so overcome by him and by you that I seemed to lose a sense of everything else.

I didn't think it was possible for you to be even more beautiful than I remembered, but you are. Perhaps it's being a mother that has given you a deeper and more captivating radiance. I'm sure it is. I wish my family would agree to get to know you, they would understand then why I love you so much. They make me ashamed for the way they are turning their backs on their grandson—they are refusing to believe he is mine, but I know that he is. It is their loss and one I am sure they will come to regret.

All the time you were here you talked about our son's little ways and how they made you think of me, and as I watched you laugh and pout and kiss him I kept thinking of how wrong it was for you to be somewhere like this. It's no place for a baby, or for you, my darling girl. I know you must have heard the shouts and jeers, the awful things that were said and I need to protect you from that.

You have made me the happiest man in the world, don't ever be in any doubt of that, but now I have to ask you not to come again. This isn't how I want to get to know my son, nor is it how I want him to get to know me. We must create wholesome and beautiful memories for him untainted by images of his father in prison.

I know you are going to find this hard, Marianne, but I have decided for your sake, and for our son's, not to send you any more visiting orders. Please understand my reasons, and please know that it is only because I love you so much that I am doing this.

If you continue to write I will, of course, write back and I will always cherish any news of our son, but I want you to think about this carefully. There is a wonderful and fascinating world out there for you to explore, one full of opportunities *and hope, and so very different to the one I am in. I want to think of you embracing that world, taking all it has to offer and showing it all to James. I don't want to picture you sitting at home writing to me, or taking long train journeys to this dreary part of our country to snatch an hour where we can.*

Please think about this with your head and not your heart, Marianne, and try to put what's best for Jamie first, and any time spent here will never be good for him. Or for you.

Tonight I shall fall asleep thinking of you in Paris and how happy we were there. I noticed you were wearing our ring when you came. Do you remember we chose it because the moonstone symbolizes love?

David

As Joely read through the next few letters it soon became apparent that Marianne had persuaded him to change his mind about visiting. In fact, she'd clearly made her way to Dartmouth with the baby at least once a month for the next several months, and seeing her and his son became, in David's words, "the focus of my world, the reason to live."

It surprised Joely to realize that her grandmother often drove Marianne all the way there and waited in the car for the single hour allowed for young Jamie to get to know his father. It was also her grandparents who'd paid for Jamie's care while they worked and Marianne continued with her studies.

The letters were moving in so many ways, including

their humor, which, though infrequent, was made all the more touching for its rarity. It mostly came in the form of a tease for something Marianne had once said, or done, or in a prideful boast about his "magnificent son." From the way he wrote commenting at length on something she'd told him, or answering her questions carefully and honestly, it was easy to imagine Marianne's letters to him. What he never told her anything about was his life inside the prison. It was only possible to gauge something of it from his assurances that the bruising on his face, or his loss of weight, or his sadness were nothing for Marianne to worry about.

His disappointment and anger at his family for the way they continued to refuse to meet their grandson, or communicate in any way with Marianne and her parents, was almost palpable from the words he used. And his pride and relief that Marianne had achieved no less than eight O levels—a year late because of pregnancy—mattered as much to him, it seemed, as the miraculous emergence of Jamie's first tooth.

He sent lists of songs and symphonies for her to listen to and play to their son, and told her how much he loved the way she wrote out the lyrics of his favorite ballads so he could hear them "inside the shell of quiet I create for myself." They exchanged poems, many by Keats and Shelley, and when Marianne sent him Elizabeth Barrett Browning's "How I Love Thee" he said it had moved him to tears. He thanked her over and over for the photographs she sent of Jamie—until suddenly, surprisingly, he asked her not to send any more. There was no explanation, and Joely wondered if other inmates had mocked or even destroyed those he already had.

After that the tone of his letters began to change, there was more sadness in them than there had been before, more concern for the way her contact with him must be holding her back, and for how his prison record was going to affect their future if they tried to build a life together.

> *I know this is hard for you to read, my love, and it's hard for me to write, but my record will always show me as a convicted sexual deviant, worse a child sexual deviant, and that isn't what I want for you and our son.*

It was apparent that Marianne had written straight back to tell him that they would change their names and move to America or Australia where no one knew them, because in his next letter he asked her to listen to "California Dreamin'." They could be safe and warm in LA.

However, by the end of that same letter he was sounding sad again, and even querulous as he feared for the kind of man he would be by the time "this hellish experience is over."

> *There is a lot of hate for me in here because of the kind of crime I committed. Even the warders despise me.*

After that the letters ran out and as Joely looked over to her mother she was already afraid that she knew why. Marianne had stopped typing now and was sitting with her head in her hands.

Going to her Joely put a soothing hand on her back and leaned in to rest a cheek on her head. Freda shouldn't have made her mother do this, she had no right to; it was time for her to leave.

"No," Marianne protested quietly as Joely asked Freda to go. "She needs to read what I've written, you both do," and getting to her feet she carried the laptop out of the room.

Realizing she'd gone to the printer, Joely looked at Freda, who hadn't spoken in so long it might have been easy to forget she was there. The letters she'd read were piled loosely on the table in front of her, but the thoughts, the feelings, the memories they'd engendered were packed so tightly inside her it was impossible to know what they were. Surely none were good for there was no doubt now that her family had not behaved kindly, or even honorably, toward Marianne or Jamie. Nor could she begin to question her brother's devotion to "the love of his life" as he'd frequently described Marianne, and their son.

Joely said, "According to those letters your mother went to visit him several times so she must have known how he felt about—" She stopped abruptly as Freda's arm rose to cut her off.

"You have no right to discuss my mother, or my father," she snapped. "We have not yet heard the whole story."

CHAPTER TWENTY-SEVEN

When Marianne came back to the room she was carrying two sets of printed pages and her laptop. She handed a set each to Joely and Freda and returned to her seat at the dining table. She didn't speak or even look at them; she simply sat quietly staring at nothing, putting Joely in mind of a defendant awaiting a verdict.

When Joely looked at the pages she saw they'd been typed in the same font Freda had insisted on for the memoir. She wondered if her mother had simply continued to use the settings because they were already there, or if she'd chosen it deliberately in order to give Freda the end for her story.

I am becoming increasingly worried about David. The depression that has come over him in recent weeks is deepening and I don't know how to help him. When I saw him last weekend he was hardly able to speak to me, and every time he looked at me I could feel the sadness inside him as though it were mine. It was mine, because that's how it is with us, we share all of our feelings, our hearts, our minds are, as he has said himself, as one.

I talked to Mummy about my fears so she asked Daddy to contact the prison to report our concerns. He was told that the matter would be looked into, but none of us really knew what that meant. Daddy said he'd talk to some other people he knows to find out if it's possible for David to be moved elsewhere, but we're still waiting for news on that.

I haven't received any letters this week, so to keep us going I've been playing Jamie the lullabies and ditties his Daddy has composed for him. I don't suppose I'll ever be a great pianist, but David keeps it very simple so I don't have much trouble following the notes. It's clear that Jamie loves the tunes; they even distract him when his gums are hurting, and sometimes, when I stop, he fusses until I start again.

I love being a mother as much as I love David. I don't care that I'm only sixteen and there are still many years to wait before David can be with us. What matters is that he will be with us one day. It's all we want, to be together.

Daddy received a call from the prison this morning to tell us that David hanged himself last night.

I could hardly take the words in, but I know I screamed and screamed because Mummy kept telling me I'd frighten the baby. I couldn't stop; I wanted to go to him, to bring him back to us, to tell him that it'll be all right. It's all my fault, I know that, if it weren't for me he'd never have gone to prison and I'll never, ever be able to forgive myself.

I know if it weren't for our beautiful son that I would do the same right now so I could be with him. I don't know how I'm going to carry on without him. I keep seeing him in the classroom laughing and blushing as we teased him, playing his guitar and encouraging us to sing. I see him driving his car with me beside him, chasing me around the garden at his uncle's cottage, the awe and passion in his eyes as we explored Paris and deepened our love for each other. I can't bear to think of him being somewhere I can't see or touch him now, where I can't hear him anymore or inhale the essence of him. I am so full of his and my despair that I'm unable to speak or move or even nurse our little son.

As the hours pass and my grief deepens beyond all bearing I come to the decision that no matter what I must go to him. I can't let him be alone in whatever place he is now. My parents will care for Jamie, he'll never want for anything, they already love him as if he were their own.

I am still thinking these thoughts, making plans, writing notes, talking to David in my mind telling him I'm coming, when his letter arrives.

My darling Marianne,

By now you will know that we won't be seeing each other again in this life. I am sorry, my angel, but this is the only way I can see to set us both free. I know we have shared many dreams, and for the past months they have been the only light in my darkness, but I cannot let you carry on believing it's possible for us to have a future together. I want you to find happiness and love with someone who is not tainted in the way I am—not only by reputation, but by the things that have been done to me in here. I am sorry,

Marianne, but I can take no more of the violence and degradation. Knowing what I have suffered. what I, as a deviant, have been forced to do, makes me ashamed to see you.

I know you will always love and take care of our son and I hope that one day you will be able to tell him about me in a way that captures only the beautiful memories we share. I thank God for them. They and your letters and visits have done so much to transport me from this hell. Yesterday, someone found the letters and destroyed them—I would prefer not to tell you how—but they also took Jamie's photos and I have no idea what has happened to them.

I am going to say goodbye to you in two ways, my darling, the first is with music, of course. Do you remember the song I once told you encapsulated everything I feel about you? I didn't play it for you enough, maybe you'll say I played it too much. I've been unable to record it myself, but along with the words that I am going to put in with this letter, you will find the name of an artiste I believe sings it very well. It is a song all about first times—the first time I saw your face, the first time I kissed you, the first time that I lay with you, and how I felt our joy filling the earth and knew it would last until the end of time.

The second way is through the poem you sent me. As beautiful and perfect a poem as it is, I have changed it to help me tell you what I most want you to know.

How do I love you? Let me count the ways
I love you to the depth and breadth and
  height
My soul can reach . . .
I love you freely,
I love you purely,
I love you with the breath,
Smiles, tears, of all my life; and I believe
With all my heart that I shall love you
Even more after death.

  Thank you, my darling, for the happiness you
have given me, and thank you with all my heart
for our beloved son. Fly now, beautiful Marianne,
live your life and know that my spirit will always
fly with you.
  David

Joely was too blinded by tears to read any further, but she could see there was more, just a few lines as though penned by the sixteen-year-old Marianne.

It's all my fault. I know that. I will never be able to escape it. If I live to be a hundred I will never stop loving him, and I will never be able to forgive myself. If I hadn't told he would never have gone to prison, then no one would have abused him and made his life so intolerable that he chose to end it like this.

  It's all my fault.
  It's all my fault.
  It's all my fault.

"Yes," Freda said, her voice cutting so sharply through the silence it made Joely start. "It is your fault."

Joely looked at her, then at her mother. Marianne's face was ashen, her eyes bright with tears.

"He would still be alive if it weren't for you," Freda declared, her tone full of contempt. "My brother, my talented, beautiful brother, who had his whole life ahead of him, would not have died in that pit of a prison if you hadn't sent him there."

Marianne didn't try to defend herself, but before Joely could speak on her behalf, Freda was saying, "There is no one else to blame. You, Marianne, are as responsible for his death as if you'd stabbed him through the heart or pushed him from a cliff. *You* are the moth that was drawn to the irresistible light that was him, but instead of burning to death as you should have done you extinguished him."

Marianne started to speak, but Freda hadn't finished: "You tore the very soul out of my family; did you know that? Did you even care? My mother never sang again after David's arrest, and she died only a year later of a broken heart. My father turned to alcohol and spent the next three years drinking himself to death. That, Marianne, is what you and your lies did to my family."

"I know it was my fault," Marianne said softly, "I accept that, but everything I've written down for you is the truth."

"And you think that makes it all right? You think that because you still have his letters, because he loved you that . . ."

"Nothing is all right," Marianne cried brokenly. "That's not what I'm trying to say. Of course I blame myself. You have my confession right there and I've never sought to deny it."

"Yet you've continued to live your life as if he never existed. You married someone else when David's son was only four years old. That was how long it took you to find another man. That's how brokenhearted you were and I don't suppose for a minute that you've ever told your son about his real father."

"Yes, I have!" Marianne shouted. "He knows everything. He *and* my husband have even read those letters."

Joely hid her shock; this was no time for it. "Perhaps," she said to Freda, "if your parents had agreed to meet their grandson . . ."

"How could they meet him without *her* being there, and believe me they had no desire to meet her."

"Yes, they proved that," Marianne broke in, "when they refused to let me come to the funeral."

"They didn't want you there. Nobody did. When does a murderer ever get invited to the funeral of their victim?"

As Marianne flinched, Joely cried, "For God's sake, Freda, in case you've forgotten, it takes two to have an affair, and your brother was twenty-five, an adult, a teacher, someone in a position of responsibility, so we should be saying that he took advantage of her. In fact, I don't think any of us can deny that he did, no matter how genuine his feelings might have been. He was weak, he shouldn't have given in to how he felt . . ."

"Ask her if she knows where he is?" Freda cut in shrilly. "Ask her why she's never bothered to find out where he's buried? Because she's never cared, th—"

"I know exactly where he is," Marianne told her. "I've

always known and I visit him. My husband used to come with me when he was alive, but now I go alone."

As stunned as Freda apparently was, Joely struggled to take it in. Her parents had visited the grave of a man her mother had loved and her father had never even known? It proved, of course, that her mother had never stopped caring, or loving, and it told her yet again what an exceptional person her father had been. He'd have gone to support his wife, to try and help her to make peace with herself and to pay respects to his adopted son's natural father. It was the kind of man he was, selfless, nonjudgmental, and a complete stranger to jealousy or any other petty feelings that could so easily corrode a person as well as a relationship.

Swallowing her emotion, Joely said what she felt sure her father would if he were here, "This all happened so long ago, Freda, that you must surely see that it's time now to let it go."

Still looking at Marianne, Freda's eyes glittered with something close to hate as she said, "Maybe I could if it had ended with David's death, or the deaths of my parents, but it didn't, did it, Marianne? You couldn't leave my family alone."

Joely looked at her mother and saw she was as confused as she was.

"What are you talking about?" Marianne asked. "I've never had anything to do with your family since David went. You've said yourself—"

"You know exactly what I'm talking about it," Freda cut in savagely. "I should have known right away it was you. He was besotted with you, he couldn't think about anything else . . ."

"Freda, who are you talking about?"

She wasn't listening. "He'd always been fascinated by the story of David's love affair, ever since he first heard about it he kept asking to hear more. It shouldn't have surprised me when he went looking for you, but fool that I am, it never crossed my mind that he would. And then he found you and just like David he fell in love with you. It was as if I stopped existing. Our marriage no longer meant anything to him; there was only you. He had to have you, he was obsessed, but you didn't want him."

Marianne was regarding her aghast. "Freda . . . I . . . This is all in your mind . . ."

"*I know it was you.* He told me. He said, "I under-stand David's passion, because she's bewitched me too. I must have her. I can't live without her.""

Marianne was still in shock. "There was someone," she said, "a few years ago. He was a stal—" She corrected herself. "I never saw him, but I knew he was watching me, following me even. He sent notes, flowers . . . In the end my husband got me to arrange a meeting with him and he went in my place. After that I never saw or heard from him again . . ."

"His name was Doddoe," Freda told her icily. "That's what everyone called him, but really it was David. Another David."

Joely regarded them in amazement and in a way awe as she considered how something that had amounted to little more than an incident, or inconvenience in her mother's world, dismissed and forgotten until now, had led to such a profound and devastating turning point in Freda's life.

"Another David," Freda repeated with scorn. "What is it about—?"

"Freda, you've got to stop this now," Joely told her firmly. "My mother had nothing to do with what happened to your husband . . ."

"*She's* who he and my brother were discussing when they took the boat out, *she's* who Christopher was trying to protect my marriage from, so if it weren't for her the accident would never have happened." Her eyes were still boring into Marianne. "And you sit there now making out like you had no idea—"

"I swear I didn't," Marianne put in hastily. "He never even spoke to me. Maybe it wasn't your husband. We could be talking about somebody else. I'm sure we are . . ."

Freda was shaking her head, clearly not prepared to listen.

Deciding it might be a good idea for Callum to come in now, Joely struggled to her feet.

"Where are you going?" Marianne and Freda asked together.

Thinking fast, Joely said, "I need more painkillers." Except she couldn't leave her mother alone with Freda, the woman was building herself up to such a pitch there was no knowing what she might do.

She was about to call out for Callum when Freda stood up too.

Joely's eyes followed her as she walked over to Marianne. It was as though time had become strangely slow as Marianne looked up and Freda leaned over to whisper in her ear—except she wasn't whispering, she was sobbing and her hands were going to Marianne's neck.

Joely threw herself forward and screamed for Callum. With her right hand she managed to shove Freda off balance. Marianne leapt up in shock and Freda clasped her hands to her face.

"What the hell?" Callum cried, running into the room.

Freda began wailing, wrenching, awful sounds coming from the desperate, tortured heart of her. She gulped and sobbed, bared her teeth and screamed as Marianne grabbed her by the shoulders.

Freda's head fell back as she howled "No!" at the ceiling.

Marianne tightened her hold, trying to draw her in.

Freda sank to her knees and Marianne went down with her holding her close as if she were a child, arms around her, shoulder supporting her head as it shook and jerked with the might of her grief. She began struggling for breath, her whole body convulsed with the enormity of her heartache and Marianne continued to hold her.

Still watching them, Joely left Callum's side and went to kneel beside them. It was hard to join in the embrace with only one arm, but she could stroke Freda's back and her mother's hair and do her best to wipe away their tears. She wondered what the ghosts of those they wept for would think if they could see them now. In an odd way she felt they were there, and that one of them, David, had brought Freda here, to the very last place she'd thought to find comfort, when in truth it was probably the only place.

CHAPTER TWENTY-EIGHT

Joely could feel herself rising from the depths of sleep, slowly, steadily through a gluey mist, not yet ready to open her eyes, but she was almost there. She couldn't think where she was, but she was lying on a bed and every part of her body hurt like hell.

"Hey you," a voice said softly.

It was Callum.

She opened her eyes.

He smiled and brushed his fingers over her cheek.

She gazed at him, taking in the silver threads in his disheveled dark hair, a couple more in his eyebrows, and the black flecks in his indigo eyes. His face was so familiar and so reassuring that she almost didn't care where she was. She found he was gazing at her too, and at the same time they both smiled.

It was as if her memory was still sleeping for she was struggling to remember everything clearly, but she sensed something awry between them, something that needed to be resolved. Maybe it had been and she hadn't yet remembered. "Are we OK?" she asked, and felt her heart tighten in anticipation of his answer.

His eyes softened more deeply into hers as he said, "You tell me. Are we OK?"

It was starting to come back, but not fully. "I hope so," she whispered. "I think we need to talk."

"Of course, but not right now."

She looked past him and realized she was in one of her mother's guest rooms. She had a faint recollection of Callum insisting she come to lie down, and no idea how long she'd slept, only that she'd felt more exhausted before he'd brought her here than she ever had in her life. Pain, drugs, emotion, had all taken their toll.

Looking at him again, she found herself thinking of all the reasons she loved him, and tears blurred her eyes. There were so many, and she wanted to tell him, but as her thoughts began to clear making way for Martha and everything else she held the words back.

She was remembering now what had happened before he'd brought her upstairs, the harrowing scene with Freda as she'd broken down so wretchedly and the way Marianne had comforted her. Where were they now?

"Your mother's downstairs talking to Jamie on the phone," Callum replied when she asked, "and Freda's in the other guest room resting. I've heard from her nephew, Edward. He's on his way back, but probably won't get here until tomorrow."

She thought of Edward on the ski slopes, tanned face and brilliant blue eyes. She pictured him hurriedly booking a return flight, and explaining to his friends why he had to go. "What did you tell him?"

"I gave him a brief outline of what I know. He was pretty upset to hear about what happened to you, and he's very worried about her. Did you know that she's had a breakdown before, presuming that's what happened here?"

Joely nodded. "Yes, he told me when he came to visit her. It was just after her husband and brother died."

339

Her eyes closed again as more pain throbbed through her left side. She tried to fathom how she felt about the secret her mother and brother had kept from her, but David hadn't been her father, so why would they have shared it with her? Perhaps her own father had cautioned against it, concerned that she would feel protective of him, and she would have.

"Is Holly back yet?" she asked.

Wryly, Callum said, "We're to expect her when we see her, and we're not to worry about her because she won't be worrying about us."

Joely smiled and rolled her eyes. "She's definitely her own person," she commented softly. She'd like to go back to sleep now with Callum lying next to her and nothing to keep them apart, but she was too concerned about her mother, and Freda, to stay here any longer. "What time is it?" she asked, as he helped her up.

"Just after seven. Are you hungry? You must be. I'll order a Deliveroo after I've helped you to dress."

Realizing she was wearing only the sweatshirt Andee had loaned her, and a pair of pink cotton panties and socks, she said, "Did you undress me?"

His mouth crooked in a smile as he said, "Only your trainers and jeans. There's clean underwear in the bag over there. Would you like to change?"

Yes, she would, but could she manage with one hand?

She found that she could, but he helped her anyway, and when her jeans were zipped and trainer laces tied he tilted her face up to his. "I'm still not sure why it started to go wrong between us," he said softly, "but I want you to know that I never stopped loving you."

Thinking of what she had to tell him, and of how

hurt she'd been when he'd left her for Martha, she said, "We have a lot to talk about, but it's good to know that, because I never stopped loving you either."

By the time they got downstairs Marianne had finished on the phone and was with Freda in the sitting room, their hands wrapped around each other's as they sat side by side talking softly. They looked up as Joely and Callum came in and Joely saw straightaway how drained, even shattered, both women looked.

"Did you have a good sleep?" Marianne asked.

Joely nodded. "Callum's going to order in some food. I thought Jak's?"

Marianne nodded. "There's a menu in the kitchen."

Callum fetched it and after everyone, including Freda, had made a selection, he went off to place the call while Joely, seeing that David's letters were still on the table, began to fold them carefully back into a bundle and retie the lace.

Freda's eyes were following her every move. "You say your son has seen them?" she said to Marianne, sounding baffled and tired and so different to the way she had before.

Marianne nodded. "After his first child was born he wanted to know about his father so my husband and I invited him to come here for a weekend. We thought it was better to do it with no one else around and I think Jamie was grateful for that."

Freda audibly swallowed. "Did he . . . What did . . . ?" She seemed unsure of what to ask next, but then the words came. "Did you tell him good things about his father?"

Marianne smiled. "There are only good things to say about David."

Freda's gaze remained fixed on the letters. "But not about his father's family?" she said.

Marianne's eyes flicked to Joely as she said, "I won't deny that he was angry about the way things had gone when he was born—"

"—and that none of us have ever tried to contact him since? Yes, I can understand that. We should have, of course. I wanted to, many times, but I was afraid to. I thought . . . I couldn't imagine that you'd welcome my interest after we'd neglected you, and him, for so long." Her head went down and her voice was barely more than a thread as she said, "Then, when I realized my husband had found you . . ."

"I swear I didn't know it was him," Marianne said gently.

Freda's mouth flattened into a painful line. "I told Joely that he was like David in his ways, but all they really shared was a love of music and a name. David would never have behaved the way Doddoe did, but I kept hoping and praying that one day he would be like my brother, full of kindness and loyalty, humor and romance, but that day didn't come." She took a breath and continued to look at David's letters as she said, "Spurning Doddoe would have been what inflamed his passion to its height and turned it into an obsession. He was like that, anyone or anything he couldn't have he saw as a challenge. He had to win, and he usually did. But you say you got your husband to send him away . . ." Her eyes closed. "Of course it made him want you all the more, so much that he told me I needed to prepare myself because it would soon be over between us. He'd never said that before so I took him at his word. I needed to find out who it was . . ." Her voice trailed away and as she looked down at their joined hands it was as though she had no idea how hers had got there.

Joely wondered what she was thinking now, if she was really as rational in her mind as she was sounding. It was hard to believe that one single explosion of emotion had been enough to settle the chaos and confusion inside her, but she really did seem calmer and strangely comforted by the contact with Marianne.

"I've spent the past hour on the phone to Jamie," Marianne told her, "and he's coming to meet you. He should be here sometime tomorrow."

Freda looked fleetingly scared, as though she might back away from this, but her voice was steady as she said, "Can I ask what you've told him about me?"

With another glance at Joely, Marianne said, "Nothing you wouldn't want me to tell him."

Realizing her mother was hoping she'd do the same, keeping to herself the way Freda had used and tricked her and come close to causing her death, Joely gave a small nod and slipped the letters into the box. There was nothing to be gained from telling Jamie any of that right now, but she knew she would one day, when the time was right.

There were only Marianne's typed pages on the table now, and as Joely picked them up Freda said, "Did I get it right?"

Joely frowned in confusion.

"The memoir," Freda explained, half turning to

Marianne. "Did I get right the way you met and fell for each other, and all that happened between you? He told me a lot when I went to see him, so I knew then how much he loved you, but you were so young; I couldn't make myself accept that you were capable of feeling the same way." She sighed shakily. "I truly believed you'd lied in spite of what he told me."

"You've captured our story well," Marianne told her. "Maybe a few things are wrong, but nothing that matters."

"The music?"

"A lot of it was right. I guess he told you about that too?"

Freda nodded. "Most of it. Some of it I added because it seemed to fit for the time and for what I knew of him and his tastes. What about the music you liked? How did I do with that?"

Marianne smiled. "I remember very well how us girls got carried away by 'Young Girl' when it came out, thinking it was about us . . . It had a powerful effect on me, and it did on David too."

Freda nodded. "Yes, he told me about that, but I didn't know about 'The First Time Ever I Saw Your Face.'"

Marianne took a breath and Joely could tell that she was recalling, even feeling, what the song had meant to her back then. "He wasn't to know," Marianne said, "that it would become a big hit right after he died. He never heard Roberta Flack sing it, but for the months, years after he'd gone, I never seemed to hear anything else. It was always on the radio or playing on someone's stereo and it kept breaking my heart, over and over again."

"Do you think he'd have liked that version?" Freda asked.

"Yes I do, but I'll always prefer the one he sang."

Freda smiled and nodded, apparently liking that.

Joely turned around as Callum came into the room.

"Food should be here in half an hour," he told them. "Can I get anyone a drink?"

"What would you like?" Marianne asked Freda.

Freda looked at Joely. "Shall we have some wine?" she asked, as if unable to make the decision for herself.

Though still thrown by the change in her client—if she was indeed still that—Joely managed a smile as she said, "Good idea. Red or white?"

"You choose."

Opting for the white, Joely was about to go and give Callum a hand when the front door opened and closed. Moments after, Holly came into the room, eyes glued to her phone, only glancing up briefly to see who was there. "Hey, Freds," she said cheerily. "What's up? You look kind of, you know."

Freds? Joely looked in astonishment at Freda as the older woman said, "I'm all right, Holly, thank you. How are you?"

"Yeah, cool, thanks." At last she looked up from the phone. "Wow, Mum, you've got a sling and everything, and check out those bruises. Looks like you lost." She laughed, clearly thinking her little quip funny.

Taking her by the elbow Joely steered her out to the kitchen, and closed the door as Callum joined them. "Freds?" she repeated to Holly, needing that answered right away.

Holly shrugged. "She didn't seem to mind. Is she OK? She looks a bit upset."

"She's had . . . a difficult day, but she's fine now, and yes, I am too, thanks for asking."

Holly leaned forward to plant a kiss on her mother's cheek. "I could do better than that," she said, "but I don't want to crush your arm. Does it hurt?"

"Quite a bit. So tell me about Freda."

With another shrug, Holly said, "She's kind of weird, isn't she? She seriously spooked me when I looked up from my breakfast and saw her holding a knife like she was going to stab me. I honestly thought she was going to, but it turned out she was just putting it back in the block. I believed her, but I still reckon she did it to get a rise out of me.

"Anyway, we had a long chat after, and let me tell you, she's got so much grief and loneliness going on it's not surprising she's weird. I felt really sorry for her. I even offered to cancel going out with Caitlin and the others to keep her company till you guys arrived, but she said she's used to being on her own so there was no need to."

Joely looked at Callum, who was opening the wine and appearing equally as amused as amazed. One relatively short conversation with a woman decades older than her and Holly had the reasons behind her mental instability sussed. Not that Joely and her mother hadn't worked out what was going on, obviously they had, but for Holly to have got there so quickly . . . "What exactly did she tell you?" Joely asked carefully.

Holly began texting as she spoke. "About how everyone in her family is dead apart from her nephews—

one she never sees, and the other is so busy he can't get down to her place very often. Actually, I think she liked having you there, Mum, and she's obviously really sorry about you ending up being locked in the house."

Joely turned to Callum again.

Shrugging, he reached into a cupboard for glasses. "We've got a delivery on the way from Jak's," he told Holly, "are you going to eat with us?"

"Deffo. I'm starving. Are we staying here tonight, or going home?"

Callum looked at Joely.

Wishing they could go home, if only so she could use their bathroom and sleep in her own bed, Joely reluctantly said, "I think we need to find out what Freda's doing first. Did she stay here last night?" she asked Holly.

"Yeah. She slept in the front guest room and wow, does she snore."

"Does she have anything with her? Clothes, toiletries?"

Holly shrugged. "Not that I saw." Down went the phone again. "Anyway, so what's with you two?" she demanded. "Have you got everything sorted out yet, because it's been kind of stressy living with you since Grandpa died, Mum, and I've worked out now that it's all about grief, just like it is with Freds, but you've got to snap out of it. It's doing my head in, and Dad's."

Joely stared at her hard. "Since when did you get to be the psychologist in the family?" she wanted to know.

Holly hadn't finished, although it was Callum's turn for the daughterly treatment now. "Just as well I moved over to Martha's with you," she informed him, "or you might have ended up staying there. Like I was really going to let that happen. But what were you thinking, Dad? I mean, Martha's OK, but she's not Mum. You've got a lot of making up to do, I can tell you that much, or have you already forgiven him?"

Joely wasn't sure whether she wanted to laugh or not, though Callum didn't seem in any doubt.

"Come here," he said to Holly, and pulling her into his arms he gave her one of his best dad-hugs.

Holly's eyes met Joely's over his shoulder and she mouthed, "How am I doing?"

Not knowing what else to do, Joely gave her a thumbs-up.

Holly's grin widened. "I totally love you guys," she informed them, "and I just know you're going to love Noel when you meet him."

Callum started. "Noel?" he repeated.

"My boyfriend. I've been seeing him for a couple of months, but I didn't want to bring him home while you two were messing each other up. If you can promise me you've stopped I'll invite him over as soon as you like."

Because she had to, Joely said, "How old is he?"

Holly's eyes narrowed playfully. "Don't worry, I'm not taking after Grandma in that. He's only twenty-four."

Joely wanted to faint, until she realized she was being wound up.

"He's seventeen," Holly informed her, "and if you want to know whether or not we've done it yet . . ."

"You better not have," Callum broke in sternly.

"You're only fifteen," Joely added.

"Still not like Grandma," Holly grinned, and giving them a little wave she left them to pour the wine.

"Did that really just happen?" Joely asked as Callum stared at the closed door.

"I think so," he replied.

"And we created her?"

"She's very much like you."

Joely's eyes narrowed and he quickly said, "In that I find her impossible not to love."

Joely laughed, and looked at the ceiling as Holly's heavy tread reached the landing. One of these days, she was thinking, she might get to have the same sort of relationship with Holly as she had with her mother, a lot of affection, easy friendship, and sharing, although she didn't see it happening soon. However, maybe they were heading in the right direction.

"I think she's right about your father," Callum said, loading up a tray with four glasses and a bowl of nuts. "I hadn't really seen it before she said it to me the other day."

Joely nodded. "Yes, she is," she confirmed, "although not quite in the way she thinks. Anyway, let's take that through."

When they reached the sitting room they found Marianne tying the ribbon around her memory box and no sign of Freda. "Where is she?" Joely asked.

Marianne looked puzzled. "I thought she came out to speak to you."

Joely glanced at Callum.

"Well, she has to be around here somewhere," he said. "She's probably gone to the bathroom." He passed Marianne a glass and another to Joely. "I guess we should wait for her to come back before I propose a toast."

Several minutes passed and when there was still no sign of Freda Joely began to get an uneasy feeling fluttering about her insides. That woman was nothing if not unpredictable, and she definitely wasn't stable, so what was going on now? "Do you think we should go and look for her?" she asked Callum.

"Yes, we should," her mother replied. "She's obviously not in the kitchen, so I'll try the TV room and you can stay here while Callum checks upstairs. Don't argue, you've lost all your color again so you need to sit down."

Minutes later Joely was with her mother in the hall as Callum came down the stairs. "She's not up there and Holly hasn't seen her," he told them.

Noticing her coat was still on the rack Joely said, "She can't have left, so she has to be here somewhere." Still feeling uneasy about this, she turned to her mother in time to see Marianne's eyes widen with shock. Following their direction Joely experienced a jolt of alarm.

Freda was standing at the top of the stairs, unmoving, and appearing to be unseeing.

Callum ran back up to take her by the hand. "Are you OK?" he asked her gently.

She looked at him and blinked as though not sure who he was.

"Come on," he said, "let's go back downstairs."

Allowing him to guide her, Freda took the stairs slowly and as she and Callum passed her in the hall Joely felt her heartbeat start to slow. What was wrong with her? Why did she look so zombified? And where had she been?

"I went to your bathroom," she replied when Marianne asked.

No one asked why when there were others in the house, even one en suite to her guest room; they simply clinked one another's glasses and decided to do without a toast.

It was as Joely took a first sip that her eyes met Freda's again and she saw that the glazed look had gone. In its place was a glimmer of something that might have been . . . humor? "If I'm correct," Freda said quietly, "you have just jumped to a conclusion about where I was. I won't ask what it was, but I know it was wrong." She raised her glass. "Presumptions," she murmured half under her breath. "Remember what I've told you about them, Joely, and yet you keep on doing it," and lifting her glass she drank the wine as if it were water.

CHAPTER TWENTY-NINE

Edward arrived shortly after eleven the following morning, looking as though he'd skied straight in from the slopes in his dove gray down-filled jacket, black woolen hat, and wraparound reflective glasses. Callum let him in, helped stow his luggage in the hall, and took him through to the kitchen where Joely and her mother were preparing lunch.

Seeing how uncharacteristically harried he looked, Joely went straight to embrace him with her one good arm. "We were afraid it was going to turn into something more serious," she told him, "but she seems calm enough. I think it'll help her to see you, though."

"Are you all right?" he asked, his blue eyes searching the injuries to her face with evident concern. "When I think what might have happened to you . . ."

"I'm OK," Joely assured him, aware of Callum watching them. "Nothing that won't heal."

"I owe you an enormous apology," he said. "If I'd had any idea she was going to do what she did . . ."

"It's not your fault," Joely told him gently. "Now let me introduce you. Callum, my husband, you've just met, and this is my mother, Marianne."

Taking Marianne's hand in both of his, Edward said, "I'm not aware of the whole story yet, but I do know that I need to apologize to you too . . ."

"No, really you don't," Marianne assured him with a smile. "I'm only glad you're here. Holly, my grand-daughter, has taken Freda to pick up the things she left at a hotel; they should be back an time now. Can we get you a coffee?"

"That would be great, thanks. And I'm sorry about my bags cluttering up your hall. I came straight here."

"Let me take your coat," Joely offered, admiring the expensive ski jacket and amused by his ruffled hair as he tugged off the hat and sunglasses.

Marianne took it all, while Callum brought over a coffee. "Milk and sugar on the island there," he directed.

"Black is great," Edward replied, and gratefully perched on the high stool Joely had maneuvered out for him. "I have to be honest," he said, "I'm still trying to get my head around everything Callum told me yesterday. I mean, I knew I had an uncle who'd died young, and I'm pretty sure I knew it was suicide, but no one ever really talked about it, at least not to me." He took a sip from the steaming mug and turned to Marianne. "I had no idea she was still so affected by David's death," he said, "although I guess it was the shock of losing my father and Doddoe a few years ago that stirred it all up again. She took that really hard; I've already told Joely about the breakdown she suffered afterward. She had treatment, of course, but when she came back from the clinic she shut herself up in that house and didn't come out for weeks, months even. It got better, after a while she ventured into town or out for walks, and when she started writing again I felt sure she was turning a corner." He shook his head in dismay. "How wrong I was, and you, Joely, got dragged into it . . . I understand now why she was so insistent that you were her ghostwriter. She obviously had it all worked out, or she thought she did anyway."

Understanding how baffling and even embarrassing this all was for him, Joely reached out to squeeze his hand.

Treating her to a grateful smile, he turned to Marianne again. "I guess the only good part of this is finding out that I have a cousin."

Marianne smiled as she nodded. "James, Jamie, is on his way over from Dublin. I think he'll be glad to have you here when he meets his aunt for the first time."

With feeling he said, "You mean his crazy aunt, given what's happened, so I'm glad to be here. At least he'll be able to see that there's one sane guy in the family. And actually, she shouldn't have to do it alone. I know you're all supporting her, which is pretty amazing I have to say, considering what she's put you through. There aren't many people who'd want to help her after that, but she definitely needs help even if she won't admit it. And I'm not only talking about her mental condition . . ." He eyes went to Joely. "I'm guessing she still hasn't told you about the cancer?"

Joely's eyes widened. "No, she hasn't, but I thought there might be something . . ."

"She swore me to secrecy," he said, "or I'd have told you before. She didn't want anyone to know, and frankly, I thought you'd finish your project with her and be gone before it became serious so there was no reason for you to know. She probably won't thank me for telling you now, but after all that's happened . . . Please don't think I'm using it to try and make excuses for her; she's always been an unusual person, eccentric, a bit bonkers even, but I hadn't realized quite how far she could go."

Marianne said, "What kind of cancer is it?"

"Follicular lymphoma. She was diagnosed about a year ago, and actually, she doesn't seem to have been too troubled by it so far. She takes medication, and has to go for regular checks, but mainly it makes her tired and sometimes light-headed."

"So how serious it is?" Joely asked, feeling a sense of care given that there were so few people in Freda's world.

He shook his head as he sighed. "The last time I spoke to her doctor he told me she needed to start accepting more treatment and at the moment she's not agreeing to it."

They all looked around at the sound of the front door opening, and as Freda's laugh carried along the hall, Edward said quietly, "Please don't mention . . ."

"Of course not," Marianne assured him.

Getting to his feet he held out his arms as his aunt came into the kitchen and Joely couldn't help feeling touched by how pleased she was to see him.

"Have I spoiled your holiday?" she asked as he hugged her.

"Completely," he assured her.

She chuckled and pulled back to look at him. "I've caused a lot of bother, I'm afraid . . ."

"Bother?" he cried. "Is this your new line in under-statements?"

She blinked and as a wave of sadness seemed to go through her she let her head fall forward onto his chest. "I miss them all so much," she said quietly, "sometimes it gets too hard."

"You've still got me," he reminded her.

"And me," Holly put in. To Edward she said, "Hi, I'm Holly, Freds's new BFF."

Freda looked up, sadness retreating. "Best friend forever," she explained to her nephew, "just in case you didn't know."

Keeping an arm around her he shook Holly's hand. "Thanks for taking care of her," he said.

Holly shrugged. "She's cool. Weird, but cool."

Freda said, "She has no idea just how weird I can be, but we can save it for later."

"I don't think we need any more demonstrations," he cautioned.

Taking the coffee Callum was handing her, she regarded him closely as she said, "You're better looking than I was expecting you to be. Have I already told you that?"

Clearly quite pleased with the compliment, he said, "You didn't, but it's OK to mention it."

"Oh God," Holly groaned, "you need to work on your taste in men, Freds."

"Do I? I'll be guided by you."

Laughing, Edward said to Joely, "So it seems we're kind of related?" His tone was ironic, but there was a tinge of regret that amused her for the way it made Callum scowl.

"It would seem so," she replied. "I haven't actually worked out how . . ."

"You," Holly told her, "are his cousin once removed, which," she said to Edward, "makes you my uncle once removed and Freds my great-aunt with nothing removed, because we say so."

As everyone laughed, Callum's phone rang. Seeing who it was he said, "Seems like your other uncle's just arrived in a taxi, and he only has euros. Now there's a surprise."

As Joely watched her brother come into the kitchen all long limbs, tousled fair hair, and merry, but cautious sea blue eyes, she saw straightaway how like Edward he was, apart from the coloring, and could have kicked herself for not realizing sooner that he, Jamie, was who Edward reminded her of.

She noticed Edward curl an arm around Freda's shoulders as Jamie greeted his mother, the bond they shared as evident as the pleasure at seeing each other. He came to Joely next, careful not to treat her to one of his more boisterous squeezes, but putting a hand gently to her cheek as he gazed at her. "I've seen you looking better," he decided, making her smile.

Not to be left out Holly pushed herself forward and was all but swept off her feet in the fiercest of uncle hugs.

"You get more beautiful every time I see you," he told her, "and so tall."

"I'm the same as Grandma now," she informed him proudly, "although she might be shrinking."

"Charming," Marianne muttered, rolling her eyes, and as Callum stepped forward to remove Holly from the limelight, Marianne took Jamie's hand in hers. "This is your cousin, Edward, and your aunt, Freda," she told him, her eyes unexpectedly welling with tears.

Edward stepped forward to shake his cousin's hand, and as the two men regarded each other with interest Joely couldn't help wondering if they recognized the

357

features they shared. "It's good to meet you, Jamie," Edward said warmly. "I confess it's a surprise, but no less welcome for that."

"It's good to meet you too." Jamie smiled, still holding Edward's hand, or Edward was still holding his. Whatever, neither of them seemed in a hurry to let go. "Likewise with the surprise," Jamie said in the droll tone Joely loved so much. "I'm looking forward to getting to know you."

"That can definitely be arranged," Edward assured him. He turned to Freda and as he pulled her in gently Joely knew from the look in her eyes that she wasn't seeing a nephew, she was searching for David. She raised her hands to his face and cupped it tenderly.

"You're like him," she murmured. "Not as much as I expected, but enough for me to see him in you."

"From everything I've heard," Jamie said, "he was a pretty special bloke."

Freda nodded. "I'm sorry you never met him."

"I did when I was a baby," he reminded her.

"But you've forgotten that. It mattered to him though. He didn't turn his back on you the way the rest of us did. I'm ashamed, Jamie, for myself, my parents . . ."

"Don't be," he told her. "These things happen."

Her hands were still on his face and noticing how they'd begun to shake, Joely said softly, "Why don't you all go through and sit down while Callum and I finish making lunch?"

After they'd left the kitchen Joely sank onto one of the barstools and reached for Callum's hand.

"Seems I came back in the nick of time," he commented wryly.

Understanding what he meant she broke into a smile. "If he weren't a relative," she teased.

"I don't think any blood's involved, is it?" he pondered.

"Ah, so I could be free to pursue things?"

"No," he replied without hesitation, "not free at all."

It was gone five by the time they'd all eaten and drunk too much wine around the dining table, and though Freda was quieter than the others she seemed to be enjoying watching Jamie—and Marianne. Joely couldn't help wondering what she was thinking, and smiled to herself as she imagined Freda warning her about second-guessing and jumping to conclusions. Still, it had to be about David, surely, and perhaps where they would all go from here.

She and Callum left without any fuss, they'd see everyone again tomorrow, although Holly had school in the morning so she'd be coming home by taxi later.

As Callum drove them through the darkening streets toward Notting Hill they talked about those they'd left at Marianne's and where everyone might stay that night. Jamie, it was agreed, would take over the guest room Joely had vacated, and maybe Freda would remain in hers—or perhaps Edward would take her home with him. It wasn't important; it was simply a way of filling the time until they arrived home.

The instant Joely walked through the glossy blue front door of their late Regency home she felt herself sinking into the familiar smells and warmth of the place and could hardly believe how long it seemed since she'd last been here. She breathed it in deeply as if it were a tonic, and watched the hall come to life as Callum turned on the lights. It was strangely as though she'd been told she'd never come home again, and yet here she was. Everything was exactly as she'd left it and she couldn't think why that surprised her. She allowed Callum to help her off with her jacket and scarf and as he draped it with his own on the coat stand behind the door she looked around. The stairs with their intricate fretwork banister and railings rose up into the darkness of the landing, the paintings collected during holidays and rummages around flea markets created large splashes of color on the teal green walls. She could remember where they'd found each one and probably, at a push, how much they'd paid for it.

"Drink?" Callum offered, starting for the kitchen.

Since she'd only had half a glass of wine with lunch she decided she could indulge in another without causing too potent a mix with the painkillers, so she said, "A sauvignon blanc, if there is any."

"Coming up."

As she joined him in the kitchen with its cluttered, countrified air and double French doors leading onto the large wooden deck she felt as though time was concertinaing weeks into hours. Once again there were all their familiar things, Joely's array of scented candles on the dresser, their favored cards slotted among china and colored bottles, jokes, photos, and drawings magnetized to the fridge, bags for life on their usual hook, Callum's trainers beside the back door, next to her gardening shoes. She noticed a stack of mail on the table, addressed to her, along with a polling card for the local elections, and the navy cardigan she'd left over the back of a chair was still there. Her eyes moved to

Callum's usual pile of newspapers in front of the place he always sat, and on to Holly's makeup bag spilling over her personalized placemat.

If it weren't for the calendar showing the change of month she might never have been away.

"Here," Callum said, handing her a glass of wine in one of the crystal glasses they usually saved for special occasions, "welcome home." Actually, it was a special occasion, she decided, considering that when she'd left she hadn't expected him to be here when she got back.

"Maybe I should be saying the same to you?" She smiled.

Though his eyes smiled back she could sense the undercurrent of his concerns as clearly as she could sense her own. They were alone now, there was much to be faced, and though she knew they loved each other, and wanted to be together, neither of them could say yet how much damage had been done. Of course they would want to repair it, she was certain he was as committed to that as she was, but she had still to tell him what she'd been holding back from him. Would he feel so committed then? They had deeply wronged each other and though they might want to forgive, she knew that betrayal could act like a slow-growing cancer on a marriage, eating away at the heart of it until it could no longer survive.

"Are you up to talking now?" he asked, regarding her closely. "You look pretty tired and I've already told them I won't be at work tomorrow."

She was tired, and the pain each time she moved seemed to be getting worse rather than better, but she wasn't going to allow herself to put this off any longer.

"Let's at least start talking now," she said, pulling out a chair to sit down. It didn't ease the throbbing in her shoulder, but it was good to get off her feet. She wondered fleetingly if the discomfort was going to make it hard to think straight, but since she was OK for the moment she watched him sit down and said, "There's something I should have told you a while ago. I wanted to . . . Actually that's not true, I didn't want to. I hoped you'd never have to know, but keeping it from you is, I know, what caused things to go wrong between us. I was so scared, so worried . . . I could hardly make myself look at you, or speak to you . . . I wanted to shut you out, or shut myself away . . ."

"Joely," he said softly, "you're not making much sense."

Aware that she wasn't she stared down at her glass and saw in its reflection everything she'd never wanted to see again, the bar, the faces, the stairs, the many rooms, the taxi, the search for her handbag, her phone . . .

"Why were you scared?" he prompted.

Deciding that the only way to do this was to come right out with it, she braced herself and said, "I slept with someone. I mean, I had sex with him. I don't know his name, it only happened once, but it happened and I've hardly been able to live with myself since. I know to some people that might not seem a big deal, but it was to me. I became terrified that I might have caught something, or what if I was pregnant? What would I say to you? I couldn't let you think it was yours if it might not be. I wouldn't be able to give it up . . ."

"Were you pregnant?" he asked.

She shook her head. "No! But I still couldn't live

with the fact that I'd done it, that I'd brought something like it into our home." Seeing his eyes widen she rushed on, "Not right inside, it didn't happen here, please don't think that, but the shame was in me, the knowledge that I was capable of being that sort of person. I couldn't tell you about it. I didn't want you to feel ashamed too, or disgusted, or tainted even." She pressed a hand to her head as the irrational panic of that time spread through her again. "He could have killed me," she cried, "or followed me and threatened Holly. Anything could have happened, and I kept thinking that it would. Every time the phone rang, or someone knocked on the door I was terrified it might be him. It never was, I don't think he has any idea where I live; he probably doesn't know my name either, but I couldn't be sure of that." She stopped, not wanting to go any further, even though she knew she'd have to.

"Can you be sure of it now?" he asked quietly.

She nodded and shook her head. "I think so. Yes . . . I . . ."

"How long ago did it happen?"

"It was about six weeks after Dad died. Do you remember you had to go to Glasgow for a conference, and Holly stayed with Mum while I had a night out with my agent and a few of his other clients. We went for something to eat at the Ivy and afterward a few of us carried on to Soho House. I got so drunk . . . I'm not sure how much I had, but it seemed to affect me much more than it usually does. I was out of control. I hardly even knew where I was, much less what I was doing."

"And that's where you met him?"

"I know you're thinking it could be someone you know, but I don't think it was. He never mentioned you and nor did I."

His expression remained grim as he regarded her. "So what happened exactly?" he asked.

Her eyes closed as she flashed on the where and how, the crazed groping on a sofa in the club, the taxi to a hotel, the room, the bed, clothes all over the floor, her lost handbag, and phone . . . "Please don't make me go into the details," she groaned. "It's hard enough telling you this much, and it didn't mean anything. Nothing at all."

He didn't press her, and she realized he was probably no keener to know the intimate minutiae than she was to describe it. "Does anyone else know about it?" he asked.

"I don't think so. My agent might have seen me flirting with him, but the others all left before I did. I swear to God I don't know what came over me. It was like all my boundaries just disappeared . . . I wasn't thinking about anything or anyone. I . . . I . . ." She halted not knowing what else to say that she wanted to put into words, or that he'd want to hear.

"So where did it happen?" he asked. "You say it wasn't here, so where was it?"

Another flash to the hauntingly decadent image of it. "Does it matter?" she countered.

"I don't know, you tell me."

She shook her head. "It doesn't," she replied with feeling. "I swear it doesn't."

He picked up his glass and took a large mouthful of the pale gold-colored wine. Seconds ticked by, drifting like a chill wind over the potential of how destructive this could be, fracturing the trust they'd always taken for granted. She was capable of being someone he didn't know, someone who'd cheapen herself after too much to drink and how could he be sure she wouldn't do it again? For all he knew she could have been fulfilling some long-held fantasy and now she'd had a taste of it . . . Of course she could remind him of what he'd done with Martha, that he'd broken the sanctity of their marriage too, but she knew in her heart that it wouldn't have happened if she hadn't pushed him away the way she had.

In the end he said, "So let me get this straight, you stopped sleeping with me because you'd had sex with a stranger?"

She nodded. "But it wasn't only the sex—"

His hand went up. "If that's all that happened you could, you *should* have told me. Is it all that happened?"

"Yes, apart from being afraid of a disease, a pregnancy . . ."

"You didn't see him again, or try to find out who he was?"

"No! All I wanted was to forget him, and try to carry on as though it hadn't happened, but I couldn't. My conscience wouldn't let me. I hated myself for what I'd done, I felt so sick of myself, every time I looked in the mirror, or saw you looking at me . . . It was *there*. It wouldn't let me go."

"You should have told me," he said darkly. "You know me, I'd have understood and tried to help you. I was aware of how much you were struggling with your father's death . . ."

365

"I can't use that as an excuse," she cried. "I know you're going to say that my emotions were all over the place and they were, and drinking so much obviously didn't help . . . It was like I was trying to blot it all out, but I can't, I won't blame it on my father."

"Not on him," Callum corrected, "on the way you were reacting to losing him. Like you said, your emotions were running high, your boundaries—"

"I don't want to tie the two together," she protested. "It's like I'm dishonoring his memory . . ."

"Joely, stop. You of all people know how grief can affect a person, how different, even crazy it can make someone. For heaven's sake, isn't that what these last weeks with Freda have all been about? She doesn't have an exclusive on it, you know?"

Joely inhaled a sob and reached for her glass. She didn't drink; she said, "According to Edward, Freda's always been odd. I don't think we can say that about me."

"But like anyone else when they're under stress you're capable of acting out of character. You had one incident, a serious one, it's true, but it's not something that we can allow to become more important than it is. We have to put it behind us, Joely. Do you think you can do that?"

She wanted to, more than anything, and now she'd told him . . .

Without waiting for an answer he said, "I should have realized something like it had happened. You've never gone cold on me like that before, and so soon after Lionel's death . . . But I'm always so busy and I kept thinking you'd get over the loss eventually."

"I did," she insisted. "I mean, actually I don't think

I ever will, because no one does when you've loved someone so much and they've been such a big part of your life, but I definitely started to find it easier to deal with than what I'd done."

"And then what did I do? I turned to your best friend for advice on our marriage and look how well that went."

She inwardly winced.

He went to fetch more wine and refilled his glass. "As I see it," he said, sitting down again, "the greater crime here is mine, by a long way, although I should come clean about this: moving in with Martha was always meant to be temporary. It was an idea that she had—and I went along with—to try and bring you to your senses. She thought if I left you you'd fight to make me stay and somehow this would sort things out between us."

Joely blinked incredulously.

"I know, I know," he groaned, "I can hear how ridiculous that sounds now I'm saying it, but I was at my wits' end and frankly I was prepared to try anything if I thought it would bring us back together."

"So you allowed her to manipulate you, to trick you . . . I hope you realize that that's what she did . . ."

"Of course I do, why do you think I came back as soon as I did? I should never have gone, obviously, but even you have to admit that we couldn't have gone on the way we were."

She wouldn't argue with that, because he was right, but for him to have fallen for Martha's blatantly self-serving answer to his problem when he'd always known she had designs on him was still hard to credit. In the end she said, "So did you sleep with her?"

He didn't meet her eyes as he nodded.

"And not just once?"

"No, not just once, but maybe we can agree that details aren't going to help the situation now."

No, they wouldn't, and realizing she didn't want them any more than he did she said, "Can I take it it's over between you now?"

It was his turn to look incredulous. "Do you think I'd be sitting here if it weren't? Like I said, the plan was always for me to go there for a few days and come back here as soon as you went off on assignment."

She regarded him steadily. "But you slept with her."

He couldn't deny it, and she could see the shame and regret burning in his eyes. Perhaps it was a reflection of what was in hers, except he hadn't been drunk, nor had he just suffered a painful bereavement. He'd been struggling to save his marriage and in so doing had slept with another woman. There was no logic to it, no excusing it either.

"And the romantic weekend away that you didn't invite Holly to?" she asked.

"It never happened, and it was never going to. I told Holly we were going away so she wouldn't be around while I told Martha that I'd made a terrible mistake and that there was never going to be anything between us."

Joely's heart remained hard. "Have you heard from her since?"

Sighing, he pushed his phone across the table. "She's texted a few times, but only to find out if I've made things up with you. You can read the messages if you like."

Not touching the phone, she said, "That sounds as

though she's still living in hope that we might not make it."

He appeared genuinely surprised. "Why? I don't understand—"

"Maybe you need to be a woman to see through that sort of artifice."

Still appearing vaguely perplexed, he said, "All I can tell you is that I made it pretty clear that I was going to do everything in my power to try and make things work with you, but even if I didn't succeed I wouldn't be going back to her."

Joely nodded slowly, imagining how Martha must have felt when he'd told her that, and how she was probably feeling now. It was hard to believe that her best friend had created such a devious and desperate plan to try and steal her husband. She must surely have known it would never work, and yet on some level she'd clearly believed that it would. And indeed for a while it must have looked as though things were going her way.

"So," he said softly, "do you think we can get through this?"

As her eyes went to his she felt her emotions shifting and falling into all the places they belonged, and yet some remained trapped in the cracks that had inevitably opened up between them. She thought of Freda and how so many betrayals followed by forgiveness had devastated her over and over again, but Callum wasn't that sort of a man. In the end she said, "I don't think we'd be sitting here talking like this if we weren't ready to try, do you?"

He smiled and she sensed the relief going through him.

Reaching a hand across the table for hers he entwined their fingers and said, "Is this the point where we ask if we can forgive each other for what we've done?"

She glanced down at their hands and back to his eyes. "I think we can both forgive," she said, "but I don't think we'll ever forget."

He shook his head. "I don't suppose we will, but maybe we can make that a good thing. It'll remind us of where we could end up if we don't talk to each other."

Liking his answer she pulled on his hand and as he got up to come around to her side of the table she tried to stand too.

Helping her up, he held her against him and put his mouth very close to hers. "We can continue this tomorrow if you like, but right now I think I need to take you to bed."

"Yes," she replied softly, "you really do."

CHAPTER THIRTY

It became clear over the following few days that no one was going to allow Freda to return to Dimmett House alone. Though she insisted she'd be fine and ordered everyone to stop fussing, Edward was having none of it, and nor was Jamie. Both nephews were ready to drive her, and probably both would have gone had Marianne not stepped in to inform them that *she* was going to do it. No one listened to Freda as she grumbled and objected, although it was plain to see how moved she was by so much determination to care for her. Eventually, it was decided that Jamie and Marianne would take her, and Edward would join them at the weekend, and when Freda finally agreed she had tears in her eyes.

"I spoke to the darling wife earlier," Jamie told Joely and Callum when they dropped around to Marianne's to wish everyone a bon voyage. "She's going to bring the kids over on Friday so Freda can meet them, and we were thinking it would be a nice idea if you guys could make it down to Devon too."

Joely and Callum exchanged glances. "Sure we can do that," Callum told him, his eyes still on Joely's, showing his understanding that Dimmett House might not be a place she wanted to revisit anytime soon. "We just have to check what Holly's doing . . ."

Susan Lewis

"She's already said she'll come," Freda informed them as she joined them at the car. "I've told her she can bring her boyfriend, Noel. Have you met him yet? A very nice lad, apart from his bizarre use of language. He says things are sick or bad when he means quite the opposite. Still at least Holly seems to understand him, and I suppose that's what counts."

Interested in this, Joely said, "When did you meet him?"

"Oh, they've called in a couple of times since Sunday," Freda replied, popping her handbag onto the back seat of the car. "So it looks as though you've forgiven him," she commented to Joely as if Callum were no longer there and she was free to speak. "I'm not sure it's a good idea; it never really worked for me, all that forgiveness. I should have told Doddoe years ago that I'd had enough. If I'd been a stronger woman I might have, and then he might still be alive." She pondered that for a moment, and said, "Yes, it's only strong women who have it in them to tell their cheating husbands they're no longer required." Her eyes darted to Callum before returning to Joely. "Think about that," she advised sternly.

Knowing Callum was bristling and almost wanting to laugh, Joely said, "There's more to the story than you know."

Freda nodded curtly. "Isn't there always?" and pulling Joely to one side she said, quietly, "You know I didn't mean for you to be in the tower for more than a day, don't you?"

"Actually, no, I didn't know that," Joely informed her.

Freda frowned. "Really? Well, it was my intention to

372

get the truth out of your mother and return again the same day, or maybe the next morning. As we know it didn't work out quite like that, which is a lesson to me not to presume I know what's going to happen."

Joely's eyebrows rose. Freda chastising herself for presumptions, this was a first. "And the music?" she asked curiously.

Freda shrugged. "I thought it would keep you company," and treating Callum to a baleful look she got into the car. "I hope you've snuffed out the moth that flew into your flame," she told him bossily.

Before Callum could respond, if he even knew how to respond, Marianne called out from the doorstep. "What are you two doing here? I thought you had an appointment at the hospital this morning, Joely?"

"We're on our way," Joely replied, going to embrace her mother as best she could. "We've just been hearing how Freda's invited everyone for the weekend."

"Or we're foisting ourselves on her. Whichever way, she's definitely not going back there alone so I've called the office to let them know I won't be in for the rest of the week, and Jamie's done the same. Did he tell you Clare and the children are flying over on Friday after school?"

"He did, and apparently you've all met Holly's boyfriend who's also joining the weekend party."

"Yes, isn't that lovely? Wait till you see him, he's quite a dish, although Holly nearly gagged when I used that word. She informs me I should have said ripped, which opened up an interesting discussion with Freda. Anyway, do say that you can make it as well. It sounds like such a beautiful place. I know you don't have the best memories of it, darling, but with us all there maybe you could create some new ones?"

Just like that. Her imprisonment and death-defying escape dismissed.

"The kids are counting on seeing you," Jamie added as he came to collect his mother's case. "And Clare's already talking about picnics and walks and horseback riding."

"Don't forget the funicular," Freda called out. "Everyone should ride it, shouldn't they, Joely?"

How could she disagree with that?

Minutes later, after Jamie had promised to call when they reached their destination, Joely and Callum stood on the pavement watching Marianne's Lexus, with Jamie at the wheel, turning out of the street.

"So no mention of the fact that she tried to kill you?" Callum muttered drily.

"Amazing, isn't it?" Joely responded, still feeling faintly dazed by the last few minutes. "Although I don't think she sees it that way. In fact I know she doesn't. She's moved on, edited it out, rewritten it . . . She has so much else to focus on now, a long-lost nephew and his family, a teenage BFF with a boyfriend, and a new soul mate, Marianne. I'm not even sure you and I really fit in, and as for the memoir . . ." She turned to look up at him and said, "I guess one thing we can say for certain, it's going to have a very different ending now to the one she imagined when she set out."

His eyebrows arched. "In anyone else's hands I might be intrigued to find out where it goes," he replied. "In hers I'm thinking about upping the life insurance."

*

It was around midday on Saturday when Callum turned the car into the driveway of Dimmett House and as Joely suspected he might, he gave a low whistle of appreciation. It really was an impressive place, especially with all the shutters open and early spring sunshine bathing the white walls.

He brought the car to a stop and as Joely looked at the house she could feel the horror of her imprisonment in the tower tightening her chest. It seemed both distant and frighteningly real. She'd known that coming back wouldn't be easy, she'd had sleepless nights about it all week, but she was here now and, she reminded herself with clenched hands, things had moved on. Freda had changed, many of her family were already inside, there would be no locking her in again, or any danger of her falling to her death.

"Oh wow!" Holly exclaimed, coming awake in the back seat. "This is totally *awesome*." She pushed open the car door and tumbled out to stretch her long limbs in all directions after the drive. Noel, the boyfriend, did the same, exposing a well-toned midriff to the chill spring air and a large strip of boxer shorts above the waistband of his drainpipe jeans.

Callum turned to Joely. "Are you OK?" he asked, clearly realizing she might not be. He'd been there for the sleepless nights, and had listened as she'd relived those terrifying minutes as though trying to exorcise them.

"I think so," she replied, adjusting her sling. This new one was purple, created from foam and cut specially to fit her injured arm and shoulder, while doing nothing to improve mobility or alleviate pain. "We're here now, so we should go in."

He looked along the drive to where Holly and Noel were joshing with each other as they walked to the house and on across the impressive façade to the gleaming, vine-covered tower. "Jesus Christ," he muttered taking in the height of it and the reality of the boulders below.

"The wisteria's starting to bud," Joely commented evenly. "It's going to look beautiful by the end of the month." Spotting her mother coming out of the front door to greet Holly and Noel she felt a truly strange shift in the world.

Her mother was in Freda's house.

Putting the car back into gear, Callum said, "Only you and Marianne could do something like this. You might have been killed trying to get out of this place, and yet here you both are taking care of the woman who—"

"We have to try and put it behind us," Joely broke in. "She needs us now, she always did, I guess, she just didn't go about approaching us in a very good way." She could see Freda now, opening the window of her writing room and stepping out onto the balcony to wave hello. *Surreal,* Joely was thinking as she waved back, *completely and totally surreal.*

With an incredulous sigh, Callum drove on up to the house and parked next to Marianne's Lexus.

"Where's Jamie?" Joely asked as her mother came to embrace her. Marianne now seemed to have taken over the role of hostess in Freda's house, just as Freda had assumed it in Marianne's.

This could all be a dream.

"He and Clare have taken the children to ride the funicular," Marianne replied, giving Callum a hug. "We've arranged to meet them at the Rising Sun for a late lunch if you're feeling up to it. Andee and her mother are joining us. They'll obviously want to see you."

Joely winced as a bolt of pain shot through her arm, "We can't leave Freda here while we all go out," she objected. "Is Brenda around?"

"She left half an hour ago, and Freda's thinking about coming with us. Holly and Noel have gone to turn the thoughts into action."

Of course they have.

"Where shall I put the bags?" Callum asked, opening the car boot.

"Dump them in the hall for now," Marianne replied. "We can take them upstairs later. You're back in the room you were in before," she informed Joely, "Edward's next door with his new girlfriend, Amanda. She's very nice, by the way, I think you'll like her. The rest of us have taken over the rooms on the top floor."

The mysterious top floor that apparently contained no mystery at all.

"I hope you haven't put Holly and Noel in together," Joely said quickly.

Marianne treated her to a scolding look. "She's fifteen," she declared. "As if I would."

Joely's eyes widened, but Marianne was already going inside to continue her hostess duties.

"She said that with no irony at all," she muttered to Callum, hardly able to believe it, but he was busy unloading the car.

Much later in the day, after a rowdy and delicious lunch at the pub, Joely and Jamie decided to walk back to

Dimmett House while the others either traveled by car, or remained in Lynmouth to watch the tide washing up over the twin beaches to flood the tiny harbor.

"OK, so how are you?" Joely asked, finally able to link an arm through her brother's for a private chat as they took their seats on the funicular to ride up to Lynton.

"It's me who should be asking you that question," he countered, nodding toward her sling.

"It'll heal," she replied. "I'm wondering how you feel about everything now you know more about your father and his family."

He cocked an eyebrow as he inhaled deeply and gazed at the gray, sun-burnished channel spreading out before them. His fair hair was being tossed about by the wind, and the new, close-shaved beard that she hadn't seen before last week suited him well. He'd always been a looker, and age was actually improving him. "I'll always think of Dad as my father," he said, squeezing her arm against him. "That's never going to change, but I'm glad to know more about David." He grimaced. "Glad" might not be the right word, but I'm sure you get what I mean."

"Of course." And as the small green carriage glided to a halt at its clifftop station, she stepped out ahead of him.

"Are you sure you're all right to do this walk?" he asked, as they started for the coastal path and he offered her his arm again.

"It won't take us long, less than an hour, and it's the best chance we have of being on our own. So, back to David—and Mum. I realize now you've heard it before, but what do you think of their story?"

ᵉᵉᵉᵉᵉᵉᵉᵉᵉᵉᵉᵉᵉᵉᵉᵉ

He gave a quiet laugh. "I guess I like it. We all want our parents to love each other, don't we, and it seems they did. Tragic though, him taking his own life like that."

Joely let a moment pass, sensing there were far deeper emotions stirring within him than he wanted to discuss.

After a while he said, "Does it sound odd to say that I felt it physically when I read it? It was like a connection that came alive inside me . . ." He grimaced awkwardly. "I'm not great with words, as you know, but it was like it had always been there without me knowing it and when I read how he died I felt it coming to life. It meant something; more than something, it meant a lot. That's kind of strange, don't you think, when I never knew him."

"Not strange, no," Joely replied softly. "Just inexplicable in the way connections and feelings often are, but it doesn't make them any less real."

He pondered that for a moment and said, "There's been a lot for me to process since the time Mum and Dad showed me the letters, but I'm doing pretty well with it, I'd say. What concerns me more right now is the way Freda got you to write the story. What the heck was that all about?"

Joely inhaled deeply and let it go in a laugh. "You're asking me to understand how Freda's mind works, and that is way beyond my powers of amateur analysis. She's different, that's for sure, 'unusual' is what Edward calls her . . ."

"And dangerous?" He seemed genuinely worried, possibly in case it was genetic.

"I honestly don't think intentionally, but she certainly

gets a kick out of mind games. You've been here all week, so how are you getting along with her?"

He didn't hesitate about that. "Pretty well, on the whole, but she keeps calling me David, which is definitely weird because I reckon she's doing it on purpose."

Joely had to smile. "Yes, that sounds like her. Do you think you'll stay in touch with her now?"

"For sure. She's my aunt, after all, and I get the feeling it would mean a lot to her, to Edward too, if I did. How about you? Will you stay in touch now that the memoir's done? I guess it is done, is it?"

Having no other answer to offer, Joely said, "It's a good question. I mean, it's not actually her story to tell, is it, so it's hard to know what she'll do with it now. As far as staying in touch with her goes, yes, I'm sure I will. We don't know how much longer she's got and the last thing any of us would want is to leave her to die alone."

Jamie said, "Ah, well that's definitely not going to happen. No one's had time to tell you yet, but Mum has now taken a sabbatical from her job so she can be here to ferry Freda back and forth for her treatments. What's more, over lunch I heard Andee's mother, Maureen, say that she was happy to help out if Mum needed any backup. So, it doesn't sound as though my batty aunt's last days—if they are her last days—are going to be spent bereft of family. My guess is we'll all be visiting a lot more often than we might think." He stopped and turned toward the view, pulling Joely in close to him so he could tilt his head to rest it on hers.

Realizing he might be talked out on a personal level for the moment, she gazed out at the perpetually moving waves with him and thought of all the different types of love there were. Right now, for her, the one she felt for her brother was the most important, but she understood that just like a tide it would yield to others, Callum, or Holly, or Marianne, or even Freda, when it mattered, and it made no one of them any less important than the other.

After a while he said, "We haven't talked about you and Callum, but as he's here I'm guessing you've sorted things out?"

Joely said, "For now, yes. For good, I hope, but let me ask you this, did you see how well he got along with Edward's partner, Amanda, over lunch? Before, I might not even have noticed it, or I certainly wouldn't have thought anything of it, but now . . . Well, I guess that's what happens when trust isn't holding you together the way it used to. Suspicion and doubt sneak in through the cracks and before you know it even innocent scenarios are turned into something they aren't." She didn't add that she was afraid it might be the same for Callum going forward, watching her with other men, but it probably would be, how could it not?

"It'll get better," Jamie assured her. "It takes time, that's all."

"You're sounding like Mum now."

"Or Dad. It's what he said to me when Clare and I ran into problems."

Joely turned to him in confusion. "You never said . . ."

"I didn't want anyone to know. Dad only found out because Clare told him. I don't think he ever confided in Mum, because she's never mentioned it."

"So you . . . ? Did you meet someone else?"

"No, Clare did, but she came back and now . . . In some ways it's better than ever. In others it's different, but we live with it and if one of us gets worried we talk about it."

Still stunned that she hadn't known any of this, Joely said, "But surely she doesn't have any reason not to trust you?"

He smiled. "I don't think that's the point. Now she knows how easy it is to meet someone else even when you're not looking, she's afraid it'll happen to me."

"Oh God," Joely groaned, and dropped her head against him not wanting to think about how corrosive mistrust and insecurity could be.

Eventually they turned to walk on, moving into single file as the path became more of a ledge until they joined hands to climb over a stony mount into the Valley of Rocks.

"Wow," he murmured, taking in the spectacular dry bowl between the moor and the sea. "It's kind of other-worldly, don't you think?" He frowned. "What's that noise?"

Joely pointed to a handful of goats clambering up the hillside. "It's their hooves clattering on the stones," she explained and took out her phone as it bleeped with a text. She was expecting it to be Callum or Holly, possibly her mother.

It was Freda.

Where are you? Please try to get back before I die. I have more to tell you.

CHAPTER THIRTY-ONE

"So, Joely," Freda said, her voice hoarse and seeming almost to float from her throat as it carried words into the warm air as if they were fledgling butterflies, "we are coming to the denouement—you know that means ending, I'm sure—and I imagine you have leapt to many conclusions by now." She smiled to herself, as though enjoying the unraveling of her thoughts, or secrets, or games, it was never possible to know exactly what was going on with her.

They were seated on the kitchen patio, enjoying the earthy scents of the meadow following a short burst of rain, and listening to the birds shrieking and twittering about the tor and soaring down to the sea. Several months had passed since Freda had sent the text summoning Joely back to Dimmett House because she had more to tell; spring had flowed and bloomed into summer, and her home had become a regular weekend retreat for most of her family, as she now termed them. True to character, she'd kept Joely waiting for details, toying with her, testing her, and occasionally, when the pain was at its worst, berating her for impatience and presumptions when none had been made.

Often she was too exhausted by her treatments to talk, or even to get out of bed to enjoy her visitors, but in between times she'd do her best to join in whatever was going on. If Jamie was around, and he and his family usually were, she spent many nostalgic hours showing him photographs of his father as a young boy. She didn't have a natural way with the children, often regarding them as if she'd forgotten who they were, but for some reason they found her fascinating and she certainly seemed to enjoy watching them romping through the meadow down to the beach. She liked to watch them wrestling with their father too, and when her gift for grim and ghoulish stories was discovered her rapt audience of two begged her to take over the bedtime routine. If she was well enough she usually obliged, but only if she wasn't in the tower writing, though exactly what she was writing nobody knew.

"I'm not going to get better," she croaked, gazing out toward the sea and cliffs dazzled into a blur by the afternoon sunshine, "so it's time for you all to stop pretending I will. I've already refused further treatment—it's doing no good so I received no resistance from the doctors. Marianne knows this, and now I'm telling you because I have a final request to make of you."

Joely inwardly balked at the use of final; of course she knew Freda was dying, but she hadn't been prepared for her to bring it up like this.

She waited, certain the request was going to be in some way related to the memoir—or perhaps it was connected to whatever Freda had been writing these past few months. They could be one and the same thing.

Freda's profile remained turned away, sharp-boned and papery thin skin against a backdrop of the gray granite rocks rising up behind her. "I want you to help me on my way should it be necessary," she said, the words coming out as simply as if she were asking for a lift into town.

Joely told herself she hadn't heard right.

Freda turned and eyed her darkly. "You didn't see that coming?" she challenged as if she'd just bowled an LBW.

Joely really hadn't.

Appearing pleased with herself, Freda nodded an urge to respond further.

"But I can't," Joely protested. "I'm not even a relative . . ."

"You're my ghost, I think that makes us even closer than relatives."

Not at all sure how she'd worked that out, actually not really wanting to know, Joely said, "I ghosted a story that wasn't even yours."

Freda clearly found that amusing. "You had no idea, did you, that it was your mother's?"

"You know I didn't."

"Have you read it yet with your mother, aged fifteen, in mind?"

"I don't need to. I can picture her in all the scenarios you described, and since she's admitted that most of them are true . . . What are you going to do with it now? Is that what you've been working on in the writing room?"

Freda raised a shaky hand and fluttered it through the air like a broken wing, following it with a small puff that had no sound. "The memoir is my gift to you and your mother," she said. "My only interest in it was to clear my brother's name, but as we know it didn't work out quite the way I'd expected." She gave a small sigh. "Life's like that, isn't it?" she said. "I believe it happens to you when you're busy making other plans."

"John Lennon," Joely stated.

Freda nodded. "'Beautiful Boy (Darling Boy).' It was written for his son, Sean, but I expect you know that."

Joely did. "I think the memoir," she said boldly, "was as much about punishing my mother as it was about clearing your brother's name."

Freda nodded slowly, absorbing the accusation and not disputing it. "That didn't really work out either, did it?" she admitted. She dabbed a tissue to her lips and let her veiny hand fall back to her lap. "I wanted to meet her," she said, her voice staging a ragged break through the hoarseness into clarity. "I hated her for what had happened to my family, but was fascinated by her as well. I wanted to find out what was so special about her, what it is that draws people to her, what she has that I don't, and look what's happened. She's drawn me in too. I can't manage without her now, and I wouldn't want to try. I look forward to seeing her when I wake up in the morning, and I think about her with fondness and gratitude as I fall asleep at night. You could say that she has become the light at the center of my world, and you would be right to, because she is. She has a luminosity about her nature, her heart, her soul that is irresistible."

Joely couldn't help feeling pleased to hear her mother described this way, but she was more concerned about Freda right now, frail and shadowed by the disease she was no longer fighting, a small shell of humanity with a livewire brain.

"How fortunate I am," Freda said, "that I didn't

succeed with my desire to destroy her. Yes, destruction was in my mind when I left here, although I wasn't clear on how I was going to achieve it." She shook her head as though considering the actions of a child and finding them lamentable and naïve. "I was too foolish to realize that all I needed to do was talk to her, she is very easy to talk to, but if I'd done that I might not have met you, Joely—and of all the blessings that have come my way these past months *you* are the one I'm most thankful for."

Joely blinked, taking a moment to absorb this for it was something else she really hadn't seen coming, especially as she and Freda had spent little time together these last few months. But then she knew only too well how capable Freda was of turning everything on its head so all she said was, "I'm surprised to hear that. I felt sure it would have been Mum you'd feel that way about."

Freda replied with enthusiasm. "Oh, certainly she is a blessing too, there's no doubt about that, and Holly—what a credit she is to you, so refreshing in her honesty and self-confidence, and if it weren't for her I'd never have known the therapeutic value of binge-watching *Game of Thrones*."

Joely had to smile at that, for she knew the box-set absorption had done as much to bond Freda and Holly as it had to help distract Freda from the awful side effects of her treatments.

"But it is you, Joely," Freda continued, "whom I hold most dear." She glanced over again, briefly but with the acutely assessing eyes that always made Joely feel as though she'd been seen through even when she had nothing to hide. "I can see that you're puzzled by this, and perhaps disbelieving; I find that I am too, because I certainly hadn't expected when you came here to end up seeing you as the daughter I wish I'd had, but that's who you are. I *like* you, Joely. You are the kind of person I'd want to be if I were able to have my time over. You're strong and loyal, intelligent, funny, caring, and you've brought gaiety into this house that hasn't had any in far too long."

Moved by this praise, Joely said, "We enjoy being here, all of us, you know that. You have a beautiful home and you're a very easygoing and generous host— when you want to be, which we have to admit isn't all of the time." She knew Freda would appreciate the teasing criticism and was glad to see the light that came into her eyes.

"You know how I value unpredictability," she responded with humor. "Now let me tell you this—I've most enjoyed the Pink Martini parties," and just as she'd expected Joely broke into a surprised smile.

There had been a few of them by now with everyone drinking cocktails by the same name while shimmying outrageously and inexpertly to the Latin and jazz sounds that Freda hadn't heard before. At the beginning she'd joined in the dancing, throwing herself into it with an abandon that had surprised them all, including her, but she no longer had the energy to let go of her inhibitions so she watched from the sidelines tapping her foot to the beat and clapping her hands.

Freda continued. "I like hearing your voice about the house when I'm in my room trying to recover from those ghastly sessions; it makes me feel less alone, if

I'm allowed to say that. I enjoy our two-person book club in spite of how often we disagree—or maybe because of how often we disagree, and of course you're always wrong. During the week while you're in London there's always a feeling of something, *someone*, missing, your mother feels it too, which is why we look forward to seeing you so much at the weekends."

Feeling a rush of loyalty toward her brother, Joely said, "And Jamie? You must look forward to seeing him too."

Without hesitation, Freda said, "He has become very special to me and not simply for being David's son, although, I confess it's hard to separate the two—and I think this is why he makes me feel sad in a way you don't." She picked up a glass of water and sipped from it. "He's made me feel closer to my brother than I have in many years; he's brought him back to life for me in a way even our memoir didn't, but I'm starting to feel close to them all now, David, Christopher, Doddoe, Mummy, Daddy . . ." She seemed to reflect a moment on the accuracy of this, and clearly decided she was describing it the way she wanted to, because she said, "I suppose that's only to be expected when I'll be with them soon." She turned her paling eyes back to Joely. "Do you believe in the afterlife?" she asked.

Remembering how she'd wrestled with it after her father's death, Joely said, "I'm not sure, but it seems that you do."

Freda let her head fall against the chair back and closed her eyes. After a while Joely realized she was dozing, so letting her be she took out her phone to check for messages. The WiFi worked perfectly these days.

There was a message from Edward confirming he'd be coming that weekend, but Amanda wouldn't be with him. She couldn't help feeling relieved about that, for Amanda wasn't the easiest company and Edward was always more relaxed when she wasn't around. There was also a message from Callum asking her to call and she wondered if he was going to delay his planned arrival for a few days. It had happened a couple of times before, work holding him up he'd explain, and unable to stop them her thoughts often turned into suspicions. It saddened her a lot, for he'd never given her any reason to mistrust him since they'd admitted to their indiscretions. Except that was too mild a label for what had happened with Martha. He'd slept with her several times knowing exactly what he was doing *and* he'd moved out of their home to go and live with her. Now she often asked herself if he could do it again.

A text arrived making the phone vibrate in her hand and seeing it was from him she felt a tightening in her heart, a sense of dread that she was about to be proved right that something had delayed him. *Can get away earlier than expected so will drive down tomorrow. Missing you. Xxx*

Freda came awake and continued seamlessly with their discussion about the afterlife. "For me it's easy," she said. "If it exists the people I love will be waiting and I will go to them, but what happens to someone like your mother? Will she go to David or to your father? Will she have to decide who she loved the most? I'm sure your father will win because of how long she was with him, but where does that leave my brother?" She flicked a hand impatiently. "You can't answer that, nobody can, I'm simply pointing out that it's more complicated for some than for others."

Since there was no arguing with that, Joely said, daringly, "If you're so certain that you're going to join your family soon, perhaps you'd like to give your nephews some guidance regarding your last wishes."

Freda stifled a small yawn as she said, "Don't worry, it's all taken care of. I haven't discussed anything with them yet, but you'll find my instructions in the top right-hand drawer of my desk. A copy of my will is there too." Her eyes slid toward Joely as if challenging her to ask what was in it, but Joely didn't rise to it.

Freda told her anyway. "Edward and Jamie are the main beneficiaries," she said, "but the jewelry is for your mother and Holly to share between them. There are quite a few heirlooms, and I think they'll appreciate them. For you . . ." She paused to take a breath and Joely knew how likely it was that she was about to say something completely unexpected, even shocking. It wouldn't be Freda if she didn't.

"Can you guess what there is for you?" she asked.

"I'm not expecting anything," Joely assured her.

Freda's bony brows lifted, apparently not believing it. "I will be your ghost," she stated as if awarding the greatest prize of all.

Joely frowned. "OK, you're starting to sound even weirder than usual now. Spooky even."

Freda seemed to take this as a compliment.

"I thought you were heading off to the great beyond to join your family," Joely reminded her. "I really don't want you hanging around here haunting me, thanks all the same."

Freda chuckled with evident delight. "It's tempting," she told her, "because I enjoy your company so much, but in typical fashion you've jumped to the wrong conclusion again. I shall be your ghost, and you will be the writer. A kind of role reversal if you like. My part is already complete. I have drafted a novel based on our short friendship, but there is a twist. Can you guess what it might be?"

Joely was regarding her warily. "I'm not sure I want to," she replied.

Freda's smile widened, showing her chemo-stained teeth. "Go on, try," she urged.

Realizing they were probably about to come full circle to the euthanasia request, Joely said, "OK, it's that I end up killing you."

Freda's laugh tripped her into a bout of coughing, and Joely got up to give her some water.

"An excellent suggestion," Freda declared when she was steady again. "How would you do it?"

Joely was shaking her head. "I'm not playing this game," she replied. "And I'm not going to help put you out of your misery either, but I must admit sometimes it's tempting."

Freda was gleeful. "It would be an outstanding way to do your research, and we could plan it together."

"It's not going to happen," Joely told her firmly.

"Think about the inquiry, investigation, arrest . . . You'd experience it all first-hand . . ."

"Freda," Joely interrupted darkly. "If you seriously think I'm going to risk going to prison . . ."

"Imagine if that happens! You'd have a ringside seat, admittedly from a cell . . . You'd be embedded, the way reporters are when they follow a war. The draft is on my desk, you're welcome to go and take a look at it now if you like. I'll be very interested to hear what you think."

"Thanks, but no," and Joely waved out to her mother and Holly as they appeared at the end of the meadow making their way back from a yoga session on the beach.

As Freda watched them approach, wading through the long grass, both carrying rolled-up mats under one arm and their honeyed skin glowing from their exertions, she gave a satisfied sigh of pleasure. "She really is beautiful, isn't she?" she murmured. "Such an aura of loveliness."

Joely would have asked who, her mother or Holly, had she not already known the answer.

"Can you believe it was fifty summers ago," Freda said softly, as Joely reached out to straighten the blanket that was sliding from her knees, "that she became the great love of my brother's life, and seeing her walking toward us like this with Holly is almost like seeing her with her younger self—the girl David couldn't resist." She was clearly sinking deeply into the moment and its connection with the past, marveling at the way time seemed to be playing tricks on her. "So beautiful," she murmured, and her eyes remained dreamy as she sighed and added, "I suppose you take after your father."

Joely tossed the blanket over her head and stifling a laugh went inside to make some tea.

Moments later her mother joined her, leaving Holly outside to help disentangle Freda from the blanket.

"Everything OK?" Marianne asked, taking four mugs from their hooks.

"Everything's fine," Joely assured her, "but I can tell you this much, she isn't going to go quietly."

Except she did.

In true Freda fashion, after setting everyone up for a dramatic exit from the world, one that would involve an assisted suicide at the very least, and a prison sentence for Joely at best, she drifted away peacefully in her sleep one night with no one helping her on her way, or even holding her hand.

"You've done it again," Joely whispered to her when she went into the room to say goodbye before the coroner arrived. "You got me thinking one thing while all the time you were planning another." She sat down on the edge of the bed and brushed a hand gently over Freda's sparse wisps of hair. "I'm going to miss you," she said, tears filling her eyes as she gazed at the gauzy thin eyelids untroubled by lashes, the unlikely barrier that would never open again to allow a connection between them. "I'm probably going to miss you a lot more than I can imagine, but please, please don't haunt me."

Ten days later Joely linked Andee's arm as they walked from the cemetery between Lynton and the Valley of Rocks to the parked cars on the grass and gravel area outside. Everyone on Freda's list of invitees had come to bid farewell to the eccentric aunt, friend, author, client, employer, and neighbor, and Joely felt sure Freda would have been startled by the tears that had been shed. She might even have been pleased by them. According to her she wasn't the kind of person to stir deep emotion in another, so she'd have been surprised

to hear her agent speak with passion about their friendship and the loyalty of her following. She probably
wouldn't have expected Edward's voice to shake as he'd
delivered the eulogy, but it had, and when he'd finished
and retaken his seat next to Joely she'd held his hand
between both of hers.

Freda's chosen entry music had been Brahms Violin
Sonata No. 3 played by her father with her uncle at the
piano; the feature music for the ceremony was Henry
Purcell's "Evening Hymn" performed by her mother, and
the final choice "to uplift everyone as they left," was
"Slippin' and Slidin" by Little Richard, because she used
to perform it with her brothers when they were young.

I haven't selected any of Doddoe's music, she'd
written in her final instructions, *because I'd like his
dance pieces to be played at the party after, but to open
proceedings we should have* "Amado mio" *by Pink
Martini especially for Joely.*

She'd planned everything, from the flowers, to the
hymns, to the notices, not because she was a control freak,
she'd insisted, but because she didn't want anyone else to
have to go to the trouble. She'd even decided on the food
Brenda was to serve back at the house, although she'd left
the wine choice to Edward. She'd also, just as she'd told
Joely she would, left him a half share of Dimmett House
and its contents, with the other half going to Jamie. The
thinking at the moment was that they'd keep it for the
family to use for weekends and holidays, but they were
all aware that could change over time. Jamie was also
now the proud owner of a small cottage in Hampshire
that used to belong to his great-uncle, and had been the
setting for most of his parents' romance.

There were many other bequests detailed in the will she'd left in her desk—the official reading was due to take place the following week—a generous recognition of Brenda's loyalty, a painting for Jamie's wife, Clare, trust funds for Jamie's children to help them through university, an ISA for Holly to mature when she was twenty-one, and David's original collection of vinyl records for Marianne. As she'd promised, there was the opening draft of a novel for Joely, about a reclusive older woman and her end-of-life relationship with a ghostwriter.

In her accompanying notes Freda had written:

It's time for you to take on a project that is completely yours. I've started this off for you simply to get you into the flow, but of course you are free to ignore it. You don't even have to become a writer, but I feel it would be a great shame if you didn't as you seem to enjoy the process and your talent is no worse than any of the popular authors being published today.

Should you go ahead with this one I have left you to decide on how the peculiar relationship could develop which will no doubt take you into fiction—we've already dealt with the reality. I told you I'd included a twist in the tale, and here it is—I have bequeathed you my library of books and have hidden within certain volumes a number of clues. When each one is solved it will lead you on to the next until eventually the conundrum will

*be solved and you will have a real shocker
of an ending.*

*I'm sure you're already trying to guess what
it might be, and as each clue is revealed
you'll be leaping to more and more conclusions, most of which you'll find to be wrong.
I think you'll enjoy the exercise—I have
certainly enjoyed putting it together.*

*Thank you, dear Joely, for all that you
brought to my life during my final year on
this planet. You cured my loneliness, understood and soothed my grief, and helped my
frozen heart to thaw.*

Be brave and be happy,
Freda

As they approached the parked cars Joely was watching her mother walking between Jamie and Edward. She said to Andee, "It's fascinating watching Mum now, isn't it? Or it is to me, because back then, when she was only sixteen, she'd never have dreamt that all these years later she'd be here at the heart of David's family in the way she is now."

Andee said softly, "Does that make you feel bad for your father?"

Joely didn't have to consider it. "No, because he was never in any doubt about how much he was loved, and he seemed to have a better understanding than most of how not to try to compete with the past." With a smile she turned to embrace her friend. "Thanks for coming today," she said. "It means a lot. And you're coming back to the house now?"

"Of course," Andee assured her, and letting go of her arm she went to join her mother and Graeme at their car.

As Joely reached Callum's car he was already opening the back door for her mother and Holly to get in. She noticed Edward standing with Jamie, heads together as they talked, and apparently sensing her watching them Edward looked up and smiled as their eyes met. She wasn't sure if she felt sad that he was on his own today, or glad that his relationship with Amanda was now over. A man like him would have no trouble finding someone else when he was ready to and not for the first time she imagined herself being that person. It wasn't going to happen, she felt sure of it, but the fantasy was as pleasing as the chemistry was real.

Feeling Callum's arm go around her she leaned into him for a moment. She loved him, maybe even more now than she had before, but that didn't mean the trust was repaired, or that he felt the same way about her. It seemed that he did in so many ways, however she wasn't going to presume her marriage would last, or that she was heading toward an affair with Edward. She was simply going to work at one and try to avoid the other while the future kept its secrets until it was ready to reveal them.

Freda would be proud of her.

Taking her phone from her pocket as it buzzed with a text, she read it and felt a ripple of shock go through her heart.

It was from her agent. *Hi, I have a great new assignment for you. Give me a call asap so we can discuss. Client says he's met you before at Soho House.*

ACKNOWLEDGMENTS

So much of what goes into a book is drawn from the research of locations. In this instance I was fortunate enough to be in the very beautiful and dramatic environs of Lynton and Lynmouth in North Devon. While there I met Betty and Dave Wilde, whom I can't thank enough for giving me so much color and detail about the area. I hope I have done their invaluable input the justice it deserves.

I would also like to thank my wonderful agent Luigi Bonomi for such an amazing and uplifting reaction to this book. It made me dance with joy.

Many more thank-yous go to the outstanding publishing team at HarperCollins, led by Kimberley Young. This is now my third book with you guys and the experience gets better all the time. (As do the parties!)

About the author

About the book

Read on

Insights,
Interviews
& More . . .

Meet Susan Lewis

Antony Thompson / www.thousandwordmedia.com

SUSAN LEWIS is the internationally
bestselling author of more than forty
books across the genres of family drama,
thriller, suspense, and crime. She is also
the author of *Just One More Day* and
One Day at a Time, the moving memoirs
of her childhood in Bristol during the
1960s. Following periods of living in
Los Angeles and the South of France,
she currently lives in Gloucestershire
with her husband, James; stepsons,
Michael and Luke; and mischievous
dogs, Coco and Lulu.

About the author

Reading Group Guide

1. Freda wants Joely to write her story in order to right a wrong. Can storytelling be used as a method of meting out justice? What are some examples of this that you've encountered in real life?

2. What do you think it is that appeals to Joely about ghostwriting other peoples' stories rather than writing her own?

3. Freda has a strong opinion on who is to blame in her story about Sir. Do you agree with her that the blame lies more with the girl, or do you think the man should be held wholly accountable for his actions?

4. On page 96, Freda asks Joely, "Would you agree that sometimes, in a memoir, it's necessary to help the facts a little, either to make them more interesting, or to bring clarity to a complex situation? Or simply to move things along." Is it ethical to stretch the truth in a memoir or other nonfiction work if you have a good reason for doing so? What might some of those reasons be?

5. On page 229, Freda says, "We can't turn back the clock to correct mistakes or untell lies, but we can punish the person who committed the crime." Is getting ▶

Reading Group Guide *(continued)*

revenge really an adequate alternative if you aren't able to change anything about the event that occurred? How do you think Freda's answer to this question would change throughout the events of the book?

6. The book includes three mother-daughter relationships: Joely and Marianne, Joely and Holly, and Young Freda and her mother. What do these relationships have in common?

7. Were you surprised to find out the truth about who the characters in Freda's story were? Did you have a different prediction?

8. What role does music play in the story?

9. Compare the ways in which Freda and Joely reacted to their grief over losing family members. What common threads do you see between their actions and the motivations behind them?

10. By the end of the book, multiple characters have made the difficult choice to forgive others for their actions. Do you agree with their decisions? Would have been able to find the same forgiveness if you were in their place?

11. Joely is initially hurt when she learns that she has been left out of a family secret, but comes to accept that it

wasn't her secret to know. Do you think she should have been told along with her brother? In what ways do family secrets like this one affect all members of a family, regardless of whether or not someone is directly involved? ❧

An Excerpt from
Forgive Me

CHAPTER ONE

Marcus Huxley-Browne looked up from the warning call he'd just received on his mobile phone. His handsome face was showing none of its usual boredom or arrogance, or the self-satisfaction that came from having so much go right in his life: being born into a wealthy family, having all the right contacts, besting someone at a deal (as he so often did). Instead it was taut with a level of fear and anger that his wife had never witnessed in him before.

It frightened her, although she wasn't sure why—yet.

"They're coming for me," he muttered. He wasn't looking at her, maybe he wasn't even speaking to her.

"Who?" she asked.

His deep gray eyes focused and sparked with ire. "You know *nothing*," he instructed her viciously. "You've seen nothing. You've heard nothing. Have you got that?"

His fists clenched. Was he going to hit her, blame her, or something worse?

Who was coming?

She knew better than to ask a second time, and stepped aside as he headed out of the room, across the hall, and into his study.

"Come here!" he shouted.

Obediently, she hastened after him and stopped on the threshold of the room she was rarely invited into. He was standing behind his desk, a Huxley-Browne heirloom, one of many others that cluttered the house with stately gloom. He looked haunted now, agitated—*hunted*—as if not knowing where to turn or what to do. Had things been different she might have felt sorry for him.

"You don't speak to anyone," he told her gruffly.

She nodded. She'd had this instruction before, but usually he didn't take any chances; he'd whisk her upstairs and lock her in one of the top floor rooms.

She used to fight it, but she'd learned not to.

She often heard things from up there, but she never saw the comings and goings outside—cars pulling up, people entering or leaving the house—as the windows were too high. However, voices carried, even if she couldn't make out who they belonged to, or what was being said.

She knew what kind of people came.

They were his set: the all-male network that he and others of his ilk had created at university, in the city, in private clubs, in various capitals—to trade information, or to start rumors, or to import and export insider knowledge. Girls came too, ▸

for the after-parties, lots of them, paid well, she imagined—and the dealers in mood- and sexual-performance enhancers came too. Shady, sinister characters from an underworld she could barely imagine.

On the nights Marcus didn't come home she guessed someone else was hosting proceedings. She never asked, and he never told her, but she'd come to recognize a comedown when it was in front of her.

There were other nights—lots of them—when he behaved like a regular family man, sober, a little tired, but happy and feeling generous at the end of a long, productive day. She could easily mistake him then for the man who'd comforted and befriended her after the tragedy of her first husband's death. She still felt strangely attached to that man and the way he'd spoken so softly to her during that terrible time—smiling into her eyes as if he couldn't believe how fortunate he was to have found her. He'd never been frightening then, just loving, attentive, interested. She'd married him believing he loved her and feeling certain it was the right thing to do—for herself and for her daughter, still devastated by the loss of her father.

Now here they were, or here she was, watching him frantically snatching files from his desk and stuffing them into an old-fashioned attaché case. She hadn't seen it before. It was a gladstone, the kind of bag visiting doctors used, or traveling salesmen.

"For Christ's sake, don't just stand there," he raged. "Get that cabinet away from the wall."

Quickly she moved to do as she was told, but the cabinet was too heavy.

He shoved her aside and did it himself, grunting, sweating, swearing . . . Was he crying? Beads of sweat? How much did she care? How afraid was she?

She wasn't surprised to see the safe behind the cabinet. She'd known it was there, but this was the first time he'd opened it in front of her.

She couldn't calculate how much cash was stacked on the five shelves inside, but it surely ran into hundreds of thousands, all neatly bundled until it was chaotically rammed into the case along with the files. Too much to fit in, but he was going to make it happen . . .

Someone knocked at the front door. Three heavy raps.

He froze. A beat later he turned to the window. Beyond was the back garden and she wondered if he was about to throw himself out onto the lawn and make a run for it.

With lightning speed, he rammed the case into the safe, spun the combination lock, and heaved the cabinet back into place.

Their visitor—or visitors—tried the bell.

Police? Drug dealers? Who else would he be so afraid of? ▶

An Excerpt from *Forgive Me* (continued)

She gasped as he grabbed her by the neck with one hand and pressed her against the wall. "Remember, you know nothing," he hissed into her face, "you've seen nothing, and you've heard nothing."

She nodded, gasping for breath, clawing at his hand.

He let her go and pointed along the hall to the door. "Answer it, but if you even think about betraying me . . ." His eyes bored into hers; he didn't have to tell her that it wouldn't end well, she already knew.

She started to move, hardly knowing who or what to expect when she opened the door.

"Stop!" he seethed under his breath.

She turned around. "I don't know where this is going to end," he growled, "but just in case you get any ideas about leaving me, you'll be watched. You won't get away, and if you try, I'll find you and by then you'll wish I hadn't."

She didn't doubt him; she never had. She knew what he was capable of, and as he turned to the door, she found herself hoping with all her heart and soul that he was about to be taken out, not taken away. ∽